Everything seemed to go still as his gaze fell on a painting that hung slightly apart from the others.

You didn't have to wear a paint-spattered smock to know that it wasn't the work of an Old World Master, dark and glorious with age, and it wasn't an Impressionist gem. It wasn't even something new, trendy or outrageously clever. The painting's only claim to fame was its subject. And she made everything else that hung on these walls fade to insignificance.

Conor moved forward, his eyes never leaving the portrait. It was of a young woman standing in the garden, her face and body angled towards the viewer. She was wearing a demure, old-fashioned dress, white lace maybe, with a high collar and long, full sleeves, and holding a wide-brimmed straw hat in her hand. Her hair, a waterfall of midnight silk, was drawn back from her high-cheekboned face and then left to spill, unhampered, over her shoulders. Her eyes were a dark shade of green that Conor knew couldn't be real but had to be the invention of the painter. Her mouth looked soft and inviting. It was the color of a budding rose and bore the faintest suggestion of a smile.

The longer he looked, the more he saw something else. The girl seemed to have both the purity of a Madonna and the sensuality of a Jezebel.

Who was she?

ROMANCE FROM JANELLE TAYLOR

ANYTHING FOR LOVE	(0-8217-4992-7, $5.99)
DESTINY MINE	(0-8217-5185-9, $5.99)
CHASE THE WIND	(0-8217-4740-1, $5.99)
MIDNIGHT SECRETS	(0-8217-5280-4, $5.99)
MOONBEAMS AND MAGIC	(0-8217-0184-4, $5.99)
SWEET SAVAGE HEART	(0-8217-5276-6, $5.99)

Available wherever paperbacks are sold, or order direct from the Publisher. Send cover price plus 50¢ per copy for mailing and handling to Penguin USA, P.O. Box 999, c/o Dept. 17109, Bergenfield, NJ 07621. Residents of New York and Tennessee must include sales tax. DO NOT SEND CASH.

UNTIL YOU

Sandra Marton

Pinnacle Books
Kensington Publishing Corp.
http://www.pinnaclebooks.com

PINNACLE BOOKS are published by

Kensington Publishing Corp.
850 Third Avenue
New York, NY 10022

Copyright © 1997 by Sandra Myles

All rights reserved. No part of this book may be reproduced in any form or by any means without the prior written consent of the Publisher, excepting brief quotes used in reviews.

If you purchased this book without a cover, you should be aware that this book is stolen property. It was reported as "unsold and destroyed" to the Publisher and neither the Author nor the Publisher has received any payment for this "stripped book."

Pinnacle and the P logo Reg. U.S. Pat. & TM Off.

First Printing: March, 1997
10 9 8 7 6 5 4 3 2 1

Printed in the United States of America

Prologue

Paris, 1988

It was April in Paris the first time Miranda Beckman saw the City of Light, but if there were chestnuts in blossom, their beauty was dimmed by the rain that fell from the dull pewter sky.

She tried to tell herself the weather wasn't an omen of things to come as she and Edouard emerged from the arrivals building at Orly Airport. A cruel wind cut through her denim jacket and she shivered a little.

Edouard put his arm around her.

"Are you cold, *ma petite?*" he said and when she nodded he laughed and said she'd be warm soon enough.

There was no mistaking what he meant. A day ago, even ten hours ago, the suggestive words, delivered in that wonderful accent, would have brought a rush of color to her cheeks and a racing sense of anticipation to her heart, but all that had changed during the flight from New York, while she and Edouard had sat crammed together in the five-across-the-row seats of a crowded Air France 1011.

Somewhere over the Atlantic, the delicious excitement had

started wearing off and doubts began creeping in. It had all seemed so romantic: slipping out of her dorm late at night and into Edouard's waiting arms, flying to Vegas, getting married by a justice of the peace who'd been too busy or too nearsighted to take a really good look at her birth certificate . . .

During the flight, she'd begun to wonder if they'd moved too fast.

Maybe she and Edouard should have driven to New York and confronted her mother. Eva might have understood.

Miranda tried to tell that to Edouard but he hushed her.

"Your mother would not have approved, *ma petite,* you know that as well as I."

He reminded her of all the things they'd already discussed. The huge difference in their ages. The difference in their nationalities. The fact that she hadn't finished school.

Miranda knew he was right, knew, too, that Eva would have started dredging up the past, rubbing her nose in all the other headstrong, stupid things she'd done. Not that marrying Edouard was one of them. Oh, no. Marrying him was the only truly intelligent thing she'd done in all her seventeen years.

Still, after they'd boarded the plane to Paris, as they flew into the night and the cabin lights dimmed, an uncomfortable silence settled over her. Edouard sensed it, put his arm around her and drew her close.

"Poor Miranda," he murmured, "you are exhausted. And who can blame you, my little treasure? If only the airline rules were not so ridiculous, we would be up front, sipping champagne."

She thought again of all the empty first class seats they'd passed on their way to the coach section, and how Edouard had explained that businesses made a habit of buying seats and then not using them.

Doubt crept into her thoughts again, which was stupid. Why on earth would her new husband lie about such a silly thing?

"Never mind the airline's champagne," he said, smoothing strands of her long black hair back behind her ears. "When we reach my *château,* we will drink all the champagne we want. Now, close your eyes, Miranda, and rest. I will help you to relax.''

His kiss brushed her lips as lightly as a feather as he tucked the scratchy wool airline blanket over the both of them. Miranda sighed as she laid her head on his strong, comforting shoulder. Her doubts faded away.

This was why she loved Edouard, why she'd loved him almost from the day he'd first come to visit his cousin, who was her roommate at Miss Cooper's School for Young Ladies. It wasn't because he was so much older, or because he was sexy and gorgeous and an honest-to-goodness Count, or even because all the other girls in the dorm had gone green with envy at his obvious interest in her.

No, she thought, snuggling closer, she loved him because he so obviously loved her and cherished her as no one ever had.

Miranda's eyes shot open. Edouard's hand had snaked under the airline blanket, slipped under her T-shirt and beneath the waistband of her jeans. She struggled to sit up but his arm tightened around her.

''Sit still,'' he said softly.

''Edouard, no! What are you . . . ?''

His hand moved again, almost as if it were not connected to him. It skimmed across her belly, intruded itself roughly between her thighs and cupped her innocence. Miranda gasped, tried to pull away, and his fingers tightened cruelly on her flesh.

''Sit still,'' he repeated, his voice harsh.

Her eyes widened in shock as his fingers began moving. He had never touched her like this, not once in the four weeks she'd known him. No one had ever touched her like this, despite what the girls at school whispered, despite what her mother thought. And, oh God, to have something like this happen for the very first time in a crowded airplane, with people all around . . .

''Someone will see,'' she hissed.

''No one will see,'' Edouard muttered, turning in his seat

so he was facing her. In the dim light, his face had taken on a mask-like quality. ''Open your legs.''

She clamped her thighs together instead. ''Edouard,'' she whispered, her voice desperate.

He bent his head to hers. ''Do you love me?''

His hand had shifted. He'd thrust his finger into her and it hurt, but he'd silenced her cries with his mouth. His breathing had quickened and he'd grasped one of her hands and snugged it against his bulging crotch, holding it tightly in place when she'd tried to pull free.

Terrified, she'd numbed herself to sensation. It was only a dream, she'd told herself, a hideous dream.

But it wasn't. It was real. And as they stood in the cold rain outside Orly, she knew she'd made the worst mistake of her young life.

A taxi pulled to the curb. Edouard reached out, opened the door. ''Get in, my treasure,'' he said, as if nothing had changed between them.

Miranda pulled back. ''I—I've changed my mind,'' she said. ''I want to go home.''

His hand fell, hard, into the small of her back. ''You are my wife,'' he said coldly. ''Now, get in the taxi and behave yourself.''

The drive through the rainy streets was long, but not long enough. All too soon, the cab pulled up before a stone building that was the same color as the Parisian sky. Edouard paid the driver. Then he locked his arm around Miranda's waist and walked her quickly up a flight of steps and through a massive door.

''Your new home, darling Miranda,'' he said, as the door slammed shut behind them. ''If it is not yet the stuff of girlish dreams, it will be—once your dear Mama provides us with an income.''

Miranda looked at the walls spotted with mold, the room almost empty of furnishings. She felt the chill in the house close around her and finally understood.

Edouard, the Count de Lasserre, had a title that spanned five centuries. But standing in the gloomy, drafty hall of his ancestral home, she realized that the money in his bank account probably wouldn't cover the next five minutes.

Her Prince Charming was broke. He had married her not for love but for her mother's money—and for what he had done to her on the plane.

Miranda tore free of his encircling arm and grabbed a poker from beside the huge fireplace that took up almost one entire stone wall.

''If you touch me again,'' she breathed, her green eyes wild, ''I'll kill you.''

Edouard's handsome face twisted. The suave features became an ugly parody of the face she knew.

She backed away as he came towards her and raised the poker over her head. He laughed, wrenched it from her hand and threw it to the floor with contempt. Then he grabbed Miranda's wrist, swung her into his arms and carried her, sobbing and beating her fists against his shoulders, up the wide, creaking staircase to his rooms.

Chapter One

New York City, 1996

Conor O'Neil lounged back on the sofa, took a swallow of cold ale, and stretched his long legs towards the fireplace while he pondered one of life's more difficult questions.

When a woman said she was going to change into something more comfortable after she'd spent the evening wearing a sexy slip of a dress that clung to her breasts and ended at her thighs, what did she mean?

Conor smiled to himself. It was almost as tough as deciding which was better—the warmth of the fire, the crispness of the ale, or the knot of anticipatory tension curling low in his belly as he waited for Mary Alice Whittaker to emerge from her bedroom.

''Conor?''

As soon as he heard that soft voice, he knew the answer. Slowly, he put down the bottle of India Pale and got to his feet.

She was standing in the arched doorway, silhouetted by the light that spilled from the hall behind her, wearing something long and black that sent his pulse rate way into the red. She'd let down her hair so that it fell like liquid gold around her face.

Something more comfortable, he thought, and smiled.

She stepped forward, just enough so the light seemed to pour into her body and turn her to flame.

"What do you think?" she said, putting her arms out and pirouetting slowly in place. "Isn't this closer to the real me?"

Conor took another look at whatever you called the thing she was wearing. A robe? A negligée? Not that he gave a damn. Whatever you called it, it was doing its job. How could something cover so much yet reveal everything that mattered?

"Oh, yeah." His smile was slow and sexy. "I'd say it's definitely closer to the real you, Mary Alice."

She laughed, a throaty chuckle that went straight to his groin, and started towards him, her high-heeled, black satin mules tapping lightly against the Italian tile floor.

"I figured you were pleased," she said. "I could tell by your smile."

Conor laughed. She'd be able to tell by more than that, just as soon as she got close enough. O'Neil, he thought, what a clever so-and-so you are! What had started as a weekend he'd figured to enjoy was shaping up as one he suspected he'd not soon forget.

"It's a terrific smile, you know." Mary Alice paused just long enough to recover the glass of white wine she'd left on the wet bar, then floated towards him again. "Sort of a little-boy-with-his-hand-caught-in-the-cookie-jar grin, if you know what I mean."

He knew exactly what she meant. It was the smile his ex-wife had described as unbearably smug. But, he thought, taking Mary Alice's hand, this was definitely not a time to think about your ex-wife. It was not a time to think about being smug, either.

The only thing worth thinking about right now was that he didn't have to be back in D.C. until nine o'clock Monday morning.

Or ten.

Or eleven.

For all he cared, they could come and drag back his desiccated body.

"I'm really glad you called me," Mary Alice said as he drew her down on the sofa. The tip of her tongue, pink and delicate as a kitten's, swept between her lips and touched the rim of her wineglass. "Really, really glad."

He bent towards her, inhaled her perfume, then caught her earlobe between his teeth and bit down gently.

"Yes," he said. "Me, too."

"Mm. That's nice."

Her voice was low and sexy with just a touch of little-girl innocence, a mind-blowing combination of Jessica Rabbit meets Rebecca of Sunnybrook Farm. It had no resemblance to her do-gooder voice, the one she'd used on him months ago when they'd ended up unlikely dinner partners at some silly Embassy reception.

"What a barracuda," his boss, Harry Thurston, had mumbled.

Considering Mary Alice Whittaker's reputation as a My-Heart-Bleeds-For-Everything lobbyist, her oversized glasses and her pulled-back hair, it had seemed an accurate description.

But not even the dress-for-success suit she'd worn had been completely able to disguise the made-for-pleasure body. And though she'd treated Conor with the scorn politically righteous reformers often reserved for members of the Washington community, he'd sensed something more.

It was like standing too close to overhead high voltage wires and hearing the faint but persistent hum of escaping electricity.

He'd waited two months, until the embassy party was long-forgotten and Mary Alice was up to her swan-like neck in some new crusade, before he'd phoned. He'd called her not at her prestigious Park Avenue office but at night, at her Gramercy Park apartment.

"Hello," he'd said, no time wasted on preliminaries, "this is Conor O'Neil."

Mary Alice hadn't wasted any time, either.

"How did you get my phone number?" she'd asked in a cool, take-no-prisoners voice.

Conor had laughed softly. "I'm the guy you called a government insider, Miss Whittaker, remember?"

"And why have you phoned me, Mr. O'Neil?"

Her voice was still chilly. For a second or two, he'd wondered if he'd read her wrong but then he'd thought, hell, what was there to lose?

"I phoned you," he'd said, "because I'm tired of wondering what you'd look like with your hair down and your glasses off."

"Good-bye, Mr. O'Neil."

"Shall I be more direct, Miss Whittaker? I have dinner reservations at The Water Club Friday night, tickets to the new Neil Simon play, and one hell of an itch to take you to bed. Are you interested?"

There'd been a pause, a long one, before she'd answered. When she had, her voice had gone soft and husky.

"The Water Club is over-rated," she'd said, "and I've already seen the play."

Conor had laughed. "You pick it, then. I'm easy."

Mary Alice had laughed, too, a low, sexy chuckle that had damned near melted the telephone.

"I'll bet you're not," she'd said—and now here he was, sitting on her sofa, the lights low, an old Eagles album playing softly in the background, with Mary Alice's bare feet in his lap.

They were well-cared for feet, he saw as he traced her polished pink toenails with his index finger. They were also vaguely oversized, which was not what you were supposed to be thinking at a moment like this, but lately his thoughts had drifted at the damnedest times. It was, he supposed, the price you paid for bedding a woman before you knew if you liked her or simply wanted her.

Not that he had any complaints. Safe, healthy, uncommitted sex was the only kind he was interested in. His job didn't allow for anything more. Besides, he'd already tried the other route, the emotional meat grinder people called love.

The pattern of his life since his divorce had been simple. You found someone you could laugh with, someone who turned you on, and you entered into a pleasant relationship that, with luck, would last several weeks, maybe even months, until one or the other of you grew bored.

It had come as an enormous relief to find that the world was filled with women who were looking for the same thing.

Mary Alice, for example, was establishing her claim to that enlightened attitude this very second, using her toes to do clever things to his rapidly hardening crotch.

"Hey." He grabbed her foot, brought it to his mouth and gently nipped her big toe. "What do you think you're doing, woman?"

She gave another of those sexy chuckles. "If you don't know the answer to that," she said, "we're in for an awfully dull evening."

Conor smiled. "Come here," he said, and with a purr of agreement, she went into his arms.

He came up out of sleep the way he always did, quickly and with a minimum of disorientation. It was, his ex had once said bitterly, the only good thing his stint in Special Forces had done for him. He wondered what she'd say if she knew him now, after the time he'd spent working for the Committee.

Mary Alice's bedroom—they'd moved there during the long night—was grey with early morning light. The soft ringing of the phone had awakened him. The waterbed sloshed gently as she rolled over and grabbed for it on the nightstand.

"Lo," she muttered, and then she shoved the phone in his direction. "It's for you."

He took it from her. "Thanks," he said, trying not to notice that her face was puffy with sleep or that the sexy, kittenish voice had given way to one that was raspy and sullen.

"I don't much appreciate having my private phone number

handed out everywhere, Conor. If you need to touch base with people—''

He reached out, cupped her breast as he scooted up against the pillows.

''O'Neil,'' he said into the phone. Mary Alice sighed as his thumb moved against her flesh.

''Did I wake you, my boy?''

Conor shut his eyes. He pulled back his hand and rubbed it over his face. The stubble on his chin and cheeks was rough against his fingers.

''No, Harry, of course not. I'm always up and alert at—what time is it, anyway?''

''It's 6:00 A.M.,'' Mary Alice said. She flopped onto her belly and dragged the satin quilt over her naked shoulders. ''Who in God's name makes phone calls at this hour on a Saturday morning?''

Harry Thurston's chuckle rumbled softly in Conor's ear. ''Did I interrupt something? If I did, I'm sorry.''

''Yeah. I'll bet.''

''But I wanted to be sure I got hold of you.''

Conor sighed. ''Well, you got hold of me. What do you want?''

''I tried reaching you at the office yesterday, four, five o'clock, somewhere around there. Rosemary said you were already gone.''

''I left at three-thirty.'' Conor shoved aside the quilt and swung his feet to the carpet. ''Come on, Harry. You didn't call me to discuss the time I checked out of the office. What's up?''

''I'm cold,'' Mary Alice mumbled. Her voice had lost some of its sullen quality. ''You pulled the quilt off me, Conor.''

He half-turned, grasped the quilt and drew it over her. She caught his hand, bit the pad at the base of his thumb none too gently, then sucked the finger into her warm, moist mouth.

The voice on the other end of the phone took on a teasing whine. ''Did you pull the quilt off, Conor? I'm ashamed of you.''

Conor shook his head at Mary Alice, smiled and gently extricated his thumb from between her lips.

"Harry," he said, "I'm warning you, I'm not in the mood for fun and games right now."

"But I am, "Mary Alice murmured. She rolled onto her back and reached out her hand. Conor caught it as it began its search for his lap.

"You've got one minute to get to the bottom line, Harry," he said.

"Anybody ever tell you you've got no sense of humor, O'Neil?" Harry Thurston sighed. "Okay, okay, here's the deal. I need a favor."

"No."

"What do you mean, no? You don't even know what it is."

"It's the weekend, Harry. I finished up the stuff I'd been working on—"

"Yeah, I saw. Nice job."

"—and now I'm off the clock."

"I told you, this is a favor. A simple one. I just need you to deliver a message to an old friend in New York. It'll take you five minutes. Ten at the most."

"A message?"

"That's right."

"Whatever happened to the telephone? Or Federal Express?"

Mary Ellen kicked off the blanket and sat up. "I'll be right back," she purred. Naked hips swinging gently, she headed for the bathroom.

"I'm only asking you to say a few words to him, Conor. We went to school together."

"And?"

"What a suspicious mind you have." Thurston sounded pained. "What's so unusual about asking somebody to say a few words to a friend?"

"I don't know, Harry. It's just a feeling I'm getting. What's this message, and who am I delivering it to?"

"Hoyt Winthrop. He has a seat on the stock exchange and—"

"I know this is going to shock the hell out of you, but I read the papers. I know who Hoyt Winthrop is."

"Then you know the President's considering him for an ambassadorship."

"So?"

"So, I just want you to tell him he's made the A list."

Conor's eyes narrowed. "As in, the FBI said he's okay?"

"Yes."

"What's the matter? Did the Fibbies get evicted from their New York office? Why don't they pass the message along themselves?"

Harry Thurston sighed. "Why must you always be so distrustful?"

"Because I'm tired of being the guy who's up to his ass in alligators while the boys in the white hats stand around pretending they don't know who the fuck drained the water out of the swamp."

"You have a way with words, Conor. Anybody ever tell you that?"

Conor heard the toilet flush. The bathroom door opened and he got to his feet, walked across the room and out into the hall.

"Listen," he said into the phone, "you want to give this the personal touch, why not call Winthrop yourself, tell him he's been vetted and all he's got to do now is stand by and wait?"

"I told you, he and I go way back together. A visit is much more personal than a phone call." Thurston paused. "And I know he was a little concerned about things. You know how it is."

Alarm bells were sounding in Conor's head. "No. I don't know," he said coldly. "What does he have to be concerned about?"

"His daughter. Well, his stepdaughter. Miranda Beckman." Thurston's voice lowered, and Conor could almost picture him bringing the telephone closer to his lantern-jawed face. ''She's a model, lives in Paris. Has for years.'' He paused delicately. ''She leads a pretty wild life, from what I hear.''

''And?''

''And,'' Thurston said, ''there's nothing for Hoyt to worry about. Well, I mean the girl's not the Virgin Queen, but she's not into heavy drugs or underage Martians of either sex. In today's world, that makes her Snow White.''

''Is that what I'm supposed to tell Winthrop? That his stepdaughter's a candidate for Miss America?''

''Just tell Hoyt things are fine. And give him my best, of course.''

''Of course,'' Conor said, waiting patiently for the other shoe to drop.

''And while you're there,'' Thurston said smoothly, ''ask him to give you the note.''

''What note?''

''The one he got yesterday.''

''Dammit, Harry—''

''Actually, it was addressed to his wife. Eva Beckman Winthrop. She owns that cosmetics firm, what's the name? Papillon, I think.''

Conor closed his eyes. Harry Thurston had come into government the old-fashioned way, because of his name, his connections, and an idealized commitment to serving his fellow man, but he'd stayed there because he was clever and competent. He never forgot details, never did anything without having planned it carefully—and never managed to scam anyone without making it obvious that he was doing just that.

''Harry.'' Conor's voice was sharp. ''Maybe I need to spell this out for you. I am not going to get involved in any more political games.''

''So you've told me.''

''I hate that crap and you know it.''

''You're good at it, though.''

Conor laughed. ''Right. That's why that congressman wanted my ass served on a silver platter a couple of months ago.''

"That's just the point. You don't give a damn, Conor. You're not interested in becoming the D.C. Poster Boy of the Month."

"That doesn't mean I'm interested in getting dragged into your pal Winthrop's situation, either."

"There isn't any situation. That's what I'm trying to tell you. You're making a mountain out of a molehill. Go see Hoyt, congratulate him for me, and eyeball this note his wife received."

"And that's it?"

"That's it. Cross my heart and hope to die."

"What heart?" Conor leaned back against the wall. "I don't suppose you know what this note says?"

"I've no idea. Hoyt left a message with my secretary. He was in and out all day and so was I. We played telephone tag for a couple of hours, then gave up."

"So, what do I do with the note after I see it?"

"Make nice-nice to Hoyt and his wife, tell them the note is nothing—which I'm certain it is—and bring it to the office with you on Monday."

"And you'll either put it in the round file or hand it over to the FBI."

"Certainly."

Conor sighed. "I can almost see your nose growing, Harry."

He could still hear his boss laughing as he jammed his finger against the *off* button and put an end to their conversation.

A couple of hours later, Conor was standing at the iron-banded door to a grey stone mansion on Fifth Avenue.

It was a cold, sunless morning with the promise of rain in the air. He'd already identified himself to a blurred face hidden behind an eye-level grill. Now, as he waited to be admitted to the Winthrop inner sanctum, he warmed himself by thinking about Mary Alice, who'd promised to take a taxi uptown and meet him on the corner in an hour.

"We can have brunch at a place I know just off 57th and Lex," she'd said.

"Brunch sounds good," Conor had answered, kissing her, "but I'll be damned if I can think of anything we can do with the rest of the day."

The sound of her husky laugh was still echoing in his ears as the buzzer to the Winthrop mansion sounded. Conor grasped the heavy brass doorknob and turned it. The door swung open and he stepped inside a small anteroom.

"Good morning, sir."

The accent was English, the attire was formal. The butler, Conor thought, without question, and though the man's greeting was polite, the look on his face suggested it was certainly not a good morning if he was going to have to admit someone like this into the Winthrop presence.

Conor gave an inward sigh. He was used to it by now but it still amazed him to find that the toadies of the rich and powerful were often twice as smarmy as their masters.

"Mr. Winthrop will see you in a moment."

"Good," Conor said, at the same time moving forward into the foyer so that Jeeves or whoever the hell he was had no choice but to step aside. He shrugged off his Burberry and tossed it at the man. "Don't bother hanging my coat away," he said pleasantly. "I won't be staying long."

Jeeves inclined his head and draped the Burberry across the back of a chair with a tapestry seat and arms and legs that ended in claws. Conor half expected the chair to growl and chew the coat into pieces.

"As you wish, sir. If you'll wait here, please?"

The butler vanished noiselessly through a doorway that led into the bowels of the house. Conor undid the button on his Harris tweed jacket, tucked his hands into his pants pockets, and balanced forward and backward on the balls of his feet while he admired his surroundings.

The foyer was handsome. The walls were paneled in the sort of rich, old wood that bore the deep luster that comes of decades of patient care. He glanced down at the carpet beneath his feet. It was old, too. Persian, maybe, or Turkish.

He took his hand from his pocket, shot back his cuff, and

looked at his watch. Five minutes gone already. What in hell was taking Winthrop so long?

Impatiently, he paced the perimeter of the room. No doubt about it, it was certainly nice to be rich. Very, very nice. That had to be a Van Gogh on the wall. His dark brows lifted. And, unless he missed his bet, that was a Jasper Johns hanging right next to it . . .

Jesus.

Everything seemed to go still as his gaze fell on a painting that hung slightly apart from the others.

You didn't have to wear a paint-spattered smock to know that it wasn't the work of anybody whose name had ever rocked the art world. This was no Old Master, dark and glorious with age, and it wasn't an impressionist gem. It wasn't even something new, trendy, and outrageously clever. The painting's only claim to fame was its subject. And she made everything else that hung on these walls fade to insignificance.

Conor moved forward, his eyes never leaving the portrait. It was of a young woman standing in a garden, her face and body angled towards the viewer. She was wearing a demure, old-fashioned dress, white lace, maybe, with a high collar and long, full sleeves, and holding a wide-brimmed straw hat in her hand. Her hair, a waterfall of midnight silk, was drawn back from her high-cheekboned face and then left to spill, unhampered, over her shoulders. Her eyes were a shade of dark green that Conor knew couldn't be real but had to be the invention of the painter. Her mouth looked soft and inviting. It was color of a budding rose and bore the faintest suggestion of a smile.

The girl in the painting was beautiful, with the guileless innocence of youth.

Or was she? The longer he looked, the more he saw something else. The girl seemed to have both the purity of a Madonna and the sensuality of a Jezebel.

With heart-stopping swiftness, Conor felt his body harden with need.

''Hell,'' he muttered, under his breath.

The last time he'd reacted that way to a picture, he'd been a randy adolescent drooling over a copy of *Playboy.* What kind of nonsense was this? If you factored in the night he'd just spent in Mary Alice's bed, what was happening to him was damned near impossible.

But it was happening, just the same.

"Mr. O'Neil?"

Who was she? He stepped closer to the painting. That smile—was it really a smile, or was it something else, an allusion to a sadness so deeply hidden it might never be revealed?

"Mr. O'Neil?"

And those eyes. That color. Surely, no artist would devise such a shade of green—

"Excuse me, Mr. O'Neil."

Conor blinked and swung around. A white-haired man with an aristocratic bearing was standing just behind him, hand outstretched.

"So sorry to have kept you waiting," the man said. "I'm Hoyt Winthrop."

Conor cleared his throat. "Mr. Winthrop." He stuck out his hand, pasted a smile on his lips and hoped he didn't look anywhere near as foolish as he felt. "It's good to meet you, sir."

"My pleasure." Winthrop gestured towards a doorway. "Let's go into the library, shall we?"

Conor nodded, smiled, did all the things a sane man was supposed to do before stealing one last glance at the portrait. And that was all it was, he saw with relief, just a portrait and definitely not a very good one.

Maybe he should have accepted Mary Alice's offer of coffee before he'd headed uptown, after all.

The library was enormous, big enough to accommodate both a grand piano draped with a silk shawl and a fieldstone fireplace with a hearth that could have easily held a spitted ox. Windows heavily draped in crimson velvet gave out onto the street.

Hoyt Winthrop waved to a grouping of leather chairs and sofas.

"Sit down, Mr. O'Neil, please. May I offer you something? I was just about to have a second cup of coffee."

"Coffee would be fine. Thank you."

"Of course. Charles?" The butler materialized at once, all but clicking his heels. "Coffee, please." Winthrop sat down on the sofa opposite Conor, waited until the door had swung shut and then leaned forward, his hands flat on his knees. "Well," he said, "it's certainly very kind of you to make time to see me, Mr. O'Neil."

Conor nodded politely. What harm was there in a little white lie?

"It's my pleasure, sir."

"How is my old friend Harry? We haven't seen each other in years."

"He's fine. He said to send you his congratulations." Conor paused as the butler entered the room carrying a silver coffee service. He waited until the coffee was poured and the door was shut before continuing. "The investigation's been completed and you passed with flying colors."

Winthrop beamed with delight. Conor had seen this same reaction before. It never failed to amuse him that men and women should look so much like little children on Christmas morning when they found out they'd passed a background check and were about to be rewarded by being appointed to jobs in which they'd almost invariably end up with ulcers or worse.

"That's wonderful news. Wonderful." Winthrop's smile dimmed just a little. "But we seem to have run into a minor glitch."

"The note, you mean?"

Winthrop nodded. "Yes."

"May I see it, please?"

"Of course. I'm quite sure it means nothing, but still—"

The door opened, interrupting him in midsentence. Winthrop rose to his feet and Conor did, too, as a woman entered the room. For one heart-stopping second, he thought it was the girl in the portrait—but it wasn't. This woman was considerably older and not half as beautiful. Still, the resemblance was strong, even uncanny.

"Hoyt, darling," she said, and came towards them. She smiled but her eyes—not the extraordinary green of the painting but a light hazel—homed in on Conor with the intensity of a laser-guided missile.

Winthrop put his arm lightly around the woman's shoulders and she offered her cheek for his kiss.

"Mr. O'Neil, this is my wife, Eva. Eva, dearest, this is Conor O'Neil. Harry Thurston asked him to stop by."

Eva Winthrop smiled politely as Conor took her outstretched hand. Her fingers were cool but she surprised him with a firm, steady handshake.

"How do you do, Mr. O'Neil? Please, sit down."

Her voice held the faintest trace of an accent. French? Spanish? Conor tried to remember what the papers had said about Eva Winthrop but he drew a blank.

"Mr. O'Neil's come to tell us the Bureau's finished its background check, darling," Winthrop said to his wife as she arranged herself on the sofa beside him.

"And?" she said, pouring herself a cup of coffee.

"And, everything's fine."

"Well, that's good news." She sipped her coffee, then put the cup down in its saucer. "Has my husband shown you the note we received, Mr. O'Neil?"

"I was just about to, when you joined us." Winthrop slipped his hand into his inside breast pocket, took out a small white envelope and handed it to Conor. "We received it yesterday morning."

Conor turned the envelope over. Eva Winthrop's name was printed in block letters on the front. There was no postmark or return address.

"Someone slipped it under the door," she said, when he looked at her.

The young man from the government nodded politely. Eva watched as he slid the note from the envelope. Had she managed to sound unconcerned? Did she look the same way? *Dios,* she hoped so. She'd practiced saying those simple words in front of her dressing room mirror for the past half hour.

If only Hoyt's friend, Harry Thurston, hadn't insisted on having the note picked up. If only they could have sent it to Washington by messenger.

If only it had never arrived.

But it had, and now she watched as a stranger named Conor O'Neil read the thing. It was taking him forever, although she couldn't imagine why. The note was only one line long. She knew it by heart.

Those who cannot remember the past are condemned to repeat it.

That was it, nothing more. And yet, if those words meant what she could only hope and pray they did not mean, the note could signal the end of everything, of the life she'd worked so hard to build.

The horror of the thought made her shudder. Hoyt turned and looked at her.

"Are you all right, darling?"

Eva smiled reassuringly. "Yes. Yes, I'm fine."

She wasn't fine. She was close to hysteria, but what else could she say? She'd said as much as she'd dared yesterday morning, when Hoyt had walked in on her just as she'd opened the note.

Of all days for him to have forgotten his briefcase. Of all days for him to have decided to come back and fetch it himself! If only he'd sent his chauffeur, or a boy from the office.

"But, what does it mean?" he'd asked, after he'd read the note.

"I've no idea," Eva had said brightly.

She'd crumpled the slip of paper as if she'd truly meant it and tossed it aside but Hoyt had reacted with all the fervor of his Puritan ancestors, retrieving the damnable thing, smoothing it out, then tucking it back into its envelope.

"I'd best report it."

"Hoyt, whatever for? It's nothing."

“I'm sure you're right, my dear, but considering the importance of this appointment, one can't be too careful. I'll phone Harry Thurston. We went to Choate together, you know.”

Oh yes. Eva knew. The great brotherhood of old money and older bloodlines, that small, select fraternity that had been closed to her until she'd made her first million at Papillon, the oh-so-private club that would not have admitted her to its ranks had she not bedazzled and married Hoyt.

“Do you have any idea who could have sent this note, Mrs. Winthrop?”

Eva looked at Conor O'Neil. She'd expected the question and she had an answer ready.

“None,” she said, putting her cup and saucer down on the table.

“Mr. Winthrop?”

Hoyt shook his head, too, his handsome face puzzled. “I'm afraid not, Mr. O'Neil.”

“Any thoughts about what it might mean?”

Hoyt shrugged his shoulders. “Not a one.”

“Mrs. Winthrop?”

Eva's eyes met Conor's. “Yes?”

“Have you any idea what the note means?”

Her gaze was clear and steady. “No.”

Conor nodded again. “Santayana,” he said.

Both Winthrops looked at him as if he'd just announced that he'd had a vision.

“The quote's from Santayana. The Spanish philosopher.”

“Oh. Of course.”

Hoyt Winthrop smiled. He had a face like an open book, easy to read and to understand. He was puzzled, and obviously so. Eva Winthrop's face bore the same expression, but Conor thought there was something else in the way she looked at him.

What was it? Animosity? Probably, and he couldn't much blame her. Her husband had endured the rigors of a government investigation and now a man from some nameless agency was sitting in her library, holding in his hands the power to start the process all over again. When you came down to it, why shouldn't she dislike him?

Conor smiled, trying to put the Winthrops at ease. He folded the note and tucked it into its envelope.

"You don't mind if I keep it, do you?" he said, as if they really had a choice in the matter.

"Certainly not," Hoyt Winthrop said.

"If you feel you must," Eva Winthrop said. Her tone was sharp, and both men looked at her. She cleared her throat. "I just think my husband's worrying about nothing. This is New York, after all. People make threats every day."

"Is that what you think this is, Mrs. Winthrop? A threat?"

Eva's eyes narrowed a fraction of an inch. "It's what my husband thinks. That's why he called Mr. Thurston."

"But you don't agree."

"Central Park is just across the street. I walk through it often. There are homeless people there. Have you ever seen them?"

"Eva, my dear," Hoyt said, "Mr. O'Neil's just trying to help."

"I'm not sure I get your point, Mrs. Winthrop."

Eva rose to her feet and the men did, too.

"If you walk past people like that often enough, you're bound to hear them muttering things. Threatening things, one might say. But I never take any of it personally. New York is full of deranged souls, Mr. O'Neil. Do you see what I mean?"

Conor smiled. She had a point, a valid one. He told her so, and she smiled back at him.

"I'm glad we agree." Eva linked her arm through her husband's and looked past him, at an antique clock on the fireplace mantel. "My goodness, I had no idea it was getting so late. May I pour you more coffee?"

It was a very polite, very proper dismissal but a dismissal, nonetheless. Conor bit back the desire to tell Eva Winthrop that he was as eager to leave as she was to get rid of him. A glance at the same clock confirmed his worst suspicions, that

Mary Alice had by now been sitting outside in a cab, waiting for him for at least twenty minutes.

"Thank you," he said, "but I have an appointment."

Eva offered her hand and he shook it. Hoyt led him from the library and into the foyer, chatting casually about this and that. Conor listened, but with only half an ear. He'd been this route before, engaging in the polite conversation that went with people trying to pretend that he might not somehow muck up their lives by uncovering secrets they'd thought were buried deep enough never to be found. He'd only spent half an hour with Hoyt Winthrop but the man seemed likeable enough. Conor wanted to tell him not to worry, that the odds were a hundred to one this note was going to end up in the shredder Monday morning.

But life, and his training, had taught him not to trust the odds. And anyway, his mind was on other things.

The portrait, for one. There it was again. There *she* was again, the girl with the smile that held a million questions and eyes that seemed to look into a man's soul.

"Mr. O'Neil?"

Conor turned around. Hoyt Winthrop was holding out his coat. Conor flushed, took the coat and shrugged it on.

"Sorry. I was—ah, I was just trying to think of some simple explanation for that note."

Hoyt gave him a hopeful smile. "And?"

"And if I were you, I wouldn't be the least bit concerned," Conor said briskly. "Your wife's right. The world's full of psychos. For all we know, the note's the first step in a solicitation by a bunch of religious fruitcakes. You know, a loose interpretation of the 'Repent, ye sinners,' kind of thing."

"Of course," Hoyt said, looking relieved. "Why didn't I think of that?" He held out his hand and Conor shook it. "Thank you again for coming by, Mr. O'Neil. And if you need anything else . . ."

"Actually," Conor said, "there is one thing."

"Yes?"

"That painting."

Hoyt's brows rose. "What painting?"

"That one. Of the girl." Conor paused. He felt as stupid as he was certain he sounded, and yet it would be stupider still not to know the answer, to leave here wondering about the girl's identity. "Who is she?"

Hoyt turned, his gaze following Conor's. "Oh. You mean Miranda."

Miranda? Of course. Eva's daughter, Miranda Beckman.

"It was painted when she was sixteen."

Sixteen? Conor thought, surprised. The girl in the painting looked older. Not wiser, just older than sixteen. He looked at her mouth again, at that Mona Lisa smile, and to his chagrin he felt that sudden tightening of his body.

"She doesn't live with us," Hoyt said quickly. "Miranda's been on her own for several years now. I'm sorry to say that we're not close, not close at all."

She lives a pretty wild life.

Harry Thurston's words echoed in Conor's head as his eyes met Winthrop's. The man's message was clear. *Don't judge me by my stepdaughter,* he was saying. *I don't have anything to do with her life and she has nothing to do with mine.*

It took nothing to offer a smile of reassurance.

"Yes, sir," Conor said quietly. "I understand."

Hoyt smiled. "Good day, Mr. O'Neil."

"Good-bye, Mr. Winthrop."

The door shut after him. Conor trotted down the steps. There was a cab parked at the curb and he hurried to it and yanked open the door. Mary Alice glared at him as he climbed inside.

"Honestly, Conor, I've been waiting and waiting. Meet me at ten, you said, and here it is, going on ten-thirty, and—"

Conor thought of Miranda's portrait. How could he have thought Mary Alice beautiful? Her eyes weren't the color of the sea; her hair didn't frame her face like ebony silk.

"—don't like to be treated this way, not one bit. If you think you can—"

What sort of man got turned on by a painting? Hell, what sort of man got turned on by a painting when he had a flesh and blood woman like this waiting for him? Conor looked at Mary Alice's blue eyes, her daffodil-gold hair. He thought about her satin thighs and the fullness of her breasts.

"—was thinking that perhaps you'd rather collect your things and go to the airport. The shuttle—"

She gasped as Conor pulled her roughly into his arms and kissed her to silence. When the kiss ended, she leaned back and smiled into his eyes.

"Oh, that's nice," she said softly. "Very nice." Reaching out, she stroked her hand over his forehead, threading her fingers into his dark hair. "I thought you'd forgotten all about me."

His smile was slow and sexy. "Not for a minute."

Mary Alice linked her hands behind his neck. "That's good, because I expect your undivided attention."

"You've got it."

"For the weekend, I mean. You do understand," she said, not unkindly. "I'm not into commitment."

Conor laughed. She was just what he needed, this woman. She was all honesty and reality and unabashed desire. As for being beautiful—a man would have to be crazy not to see that she was.

Whatever nonsense had spooked him in the Winthrop house would wither once he and Mary Alice Whittaker took another ride in her waterbed.

They shared a long brunch and then they took an equally long carriage ride through Central Park. In late afternoon, Conor bought a couple of bottles of Chardonnay at a store that looked more like a place that sold magic elixirs than booze and then they stopped at Zabar's for Brie, English water biscuits and smoked Scotch salmon.

They taxied to Mary Alice's apartment and while she changed to another incredibly sexy gown that seemed to be woven of cobwebs, Conor chilled the wine, lit a fire in the fireplace and tossed the throw pillows from the sofa onto the carpet. They made love slowly, by the light of the dancing flames. It was all perfect . . . and yet, at the last minute, Conor hesitated.

"Conor?" Mary Alice whispered as he went still above her.

He looked down at her upturned face. "It's all right," he said, bending to kiss her.

And it was all right, just as soon as he closed his eyes and substituted the inky spill of Miranda Beckman's hair for the soft strands of gold that actually lay spread over the pillows, the unfathomable green eyes for the greedy blue ones.

It was the first time in his life he'd ever made love to an imaginary woman. It was a new feeling, and he was not sure he liked it, but it brought him to a shattering climax that somehow still managed to be incomplete.

At dawn, he arose from Mary Alice's bed.

"Wha' time issit?" she said sleepily.

"Go back to sleep," he said. Then he kissed her gently on the mouth, showered and dressed, and caught an early morning flight back to Washington.

Chapter Two

Monday morning and It was still raining, in New York and in D.C. But the six o'clock shuttle touched down at Dulles right on schedule.

Conor swung his carry-on bag from the overhead compartment, made his way out into the terminal along with a hurrying bunch of yawning, early-morning business travelers and headed for the lot where he'd left his car. He slung his bag into the rear seat of the vintage Thunderbird, got behind the wheel and headed for the Beltway.

Traffic was heavy. It always was. Sometimes Conor had the feeling that everybody who worked in Washington spent half their time sitting in their automobiles, driving the road that encircled the city.

Things eased off, once he headed into the Virginia countryside. Office buildings weren't jammed in here the way they were in town. Traffic was moving pretty smoothly by the time he reached the turn-off for the complex where the Committee had its offices. It was still raining, but that was okay.

The rain suited his mood.

The weekend that had begun with so much promise had

ended on an off-key note and he had nobody to blame but himself.

Why in hell had he agreed to do Thurston's "little favor?"

"Little favor, my ass," he muttered as he took the off-ramp faster than was sensible, considering the rain. The 'bird slipped a little on the wet macadam and Conor eased his foot from the gas pedal.

Despite his assurances to the Winthrops, every instinct he possessed told him there was more to that seemingly simple note than he'd pretended. Those same instincts told him that Eva Winthrop knew it, that she knew one hell of a lot more than she'd admitted.

And then there was that portrait.

Conor's hands tightened on the steering wheel. Why couldn't he get it out of his head? It was as if the image of the girl had burned itself into his brain. All he had to do was shut his eyes and he could see that perfect oval face, those green eyes, that mane of black hair.

What kind of stupidity was that?

He was not a man given to romantic daydreams, especially about females who were, what? Sixteen? Wasn't that what Hoyt Winthrop had said Miranda was, in the painting? As for sexual fantasies—like any other man, he'd had his share. A beautiful woman strolling past, hips swaying just so. A quick glance, a smile, and he could amuse himself with some very interesting scenarios during a dull meeting an hour or two later. But he never toyed with fantasies when he had a stunning, eager-to-please woman in his arms—and yet, he'd left Mary Alice's bed in the dark hour just before dawn, not so much because he couldn't sleep but because there was something unsettling about the possibility of making it with her again while conjuring up an image of Miranda Beckman.

Conor's jaw tightened as he pulled into the parking lot. Okay, so maybe the girl's face was stuck in his head. But it wasn't his hormones that kept it there, it was instinct, the same sixth sense that told him that her mother knew lots more than she was letting on.

Miranda Beckman, Miranda Winthrop, whatever Eva's daughter called herself, was somehow part of what was going on. He wasn't sure how or why, only that the note, and the girl, were linked. Despite what he'd told Eva and Hoyt, the note meant business. And it had something to do with Miranda.

Conor trotted up the marble steps of the building that housed the Committee's offices, walked through the doors as they opened soundlessly and made his way across the lobby. He bypassed the bank of public elevators for three others that were tucked away in an alcove, keyed in the code that opened one of them and stepped inside. The doors shut and a disembodied electronic voice asked him to place his fingertips against a glowing panel in the wall. He did, and the same toneless voice asked him to select a floor.

"Seven," he said.

The elevator rose noiselessly.

On the other hand, he wasn't going to tell any of that to Harry Thurston.

For one thing, it was all speculation. For another, he absolutely, positively had no intention of getting drawn into an investigation that was none of his business. The elevator doors opened and he stepped out onto the seventh floor. There was no reason to get drawn in. The Winthrop thing was in the FBI's lap, not CIA's, not the Committee's, and surely not—

"You're late, Mr. O'Neil."

Conor sighed. For all the electronic and digital coding that guarded the inner workings of these offices, it was still a human being who decided who got through the last set of doors. Sybil Aldrich, Harry Thurston's plump, fiftyish and formidable secretary, guarded her boss's lair with unwavering ferocity.

Conor looked at the old-fashioned clock that hung on the bilious green wall beside Sybil's desk. It was 8:03. He'd phoned Harry from the plane and told him he'd be in to see him around eight.

"Did you hear me, Mr. O'Neil? I said, you're late."

"And good morning to you, too, sweet Sybil."

"Mr. Thurston expected you promptly at eight."

"He expected me whenever I showed up." Conor paused at Sybil's desk, bent towards her and took a dramatic sniff. "Mmm. What wonderful, exotic fragrance are you wearing today, I wonder?"

"It's Ivory soap. And you should know by now, your nonsense doesn't impress me."

Conor smiled. Theirs was an old routine. At least, it was a routine on his part. He was never quite certain if Sybil played at being a junkyard dog or if she really was one.

"Try and remember I take my coffee with sugar and cream this time, will you, Sybil, love?"

"Try and remember that asking a secretary for coffee is a sexist act."

"Two lumps, okay? And make sure you use cream, not that powdered stuff you pawn off on the peasants." He shot her a smile, opened the door and stepped inside Thurston's office.

The head of the Committee was seated behind his government-issue tan metal desk, his swivel chair turned so that his back was to the room and he was facing the window and the grey, steady rain. Conor walked to the desk and sat down in one of the leather chairs that faced it. The chair was government-issue, too, which meant that it was almost as uncomfortable as it was unattractive.

"Your kind of day, Harry?"

Thurston chuckled as he swiveled his chair around. He was a slender, fine-boned man of indeterminate years who would have looked more at home as a professor at an Ivy League university than as head of a group that few people inside government, and no one outside it, knew existed.

"It's a brook trout's kind of day, my boy. I was just wishing I could take the morning off and head up to a little pool I know in the mountains." Harry folded his hand on his desk. "How was your weekend?"

"Great."

Harry sighed dramatically. "It must be wonderful to be young, single and a shoe-in for the next James Bond."

Conor smiled. He dug into his pocket, took out the note Hoyt Winthrop had given him and tossed it onto the desk.

"Only if Bond's an errand boy, Harry. There's your note."

"And here's something to keep you busy, while I read."

Thurston pushed a slender file folder across the blotter. Conor picked it up and flipped it open. Inside was a summary of the background checks that had been done on Hoyt and Eva Winthrop. He skimmed the notes on Hoyt but there was nothing there he didn't already know. The man was Old Money, through and through.

The stuff on Eva was only a little more interesting. She'd been born in Argentina, where she'd met and married a young Marine named James Beckman who'd been assigned to the American Embassy. When his tour of duty ended, Beckman took Eva home with him to the States. He'd died in a car crash shortly after their daughter, Miranda, was born. Eva had gone on to cleverly parlay a door-to-door cosmetics business into a multi-million dollar company.

Conor closed the file folder and dropped it on the desk.

"Interesting," he said politely.

Harry looked up from the note. "So is this." He folded the note, tucked it back inside its envelope and pushed it across the desk. "Conclusions?"

"Could be anything," Conor said, without acknowledging that the note was sitting in front of him.

"A shopping list? A birthday message for Grandma?"

"Come on, Harry, you know what I mean."

Thurston smiled. "Humor me."

"Well, it could be from a crank, just looking to keep the President's newest appointee on his toes."

"By goosing the appointee's spouse?"

"Ask Sybil to clue you in on the subject of sexual equity sometime," Conor said with a wry smile.

"What else?"

"Could be it's from a run-of-the-mill crackpot, somebody who spotted Eva Winthrop's name someplace and wants to shake her up a little."

''Why?''

''How should I know why?'' Conor leaned back in his chair, folded his arms and crossed his legs. ''She runs a cosmetic company, remember? Maybe it's from a dissatisfied customer.''

''Would you care to figure the odds on a customer sending Eva Winthrop a quote from Santayana because she doesn't like the color of the lipstick she just bought?''

Conor's eyes narrowed. ''I didn't know you were a student of philosophy, Harry.''

Thurston chuckled. ''Hoyt and I finally connected by phone this morning. He told me what the note said, told me what *you'd* said, and that he was impressed with how you'd handled things.''

''Yeah, well, that's only because I lied through my . . . '' Conor broke off but it was too late. Harry was looking at him with his eyebrows raised.

''Lied through your teeth? When you told my old friend the note was meaningless?''

''You wanted me to reassure him, right? Well, I reassured him.''

''But you don't think the note is just from some nut case.''

Conor shoved back his chair and got to his feet.

''Look, let's stop playing games. Hoyt Winthrop's up for a presidential appointment. His wife got a note from a person or persons unknown. It's not a note that says 'Have a nice day,' or even 'Watch yourself or I'll blow you away,' which would at least make some sense, it's a note that's pretty much open to interpretation, all of which adds up to mean—as you and I both know—that somebody should probably check things out.''

''Somebody?''

''Somebody,'' Conor repeated coolly. ''Meanwhile, I'm glad to hear that Winthrop was pleased with my visit. You be sure and ask him to write a note of recommendation for my file. Now, if you don't mind, I've got work to do.''

''Conor, let's not play games.'' Thurston plucked the note from his desk and stood up. ''This thing has a bad smell and you know it.''

"Maybe. On the other hand, it could be just what I said, a crank note with no more meaning than a crank phone call."

Thurston's brows lifted. "Did they get a phone call, too?"

"No! Dammit, Harry, I'm just making a point. The note might be something to worry about or it might not. Hand it over to the FBI and let them check it out."

"Is that your best advice?"

"It's my only advice."

"I'm surprised. I never realized you were so fond of the establishment."

"It's their job," Conor said, refusing to be baited, "not ours."

"I agree."

"Good. End of story. When you've got something for me to start on, give me a ring."

"The President doesn't want anybody's dirty laundry showing when he makes this appointment."

"Right." Conor strolled to the door. "And I'm sure the FBI will do a bang-up job of seeing it doesn't."

"And Hoyt would be devastated if something went wrong."

"Uh-huh. My heart goes out to him."

"Remember the last time the Oval Office put its stamp of approval on an appointee?"

"Of course I remember. They almost got ridden out of town on a rail."

"So did the poor bastard who was up for the appointment, and all because there was a screw-up in the investigation."

"So, let the White House tell whoever handles this to make sure they don't screw up this time."

"Conor, come on." Thurston offered his most engaging smile as he walked towards Conor, the note held out in his hand. "How often can you do a favor for the President's men and for a friend, all at the same time?"

Conor looked at the note, then stuffed his hands into his trouser pockets.

"To tell you the truth," he said, "I've never much wanted

to do a favor for the President's men. As for doing one for a friend . . . Winthrop's your buddy, not mine."

"I meant, do it for me," Thurston said, with a wounded look. "What will it take? A day of your time? Two, maybe? Check things out, write me a one page report—"

"I'm not writing anything. I've been around long enough to know that the minute you put pen to paper in this funhouse, you sign on for trouble, especially when what you're doing is supposed to be somebody else's job."

"All right, don't do this on an official basis. We'll keep the Committee out of it."

"Must I spell it out, Harry? I don't want any part of this."

"Any part of what? What's the matter with you this morning? You're making a hundred times more out of this than it's worth."

A muscle twitched in Conor's jaw. He wanted to tell Thurston that he was wrong, that he wasn't making more of this than it was worth—but how could he, when it was the truth? Whatever the note meant, whoever had sent it, checking it out wouldn't be difficult. A couple of days work at the most, and he'd have everything he needed to know. The FBI had already done a job on the Winthrops; he'd have all that info at his disposal, which would surely make things simpler.

As for this not being the Committee's business . . . hell, as far as this town knew, nothing but sweet, simple commerce was the Committee's business. No more than a dozen people with the right kind of top-level clearance knew the truth.

Thurston, sensing Conor's mood change, moved in for the kill.

"Conor, my boy, come on. I've done you favors, haven't I? Remember that time you wanted to put in another year in Vienna and the brass had already figured you for a stint in Moscow?"

"You calling in old favors?"

"I'm simply pointing out that we're compatriots who go back a long way. Besides, this is a simple deal. There's no problem, is there?"

The portrait. That was the problem. The portrait in the Winthrop mansion. Conor didn't want to see it again, that hint of darkness in those wide green eyes, the isolation of that figure that hovered on the brink of womanhood.

"*Is* there?" Thurston repeated, with polite interest.

Conor cursed under his breath, snatched the note from Thurston's outstretched hand and shoved it into his pocket.

"You owe me one," he growled, and he strode from the office.

The lab was the first logical stop.

A woman in a white coat looked at the note, sniffed it, looked at it again before putting it under a microscope. She told Conor that the paper was a fine quality linen, a European brand, according to the watermark, but she added that you could buy the stuff in at least a couple of dozen stores on the East Coast and probably almost as many on the West.

The ink was standard, black and waterproof, that could be found virtually anywhere between here and Beijing, unusual only in that it hadn't come from a ball point pen. As for fingerprints . . . Conor hadn't figured on getting any help there and he didn't. There were his own prints, and Thurston's, though both men had been careful to handle both the envelope and the note inside by its edges. And there were Hoyt Winthrop's and others he'd bet were Eva's. The handwriting was right-handed.

"Could be a man's," the tech said in a bored voice, "or a woman's. Could be European or American. Could be anyplace from thirty to, say, sixty."

"That certainly narrows things down," Conor said pleasantly, and he pocketed the note and made his way to the third floor library. He found the volume of Santayana easily enough, found the specific line used in the note, too. Unfortunately, reading it in context made no more sense than reading it out of context.

In midafternoon, he telephoned the Winthrop mansion. To

his surprise, Eva answered the phone herself. Conor asked if he could see her for half an hour or so. He had expected her to ask him the reason but she didn't.

"When?"

He glanced at his watch. "How about this evening? I can catch a flight at six and be in Manhattan by eight."

"I'm afraid that's impossible. My husband and I are having dinner with the mayor tonight."

Conor smiled. He suspected he was supposed to be impressed.

"Tomorrow morning, then. You name the time."

"Tomorrow's no good either," Eva said. "I have business meetings all day. Actually, this isn't a very good week, Mr. O'Neil. My schedule is quite full."

"What time is your dinner appointment, Mrs. Winthrop?"

"I'm meeting my husband downtown at quarter of eight. We're due at Gracie Mansion a few minutes later. So you see, unfortunately, I just won't be able to—"

"I'll see you at six, then."

"Six? But I thought you were in Washington."

Conor looked at his watch again. "Six," he said, and hung up the phone. He had to hurry if he wanted to make the airport in time.

The same butler let him in.

"Mrs. Winthrop is expecting you," he said, in a tone that made it clear he didn't approve.

Conor grinned. "Ah, the things one must tolerate in this life, hmm, Charles?" He took off his Burberry, dropped it into the same chair as yesterday, deliberately avoided even a glance at the painting and followed the man's stiff back to the library.

Eva Winthrop was seated before the fireplace. She was wearing an off-white dress dotted with tiny gold sequins that reflected the flames from the hearth. Her dark hair was drawn back from her face in the kind of severe style only a woman with bones like hers could hope to pull off.

She rose when Conor entered the room and held out her hand.

"Mr. O'Neil," she said politely, "how nice to see you again." She shot a quick but meaningful glance at the clock. He knew she'd done it to remind him that her time was limited. "May I offer you some coffee?"

"No, thank you. I had coffee on the plane." He smiled. "Actually, I think it was more like a straight cup of caffeine."

Eva smiled back at him, though the smile didn't quite reach her eyes. "That will be all then, Charles." She waited until the butler had shut the door and then she looked at Conor. "Well, Mr. O'Neil, what can I do for you?"

Did she want to get straight to the point? Or did she hope to get rid of him quickly? Either way, for all her sophisticated aplomb, he could see the tension in her hazel eyes, and suddenly he thought of the green eyes of her daughter, of the haunted look in them.

Conor frowned and cleared his throat.

"I thought you'd like to know that we've done some preliminary work on that note."

"And?"

"And, we haven't come up with anything."

Eva nodded, her expression impassive. "I see."

"The other day, I asked you if you could think of anyone who might send you a message like that."

"Yes. And I told you I couldn't. If you came all this distance to ask me the same question again, Mr. O'Neil—"

"Do you have any enemies, Mrs. Winthrop?"

"Enemies?"

Did her tone suddenly reflect the same tension Conor saw in her eyes?

"No," she said quickly. Too quickly, Conor thought. "Why would I have enemies?"

"Well, you're CEO of Papillon Cosmetics."

Eva smiled for the first time. "Yes. And its founder and president."

"Surely, you've made enemies on the way up."

"I suppose I have, but if you're going to ask me if somebody I fired or somebody I bought out could have sent me that note, I'd have to tell you it's impossible." She smiled again. "None of them is literate enough to quote a philosopher."

Conor laughed. "People can surprise you, sometimes."

"People never surprise me," she said flatly. She looked pointedly at the clock, then turned and made her way to the door of the library. "Now, if that's all, Mr. O'Neil, I'm afraid I really must—"

"What about your daughter, Mrs. Winthrop?"

Eva swung towards him, but not before he saw her shoulders stiffen.

"What about her?"

"I understand that she lives in Europe."

"Yes."

"In France."

"Yes."

"And that she has, for several years."

"Yes," Eva said again.

Did she think this was going to be a game of Twenty Questions? The woman's tone was as unyielding as her posture.

"Are you suggesting that my daughter had something to do with that note?"

Conor shrugged his shoulders. "I'm not suggesting anything, Mrs. Winthrop, not yet, anyway. I'm just trying to get a handle on things."

"Of course." Eva cleared her throat, glanced at her watch, then took her hand from the doorknob. "I'm going to be late for my dinner engagement."

"Just a few more minutes and I'll be out of your way, I promise."

She nodded. "Well, then, perhaps I'll only miss the cocktail hour and not dinner." She smiled stiffly, and Conor caught a whiff of her perfume as she made her way past him to a wet bar on the far side of the room. "Won't you join me in a drink, Mr. O'Neil?"

His first instinct was to decline her offer. He never drank

when he was on the job and even though he wasn't on the job, not officially, this visit wasn't a social one. Besides, his particular passion was for ale, something he'd long ago figured was about the only thing he'd inherited from his old man, and he was pretty damn certain the Winthrops weren't given to stocking ale in the refrigerator. But Eva was looking at him as if her life hung on his answer and he realized suddenly that she wasn't just being polite. She needed that drink.

"Thank you," he said, "a drink would be perfect."

She let out an audible breath. "What would you like?"

Conor hesitated. If he couldn't get ale, he'd settle for Irish whiskey, straight up. But Irish whiskey, no matter how fine the label, was hardly what Eva Winthrop would be pouring for herself.

"Whatever you're having."

She nodded, dumped ice into two glasses, then poured a generous amount of vodka into each. She handed him a glass, drank down half of her own, and looked at him.

"Miranda lives in Paris," she said. "She's a model, sought after by all the *couturiers* and by the top fashion magazines."

"You must be very proud of her," Conor said politely.

The ice cubes in Eva's glass clinked together as she raised the glass to her lips.

"Any mother is pleased by her child's success."

"Of course," he said, even more politely, but what he thought was that Eva might just as easily been talking about the daughter of an acquaintance. "When was the last time you spoke with your daughter, Mrs. Winthrop?"

"I fail to see the relevancy of—" Eva took a deep breath. "On her birthday, I think."

"And that was . . . ?"

"Last March."

Conor struggled to keep his surprise from showing. He wasn't particularly proud of his own record for keeping in touch with his old man but ten months without so much as a phone call seemed a bit excessive.

"We are not close, Miranda and I," Eva said stiffly.

The understatement of the year, Conor thought. He smiled politely.

"And when did you last see her?"

"Eight years ago this past April."

"I see," he said, struggling to keep his face a mask.

"You don't see, but that's quite all right. It would be difficult to explain—and I've no intention of doing so." She turned and looked him squarely in the eye. "My relationship with my daughter is a private matter."

"Nothing is a private matter," Conor said bluntly, "not when your husband is a presidential appointee."

Eva looked at him for a long moment. Then she turned away, picked up the bottle of Absolut and refilled her glass.

"You're right, of course. And if I'm honest, I suppose I must admit that the note might very well be connected to my daughter."

"Connected? In what way? Perhaps you'd better tell me what you know, Mrs. Winthrop."

Eva hesitated. Then she sighed, sat down in a silk-covered armchair and motioned Conor into the matching chair opposite hers.

"Yes, I might as well. You can find out easily enough." She put down her glass, crossed her legs and folded her hands on her knees. The action brought her forward in the chair so that she seemed to be leaning towards him. "This isn't easy for me, Mr. O'Neil."

"I'm sure it isn't," Conor said in a soothing tone.

"Eight years ago, Miranda was in her junior year at a boarding school in Connecticut. Miss Cooper's. Perhaps you've heard of it?"

"I went to a high school in the Bronx," he said with a smile meant to put Eva at ease. "I'm afraid we didn't play any football games at Miss Cooper's."

She smiled. "No, I suppose not. Well, Miss Cooper's was—is—a fine school. Very Old World, if you know what I mean. There were curfews, you had to study so many hours an evening, you were restricted to your room after nine . . . The girls were expected to live by certain standards.''

Rules, Conor thought, not standards. But he'd grown up under rules himself, and he'd have bet his last dollar that the rules laid down by Detective-Sergeant John O'Neil, NYPD, had been a hell of a lot tougher than the ones at a high-priced girls' school.

Eva seemed to be waiting for him to say something so he smiled a little, nodded his head, and made a non-committal sound.

''Miranda didn't care for the place,'' she said.

''Too strict?'' he asked politely.

''So she claimed.'' Eva's mouth thinned. ''But I was at my wits' end. She'd already been expelled from other schools for various infractions.''

Drugs? Booze? Boys? He waited, saying nothing.

''Broken curfews. A disrespectful attitude. Marijuana. And finally, some unpleasantness about a boy in her room when the rules clearly said—''

''So you sent her to Miss Cooper's as punishment?''

''I sent her there so she could learn to curb her excesses.'' Eva shot to her feet, marched to the bar and refilled her drink. ''And a lot of good it did me.''

''But did it do your daughter any good?'' Conor heard himself ask. He frowned as Eva spun towards him. ''I mean, did she change?''

Eva smiled bitterly. ''Indeed she did, Mr. O'Neil. She gave up the small stuff and went for the brass ring. A month after she turned seventeen, she seduced her roommate's cousin, the Count Edouard de Lasserre. He was thirty-two years old, a sophisticated man of the world, but he was no match for Miranda. She ran off with him to Paris.''

Conor rose to his feet as Eva walked past him and flung open the door. He put down his untouched drink and followed her into the foyer, to the portrait on the wall.

The painting couldn't have changed. It had to be his perception of it that had undergone a subtle shift. Yes, Miranda was smiling but he was certain now that her smile was tinged with sadness.

"She was sixteen when that painting was done," Eva said, her voice trembling with righteous indignation. "Spoiled, self-centered . . . just look at her face and you can see what she was like."

Conor looked. Was Eva right? Was that sadness he saw in the curve of Miranda's lips, or was it smug satisfaction?

"Of course," Eva said, "I flew to Paris the moment I found out what had happened but I was too late. Miranda had talked Edouard de Lasserre into marrying her. Well, of course, I knew she was far too young to marry anyone, let alone a man so many years her senior. I agonized over how I'd get her out of his clutches." Eva smiled tightly. "I needn't have worried. By the time I caught up to them, de Lasserre had come to his senses. He was more than eager to grant Miranda a divorce. For the right price, naturally."

"How much did it cost you?"

Eva's breathing grew ragged. "Everything," she whispered.

He turned and looked at her. Her eyes were wet with tears; her face was pale.

"His price was exorbitant, hundreds of thousands of dollars, but what mother would do less for her child?" Eva clasped her hands to her bosom. "And do you think Miranda thanked me? No, she did not! She turned on me in a rage, furious that I'd interfered."

Conor looked at the portrait again. "Did she love him that much?"

"Love him? Miranda?" Eva gave a brittle laugh. "She never cared for anyone but herself. She hadn't seduced the man or married him for love. She just wanted to be free of me and my attempts to turn her into a responsible young woman. That was why she'd run off with him, because she knew she could twist him around her finger and live a life she preferred."

A wild life, Conor thought, a life on the edge, and for reasons he didn't pretend to understand or want to dwell on, his gut twisted. But when he spoke, his voice gave nothing away.

"It must have been a difficult time for you," he said.

Eva laughed bitterly. "It was hell."

"So, your daughter convinced Edouard de Lasserre to change his mind?"

"To keep her and give up half a million dollars, you mean? Not a chance. The Count was pleased with our arrangement. But Miranda—Miranda told me she never wanted to see me again."

"I don't understand. I thought you said she was a minor."

"She was." Eva turned, walked back into the library and headed straight for the bar. Conor gave the painting one last glance, then followed after her. "But she was no longer a child. That was what she told me in the taxi en route to the airport. I told her I was taking her home, that we'd work things out together. But Miranda said she was a woman now, not a little girl, and that she liked Paris and was going to stay there."

"A seventeen-year-old girl? And you let her?"

Eva spun towards him. The vodka in her newly freshened drink sloshed over the top of the glass.

"You're damn right I let her! She called me the most terrible names, said the most cruel things . . . " Tears glittered on her lashes. "You cannot know what it's like to have a child you've loved and nurtured turn on you! What could I do? Fly her back in chains? Lock her in her room when we got home?" Her chin rose. "I had already given more of myself to my daughter than she deserved. It was time for me to think of my husband. Of Hoyt. 'You want to stay in Paris?' I said, 'very well. Stay! I'll send you money each month and when you've had enough, let me know and I'll send you a ticket home.' "

"You've supported her, then, all these years?"

"Yes, of course. Well, until she became a successful model."

"She never wanted to come home?"

Eva shook her head. "Never," she said, her voice breaking. "I should have known that Miranda would never have enough of the kind of life she leads."

"And your husband knows all of this, Mrs. Winthrop?"

"Certainly. There are no secrets between Hoyt and me. He knows. And he agrees that I did the right thing."

Conor thrust his hands into the pockets of his trousers. "You told the FBI none of this," he said softly.

"No." She smiled thinly. "They didn't ask, and I didn't volunteer it. What mother would be proud of such failure? Besides, I didn't see that it was important but now, I suppose . . ."

"Now, you think your daughter's somehow involved in this."

Eva's eyes flashed. "She moves in decadent circles. I'm sure she knows people who'd think nothing of trying to embarrass me."

"You could have saved us all a lot of trouble if you'd told me this last night, Mrs. Winthrop."

"And I tell you again, what mother would be proud of talking about such awful failure?" Eva pulled a lace handkerchief from her pocket and dabbed at her eyes. It crossed Conor's mind that he'd never seen a woman take out a lace handkerchief except in an old movie. "Why, Miranda wouldn't even talk to me on the phone until just a year or two ag- . . . " She began to weep, very quietly. "I'm sorry, Mr. O'Neil, but I'm afraid I'm going to ask you to leave."

"Of course." Conor took out his wallet, pulled a card from it, reached past her and put it down on the bar. "If you think of anything more to tell me, Mrs. Winthrop, please give me a call."

He shut the library door after him, walked to the chair where he'd left his coat and scooped it up. The FBI investigation hadn't turned up the story of Miranda's elopement but he wasn't surprised. The incident was years old; Eva had moved quickly to hush it up and she'd succeeded. Besides, the investigation had centered on Hoyt Winthrop, not on his stepdaughter.

What did surprise him was the performance he'd just witnessed. And he was almost certain that was exactly what it had been. But why? Was there more to the story than Eva claimed?

Was she putting on an act in hopes of keeping him from digging any further?

He turned around slowly and stared at the portrait. The Mona Lisa was supposed to have the most mysterious smile in the world.

Then again, the odds were damn good that whoever had come to that conclusion had never laid eyes on this painting of Miranda Beckman.

Chapter Three

Eva had told him the truth . . .

About her husband knowing the details of Miranda's elopement, anyway. Conor's unannounced visit to Hoyt Winthrop's Wall Street firm the following day confirmed it.

The building that housed Winthrop, Winthrop and Winthrop was one of lower Manhattan's tallest and most impressive. Hoyt's company filled the top three floors; his private office took one enormous corner of the upper two. Thanks to its size and to two walls made almost entirely of glass, walking into it was like walking into an aerie.

Hoyt rose from behind a massive mahogany desk to greet him.

"Mr. O'Neil," he said, rounding the desk with his hand outstretched, "it's good to see you again."

"Thank you," Conor said politely.

"Sit down, please." Hoyt gestured to a group of chairs clustered around a marble-topped coffee table. "Can I get you anything?"

"Nothing, thank you." Conor sat and Hoyt settled across from him. "Mr. Winthrop, I was wondering if we could discuss your daughter."

"Stepdaughter," Hoyt said with a little smile.

"Yes, of course, sir. Your stepdaughter. Would you describe your relationship with her as close?"

Hoyt sighed. "It was, when I first married her mother. Miranda was, what, six or seven, I guess." He smiled. "A beautiful little girl, Mr. O'Neil, and the sweetest child imaginable. Eva and I had our concerns, you know, that it might be difficult for her to adapt to having a stepfather—her own father had died when she was only a baby—but she took to the new arrangement like a fish to water. Why, it was only weeks before she asked if she might call me Daddy."

"And you said . . . ?"

"I said it would be fine. I'd waited a bit longer than most men to marry, you see. The thought of having an instant family was most appealing."

Conor nodded. "So, you and Miranda got along well."

"Yes." Hoyt's aristocratic forehead wrinkled. "We did, until Miranda changed."

"Changed, sir?"

Hoyt rose to his feet and paced to the wall of glass that looked out over the Hudson River.

"At first, we thought it was simply prepubescent nonsense. You know the sort of thing. Temper tantrums, disobedience . . . we were sure she'd grow out of it."

Conor rose, too, and walked towards Winthrop. Far out on the river, toy boats chugged their way upstream.

"But she didn't?"

"If anything, her behavior got worse. She began to lie, to cheat at school. Well, they wouldn't put up with that, of course, so we took her out and placed her elsewhere. Not that it did any good. She was asked to leave that school and the one after that. And the next, if I remember correctly." He looked at Conor and shook his head sadly. "To be honest, I've lost count of how many places she was in and out of before she finally went to Miss Cooper's."

"You agreed with your wife's decision to put her into a school as strict as that?"

"Certainly. It was what she needed."

"And?"

"And, as my wife has already told you, Miranda disgraced herself completely at Miss Cooper's, enticing her roommate's distinguished cousin into an escapade only she could have devised."

"You hold your stepdaughter responsible, then?"

"I wish I could say otherwise, but I know Miranda."

"How do you mean that, sir? Did she have a history of promiscuity?"

Hoyt swung around and looked at Conor. "Promiscuity, and of orchestrating things to suit herself. She wanted freedom from Miss Cooper's and from parental control."

"And she thought eloping with a man almost old enough to be her father would provide that freedom?"

"That's my assumption. It was not a practical decision but then, practicality was not Miranda's strong suit."

Conor nodded. "You didn't accompany your wife to Paris, to confront the girl?"

"No." Hoyt sighed deeply. "I regret it, to this day. I wonder if things might have gone any differently if I'd been there to give Eva strength."

"You don't agree with how she handled things, then?"

"Offering Count de Lasserre money for an annulment, you mean?"

"Buying it from him, yes."

Hoyt went to his desk and sat down. "I suppose she did the only thing that seemed appropriate."

"Then, what did you mean when you said things might have gone differently if you'd been with your wife?"

Hoyt reached out and picked up a double silver picture frame that stood on his desk. Eva Winthrop smiled out from one side; Miranda looked out from the other. With a little start of recognition, Conor realized it was a photo that must have been used as the basis for the painting in the Winthrop foyer. There were the same wide, shadowed eyes, the same tremulously curving mouth.

"I mean," Hoyt said, looking at the picture, "that if I'd been along, perhaps things might not have ended so badly between Eva and Miranda." He shook his head as he put the picture down. "It's damn near broken my wife's heart, you know, this long estrangement."

Conor thought of the coldness in Eva Winthrop's eyes and voice when she'd spoken of her daughter, the way she'd snapped at him for having seemed surprised that she'd left a seventeen-year-old girl to her own devices on the streets of Paris.

"I'm sure it has," he said smoothly.

"Then again, Eva always had much more influence over Miranda than I. If she couldn't convince her to return home, no one could have."

"Aside from the issue of estrangement, how did you view your wife's decision to let the girl remain in Paris on her own?"

"I supported it completely."

"Despite the fact that Miranda was a minor?"

Hoyt laughed. "A minor? Miranda was an accomplished liar. A cheat. She'd managed to seduce a man old enough, worldly enough, one would think, to have resisted her. No, Mr. O'Neil. My stepdaughter was a minor only in the eyes of the law."

"You think she was capable of handling herself in a strange city, then?"

Hoyt Winthrop's eyes narrowed. "I know she was," he said coolly. "Furthermore, I don't care for your implication."

"I'm not implying anything, Mr. Winthrop."

"I think you are. I think you're suggesting my wife erred in finally admitting the girl was beyond our help. And I resent it."

Conor smiled tightly. "I can't help what you feel, Mr. Winthrop. I'm only trying to get at the facts."

"What facts? Your assignment, as I understand it, is to determine who sent Mrs. Winthrop that note."

"And that's exactly what I'm trying to do."

Hoyt blink. "You mean, you think Miranda . . . ?"

"Maybe."

"But why? What reason would she have for doing such a thing?"

"I'm not sure." Conor reached down, picked up the double silver frame and looked at it. "Maybe just for kicks. Then again, considering the circle she apparently moves in, one of her pals might have sent that note." He looked up and smiled. "You can never tell what passes for humor with some people."

"For . . . ?" Hoyt's mouth tightened. "I see what you mean, Mr. O'Neil. But I can't imagine—well, I mean, I suppose I can, but still . . ."

"That painting of your stepdaughter. Was it done from this photo?"

"It was."

"Who took the photo, do you know?"

"I did." Hoyt smiled as Conor looked at him in surprise. "I did the painting, as well."

"You, Mr. Winthrop?"

"Painting has been my hobby for years. I did the picture as a gift for my wife just a month or so before Miranda ran off."

Conor nodded. Why should the news seem so unexpected? The portrait had been well done but he'd known right away that it lacked technical quality. He glanced down at the photo.

"I take it Miranda wasn't happy to pose for you," he said.

Hoyt laughed. "An understatement, if ever I heard one, but what tells you that?"

"Well, the look on her face. That sad smile."

"Sad?" Hoyt frowned and took the picture frame out of Conor's hands and put it back on the desk. "Seems to me she was in one of her rare good moods the day I took this. In fact, she looks quite happy to me, Mr. O'Neil—but then, if you'd ever met my stepdaughter, she'd probably confuse you, too. Miranda wasn't one to give away how she was feeling," he said, shoving back his chair and rising to his feet. "And now, if you'll forgive me, I've a meeting in a few minutes."

"Of course." Conor put out his hand. "Thank you for your time."

"Thank *you* for handling this matter so promptly and with such discretion." Winthrop clapped Conor lightly on the back and strolled with him to the door. "It's just pitiful that Miranda would stoop to sending upsetting notes to her mother."

"That's if she's the person who sent it."

"Well, of course, but now that you've suggested it, it makes perfect sense. It's just the sort of childishly sly thing she'd do. But I must admit, I'm relieved." He paused, his hand on the doorknob. "At least it means we can forget about the note, can't we?"

"I'm almost certain you can, sir."

"Almost," Hoyt said, and smiled. "What will it take to convince you?"

A couple of hours later, Conor slammed the door of his rental car and looked up at the rambling stone buildings of Miss Cooper's School for Young Ladies.

This was what it would take, he thought as he followed a sign towards the administrative offices, a visit to the school Miranda Beckman had attended, though he wasn't quite certain what he expected to find here. Closure of some sort, enough to satisfy Harry Thurston and himself that the note was nothing but a tasteless joke.

The headmistress's office was on the first floor. It was a cold place, smelling of chalk dust, mice, and, Conor thought, childish despair.

Agnes Foster was a stereotypical old-maid schoolteacher if ever he had seen one. She shook his hand, seated him in a chair almost as angular as herself, listened politely as he flashed her his most charming smile and explained that he was trying to get some information about a former student named Miranda Beckman. The name made her thin lips compress into an even thinner line but she smiled frostily and assured him that it was her policy never to discuss students, past or present, with anyone.

So much for charm, Conor thought. He turned off the smile,

replaced it with what he thought of as a Washington face, and dug into his pocket for the leather case with the gold-plated shield and the picture ID that bore the initials of a government agency that had never existed.

"Perhaps I should have said that I'm here on official business."

It worked like a charm, as it always did with people like Agnes Foster. She looked at the shield, the official-looking seal and his photo and turned into a cooperative citizen.

"Of course," she said. She came out from behind her desk, carefully shut her office door, and pulled open the bottom drawer of a battered metal file cabinet. "Beckman," she muttered, as she leafed through the contents, "Beckman . . . Yes, here is the girl's record." She tossed a file folder on the desk in front of Conor and sat down opposite him again. "Not that I've forgotten anything in that file, sir. One does not forget the Mirandas of this world."

"Was she a problem student, Miss Foster?"

The headmistress smiled pityingly. "All our girls," she said, making it sound like *gels,* "are behaviorally challenged, Mr. O'Neil."

He nodded and concentrated on keeping his expression serious.

"Do you recall in what particular way Miranda was, ah, behaviorally challenged?"

Miss Foster pursed her lips. "It would be simpler to tell you in what ways she was not." She reached across her desk, opened the file, and pulled out the top page. "By the time she came to us, she had been expelled from three other boarding schools for everything from being intoxicated to inappropriate sexual behavior."

"Inappropriate sexual . . . Could you be more specific, Miss Foster?"

Agnes Foster fixed him with a cold eye. "I see no reason to, Mr. O'Neil. I think the term speaks for itself."

It probably did. And it didn't really matter if the phrase meant Miranda had been caught behind a dorm with a local lad or if she'd been found in bed with the entire football team from a neighboring boys' school. He didn't need the information.

Not officially.

Conor frowned and shifted in the uncomfortable chair.

"I understand she ran away from here," he said. "Is that right?"

"Indeed. It was a terrible scandal, for us and for her poor mother."

"Who did she run off with, Miss Foster? Do you recall?"

"Distinctly. Count Edouard de Lasserre, the cousin of Miranda's roommate, Amalie." The headmistress's nostrils flared delicately. "To think that members of such a fine old French family should have been compromised by that girl . . . oh, it still makes my hackles rise!"

"It was Miranda's doing, then?"

"Of course it was! Amalie was beside herself, and her parents were furious. They removed her from our school at once and she returned to France. As for the Count—I must say, I felt pity for him."

"You don't hold him responsible for what happened?"

"I do not. Miranda was a corrupting influence, even at her tender age. She lured him into the situation. I am sorry, Mr. O'Neil, but I must be blunt. The Count de Lasserre should have been wiser but he had every man's appetites and weaknesses and Miranda played upon them."

Conor looked up from the file. Agnes Foster's wrinkled cheeks were flushed. She wasn't sorry, she was simply delivering the gospel she lived by. He thought of telling her that men who let their gonads lead them around were no longer considered helpless creatures—but then he thought of the portrait of Miranda, and his embarrassing reaction to it, and changed his mind. Besides, arguing with this old battleaxe would get him nowhere.

"How did her mother and stepfather react to the elopement, Miss Foster?"

"How would you expect them to react, sir? They were beside

themselves with worry. Why, Mrs. Winthrop chartered a plane and flew right to Paris."

"And?"

"And, that's all I know. I explained to Mrs. Winthrop, before she left, that we could not possibly re-admit her daughter. She asked me to recommend another school and I did, a very fine academy in Chilton known to have excellent results with difficult students."

Conor frowned and thought back on his talk with Eva Winthrop. "She wasn't going to take Miranda home to live, then?"

"No, certainly not."

He nodded. Perhaps he'd misunderstood Eva. "So, you recommended a school, and . . . ?"

Miss Foster's bony shoulders rose and fell in an expressive shrug. "The girl never put in an appearance."

"You've no idea what happened to her?"

"None."

Conor pushed back his chair. "Well, Miss Foster, thank you for your time."

"It's just a pity, really. Miranda was really quite bright." The headmistress stabbed her index finger against the records file. "Just look at these grades."

He looked at the neatly printed course names and the letters after them. A in math. A in science. In French. In philosophy.

"Philosophy?"

"Certainly." Miss Foster smiled. "We are great believers in the benefits of a well-rounded, classical education."

Conor hoped his smile was at least the equal of hers. "As in Plato?"

"We teach all the greats, sir. Plato. Kant . . ."

"Santayana?"

"By all means."

Conor nodded. That was it, then. The girl had sent the note, just to get under Eva's skin. He'd stake his reputation on it. He'd fly back to D.C., tell Thurston to phone his pal, Winthrop, make sounds of reassurance to him and his wife, and consider the matter closed.

He sighed, pushed back his chair, got to his feet and told himself he was happy to be done with the mess.

"Thank you very much for your time, Miss Foster."

"I hope I've been helpful, Mr. O'Neil." The headmistress rose, too, and came around the desk towards him. "Please be assured that, unlike Miranda Beckman, most of our girls profit by their experience here and—"

Her hip brushed the records folder. It fell to the hardwood flooring. Papers spilled in all directions, along with a small, black and white photo.

Conor bent down, retrieved the papers and the folder and put them on Agnes Foster's desk. But he held on to the photograph, his eyes riveted to the grainy image.

It was a picture of Miranda.

She was seated in the grass, her back against a tree, her legs tucked gracefully beneath her. There was a book in her lap—he couldn't read the title but it seemed to be a slim volume—and from the startled look on her face, he knew the photographer must have surprised her. Her dark hair was wind-tossed; she had one hand raised as if to brush it back from her eyes. The other hand lay curled in her lap, clutching something white. A handkerchief, he thought, or a tissue. And she was smiling. Really smiling. Not mysteriously but happily, as if all of life's most wonderful secrets were about to become hers.

". . . have to clean out these files!"

Conor pulled his gaze from the photo. Agnes Foster was glaring at it as if it were a personal insult.

"Sorry, Miss Foster. What did you say?"

"I said, I can see that I'm going to have to go through these old files and sort them out."

"When was this snapshot taken, do you know?"

The headmistress took the picture from him. "Well," she said, "in the early spring, I should think. That's a dogwood tree. Do you see how it's starting to bloom?"

He did, now that the woman had pointed it out. He saw, too, that what he'd taken for a tissue or a handkerchief in Miranda's hand was, in fact, a creamy dogwood blossom.

"That's the sort of girl she was," Miss Foster said coldly. "Sitting on the grass when she knew it was forbidden, thoughtlessly plucking blossoms from the tree. I assure you, she would have been reprimanded for that."

"This was taken just before she ran away with the Count de Lasserre, then."

"Yes. In fact, I suspect he must have taken it." The headmistress's mouth tightened. "It was found in Miranda's closet, along with a few other things."

"Such as?"

"I don't recall, exactly. Some candy, I think, and a trashy book. Things she surely knew were forbidden. We pride ourselves on teaching self-discipline, Mr. O'Neil." Agnes Foster's nostrils flared. "Not that it did Miranda any good."

"Oh, I can see that," Conor said evenly. "A girl who'd walk on the grass, sneak chocolate into the dormitory . . ."

"They may seem minor infractions to you, sir, but our girls come to us with problems. They need a stern hand to guide them and I assure you, we attempted to offer that to Miranda. But it was too late. She was set in her ways, just as her mother and stepfather had warned us. She was self-centered. Selfish. A liar and a cheat." The headmistress's mouth twisted. "And promiscuous, to boot. I'm sorry to speak ill of a former student but I see no point in lying."

Conor took the photo from the woman's bony hand. "I'd like to keep this, if I may."

She looked as if he'd just suggested absconding with the school's funds.

"That's out of the question, I'm afraid. The photo is school property. I cannot hand it over to just anyone."

Lord, give me strength, Conor thought, but he gritted his teeth, drew himself to his full six feet two inches, and even managed a smile.

"But I'm not 'anyone,' Miss Foster, I'm . . ." What? What ID had he shown the old broad? "I'm in charge of dealing with this matter,'' he said briskly. ''And I'll be more than happy to give you an official receipt.''

Agnes Foster beamed. ''In that case, the photo is yours.''

He stopped at the first rest area on the highway, called Harry Thurston and told him what he'd learned.

''So, you think the girl sent Mama the note?'' Thurston said.

Conor undid his collar and loosened his tie.

''Yeah, that's my best guess.''

''Why? Is she planning on blackmailing her?''

''Maybe.'' An eighteen-wheeler roared past. ''Or maybe she just wants to shake her up. I'm not sure. Either way, it looks like it's all in the family.''

''Yes, well, thanks for doing the leg work, my boy. You come on in, write it up and I'll hand your report to the Committee and that'll be the end of it.''

Those were the words Conor had been waiting for. So why was he taking a deep breath, turning his back to the noise of the traffic and running the tip of his tongue over his dry lips?

''Listen, Harry, I've been thinking about what you said. Hoyt Winthrop's a personal friend of yours, right? It would be really bad news if it turns out that I'd overlooked something, especially after I put all this time into the preliminaries.''

All this time? He'd been at this, what, a grand total of forty-eight hours?

''Such devotion and loyalty,'' Thurston said with a wry chuckle. ''What's the bottom line?''

''I think somebody should check out Miranda Beckman.''

''That seems logical.''

''And this de Lasserre character, too.''

''Meaning?''

Conor took another deep breath. ''Meaning, a couple of days in Paris and I'll be able to nail the lid on this thing.''

''You? Go to Paris?''

"Check my passport, Harry," Conor said drily. "I've been there before."

Thurston laughed. "Oh, you are a clever one, O'Neil. You didn't want to touch this with a ten-foot pole but now that it means a couple days strolling the Champs Elysées, you figure, why not?"

Conor laughed, too. "You know me. 'Ask not what your country can do for you . . .' "

"Well, why not? Go to France, parlay fransay with Miranda Winthrop . . ."

"Beckman."

"Beckman, Winthrop, whatever. Sacrifice yourself on an altar of mademoiselles, *fromages* and *vin rouge,* and we'll put this one to bed."

Conor laughed again. Then he hung up the phone, pulled the picture of Miranda Beckman from his pocket and looked at it. After a long minute, he got back into his rental car and pulled out onto the road.

He flew Air France, business class, and though he was usually good at catching a long nap on a flight, he couldn't manage it this time.

He asked the hostess for a couple of magazines and she obliged with a *Time* he'd already read, a *Forbes* that didn't interest him, and a copy of something French.

Miranda was right inside the cover, smiling that cool, Mona Lisa smile.

It was an ad for perfume, maybe, or jewelry. He had no idea which and it didn't matter. He just thought that only a photographic trick could make a woman look so innocent and so sexy at the same time. And when his body reacted, the blood pooling hot in his loins in a way that had become increasingly familiar over the past few days, he finally admitted the truth to himself.

He wasn't going to Paris to close out the Winthrop file. He was going because he needed to take a cold, in-person look at

Miranda Beckman and put an end to whatever in hell was going on inside his head and in other, more primitive parts of his anatomy.

Boys got hard-ons from pictures, not men. And he had left boyhood behind, a long time ago.

Chapter Four

Paris, two days later

The thin, bright light of the early January morning spilled over the glass pyramid that was the entrance to the Louvre.

Conor had seen the pyramid before, when he'd been assigned to the Embassy as a "cultural liaison," meaning he'd spent his time trying to look inconspicuous instead of slipping across the Iraqi border on moonless nights or meeting with armed rebels on mountaintops in Eastern Europe.

A smile tilted at the corner of his lips as he headed towards the pyramid over the centuries-old stones of the courtyard. Looking inconspicuous was going to be a tough order this morning, considering that there was a fashion show being held here today.

Ted Hamlin, an old friend at the embassy who'd snagged him an admission ticket, had known better than to ask why Conor needed it, but that hadn't kept him from damn near laughing his head off.

"You? At a fashion show?" Hamlin had rocked back in his chair. "Oh pal, are you gonna be in trouble. Unless you develop a lisp real fast or figure out a way to double for Rod Stewart, you're gonna stand out like a hound dog at a chihuahua convention."

Conor had given Hamlin a cool smile. "I just love that country-boy humor of yours," he'd said, pocketing the ticket and walking off, but he suspected Ted was right.

Once he reached the entrance to the showing, which was being held inside the Cour Carrée, he was sure of it.

The guy manning the gate looked at Conor's pass and then at him. His eyes narrowed with suspicion. Conor returned the favor. How else would you look at somebody with fuschia hair who was wearing a ripped Mickey Mouse T-shirt, jeans that could easily turn a man into a castrato, and combat boots? Six silver studs climbed the lobe of one ear and three tiny gold hoops dangled from the other. Assorted goodies pierced everything from the guy's eyebrows to his lips but the *pièce de résistance* was a diamond-studded safety pin that was clipped straight through his nostrils.

Conor realized he'd been staring.

"*Americain?*" the ticket-taker asked, his safety-pin quivering with disdain.

Conor smiled. Clearly, his grey tweed jacket, charcoal trousers, white button-down shirt and maroon knit tie didn't pass muster.

"Yes," he said pleasantly. "And you? Martian?"

"Very funny," the guy snapped, in perfect English. "The seats with the ribbons around them are reserved for important guests. The others are available to people like you—if you're lucky enough to find one that's not in use."

Conor grinned. "Thank you so much," he said, and made his way inside.

It was like stepping into organized chaos. Hot lights glittered, heavy metal music blasted, and a wave of perfume strong enough to choke an ox filled the air. Chairs, most of them filled with women dressed in what Conor supposed was the height of fashion, were lined up in tight rows from where he stood to the front of the room, where they were bisected by a catwalk that extended out from a stage draped in scarlet silk.

Ted Hamlin had been right about the men. There weren't many of them, but Conor certainly couldn't have fit into their ranks. One, who seemed to be taking all this very seriously, was dressed in a pink velvet suit. Another, who just had to be a drag queen in full regalia, sat on an aisle, and to his—or her—left, an aging but still famous rocker sat between two stunning women whose outfits were no match for his.

"No pictures, no pictures," the rock star was saying loudly, even though there wasn't a camera pointed anywhere near him.

Conor sighed. A fox would have an easier job blending into a hen house than he had of blending in here. Not that he had any intentions of even trying. He just had to figure a way to slip backstage so he could find Miranda Beckman, talk to her, try to make some sense out of what was going on—for the Committee, of course, because a night's sleep had made him realize that whatever else he'd thought he'd felt was nonsense.

One look and the Beckman babe would turn into what he already knew she was, a spoiled brat who'd never quite grown up, a gorgeous piece with the morals of a slut—and then he could stop thinking about her, stop imagining those sad eyes and that secretive smile . . .

"Monsieur?"

A hand tugged sharply at his sleeve. Conor looked down. A tiny woman with a fox-like face was giving him the same sort of look he'd already gotten at the door.

"What are you doing here?" she demanded in swift Parisian French.

Conor fumbled in his pocket. "I have a pass," he said, in French almost as swift as hers. "I assure you—"

"Merde!" Her fingers bit into his wrist. "Do not show me your card here, you fool. Do you want everyone to know who you are?"

"Madame?"

"Oh, *mon dieu,* I am so weary of dealing with stupid people. It is bad enough you stand out like a sore thumb dressed in that stupid outfit. Must you also wave your identification card around and announce to the world that you are Security?''

John O'Neil had not raised a stupid son. ''Certainly not,'' Conor said, with just the right amount of chagrin.

''We need coverage backstage. That is where you should be.''

''Of course.''

The woman's eyes narrowed. ''You *are* Security, yes?''

Conor rolled his eyes. ''Look,'' he said, reaching into his pocket again, ''let me show you my—

''No, no, don't do that!'' The woman jerked her head towards the stage. ''Go on,'' she hissed, ''get to work. Remember, no one gets into the dressing room without a special pass. I don't care if it's Mother Theresa herself, you understand? You will protect Monsieur Diderot's designs with your life!''

Conor did his best not to click his heels and salute.

''*Oui,* madame,'' he said.

A moment later, he'd vaulted onto the stage, parted the curtains and stepped into another world.

If it was chaos out front, it was a madhouse back here. There was no other word to describe it, he thought, staring around him in bemusement. The noise. The clouds of hair spray. The smoke from what had to be a zillion unfiltered Gauloises.

And the people. Conor had never seen anything like this mob. There were fat women. Skinny women. Young ones and old ones. There were men, too, most of them garbed in tight black leather and draped with enough chains to outfit an Alabama work gang.

What in hell were all these people doing? Racing around in circles, from what he could tell.

How would he locate Miranda Beckman in this crowd? He'd assumed it would be easy enough, considering that he'd seen her portrait and that he had a photo of her in his pocket.

How wrong could a man be?

It wasn't that he couldn't pick out the models. They were the only people not rushing around in a frenzy. They were draped languidly in chairs, or perched on stools, looking bored while the men and women buzzing around like bees made up their faces and their hair.

It was just that they all looked alike.

The girls who'd already been fixed up all had faces powdered white, eyes outlined in black and mouths painted into blood-red pouts. The ones who hadn't were almost as impossible to tell apart, with their elegant bones, wide-set eyes, swan-like necks and long, slim bodies.

Conor breathed a sigh of relief. The room was filled with Mirandas. He knew now, for certain, that there was nothing special about her.

Slowly, he made his way into their midst. He hadn't seen this much carelessly exposed female flesh at one time since a long-ago weekend at Columbia, when he and half a dozen drunk fraternity brothers had burst into the women's locker room on a dare. He'd been too bombed to fully appreciate the sight then and hell, he wasn't really appreciating it now, either. Maybe it was the atmosphere, or maybe it was the bored, vapid looks on the women's faces, but the view just wasn't a turn-on.

"Regardez!"

Conor jumped back as a trolley loaded with black wigs raced towards him.

"Pardon," he mumbled.

He made the same apology another half a dozen times before he finally gave up. Nobody heard him and even if they did, nobody cared. And yet, things weren't as frenzied as he'd thought. There was an order in the insanity. Clothing was here, makeup tables were there . . .

Oh, hell!

There she was. She was sitting on one of the stools, wearing a blue smock that fell to mid-calf. Her back was straight, her hands were folded in her lap, and her face was tilted towards the man who was painting it.

Conor told himself it was plain luck he'd been able to pick her out. He told himself it was just a trick of the light that made her look different. He told himself there was nothing special about her.

Hell, he thought again, and let out his breath. What was the sense in lying to himself?

Miranda Beckman's beauty shone as brightly as the sun.

Miranda was trying her best not to tick Claude off.

He wasn't in a good mood today but then, he never was. Claude had the temperament of an *artiste,* people said. Personally, she thought he had the temperament of a barracuda but there was no point in pretending that he wasn't the best makeup-artist this side of the Atlantic. Rumor was that Jacques had paid him a fortune and a half to agree to design the *maquillage* for this showing of summer *couture* and to agree that he'd personally do the faces of the top girls.

Claude himself had made it clear he wouldn't tolerate any nonsense.

"If you come to the Master with bags under the eyes," his assistant, Françoise, had warned, "or if you do not sit absolutely still while the Master works, he will dismiss you, poof, just like that!"

Well, Miranda thought, she had come to the Master with bags, thanks to the party Jean-Philippe had taken her to last night. She'd danced and laughed and drunk champagne until the small hours of the morning, all in honor of the Sultan of Something-of-Other, who'd been celebrating his birthday, or maybe the birthday of one of his three wives. Jean-Phillipe hadn't been certain, he'd only known that he absolutely *had* to attend—which meant that she had to attend with him.

"I am lost without you, *chérie,*" he'd murmured when he'd shown up to ask her to go to the party during yesterday's run-through, and Nita, who'd overheard, had rolled her eyes and said, in a honeyed drawl that was as phony as Claude's lineage, that if *le sex pot* movie star of *la belle France* were to say such a thing to her, she'd be his slave forever.

Miranda smiled. Nita had nothing on her. She was more than

willing to do anything Jean-Philippe wanted, and for the rest of her life. He was wonderful. He was everything . . .

And he wasn't here.

He'd promised he would be. He knew she never did a show without him in the audience to cheer her on, right from the beginning, all those years ago when she'd done her first *prêt à porter* and one of the other girls had almost had to shove her out onto the catwalk.

"Stop moving," Claude snapped. "How will I disguise these bags beneath your eyes, mademoiselle, if you do not sit still?"

Miranda complied. She was getting a crick in her neck, thanks to the angle he'd demanded she keep her chin at. But Claude hadn't done as Françoise had threatened. He wasn't about to dismiss her, poof, just like that, not while she was still at the top of the heap along with Jacques Diderot's crazy, and crazily expensive, designs. Not even Claude was foolish enough to distance himself from so much success—but he could damned well screw up her makeup. She'd seen it happen before, the brush stroke that went just a little off, the color shade a bit too dark.

Claude drew back and glared at her again and she realized she must have moved, or twitched, or maybe just breathed too hard. Heaven knew she was trying not to breathe at all because Claude was exhaling clouds of garlic and red wine straight into her face.

"I am almost *fini,*" he snapped, "and although you are not deserving of it, I have made you my masterpiece, Miranda. Do what you must to keep entirely still for a moment longer, if you please."

"Do what you must to get done," Miranda said, without moving her lips. "I mean," she said, when he glared at her again, "I am very grateful, Claude, but my neck is getting stiff."

"Kohl," Claude snapped, and held out his hand. Françoise slapped a pencil into his palm. "Brush." She slapped that into his other hand. The Master bent closer to his canvas and Miranda held her breath. "Your neck is a small price to pay for my genius, mademoiselle. Look up. Look down. Now, look to the side. No, do not *turn* to the side, you stupid girl, *look* to the side. The eyes move, nothing else. You understand?''

''Umm,'' she said, and did as he'd asked . . .

And saw the man.

Who was he?

Why was he staring at her?

She didn't know him. She had never even seen him before. She was certain of that, even though she couldn't really get a clear view of him. Her head and eyes were at a strange angle and he was too far away. Still, she knew he was watching her, she could feel it, and with such intensity that it sent a funny feeling up her spine.

She scowled, trying to bring him into focus. Claude let loose with a blistering string of obscenities in a breathtaking *mélange* of languages.

''*Qu'est-ce que tu fous?*'' he said furiously. ''What the hell are you doing, you stupid girl? Would you like me to stop? I can leave you this way, if you wish, with your left eye only half-finished!''

Miranda shook her head the slightest bit.

''Look at me, then, and do not move.''

She did as he'd ordered. Long moments passed and then Claude tossed the brush at Françoise, put his hands on his hips and stepped back.

''I have done you,'' he announced.

Nita Carrington, seated on the stool next to Miranda's, gave a throaty laugh.

''Not on your best day, Claude, baby,'' she said. ''Miranda and I don't give no pity-fucks, isn't that right, girlfriend?'

Claude drew himself up to his full five feet, two inches.

''Françoise will do your face, Mademoiselle Carrington,'' he said coldly, and marched away.

''Françoise was gonna do me anyhow, weren't you, sweetness?'' Nita said. She sat up straight and tilted her face towards Claude's sour-faced assistant. ''Go on, girl. Do your worst.''

Françoisė set to work. Miranda waited a minute, then slid her gaze sidewards.

The man was still there.

"Nita," she hissed.

"Hmm?"

"Can you see the stage?"

"A little bit of it. Why?"

"Who's that man?"

"What man?"

"The one near the stage, dammit! Aren't you listening to me?"

Nita shifted her gaze. "I don't see nobody."

"What do you mean, you don't see anybody? You can't miss him."

"Mademoiselle," Françoise said petulantly, "if you move . . ."

"Nita, try again. See? The guy in the tweed jacket?"

"The guy in the what?" Nita bit back a giggle. "What are you flyin' on, girlfriend? Ain't nobody here gonna be wearin' a tweed jacket."

"This man is," Miranda said impatiently, "and do me a favor and ease off the down home talk, okay? There's nobody around to appreciate it."

"Says who?" Nita slipped into perfect upper-class American diction. "Besides, I have to keep in practice. In these parts, 'down home' is lots more exotic than Ivy League. Haven't you ever heard of Josephine Baker?"

"Haven't *you* ever heard of Colin Powell? Why's he watching me?"

"Colin Powell?"

"Nita, I'm warning you—"

"Come on, Miranda. There's a guy watching you. So what?"

"He hasn't just been watching. He's been staring."

"Everybody stares at you. You'd be collecting unemployment if they didn't. What's with you? I'm the one gets the jitters right about now, not you."

Miranda took a deep breath. Nita was right. She never got edgy before she went out on the catwalk, not since the first time. As for people watching . . . so what? Nita was right about that, too. She was paid to let people watch her.

Why was she getting antsy because this one guy was looking?

Maybe it was the way he was watching her. As if he were some kind of scientist and she a bug he'd never seen before. This wasn't the long, hungry look that went with the territory of her profession. This was . . . different.

Françoise dusted a powder puff over Nita's face and then stepped back, hands on her hips, in a perfect, if unconscious, parody of her boss.

''Et voilà,'' she said, ''you are done.''

''And so are you,'' Nita said, slipping off the stool and turning to a mirror behind her, ''if I don't look fantastic.'' She peered at her reflection. ''Good God almighty, I look like somethin' that would make the Ku Klux Klan fire up another cross!''

Miranda laughed. ''Wait until you put on your wig,'' she said, ''and then . . . Shit!''

''Oh, come on. It's not that bad.''

''He's heading this way.''

''Claude?''

''That man.''

''What man?''

''Nita, dammit all, I am not in the mood for—''

''Wow. You were right. The guy's wearing a tweed jacket.''

''Told you so.''

''And he's heading straight for us,'' Nita whispered. ''Straight for you, anyway. My oh my, I have seen intensity before, girlfriend, but not like this! He hasn't even blinked.''

Miranda would have known that without Nita telling her. She could feel the stranger's gaze still locked onto her.

''Maybe he wants my autograph.''

''Uh-uh. Man's not into autographs, babe, trust me.'' Nita's voice dropped dramatically. ''You sure you don't know him?''

''Positive.''

''And no wonder, considerin' he's wearin' tweed. On the other hand, even I might make an exception about tweed for a guy looks like this one. Bet he's got muscles where a man should have muscles, if you know what—''

''Miss Beckman?''

He had a good voice, Miranda thought, she had to give him that, deep and just a little husky.

''Excuse me, Miss Beckman, have you got a minute?''

And he was polite, too. Then, why was it so hard to turn around? Stop being an ass, Miranda told herself, and she swung towards him.

He was tall, that was her first thought, tall enough so she'd probably have had to look up at him even if she'd been on her feet and wearing heels. Not many men could meet that qualification. And he was good-looking, as Nita had said, if you went in for the rugged type. Broad shoulders beneath that oh-so-proper grey tweed jacket, good chest, narrow waist and long legs.

The rest wasn't bad, either. Black hair, thickly lashed blue eyes, a nose that looked as if it had once taken on a bit of trouble, a wide mouth set above a square, cleft chin. The camera would probably love him, except for the cold, cold look in those eyes.

Why was he looking at her that way, as if he'd seen her somewhere before and wasn't quite sure if they'd parted as friends or enemies? Nita was wrong. His interest in her wasn't sexual. His gaze was steady and cool, maybe even a little mocking. He was looking at her in a way men never did, and she didn't like it.

''How do you do, Miss Beckman?'' he said. He held out his hand. ''My name is Conor O'Neil.''

Miranda looked pointedly at his outstretched hand. Then she looked at him.

''How nice for you,'' she said coolly. She heard Nita swallow a giggle.

His hand dropped to his side. She could see the swift flash of anger in his eyes but his tone remained polite.

''Can you give me a few minutes?''

''I don't give interviews, Mr. . . .?''

"O'Neil. Conor O'Neil."

"Oh yes, you already told me your name, didn't you?" Miranda leaned forward, peered into the mirror behind Nita and touched the tip of one finger to her lips. "Well, as I said, I don't give—"

"I'm not a reporter."

"Really," she said, the single word making it clear she didn't care what he was. "Well, then, if you've come for an autograph—"

"I don't want an autograph, either."

His voice was tight now. Good. The balance of power was shifting.

"I'm glad to hear it, Mr . . . O'Neil, did you say? Because if you did, want an autograph, I mean, you'd have to stop by and see Annick—she's that woman over there, do you see her?—and tell her to give you a signed picture."

"I just told you," he said through his teeth, "I'm not interested in an autograph."

Miranda turned and looked at him. "No?"

"No."

"What are you doing here, then? For that matter, how did you get in? No one's permitted backstage, Mr. . . . Mr. . . ."

"O'Neil," he growled. "O-apostrophe-N-E-I-L. Is that too difficult for you to remember?"

Nita laughed out loud. Miranda looked at her and smiled. Then she turned her back on Conor O'Neil.

"So," she said to Nita, "what do you think? Should we go to that party after the showing or . . . hey! Hey, what do you think you're doing?"

Conor's hand had closed tightly on her shoulder. He swung her towards him, fighting to control his temper.

"Maybe that act works with clowns like the guy who was painting your face," he said. His voice was soft and cold and as hard as the press of his hand. "Maybe it works with all the other monkeys who swing around after you."

"Let go of me!"

Conor's fingers bit into her flesh. "But I promise you, Miss Beckman, it sure as hell isn't going to work with me."

He took his hand from her shoulder and watched her face. It was hard to read, under all that gook, but she was shaken, he could tell. Well, hell, he was shaken, too. Losing control was never a good idea but who could blame him? Even from across the room, he'd known when she'd become aware of him and known, too, how readily she'd dismissed him as a man beneath her notice.

It was one thing to be treated rudely but to be treated as if he were something messy Miranda Beckman had found on the bottom of her shoe was something else again.

She was beautiful, yes, and beyond his wildest imaginings. She was also everything he'd been told she was, and more. Aloof, spoiled, self-centered, and with one hell of an attitude.

No wonder nobody had a decent word to say about her.

The fat little man with the paunch had painted her face so she looked like a cross between Morticia Addams and the bride of Frankenstein. Close-up, he could see that her mouth was outlined in black and filled in with a red that reminded him of blood. Her green eyes had been so heavily circled with something that looked like ink that he could hardly see their true color. Her hair had been pinned back, probably so she could wear one of the ugly black wigs he'd seen piled on the cart that had almost run him down.

And yet, for all of that, her natural beauty managed to show through—on the outside, anyway.

A memory flashed into his head. One Christmas when he'd been little, maybe a year or two before his mother had died, she'd taken him into Manhattan to see the sights. The animated displays in the Lord and Taylor windows had enchanted him, and the Santas on every sidewalk, but what had sent his heart soaring had been the beautiful Christmas tree in Rockefeller Center.

When the cold had gotten to be too much, his mother had dragged him away only by promising she'd take him to Macy's, where he could pick out a special decoration for their own tree, back home. But when they got into the store, Conor had taken one look at the white trees hung with gold and silver balls that decorated the place and announced, with perfect childish logic that he didn't want a decoration, he wanted one of those trees.

He'd pleaded. He'd argued. He'd almost wept, though his father had already taught him that little boys never cried. But his mother kept saying he couldn't have one and finally, he'd sat down cross-legged on the floor beneath the biggest white tree and refused to move.

Angry, embarrassed, his mother had swept him up into her arms to carry him off. Desperate, Conor had reached out and grabbed the white Christmas tree . . .

And discovered the truth.

The tree, beautiful beyond his wildest dreams, wasn't real. It was gilt and tinsel, straight through to its phony core.

He remembered his disappointment. "You should have told me," he kept saying to his mother, and his mother had given up her scolding, held him close and said if she had, he'd never have believed her.

Twenty-eight years later, he was older but not smarter. People had told him what to expect of Miranda Beckman, but he knew that he hadn't really believed them.

Now he did.

Whatever he'd thought he'd seen in the painting of her, and in the snapshot, had been put there by his imagination. Her smile wasn't mysterious, it was vain. Her eyes weren't sad, they were empty. She was as one-dimensional as her portrait.

Conor felt a rush of relief. It was over. Now he could admit to himself that thinking about Miranda Beckman had been some kind of weird obsession. It had not been pleasant, walking around, knowing he was almost out of control and hating himself for it, but that was finished. If she was the one who'd sent the note to Eva, she'd have to be dealt with. If she wasn't, he'd walk away and forget her.

All he needed were the answers to a few questions, and that would take some doing. It didn't take a genius to figure out that she was used to dominating men with her looks. Well, he was immune to it. He knew it, she knew it, and she didn't like it. He could see it in the way she was looking at him, and the realization made him smile.

Color streaked across her high cheekbones.

"Miranda?" The girl standing beside her moved closer. "Should I call Security?"

Conor laughed. "I *am* Security."

Miranda stood up. She was tall, but the top of her head only came to his shoulder.

"It's all right, Nita." She took a deep breath. "What do you want with me, Mr. O'Neil?"

"I told you. I need to talk to you."

"About what?"

"A private matter."

She held herself straighter and put her hands on her hips.

"Nita's my best friend. You can say whatever it is you have to say in front of her."

"I'm afraid that's impossible."

"*You're* afraid?" Miranda laughed; he could see her regaining control of herself. "Just who the hell do you think you are? Do us both a favor, please. Get to the bottom line fast. I've got a show to do."

He stepped closer to her, turning so that Nita was shut out of their conversation.

"Hoyt and Eva Beckman Winthrop. Is that 'bottom line' enough to suit you?"

He watched her face closely. He had made the reference to her mother and stepfather obtuse in hopes it would draw a reaction he could read but her expression didn't change. Only her eyes seemed to darken, or perhaps it was his imagination.

"I don't understand," she said. "Has something happened to my—to Eva?"

"Why would you think that?"

"Why else would you be here?"

"Nothing's happened to your mother, Miss Beckman."

"Then what—"

"I told you, I'd rather not discuss it here. It's a private matter."

"There are no private matters between Eva and me. Even if there were, they certainly wouldn't involve you."

Conor felt his composure slipping. "Listen, lady," he said, "I'm not here to play games."

A bell sounded. Somebody gave a ladylike whoop. "Time, girls," an English-accented voice called out.

Nita slipped from her stool. "Darn," she said, "and just when things were getting interesting."

"Good-bye, Mr. O'Neil."

"I'm not going anywhere, Miss Beckman."

"But I am." She reached for the buttons on her smock. "And I assure you, I've absolutely nothing to say to you about my mother."

Conor's jaw tightened. She was undoing the buttons, undressing in front of him as if he weren't even there.

"Do you like working in Paris, Miss Beckman?" he asked in a pleasant tone.

Miranda's head snapped up. "What's that supposed to mean?"

He shrugged. "Nothing much. I was just wondering if it's as tough to get a work permit as I've heard—and as easy to have one taken away."

"Are you threatening me?" She took a step towards him, eyes flashing. "You get the hell out of here, mister, before I have you thrown out!"

"Miranda?" A girl came hurrying towards them holding out a jumble of clothing. "Miranda, *s'il vous plaît, c'est le moment!*"

She glared at him but he didn't move.

"Okay," she said, "okay, O'Neil, you want a free show?" Her chin lifted in defiance. "You got one."

The smock slipped from her shoulders, revealing a white silk teddy. It was unadorned and plain and for all that, as sexy as anything Conor had even seen.

He told himself to turn around but how could he, when she

was deliberately exhibiting herself before him, telling him with her body and her cool eyes that he was beneath contempt? Besides, a man would have to be a stone saint not to look at legs that were as long and as lovely as hers, at the high-cut lines of the teddy that defined the soft roundness of her thighs.

His gaze rose further, until he could see that she was braless under the silk. Her breasts, as firm and round as apples, thrust against the fabric; her nipples were shadowed and mysterious.

Without warning, he felt his body clench.

"Like what you see, O'Neil?" she said gently.

Conor jerked his eyes to Miranda's face. She was smiling like a cat that had just dipped its paw into a dish of cream, her green eyes slanting slightly upward at the corners, her carmine-red mouth curving with pleasure, and he knew that she'd read his every emotion.

"Because that's all you're ever going to do, you know." She smiled and stroked her hands lightly down her throat, to her breasts. Her hands cupped them and her smile tilted, became a promise of pleasure beyond endurance. The pink tip of her tongue slicked across her crimson lips. "You can look, like all the rest, but you're never, ever going to be able to touch."

Conor's hands fisted at his sides. The urge to reach out and slap that beautiful, taunting face was almost overpowering. It took a minute until he could return that clever, disdainful smile.

Have you ever done any mountain-climbing, Miss Beckman?" He saw the smile slip from her mouth, saw confusion blur those knowing eyes. "No? Well, I have. Not much, I admit, but just enough to have learned a couple of things about myself. One is that there's no satisfaction in accomplishing something that's already been done by too many men before you. The other is that no matter what anybody says, just because the mountain's there doesn't mean it's worth climbing." Her face seemed to whiten, even under the heavy makeup, and it made his smile genuine. "I'll see you later, after you've finished making believe you're a real woman for the paying customers."

Nita let out a long, sighing breath as he turned and strolled away.

"Like I said the first time," she said, "wow!"

"The bastard," Miranda said. Her voice trembled.

Nita turned and looked at her. Miranda's hands were balled into fists at her sides.

"Hey," she said, "come on, girlfriend. The guy was just getting even. I mean, you got to admit, you chewed him up pretty good." She slipped her arm around Miranda's shoulders. "You hear me?"

"Yes." Miranda nodded, her eyes glued to Conor O'Neil's retreating back. He was almost at the exit door. "I hear you."

"Well, then, put on a smile. And let Annick help you get dressed. Poor thing is standing here, wringing her hands." Nita grinned. "It's time to get out front, give the guys a heart attack and make the ladies drool. You know, do your thing!"

Make believe you're a real woman.

A pain Miranda hadn't felt in years and years stabbed through her heart.

"Oh, look it there," Nita screeched. "It's Jean-Phillipe!"

Miranda spun around. Jean-Phillipe was hurrying towards her, drawing smiles from even this jaded, sophisticated group. But his eyes were fixed on her and when he saw her face light at the sight of him, he held out his arms.

"Chérie," he said, as he caught her, "forgive me. I meant to be here sooner."

"It's all right," she said, and wound her arms around his neck.

Some sixth sense made her look towards the exit. Conor O'Neil hadn't left yet. He'd paused, his hand on the door, and now he was turned in her direction and looking at her—at her, and at Jean-Phillipe.

Miranda's head lifted. She smiled, straight at him, and then she put her hands on Jean-Phillipe's shoulders, rose on tip-toe and pressed her mouth and her body against his.

Conor's vision clouded. He felt his hands curl into fists, felt the muscles in his arms and shoulders knot until they were rock-hard. Two minutes, that was all it would take, two minutes to close the distance between them, beat the too-handsome son of a bitch holding Miranda into a bloody pulp and then he'd throw her down on her back, part her legs and do what needed doing . . .

"Fuck!" he snarled, and he slammed his fist against the door and got the hell out of there while he still could.

Chapter Five

All right, he had blown it.

So what?

Conor stubbed out his cigarette—the first he'd smoked in, what, five years?—and caught the waiter's eye.

A second bottle of ale appeared at his elbow, along with a little basket of crackers.

Conor nodded his thanks, declined the glass, just as he had the first time, and wrapped his hand around the bottle. The ale wasn't India Pale, it wasn't even American. But it was icy-cold and just bitter enough to suit his mood and when he lifted the bottle to his lips and took a long, slow drink, the stuff slid down his throat as cool as silk.

What an ass he'd made of himself. He couldn't stop thinking about it, not even after a brisk walk along the Seine with the wind blowing raw and cold in his face.

Miranda had made a fool of him.

Conor scowled and tilted the bottle to his mouth again.

Correction. He had *let* her make a fool of him, and that was even worse.

He'd gone in there knowing what she was, a woman who

specialized in getting men to do what she wanted, and he'd still ended up letting her get to him.

Expect the unexpected, his instructors at Special Forces had said.

He always did. It was how he'd survived dark cul-de-sacs, fetid jungles and even, one memorable night, what had come at him in his own apartment.

Conor lit another cigarette. He took a long drag, coughed, looked at the slim white tube with distaste and then mashed it to death in the ashtray.

A fashion show wasn't his kind of jungle but he should have been prepared for something down-and-dirty. He knew what Miranda Beckman was. He should have gone in there with a smile on his face and his hands over his *cojones.*

He glowered at the bottle of ale as he raised it to his lips again.

The bitch! Peeling off her clothes as if he hadn't existed, letting him glimpse that lithe, tanned body and think about what it would be like to lay claim to it. What pleasure it must have given her, when his mask had slipped and she'd seen the hunger in his eyes.

Even now, hours later, the words she'd flung at him still burned in his brain.

You can look, like all the rest, but you're never going to touch.

And then the final insult, the show she'd put on with the Frenchman with the pretty face, climbing all over the guy, giving him a good, long look at what it was like for the men she did allow to touch.

But she'd miscalculated. She couldn't operate him the way she did others. Besides, his turn was coming.

A smile twisted across Conor's mouth.

Miranda Beckman had sent that note to her mother. It was just the sort of smug, aren't-I-clever thing a babe like that would do.

I'm bored, so I'll just rattle Mommy's cage for fun.

It was a stunt with all the markings of an amateur. Somebody who was serious, a blackmailer who wanted money, would have followed through with a demand. Even a looney-tunes looking for kicks would have come up with a P.S. by now.

No question about it, the note was Miranda's, sent to shake her mother's composure, to put Hoyt into a sweat and generally remind them both that life was never simple with a loving daughter like her dancing around behind scenes.

Conor drank down the last of the ale.

He'd solved the mystery, such as it was. Unfortunately, there was still a bit of a problem to overcome because what he'd come up with was all theory. He couldn't prove a damned thing. On the other hand, that was one of the pleasures of working for the Committee.

Conor smiled. His chair squealed against the marble floor as he shoved it back and got to his feet.

He didn't *have* to prove anything. The only thing he had to do was get Miranda to admit she'd written the note and then convince her she'd sooner get caught in an earthquake than try and pull a stunt like this again.

He tucked a hundred-franc note under the edge of the pack of Gauloises. The waiter could have both, the money and the cigarettes, and more power to him. As for Miranda Beckman . . . he'd intended to identify himself to her as a low-level embassy flunky, doing a routine checkup now that her stepfather was up for a presidential appointment, but what was the sense in coming on so nice and easy?

A little session of question-and-answer, complete with some hard-ass assurances that she wouldn't much like the things that could happen to spoiled little girls who played nasty games, and that Mona Lisa smile would disappear.

Eva could go back to worrying about Papillon's next shade of nail polish, Hoyt could take his tux out of mothballs, and he could fly back to Washington and tell Harry Thurston what to do with himself the next time he decided to toss a mess in his direction. And if, in the process, Miranda Beckman learned that some men weren't to be played with . . .

Hey, some things were just too good to pass up.

Whistling jauntily through his teeth, Conor belted his raincoat and stepped out into the biting chill of the night.

The party that followed the showing was held at Jacques Diderot's mansion on the Rue St-Honoré.

Jean-Phillipe said that two centuries ago it had been the home of a mistress of Louis XVI, but Miranda suspected that even before the lady's head had parted company with her body, courtesy of Madame Guillotine, the house had probably never seen a party more extravagant than this.

On the street, strobe lights flashed against the night and video cameras whirred. Photographers and reporters fell on each arriving limousine like lions pouncing on impala.

Inside, Italian principessas rubbed shoulders with Seventh Avenue princes. The buffet tables groaned under the weight of Beluga caviar and Strasbourg *foie gras;* the champagne was vintage Moët et Chandon. It was the kind of scene that Miranda knew best. The envy of the women, the hunger of the men . . . and the comfort of knowing that Jean-Phillipe was never more than a moment away.

Parties like this were always fun.

But not tonight.

Tonight, she found it difficult to smile and mingle. She felt as if everyone could see that she was wearing a mask. Was it the morning's run-in with Conor O'Neil that had left her feeling this way? Was it wondering whether Eva was in some kind of trouble? That didn't seem possible. She didn't give a damn about her mother and, heaven knew, the feeling was mutual. As for O'Neil—why would she waste time even thinking about the man?

Still, she felt out of sorts and out of place. Jean-Phillipe, who was always attuned to her emotions, noticed.

''You are so quiet, *chérie*. Do you feel ill?''

Not ill, she almost said. Just—just strange.

But she didn't say it. Mentioning Eva would only lead to an argument. Jean-Phillipe, who'd lost both his parents in infancy, had a sentimental view of mothers that nothing could shake, not even the reality of one like Miranda's.

"Your mother made mistakes, *oui,*" he'd said at least a dozen times over the past couple of years, "but time has passed. Perhaps you should try and make things better between you."

No, she didn't want to hear that lecture again. And she certainly didn't want to talk about that boor, Conor O'Neil. It was a long time since anybody had gotten to her the way he had. Who did he think he was? Even now, hours later, she wished she'd slapped that contemptuous look from his face.

So she answered Jean-Phillipe's question by not answering it. Instead, she linked her arm through his and gave him a bright smile.

"Maybe I'm just getting too old for this business," she said.

He grinned. It was a joke, but one that had some truth to it and they both knew it. Not many models could endure almost eight years in the merciless glare of the spotlight.

"Over the mountain at twenty-five! *Mais oui,* the crows' claws are forming at your eyes even as I watch."

"Crows' feet," she said, laughing up at him.

"Feet, claws, what does it matter?" He leaned closer and spoke softly to her. "We will leave early, *chérie,* yes? I only want to track down this man my agent told me about, a Hollywood producer with very deep pockets who is supposed to be here tonight. Will you be all right if I leave you for a while?"

"Of course." She kissed his cheek, then wiped away the faint trace of pink lipstick she'd left. "You go find Mr. Moneybags and turn on the charm."

Jean-Phillipe vanished into the noisy crowd. Miranda took a flute of champagne from a passing waiter. A hand dropped lightly on her shoulder.

"Hello, Miss Beckman," a husky male voice said.

She went very still, and then she twisted away from that proprietary hand and turned to face its owner.

"Mr. O'Neil," she said coldly, "if you don't stop following me . . ."

But it wasn't Conor O'Neil who'd come up behind her, it

was someone else. A stranger, smiling politely and with that look of interest she knew so well in his eyes.

Something trembled deep inside her. Disappointment? No, certainly not. It was just a let-down, all that adrenaline surging in preparation for the chance to tell O'Neil off, and now it wasn't going to happen.

Miranda smiled. "Sorry. I thought you were someone else."

"I'm glad I'm not." The stranger smiled, too. "You didn't sound happy to see this person."

"I'm not. I mean, I wouldn't be." She laughed and held out her hand. "Never mind. Let's just start again, shall we? I'm—"

"Miranda Beckman. Of course. And I'm . . ."

He had an American accent but a foreign-sounding name, a melodious one that got lost in a sudden burst of nearby laughter. He was good-looking, well-dressed and, Miranda supposed, charming. He started a pleasant conversation and she smiled when she knew she should and nodded her head, but she couldn't concentrate on anything he said. Her thoughts kept returning to Conor O'Neil.

Who was he, anyway? A man who thought a lot of himself, that was for certain, but who was he, really? Had he told her the truth when he'd said he had some connection to Eva? It didn't seem likely. How could a man with such hard eyes be associated with a woman as elegant as her mother?

"Miranda." She looked up. Jean-Phillipe had come up beside her, her cape and his evening coat draped across his arm. He smiled politely at her and then at her companion. "Forgive me for intruding, *chérie,* but would you be terribly distressed if I suggested we leave now?"

Miranda gave him a dazzling smile. "Of course not." She put her hand lightly on the arm of the man she'd be talking to. What *was* his name? The hell with it, she thought, and flashed him a smile, too. "It's been nice talking with you."

The man bowed, took her hand and lifted it to his lips.

"Until we meet again, Miss Beckman," he said.

Jean-Phillipe shook his head as they made their way out of the gilt-trimmed *salon.*

"Someday," he murmured as he drew her cape around her shoulders, "someday, little one, you are going to get yourself in trouble with your games."

"What games? I was behaving like a perfect lady."

"Perfect ladies do not exchange pleasantries with gangsters."

"Gangsters?" Miranda said in amazement. She craned her neck and tried to look back into the *salon* for another look at the man, but it was too crowded.

Jean-Phillipe's hand tightened on her arm.

"Behave yourself," he said sternly, "and remember to smile for the cameras as we go out the door."

"Was that man really a gangster?" she whispered as they threaded their way through the gaggle of photographers that lined the steps and sidewalk.

"So it is said, and for God's sake, must you sound so delighted?" There was a studio limousine waiting for Jean-Phillipe. The driver leaped out, opened the door, then shut it after them. "I suppose you would not have looked so bored had you known, eh?"

Miranda laughed. "Did I look bored?"

"Completely so."

She sighed, kicked off her shoes and wiggled her toes against the deep pile carpet of the limo.

"I'm sorry, Jean-Phillipe, I'm just in a bad mood tonight, I guess."

"Any special reason?"

Yes, she thought, and his name is Conor O'Neil.

"Miranda?"

"No," she said quickly, "no reason at all. I'm just tired."

"Well, you did not look tired, on the runway this morning, *chérie.* You looked beautiful."

"And you're prejudiced," she said, smiling, "but thank you anyway. What about you? Did you connect with the Hollywood money man?"

"Unfortunately, no. Apparently, he changed his mind about attending."

"Ah. Too bad." She looked at him, her eyes twinkling. "I hope the night wasn't a total waste. Did anybody catch your eye, at least?"

Jean-Phillipe chuckled. "I never kiss and tell, *chérie,* that is one of my charms, *non?*"

She laughed and took his hand in hers.

"The other is your humility," she said, as the big car moved through the brightly lit streets.

Jean-Phillipe offered to see her to her door but Miranda told him to go on home.

"You're tired and I'm tired," she said, "and we both know that if you come up, I'll offer you a cognac and we'll end up talking half the night, dishing the dirt on everybody."

"What you really mean," he said, with a mock frown, "is that I will ask you why I rated such an effusive welcome at this morning's showing."

"You already asked me." Her tone was light. "And I told you, I missed you."

Jean-Phillipe touched his finger to the tip of her nose. "Did it have something to do with that handsome fellow I saw?"

"What handsome fellow?"

"You know exactly the one I mean, *chérie.* The one who was hurrying off with a face like a thunderbolt."

"Thundercloud," she said, with a little smile, "and no, it had nothing to do with him."

"Who was he?"

"He was just a man. An annoying one. No, no more questions! It's late. I'm tired. And if you don't get some sleep, those little bags under your eyes are going to have babies."

"Ah, Miranda, you know how to strike terror into an actor's heart." He clasped her hand, brought it to his mouth and kissed it. "*Bonne nuit, chérie.*"

She leaned forward and pressed her lips lightly to his cheek.

"Good night, Jean-Phillipe."

His driver waited while she dug out her keys and unlocked the ornate iron gate that barred entry to the courtyard of her apartment building. The three-story, U-shaped structure had once been a Bourbon palace. Now, it was home to an eclectic assortment of executives and artists.

The gate clanged shut behind her and the lock slid heavily into place. Miranda's high heels clicked loudly against the old paving stones that led to the massive front door. Her key slid home again and she pushed the door open.

"Good night," she mouthed, turning to wave.

Jean-Phillipe had rolled down his window. He blew her a kiss and the car rolled away.

Miranda stepped inside the building and the door swung shut.

The lobby was huge and had a high, vaulted ceiling. There was a stone fireplace at one end and a grouping of velvet-covered chairs and sofas no one ever sat in at the other. Just ahead, the *concièrge's* desk stood unattended. It was after eleven and Madame Delain had retired for the night.

Beyond, shadowed in darkness, the ornate wrought-iron elevator cage waited.

She hesitated. Was the lobby always this dark and silent?

What on earth was wrong with her tonight? Of course it was dark, and silent. It was almost midnight. She'd come home at this hour hundreds of times before. Actually, she'd come home far later.

But she'd never felt so uneasy, so—so . . .

Miranda frowned, marched to the elevator and stepped inside. The door clanged shut and she pressed the button for the third floor. The car rose slowly, as it always did, and with its usual accompaniment of rattles and moans. When she'd first moved in here, a couple of years ago, the sounds had struck her as spooky.

Now, for some silly reason, they sounded spooky again.

At the third floor, the car groaned to a shuddering halt and as it did, the bulb that lit the hall that stretched ahead of her blinked out.

Miranda swallowed dryly. So what? She didn't need the light to guide her. She'd made this walk in the dark before. The wiring in the old building wasn't good; lights were always going on and off for no reason. Tenants grumbled about it to each other all the time.

But there was a tight feeling in the pit of her belly. She didn't want to put her hand on the brass knob of the elevator door, turn it, and step outside.

It would take just a couple of minutes to go back downstairs and rouse Madame Delain. Madame would roll her eyes but her husband, a plump little man with a sweet smile, would be more than happy to take a flashlight, ride upstairs with her and walk her to her door.

And wouldn't she feel like a fool, if he did.

Whatever is the matter with you tonight, Miranda?

She gave herself a little shake, opened the elevator door and hurried to her apartment. Her hands were unsteady and she fumbled with the key before she managed to get it into the lock but finally the door swung open.

She stepped inside, let out a sigh of relief, shut the door behind her and reached for the light switch.

Click.

The room remained dark.

The hair stirred at the nape of her neck. Was this bulb out, too?

Coincidence, that was all it was.

Wasn't it?

Her nostrils dilated. What was that scent in the air? It was very faint. Perfume, or cologne.

But not hers.

Her heart started to race. She put her hand over it and told herself to stop being silly. Of course, the scent wasn't hers. She'd just come from a party where the guests had been packed in like sardines in a can. Clouds of stuff had filled the air. This wouldn't be the first time she'd come home with drifts of someone's Opium or Blue Water, whatever, in her hair and on her clothes.

Her heart banged again.

Where was Mia?

She'd had the cat for almost three years and in all that time, Mia had never missed the chance to come racing to the door and weave around her ankles while she said "Hello, where have you been all this time?" in a discordant, Siamese purr.

Miranda stared into the darkness. She could see nothing, hear nothing, but the racing thud of her heart.

"Mia?" she whispered.

Nothing moved.

She thought again of Monsieur Delain. She could still go down and get him. She had plenty of time to get out; she was barely inside the apartment and . . .

Get out? What for?

She was in her own home. She was completely safe. There had never been so much as a break-in here. Never. There was the bolted gate. The heavy, locked front door. There was Madame, standing guard like a short-tempered lioness.

But not at this hour.

So what? There was still the gate, and the locked downstairs door. And this door, the one to her apartment, had not been tampered with. Surely, if someone had broken in . . .

"Stop it," Miranda said firmly, and she walked briskly through the inky shadows and reached for the lamp she knew stood a few feet away.

Light, soft and warming, flooded the foyer. In its glow, she could see that everything was just as it was supposed to be, even Mia, blinking her great sapphire eyes as she looked up from a corner of the white sofa.

Miranda laughed shakily and let out a gusty sigh. She dropped her cape and her purse on a chair and scooped the Siamese into her arms.

"Naughty girl," she crooned, rubbing her face against the cat's chocolate brown fur, "why didn't you come to say hello?"

The cat meowed and butted its head against Miranda's chin.

"Are you angry because I've been gone so long? Well, suppose I open a can of tuna, hmm? No cat food for you to—"

The Siamese hissed, dug its claws in hard, then leaped to the floor and took off running.

"Mia!" Miranda rolled her eyes. The only thing more temperamental than a woman, Jean-Phillipe had once said, was a cat—and he was right.

"Mia," she said sternly, "it's late and I've had a long day. The last thing I'm in the mood for is a game of Siamese hide-and-seek!"

Mia skidded down the parquet-floored hall towards the bedroom. Her sinuous, chocolate-tipped tail disappeared around the half-open door just as Miranda reached it.

"For goodness' sakes, cat, what's gotten into—"

Oh God!

The blood in her veins seemed to freeze. The faint light from the street cast an eerie illumination over a room that suddenly didn't seem to be hers.

What had happened here? The bed was rumpled. The closet was open and clothing lay strewn over the floor. The doors of the cherrywood *armoire* were open, too, and her silk and lace underwear was spilling out of the top drawers.

Someone had been here.

Here, in her apartment.

In her bedroom.

Someone had been here, and whoever it was had lain on her bed, had taken her clothes from the hangers, had handled her panties and bras . . .

The doorbell rang.

She spun around, her skin icy with fear.

Who would come calling at this hour? No one had rung the courtyard bell. You had to ring the bell, unless you had a key to the gate. And no one had a key to that gate, except for her.

And Jean-Phillipe.

Yes. It could be him. Jean-Phillipe could have come back.

She'd told him to go home, that it was too late for a drink

but so what? This wouldn't be the first time he'd decided to ignore her saying something like that.

The bell rang again.

Miranda moved slowly down the hall.

"Jean-Phillipe?" she whispered.

Knuckles rapped against the door.

"Yes," she said, oh yes, of course it was him, who else would it be? A sob burst from her throat as she flew to the door and flung it open.

"Oh, Jean-Phillipe, you can't imagine how happy I am to see—"

"Good evening, Miss Beckman."

Miranda screamed.

Jesus H. Christ, Conor thought, and even as he was thinking it, Miranda Beckman tried to slam the door in his face.

He reacted instinctively, thrusting his foot into the opening, driving his shoulder against the ornate paneling, and the door flew open, hurling her back into the room. She scrambled to her feet and came at him in what had to be the worst impression of a karate crouch that he'd ever seen in his life.

"Miss Beckman . . ."

Grunting, she kicked out with her right foot. Conor danced back easily.

"Okay," he said, "I didn't exactly expect you to greet me with open arms—"

"You sonofabitch!"

"Lady, if you'd just let me talk—"

"Talk? Talk?" She spun around, then kicked out. Her foot caught him a glancing blow. It didn't hurt but it sure as hell surprised him. "You don't want to talk, you want to—you want to—"

She came at him a third time. She had as much finesse as an elephant but it didn't matter, not when she had so much determination. Conor knew he could stop her, but he didn't want to hurt her. On the other hand, he didn't want to end up with what looked like a shoe equipped with a four-inch spiked heel embedded in his groin.

"Miss Beckman," he said soothingly, "Miranda, listen."

She wasn't listening. She was intent on killing him.

"Hell," he muttered, and he moved fast, got inside her stiffly outstretched arms and past her flailing kick, grabbed her wrist and tossed her to the carpet.

She went over backwards, hit with a thud and gave out a high, wild cry. Even as he came down on top of her, the last Pink Panther movie he'd ever seen flashed through Conor's head and dammit, he couldn't help it, he started to laugh.

Miranda hissed like a snake and went for his eyes.

"Damn!" He caught her wrists in one hand, drew her arms above her head and pinned them there. "Are you crazy?"

"I'll kill you first," she said, and before he could ask her what in hell that was supposed to mean, her lips parted and he knew she was going to scream. For one crazy instant, he thought of shutting her up by kissing her—but then sanity returned. He slapped his free hand over her mouth, and just in time. The muffled shriek that burst from her throat would surely have been enough to call up every *gendarme* within miles.

"Okay," he growled, "that's enough."

She said something against his hand. It wasn't pleasant, whatever it was, and probably wasn't very ladylike but then, Miranda Beckman didn't look very ladylike, lying sprawled beneath him, her hair a tangle of black silk, her eyes hot and dark in her flushed face. She was wearing what he thought women called slip dresses although this one looked more like a bathing suit, for God's sake, with its skinny black straps and the way it exposed the curve of her breasts, and the way it had ridden up her thighs.

Conor felt his body stir.

Stop it, he told himself furiously, what the hell is wrong with—

Her teeth sank into the heel of his hand. He yelped, pulled his hand back, and she almost scurried out from under him. He came down harder, his chest pressed to her breasts, his knee jammed between her thighs, and he held on to her wrists with one hand while he clamped the other around her throat and jaw, hard enough to get her attention.

''Okay,'' he said roughly, ''here's the deal.''

She made a sound but the pressure of his fingers stopped it. Her eyes were wild with fear. That was okay with him. She deserved a good scare. Maybe, if she was scared enough, she'd start to listen.

''I'm only going to say this one time. You got that?''

Her blue eyes gleamed with hate. Conor applied just a little more pressure.

''Do you understand me, Miranda?''

His thumb bit into the hollow of her throat. She nodded.

''You scream,'' he said, ''or bite me again, or try any crap at all, you try to do anything but listen to every word I say and I'll be forced to get your attention the hard way.'' After a few seconds, he shifted his hold on her jaw, forcing her head up and back. ''Blink if we've got a deal.''

He had to give her credit for guts if not brains. He had every advantage, size and weight and position, but she still wanted to defy him. He could see it in the rush of conflicting emotions that swept over her face. But she wasn't a complete fool. A minute passed, and then she blinked.

''Was that a yes?''

She blinked again.

''All right. I'm going to lift my hand from your throat. Just remember what I said. Any funny stuff and you'll regret it. *Comprenez-vous?*''

Slowly, he eased his hand from her neck.

''You still with me?''

The tip of her tongue snaked across her lips.

''Do you know who I am?''

Her mouth twisted with undisguised contempt.

''I'm not a moron, O'Neil.''

''And I'm not the bogeyman, or whoever in hell you mistook me for.''

"You'd better get out of here," she said. "I called the police."

"Yeah? Well, maybe we should call a doctor." He drew back, his knee still wedged between her legs, and shot a quick look at his hand. The tiny marks of her sharp teeth stood out clearly against the skin. "I hope you've had your rabies shots, Beckman."

"The police station is only a block away. They'll catch you, if you don't—"

"And charge me with what? Defending myself against an attempt on my life?"

"Let me up!"

"Why? So you can launch another attack?"

"Dammit, O'Neil!"

"What in hell's wrong with you? Or do you always greet your guests that way?"

"You're not a guest," she said furiously, "you're an intruder. A—a pervert!"

"A what?" he said, and laughed.

She didn't blame him for laughing. Whoever Conor O'Neil was, whatever he was, she somehow doubted if he'd get his kicks by messing around in a drawer filled with women's underpants.

But he'd caught her by surprise. She'd expected to see Jean-Phillipe's familiar face when she'd opened the door. Instead, she'd been faced with this—this barbarian.

"Get off me," she snapped.

"First you tell me why I rated such a welcome." His teeth flashed in a humorless smile. "I know I'm not on your list of favorites, Beckman, but—"

"Will—you—get—off—me?" she said and when he didn't move, Miranda twisted beneath him and tried to roll him off.

In a heartbeat, she knew it hadn't been a very good idea.

So did he.

If only she hadn't moved.

One minute, adrenaline had been pumping through Conor's system at about a gallon a minute while he'd tried to figure out how to deal with the crazy woman pinned beneath him and the next . . . the next, his body was doing it again.

At least, this time, it made sense. He wasn't reacting to a portrait, or a photograph, or to a woman going out of her way to give him a peep-show. He was reacting to the real thing. Male anatomy and female anatomy. Yin and yang. Hard muscles against soft, sweet-smelling woman . . .

A woman who was terrified of him.

Dammit to hell, he thought furiously, and he rolled off her and shot to his feet.

"Get up," he snarled.

She stood up, her face stony and her eyes cold. But she was trembling, and that only made him angrier. He thought of the ads he'd seen her in, of that sexy pout she offered the camera; he thought of the way she'd greeted the Frenchman with the too-pretty face this morning, damn near climbing the guy's leg like a bitch in heat.

So she'd felt his erection. So what? It would hardly be the first time.

Who was she kidding, standing there in a dress that molded itself to her breasts and ended at her thighs? He'd be damned if he'd apologize for an act of biology she specialized in causing.

"Well, Beckman?"

"Well, what?"

"Are you going to tell me why you tried to kill me?"

Her eyes narrowed until they were slits.

"Get out of my apartment, O'Neil."

"I take it that's a no."

"Did you hear me?" Her voice shook; but the hand she pointed towards the door was rock-steady. "Get out!"

"Okay, don't tell me. I'm not even sure I want to know. It's been a long day. I'm tired, I'm hungry, and I'm as eager to see the last of you as you are to see the last of me. If it makes you feel better . . ." He went to the door, opened it a few inches, then turned and looked at her. "How's that? We'll leave the door ajar, I'll ask you a couple of questions, and then I'll leave."

"I'm not answering any questions. I told you that this morning."

Conor sighed. He dug into his pocket, came up with an ID card that bore his photograph and flashed it at her.

"This is an official visit, Miss Beckman."

As he'd hoped it would, that caught her attention. "Official?"

"Yes."

Some of the color was returning to her face and with it, that look of haughty disdain.

"I should have known," she said. "What are you, O'Neil? Some government flunky come to chat about my childhood?"

Conor looked at her. "Why would I want to do that?"

"Oh, come on. I'm not stupid. You said you wanted to talk about my mother and Hoyt. And Hoyt's up for—what? A U.N. post?"

"An ambassadorship."

"Whatever," she said, shrugging her shoulders. "It's time to open the closets and sweep out all the dirt."

Conor smiled pleasantly. "Is there dirt to sweep out?"

Miranda's eyes flashed. "Only me," she said, her voice steady and cold.

"Well, then, you won't mind answering my questions."

"That's where you're wrong." She strode past him, shouldered the door fully open, and stood beside it with her arms folded. "Eva should have warned you. I'm not into accommodating authority figures. So you can take your government badge and your notepad and shove them—"

"I'm not with the government," Conor said with a smooth smile.

"No?"

"No."

Miranda's eyes narrowed. "You just said—"

"I said I was here on official business, and I am." He didn't even think about what lie he'd tell her. It was one of the things about his profession, he thought with bitter satisfaction; lying came as easy as breathing. "I'm working for your mother."

She laughed. "Right. And I'm a candidate for mayor."

"I'm a private investigator."

"A what?"

"An investigator. A private detective."

"You're joking."

"I never joke about my profession," Conor said with such sincerity that he gave himself a round of mental applause. "Can we sit down and discuss this?"

"We are discussing it. Why would Eva need a private eye?"

"Someone sent your mother a note."

"How fascinating."

"It was a strange note, and unsigned."

"So? What's it have to do with me?"

"That's what I'm here to find out."

Nothing showed on Miranda's face. If she'd sent the note, she was hiding it well.

"Look, O'Neil, I'm sure this is leading somewhere but it's getting very late—"

"The note may have been a threat."

"A threat?" she said, her eyebrows lifting.

For a woman who'd written the note, she looked absolutely blank.

"Maybe. It was cryptic."

"And?"

Here it came, The Big Lie. He didn't think she'd be able to keep that stony look on her face after this. If she'd written that note, he'd know it.

"The note mentioned your elopement," Conor said, and waited. But her reaction wasn't anything he'd expected. She didn't look caught off guard, she simply looked baffled.

"That's ancient history. Why would anybody send Eva a note about that?"

If she was putting him on, she was doing a damned fine job of it. Conor decided to switch tactics.

"That's what bothered her. She's worried. About you, I mean."

Miranda's eyes narrowed. "Try another line, O'Neil. Eva hasn't worried about me since I was twelve."

"Still," he said, "she's concerned."

"Why?"

"Well, if the note is some sort of threat, it could very well be directed at you.

"That's ridiculous. Why would anybody want to threaten . . ."

She went still so suddenly that the silence seemed to have a physical presence. Then she made a little sound of distress and sank down on a chair.

"Shut the door," she whispered.

He did, and then he looked at her. "What is it?"

She stared at him. The color was creeping back into her cheeks but when she got to her feet, she seemed wobbly.

"Here's the chance of a lifetime, O'Neil," she said. "How'd you like to take a tour of my bedroom?"

She didn't wait for him to answer; she simply set off down the hall. Conor stared after her. Then he took a deep breath and started walking.

Chapter Six

The coffee in Conor's cup was murky black. He looked down at it, scowled, then lifted it to his lips and took a long swallow.

The stuff tasted like something that ought to be poured down the drain, but when you needed a jolt of caffeine as badly as he did, you took what you could get and you took it straight, without sugar or cream.

He sighed, put the cup down and scrubbed his hands over his face. What he really needed was to fall into bed, clothes and all, and sleep for ten hours straight.

How long was it since his plane had touched down on French soil? A day? A week? A month? He didn't know anymore, and he wasn't sure he was functional enough to figure it out. Exhaustion and jet lag were doing him in. His legs felt numb, his tongue felt thick, and his eyeballs felt as if they'd been sandblasted.

"Welcome to Paris, O'Neil," he muttered. He'd have laughed, too, if he'd had the energy.

Conor picked up the cup and forced down another mouthful of coffee. What was he doing here, sitting in Miranda Beckman's apartment in the middle of the night? He was supposed to be in his place in Georgetown, snug and cozy in his own bed. Or was it only evening back home? At this moment, figuring out the time change seemed a challenge for a genius.

Not that it mattered. Whatever the hour, he'd bet that Harry Thurston wasn't sitting around in a daze, with the floor spongy under his feet and his stomach snarling and saying it couldn't remember the last time something other than coffee acid had been dumped into it.

Thurston, the bastard, was eating dinner. Or watching a movie. Or sleeping soundly. Whatever he was doing, it was better than this.

Conor's mouth thinned. Thurston, he thought grimly, Thurston, you no-good—

Hell. Who was he kidding? He couldn't blame Harry for this mess. It had been his idea, and his alone, to fly to Paris. And why? To question Miranda Beckman, and to get a look at her.

"Okay," Conor muttered, staring down into his cup where blobs of oil from the coffee floated like debris on the Potomac, "you got a look. And now you're sitting here at something o'clock in the morning, brain-dead, and you know, you *know,* you're getting drawn in deeper and deeper."

Shit.

He got up, dumped the contents of both his cup and the coffee pot into the sink and rinsed them out.

He'd come here to ask Miranda a couple of questions, get her to admit what had seemed such a basic truth that he hadn't questioned it. She'd written the note, she'd acknowledge it under his prodding, and he'd go back to the States, the investigation concluded and his basic male curiosity satisfied.

What was it Robbie Burns had said about the best-laid plans of mice and men?

Conor puffed out his breath, took down the coffee canister he'd put away only moments before, and glared at it.

All those best-laid plans had gone up in smoke. Miranda hadn't reacted the way she'd been supposed to, when he'd mentioned the note and then lied about its contents. Instead, her face had gone white and the next thing he'd known, he'd been standing in a bedroom that looked as if it had been sacked by the Huns.

The closet was open and the clothing from it was everywhere, on hangers, off hangers, a tangled mess of stuff strewn all around the room. The doors of what she'd insisted on calling an *armoire* were open, too, and underwear as lacy and silken as any man's dream was spilling out of the drawers. The bed was messed up, the pillows dented in as if a head had laid on them.

None of which proved anything.

Conor filled the electric kettle with water and plugged it in.

For all he knew, the woman always left her bedroom like that. He'd seen enough boudoirs in his time to know that not all females subscribed to the belief that neatness counted, especially when they were getting dressed to go out.

As for the bed—so what if both pillows were dented? Miranda had made a big point of telling him that she slept only on the right-hand side of the bed, that she only used the right-hand pillow.

That didn't mean her lover hadn't used the other one.

Conor had had a sudden image of her naked on that bed in the arms of the Frenchman with the pretty face.

He leaned back against the sink, arms folded and mouth thinned.

That was the exact moment he should have turned to her and said, I'm out of here, but how could he?

Either she was lying, trying to divert his attention and convince him she hadn't sent Eva that note, or she was telling him the truth, and somebody had been in the apartment while she was out.

Maybe some poor, demented bastard had seen her wearing that come-and-get-me smile one time too many and had finally decided he just had to jimmy the door and sniff her underwear—and maybe not. Maybe she'd been paid a visit, but not by a sexual sicko. There could just be a connection between the note sent to Eva and whatever had gone on here tonight.

It was Conor's job to find out.

He'd checked the door. The lock was easy, the kind of thing you could open without raising a sweat, assuming you knew your stuff.

Would a sicko have known his stuff? Would a nut-job have been able to slip the lock without leaving a scratch?

Which meant, he thought glumly as the kettle sent up a shriek, which meant that there was a chance that Miranda was telling him the truth, that she hadn't sent the note, didn't know anything about it, and that maybe, just maybe, she was the quarry in a scheme that was somehow connected to it, and to Eva.

He was starting to think that she was. She could have faked the messy room but could she really have faked the way she'd looked at him as he'd set out to check every nook and cranny in the apartment? It was possible but he wasn't taking any chances. So he'd told her to calm down, make some coffee and they'd talk.

And she'd looked at him with those big green eyes, with her soft mouth trembling, and the contrast between the frightened innocence in her face and the sexy voluptuousness of her body poured into the too-short, too-tight, too-everything dress had turned his brain to mush and he'd had all he could do to keep from taking her in his arms and saying that it was all right, he wouldn't let anything hurt her.

He hadn't done that, thank God. He might be jet-lagged but he wasn't crazy. Not completely. They'd moved into the kitchen, he'd perched on a high stool at the central island counter while she made coffee. Then she'd opened a box of cookies, sat down beside him and they'd drunk all the coffee and munched most of the cookies while he'd asked her half a dozen questions half a dozen times.

Finally, she'd said she couldn't think straight anymore.

Hang in just a little bit longer, he'd said.

What he hadn't said was that not thinking straight was the general idea.

If she couldn't think straight, her tongue might trip her up. She might begin changing the answers she gave him. She might slip and admit she'd written the note to Eva or that she'd thought fast, lied about someone having been in her bedroom.

But she hadn't. What she'd done, eventually, was groan, bury her face in her hands and say she had to splash cold water on her face or she'd fall asleep where she was.

Conor had yawned.

"Go on," he'd said wearily, "and I'll put up another pot of coffee."

Another bit of volunteerism gone bad, he thought, glaring at the coffee maker.

It wasn't a pot you plugged in. It wasn't one you put on the stove. It wasn't a filter job or a plain vanilla Chemex.

The coffee maker was what she'd called an infuser. He'd never used one, never even seen one before except when a smaller version had been plunked down at his elbow in a little place in Cornwall, or maybe Normandy. He didn't remember, didn't care, didn't give a damn about this thing Miranda used to make her coffee except to know that he'd need to be Betty Crocker to figure out how to work it, which probably explained why the coffee he'd brewed a while ago had looked and tasted more like ink than—

"O'Neil?"

He looked up. Miranda was standing in the kitchen doorway and if the way she was staring at him meant anything, he looked as bad as he felt. Worse, maybe, though he didn't know how that could be possible.

She, on the other hand, looked fine. Better than fine, he thought, as his sandblasted eyes took in the picture she presented.

She'd done more than splash cold water on her face. She'd showered. He could tell by the way her hair hung down her back, loose and damp and curling around her shiny, scrubbed-clean face. The dress that wasn't a dress had given way to shapeless grey sweats with a pair of fuzzy pink slippers peeping out from under the pants.

All she needed was a backdrop of flowering dogwood.

Something of what he was thinking must have showed in

his face because she frowned uncertainly and made a little fluttery gesture with her hand.

"What?" she said.

He was just tired enough to think of giving her a real answer. *I'll tell you what,* he'd say. *I don't know who you are or what you are. I don't know if you're guilty of screwing with your mother's head and maybe now with mine or if you're as innocent as you look right at this minute. I'm not even sure I know what I'm doing here. So the way I'm going to sort things out, Miss Beckman, is to haul you into my arms, carry you into the bedroom and make love to you until one of us—hell, until both of us—collapse with exhaustion.*

"O'Neil? Is something wrong?"

Conor dragged air into his lungs.

"Yes," he said. He turned away from her, stared at the coffee pot he still held in his hands, then carefully set it down on the counter. "I can't figure this mother out."

She laughed.

"It's simple." Her arm brushed his. "Sit down," she said. "I'll take care of it. Although I don't know why I'm bothering." She yawned. "All the caffeine in the world won't keep me awake much longer."

Why bother arguing? He felt exactly the same way.

"One last go-round," he said. "Then we'll quit for the night."

Miranda hitched her lip onto a stool. "I've already told you everything I know, O'Neil, ten times over."

Conor nodded. He leaned back against the counter and stuffed his hands into his trouser pockets. Sometime during the past hours, he'd peeled off his coat and tweed jacket, unloosened his tie and rolled up his shirt sleeves. He felt rumpled and weary and in desperate need of a long, hot shower, especially now that Miranda had come sailing back into the room, smelling of lilacs and soap.

God, he was more tired than he'd realized. He cleared his throat, frowned, and looked at her.

"Let's go over your day again, Beckman. You did the show this morning, you stood for some photos afterwards. Right?"

She sighed, shut her eyes and let her head droop. Her hair fell forward, slipping over her shoulders like silk.

"Right."

"And?"

She sighed again. "And then I had lunch."

"Who with?"

"Nita. I told you that. We were going to order in but Nita said she was desperate for some fresh air so we went around the corner to that *bistro.*"

"What *bistro?*"

She groaned, lifted her head and ran her hands through her hair.

"I don't remember the name. I told you that, too. It's just a restaurant, for heaven's sake. You want to know the name, go check it for yourself."

"How come you didn't have lunch with Pretty Boy?"

"Who?"

"The Frenchman. Lunch, maybe a quickie. Wasn't he interested?"

She sat up straight and glared at him. "His name is Jean-Phillipe Moreau. He's an actor. And do you always go out of your way to be offensive?"

"Me? Offensive?" His smile was all innocence. "I'm only stating the obvious, Beckman. From the way you and Pretty Boy went at each other, I figured you had afternoon plans. Was I wrong?"

"Yes," she said, clearly and deliberately, "you were. Neither Jean-Phillipe or I would ever dream of rushing a fuck."

She saw the quick rush of crimson across his cheeks. Good, she thought, coldly, he deserved it.

Then, why did she feel as if she ought to have her mouth washed out with soap? She was a grown woman; she had a reputation for doing and saying whatever pleased her.

And he'd *definitely* deserved it.

Conor O'Neil had shouldered his way into her life without

being invited. She didn't trust him, not one bit. All that stuff about his working for Eva . . . Who was he kidding? She couldn't imagine Eva caring enough about her welfare to send somebody to check on her. She couldn't imagine O'Neil taking orders, either, especially from someone like her mother.

There was something missing in the equation.

O'Neil was more complex than he appeared. There was something urbane and sophisticated lurking just underneath the tweedy surface. Something scary, too, but in a way that was strangely comforting. In fact, once she'd got over the shock of opening the door and seeing him, she'd found herself thinking that it was just as well he'd turned up instead of Jean-Phillipe. She loved Jean-Phillipe dearly but the truth was that he dramatized everything and the last thing she'd needed tonight was somebody to make more of that messy scene in the bedroom than she'd already made of it herself.

O'Neil hadn't done that. He'd looked the room over, then turned to her and issued a terse command.

''Stay put,'' he'd said, and no one in their right mind would have argued with him. He'd gone through the rest of the apartment, room by room, moving silently and purposefully and in a way that had made her feel protected and safe. No question about it, Conor O'Neil was very definitely the man you wanted around when you were frightened.

It was just too bad she didn't trust him.

Or like him.

The feeling was clearly mutual. He despised her; the message was in his eyes each time he looked at her.

But he wanted her, too.

The realization pleased her. It made him as predictable as every other man she'd ever dealt with. Sooner or later, he'd try to bed her. They always did, and they always ended up wondering what had hit them on their way out of her life. He would, too. This was a game she never lost. The rules were hers and the outcome was inevitable.

The thought made her smile.

''Something amusing come to mind, Beckman?''

Miranda looked up. O'Neil's face was stony, his gaze contemptuous. Her smile curled at the corners.

"Nothing you'd understand," she said.

His expression didn't change. "I'm still waiting to hear about the rest of your day. Lunch with Nita, no afternoon assignation with the boyfriend . . ."

"That's right. If you were hoping for a play-by-play account, you're out of luck."

A muscle ticked in his jaw. "What did you do after lunch?"

Miranda sighed. She pressed down the filter top of the infuser and watched as it slowly plunged to the bottom of the carafe.

"Nita and I went to the Diderot showroom on Rue du Faubourg St-Honoré. There was a photographer waiting. He took some more pictures."

"And?"

"And, that was it."

"You came home?"

"Yes. No." She shot him a narrow-eyed look. "Are you trying to confuse me?"

"Just answer the question, please. And hurry up with that coffee before I pass out."

She poured two cups of coffee, gave one to Conor and kept the other for herself. Then she leaned back against the sink, holding her cup with both hands.

"Where was I?"

"You were having your picture taken, at the Diderot showroom."

"Right. Well, by the time we finished, it was late. So I sat around for a while and took it easy. Then I dressed for the evening."

"You didn't come home to get dressed?"

"No. There wasn't any reason. Jacques had asked me to wear one of his designs to the party I was going to tonight. Last night. You know what I mean."

Conor's brows lifted. "That thing you were wearing was a dress?"

She laughed. "An eight-thousand-dollar dress."

"Yeah, well, it only goes to prove that there's no accounting for taste. So you got dressed at the showroom. And then you met Pretty Boy."

"Jean-Phillipe," Miranda said coldly.

"Right. You met him for drinks. And afterwards, you went to, what was it? La Tour d'Argent for dinner?"

"We went to Taillevent. This is childish, O'Neil. Trying to trip me up as if—"

"Then you and Moreau went to a party."

Miranda nodded wearily and put down her coffee cup. She closed her eyes, tilted her head back and massaged her temples with the tips of her fingers. Her hair tumbled down her back, exposing her ears and throat.

Conor stared at her. She had beautiful skin. It reminded him of peaches and cream. Would it taste that way, too?

His jaw tightened. He looked down at his coffee, raised it to his lips and took a swallow.

"Tell me about the party," he said.

"I told you about the party."

"Tell me again."

She sighed and looked at him.

"It was on the Rue St-Honoré. A big, handsome house, owned by some English diplomat."

"You had some champagne, you chatted with some people . . ."

"One person," she said wearily. "Just one. And before you ask me again, I still don't remember his name."

"You didn't ask?"

"I told you, he introduced himself. But the place was noisy. And crowded."

"So you had this long conversation with some guy whose name you didn't know?"

"This may come as a shock, O'Neil, but very few people check someone's ID before they carry on a conversation. Any other questions?"

"Yeah. Try harder to come up with the guy's name."

Miranda groaned. "It was foreign, I think. American."

"Which was it? American or foreign?"

"He was American. But his name was European. Italian, maybe."

"So, you wouldn't know how to get in touch with him?"

"Why would I want to get in touch with him?"

"I don't know. You said he was pleasant. Good looking. Made nice chit-chat."

"So what? I meet a lot of people like that."

"Men, you mean." His smile was quick and chill. "Might be a good idea to sort them out, you know? Keep a scorecard."

There was no mistaking what he meant. She bit back the rush of anger, knowing it was just what he wanted, swung away and dumped her coffee into the sink.

"An excellent suggestion. Now, if you don't mind, I'm tired, and my nerves are jingling from all this coffee." She turned towards him again, her hands on her hips. "Let's just get this over with."

"Moreau drove you home?"

"Yes."

"But he didn't bring you to your door."

"No. There was no need. This building is perfectly safe. There's the locked gate . . ."

"Oh, right. The locked gate." Conor shook his head, dug into his pocket and took out a small Swiss Army knife, the kind she'd always figured was useless for anything more complicated than clipping off a thread. "A minute with this and I was in."

"Well, not everyone has your talent," Miranda said sweetly.

"Anybody with the least bit of determination could have been inside this apartment in less time than it takes to tell. The gate's a laugh, and so is the lock on the door downstairs."

"You opened that with a penknife, too?"

He grinned. "Actually, I used my American Express card. Never leave home without it."

She laughed before she had time to think about it. It was a nice laugh, Conor thought, and real. Her eyes met his; it was almost as if she'd realized what she was doing. She stopped laughing, turned away and began slamming the doors to the cabinets over the sink.

"What are you doing?"

"Looking for chocolate."

"What?"

"I'm going to fall on my face in about five seconds, thanks to this inquisition. Caffeine's not helping, so I'm hoping chocolate will." Rising on her toes, she felt along the cabinet shelves. "I always keep some in the house. Not where I can find it too easily, but somewhere . . ."

Her words trailed off but it didn't matter. Conor wasn't listening. How could he, when he was watching her every move? Her sweatshirt had ridden up. Not much, just a couple of inches—just enough to bare a narrow band of smooth, silky skin and the delicate tracery of her spine.

". . . never find it when I want it . . ."

She grunted as she stretched higher; the shirt climbed another inch up her back. Conor's mouth went dry. He knew that a gentleman would offer to help but hell, he wasn't a gentleman. He was a man transfixed by a sudden vision of himself crossing the room to where Miranda stood, slipping his hands under her shirt and cupping her breasts while he bent his head, nuzzled her hair from the nape of her neck and tasted her skin with his tongue.

The coffee still left in his cup dumped into his lap.

"Dammit," he yelped, and shot to his feet.

Miranda spun around, a little box of Fauchon's chocolates in her hand.

"What happened?"

"Nothing. I spilled the damn coffee, that's all."

She put down the box, picked up a dish towel and leaned towards him.

"Here, let me—"

"No!" He jerked back from her outstretched hand, then took a deep breath. "That's okay. I'll go and wash up."

"Listen, O'Neil, why not do us both a favor and leave? It's late and we're both exhausted . . ."

She was talking to herself. O'Neil had already disappeared down the hall.

Miranda sighed, walked into the living room and collapsed onto the sofa with her feet up. Mindlessly, she opened the box and took out a chocolate. Cookies, and now candy. Well, just one wouldn't hurt. She could skip breakfast tomorrow. Or today. Whatever it was; she didn't know anymore. The minutes and hours had all run together, thanks to the mess she'd come home to.

And what an ugly mess it had been.

She thought again that it was a good thing Conor O'Neil had turned up tonight. So what if he didn't like her? If he thought she was wild, and immoral, and all the things she'd worked so hard to make the world believe she was. He could think what he liked about her; she didn't care . . .

"Okay, let's talk."

She swung her feet to the floor and sat up. Conor was standing over her, his hands on his hips. His hair was wet; he must have ducked his head into the sink. Her eyes went to his face. It was a good face. Strong. Very masculine. She supposed there were women who'd find him handsome, with those prominent cheekbones and that nose that tilted just slightly to the side, as if it had once been broken. The rest of him suited the face: the wide shoulders, leanly muscled body, the aura of danger that was so wonderfully sexy.

A pulse leaped in the hollow of her throat.

I'm tired, she thought, that's what all this is about, I'm tired and I'm not thinking straight.

"It's late." She stood up, the half-empty box of chocolates dangling from her hand. "I can't answer any more questions."

Conor had had a long talk with himself in the bathroom. The talk, and a sinkful of cold water, had cleared his head. He was good at what he did. His emotions didn't get in his way. Hell, according to the woman who'd once been his wife, his emotions *never* got in his way.

He'd let the water out of the sink, looked himself in the eye in the mirror, and told himself he was done behaving like an ass.

So why was he standing here now, looking at Miranda and wanting to—wanting to—

Hell, she was right. It *was* late.

"Okay," he said briskly. He tore his eyes from her face and began rolling down his sleeves. "We'll pick up tomorrow."

Miranda groaned. "Tomorrow?"

"Yes." He looked up. "You've got—you've got . . ."

"What?"

His eyes met hers. "You've got chocolate on your mouth."

It wasn't what he'd meant to say. What in hell was the matter with him?

She shot a guilt-filled look at the box in her hand, then dumped it on the sofa behind her while a rush of bright color climbed her cheeks.

"Is it gone?" she said, rubbing her hand over her lips.

He saw himself walking to where she stood. "No," he'd say, and before she could react he'd bend his head to hers, run the tip of his tongue over her mouth.

Heat raced through his blood. It took everything he had not to move.

"Yeah." He cleared his throat. "Yeah, it's gone. Look, I'll come by tomorrow morning, tie this thing up, okay?"

"I suppose. But I don't know what questions you can ask that I haven't already answered."

"I'll think of something." He tried for a smile. "By morning, my brain ought to be functioning again."

He plucked his jacket from the back of the chair where he'd left it and started towards her, hoping she'd step aside before he reached her because he wasn't really sure what would happen if she didn't. But she didn't move, she just stood there looking soft and vulnerable and all at once he felt something give inside him.

"Hell," he said, and he reached out, pulled her into his arms and kissed her.

Miranda made a little sound of protest and tried to pull back, but Conor wouldn't let her. He drew her closer, kissed her harder.

She melted into him.

There was no other way to describe it. One second he was holding her, forcing her to suffer his kiss. The next, her arms were around his neck and her mouth was clinging to his.

They drew back at the same instant, both of them breathing hard.

"I'm not going to apologize," Conor said, "or to say I didn't know what I was doing—"

Her fist blurred through the air and slammed into his mouth.

"Get out," Miranda said, "get out and don't you ever touch me again. Do you understand me, O'Neil? Because if you do, if you do . . ."

Her voice shook, but hatred for him burned bright and steady in her eyes. There was nothing soft or vulnerable about her now. She looked tough and determined and when Conor touched his lip, he wasn't surprised to see a smear of bright red blood on his fingertip.

"Lock the door after me," he said, as calmly as if nothing had happened, "and put on the chain. Don't open the door for anybody, not even for Pretty Boy. Not that you have to worry. Whoever did this isn't going to put in a return appearance tonight. I'll arrange to have a new lock installed first thing in the morning."

"Do you really think I'm going to take orders from you?"

He put on his jacket and draped his raincoat over one shoulder.

"Yes," he said. "That's exactly what I think."

"Damn you, O'Neil! You can take your orders and—"

"Give it up," he said, very quietly. "That may have worked with Mama and Hoyt and all those fancy schools. But I promise you, Beckman, it sure as hell isn't going to work with me."

The street was dark, the night was cold.

It was very late, but there were still taxis cruising the Rue de Rivoli. He stepped off the curb, started to signal for one, then changed his mind.

A long walk was just what he needed.

Conor turned up the collar of his coat and tucked his hands into his pockets. He needed to clear his head and think about the growing complexity of the Winthrop situation.

Instead, he thought about Miranda.

He'd kissed her and he wished he hadn't, but he didn't blame himself for it. He was a man, not a saint. Just this morning, she'd teased him almost beyond tolerance. In another time and place, a man would have done more than kiss a woman under such circumstances, no matter how unwilling she was.

But that was just the problem. She hadn't been unwilling.

Yes, she'd slapped his face. She told him what she'd do if he ever tried to touch her again, but that was after she'd given herself up to the kiss.

Had she done it deliberately? She might have. She was a woman who'd do anything to confuse a man.

But the kiss had seemed so real. As real as the photo he had in his wallet, of Miranda under the dogwood tree.

Conor's jaw tightened. Forget it, he told himself. He'd kissed her, and now it was over. He had to concentrate on what mattered. The note. The fact that someone seemed to have tossed her apartment. The wariness in Eva's eyes.

It worked, for a few minutes, but after a while, as he made his way along the dark streets of the sleeping city, Conor gave up trying to think about anything but the warm, silken magic of Miranda's mouth under his.

Chapter Seven

Miranda was in the shower when the phone rang early the next morning.

Maybe it was Jean-Phillipe. She'd tried to reach him almost an hour ago but his answering machine had picked up and she'd ended up saying no more than "Hi, it's me, give me a call when you can."

It just hadn't seemed possible to tell a machine that your apartment had been broken into and that somebody had rifled through your clothing.

She grabbed for a towel, wrapped herself in it and raced for the phone.

"Hello," she said, sitting down on the edge of her bed, "oh, I'm so glad you got my message!"

"Did you leave a message for me, darling?" Conor purred. "I'm really touched."

Miranda stiffened. "O'Neil?"

"I take it you were expecting somebody else."

"What do you want, O'Neil?"

"A bright and cheerful good-morning would do for starters."

"Listen, I was taking a shower when the phone rang and

now I'm dripping puddles all over the place. Just tell me what you want, okay?''

You, Conor thought, with water beading on your shoulders and the smell of soap rising from your skin . . .

''O'Neil? Why did you call?''

''Just checking,'' he said, and cleared his throat. ''Any problems during the night?''

The question made her want to laugh. Did half-jumping out of your skin at every little creak of the building constitute a problem? How about trying to sleep on the living room sofa because you couldn't stand the thought of going into your bedroom? Did you categorize that as a problem?

''No,'' she said easily, ''none at all.''

She sounded almost bored, as if she'd all but forgotten the break-in. Conor almost laughed. It was a good thing she couldn't know that he'd spent the night wondering if he'd been stupid to have left her alone and the other half telling himself he'd have been even stupider to have stayed.

''Is that all, O'Neil?''

''No,'' he said curtly, ''it's not. There'll be a locksmith at your door in half an hour.''

''A locksmith?''

''That's what I said.''

''Thank you, but if I need a locksmith, I'll make my own arrangements.''

''You need one. And I'm making the arrangements.''

''I didn't authorize you to—''

''No. You didn't. On the other hand, if you know some guy who can be trusted to install a pick-proof lock on the door of the apartment of the famous Miranda Beckman without being tempted to blab about it over a glass of *vin ordinaire* down at the local *café* a couple of hours later, be my guest.'' He paused. ''Unless, of course, you want that kind of publicity.''

She didn't, and he knew it. Miranda sighed and gave in to the inevitable.

''All right. Tell your locksmith to come over.''

''I already did. His name is Pete Cochran. He's tall and

skinny and he's got hair so red it can stop traffic. He'll have an ID card with an embassy stamp on it. Ask him to show you the card before you let him in."

"The American Embassy?"

"Yes."

Miranda's brows lifted. "You have friends in high places, O'Neil."

"Yeah, my connections are impressive," Conor said smoothly. "It's one of the reasons your mother hired me. I'm probably the only guy you'll ever meet in Paris who's owed a favor by somebody used to make his living breaking into the homes of the rich and infamous."

"I'm sure you only move in the finest social circles," Miranda said sweetly.

"Half an hour, Beckman. And try and be dressed by the time Cochran gets there, will you? He's got a wife and four kids and, for all I know, a weak heart."

"Don't tempt me, O'Neil. I've always wanted to add a married, red-headed thief to my list of conquests and here you are, serving him up for breakfast." Her voice hardened. "Have a nice day," she said, and slammed down the phone.

Conor glared at his telephone, mouthed a couple of very creative obscenities, and then headed for the bathroom to shave.

Half an hour later, Miranda's intercom rang.

It was Madame Delain calling to say that there was a gentleman called Monsieur Cochran—she pronounced it Cookrain—in the lobby.

"He says," madame said with obvious displeasure, "that he is expected."

"Yes, that's right. Send him up, please."

Madame sniffed and broke the connection. Miranda knew she'd expected an explanation of why Monsieur Cookrain was expected but she offered none. The *concièrge* was discreet but her husband was not and, as Conor had said, she didn't want the story of the break-in getting around.

When the bell rang, she started to reach for the doorknob. Then she remembered Conor's warning. It seemed stupid to ask for the locksmith's ID when madame had just rung to say he was on his way, but she decided to go along with it.

"Yes," she said, "who is it?"

"Pete Cochran."

He held his card to the peep-hole. Miranda looked at it, then looked at Cochran's pleasant, mid-Western American face.

"Okay," she said, and let him in.

Except for the bright red hair, Cochran was a nondescript-looking man carrying an equally nondescript canvas satchel that looked as if it had seen better days. He shut the door, put down the satchel, and gave her an appraising look followed by an easy smile.

"Nice."

Miranda didn't return the smile. "You're here to change the door lock, Mr. Cochran," she said coolly.

Cochran grinned. "That's what I meant," he said, running his hand over the door. "It's nice wood. Mahogany."

After that, he was all business, working methodically and neatly but that didn't surprise her. For all his swagger, it was the way Conor worked, too. The people he relied on would do the same.

Miranda leaned back against a small, marble-topped table—a find she'd picked up during one of her forays to the flea market—and folded her arms.

"So," she said, "you and O'Neil are old friends, hmm?"

Cochran picked up a small drill and plugged its cord into the nearest outlet.

"Old acquaintances, you might say."

"Have you known each other long?"

"Long enough, you might say."

The drill whirred as he turned it on and attacked the screws that held the old lock in place.

"Where did you meet?" Miranda asked, raising her voice over the sound of the drill. "In New York?"

Cochran looked up at her and smiled. "You might say."

Miranda narrowed her eyes, bit back the sudden desire to ask him if he had any idea if the sun rose in the east, and left him to his work.

The phone rang again, just after she'd shut the door on Pete Cochran and slid home the bolt on the new lock.

"Yes," she said crisply, putting the phone to her ear, "your locksmith is all done. He's quite the conversationalist, your Mr. Cochran, but I suppose you already know that."

"Miranda?" Jean-Phillipe said cautiously.

Miranda sighed and sank down on the sofa.

"Jean-Phillipe. You can't imagine how glad I am to hear your voice!"

"I take it you were expecting someone else."

"Unfortunately," she said with a little laugh, "I was."

"I have never heard you mention someone named Cochran, *chérie.*"

"No. I mean, that's not who I thought you were."

"Miranda? You sound—how do you say?—upturned."

"Upset. And you're right, I am. Or I was, until I heard your voice." She looked at her watch. "Could I interest you in breakfast?"

"I am afraid I have already had my croissant and coffee this morning."

"I meant an American breakfast," she said, dropping her voice to a deliberately seductive whisper. "Orange juice, hot-cakes with syrup and sausage, hash browns, eggs . . ."

Jean-Phillipe made a sound of soft distress. "McDonald's?"

"McDonald's," she agreed, "in half an hour. What do you say?"

He chuckled. "Make it fifteen minutes, *chérie.* If I must wait any longer than that, I will expire of anticipation."

At a few minutes past ten in the morning, the big McDonald's on the Champs Elysées was almost empty. The breakfast crowd was gone; the lunch crowd had yet to arrive. Jean-Phillipe, dressed for what he'd claimed would be anonymity, was waiting just inside the door.

"Oh yeah," Miranda said, giving him the once-over, "you're anonymous, all right."

"I did my best," he said staunchly, but there was the hint of a smile on his lips.

And well there should have been, Miranda thought wryly. She was bundled from head to toe in a grey wool coat, her hair invisible beneath the brim of a squashed-down cloche. Her sunglasses were dark and covered half her face. He, on the other hand, was resplendent in a full-length black leather coat, silver Tony Lima lizard-skin boots and the latest rage in oval designer shades. With his trademark blond hair blown dry in artful, shoulder-length disorder, Jean-Phillipe was about as anonymous as a macaw in a flock of starlings.

He bent down, kissed her on both cheeks and took her hands in his.

"Such cold hands, Miranda."

"Well, it's chilly out."

"And what I can see of your face is very pale." His brow furrowed. "What is it, *chérie?* Have you something to tell me?"

Miranda hesitated. Had she chosen the right place to tell him about the break-in at her apartment? They could have had breakfast at the Grand or the George V, where they'd have been safely secluded at a quiet table. Instead, she'd deliberately chosen McDonald's, not just because Jean-Phillipe had a very un-Gallic weakness for its bill of fare but for its bright, uncomplicated atmosphere.

Maybe here, with Ronald McDonald grinning down from the wall, she could think about, talk about, what had happened last night without shuddering.

"Miranda?"

Jean-Phillipe's dark blond eyebrows were drawn together above his long French nose. Miranda squeezed his hands in hers.

"Yes," she said, "I do have something to tell you. But let's get our breakfast first, okay?" She smiled. "I need a caffeine fix, and the thought of an Egg McMuffin is driving me crazy."

"Ah," he said, and smiled back at her, "*chérie,* you are still *une américaine* at heart."

A bunch of young cashiers had already collected at the counter to giggle and gawk at Jean-Phillipe. He let Miranda draw him there, even though the idea of breakfast *à la McDonald's* was no longer quite so appealing. Miranda was upset—he had sensed it yesterday, when she had greeted him so effusively at the Diderot showing and again last evening, at the party—and it worried him.

There was no point in demanding explanations. She would explain in her own good time and meanwhile, he would see to it that she ate something, despite her attempt at trying to get away with having only coffee.

"Nonsense," he said briskly, and ordered enough food to feed a small army. Then he autographed a couple of place mats, a Big Mac wrapper and, as the *pièce de résistance,* the breast pocket of one of the blushing cashiers.

"Now," he said, lifting their heavily laden tray, "mademoiselle and I shall have our feast."

The hazel-eyed blonde who now bore Jean-Phillipe's signature across her left breast looked at Miranda.

"Are you someone special, mademoiselle?"

Miranda shook her head. "Sorry, no."

"Ah," Jean-Phillipe said, "that is not so. She is—"

Miranda's boot-clad foot landed on his instep.

"I'm just one of M. Moreau's worshipful fans," she said solemnly.

"Just another fan, indeed," Jean-Phillipe muttered as they set off for a corner table. "Why do you hide your fame under a basket?"

"It's a bushel. And you flaunt yours enough for the both of us."

"I?" he said with a wounded smile.

Miranda sat down, slipped her coat back from her shoulders and tugged her dark glasses down on her nose.

"You love the glitter of the bright lights," she teased. "Admit it."

"Certainly, I do." A grin lit Jean-Phillipe's handsome face. "But I hide it well, yes? I am becoming a better and better actor, Miranda. Even my drama coach tells me this."

"The little girl with the hazel eyes is still looking at you," Miranda whispered, leaning towards him. "I'll bet she never washes that blouse, now that you've signed it."

"Such is the price of fame," he sighed dramatically. "Now, drink your juice. And eat your Egg McMuffin. You are too thin, *chérie.* Unlike that fool, Diderot, I prefer you with some meat on your bones."

She tried, but each mouthful seemed to stick in her throat. After a while, she shoved her breakfast aside and concentrated on her coffee.

"You are not eating?"

"I ate," she said defensively. "I finished almost half my McMuffin."

Jean-Phillipe looked at her. Then he collected everything except their coffee cups and dumped it into the nearest trash bin.

"Now," he said, sitting down not across from her but beside her, "tell me what is wrong."

"Am I that transparent?"

"To me, yes. Tell me what troubles you."

She hesitated, looked up at a grinning Ronald McDonald again, and took a deep breath.

"Someone broke into my apartment yesterday."

Jean-Phillipe's face went chalk-white beneath its year-round tan.

"My God," he whispered, reaching for her hand.

"I don't know exactly when it happened, but I suspect it must have been in the evening, after Madame Delain locked the front door." Miranda tried for a smile. "You know how she is. She'd never have let anyone slip past her."

Jean-Phillipe's hand tightened on hers.

"A burglar, in your apartment?" He shuddered. "Thank God you were not home when it happened."

"I know. I keep thinking that, too."

"What was taken, *chérie?* Not that it is of any importance. Possessions are always replaceable."

"That's just it," Miranda said quietly. "Nothing was taken."

"Nothing?"

She shook her head.

"The thief was surprised in the act, then?"

"I don't think so. Whoever broke in just poked around in my bedroom, went through my things . . ."

"He touched your possessions?"

She nodded. "My clothing. And—and apparently, he laid on my bed."

Her voice quavered and she fell silent. Jean-Phillipe let out a string of French oaths she barely comprehended. His hand tightened around hers, hard enough so it hurt, but she didn't mind. The pain was an anchor to reality.

"Did you call the police?"

"No."

"And you did not call me. Why not? I would have come to you at once, you know that. *Mon Dieu,* you should not have been alone!"

"I wasn't. Do you remember that man at the showing yesterday morning?"

"What man?"

"The one I was talking to when you came backstage to wish me luck."

Jean-Phillipe frowned. "The one who looked as if he would have liked to carry you off?"

"Don't be silly."

"That is how he looked, Miranda, as if he wished he could kill me and have you all to himself. *Oui.* I remember." His face darkened. "You are not saying it was he who did this thing?"

"No. No, it wasn't him. But he came to the door, right after

I found—right after I got in last night.'' She reached out, touched the tip of her finger to a scattering of bread crumbs on the table top. ''In fact, when the bell rang, I thought it was you.''

''Instead, it was this stranger?''

''Yes. His name's Conor O'Neil. He's American.''

''And what does he want with you?''

''Well, he's a detective. He's working for my—for Eva.''

''But why does she need the services of a detective? And why has he come to see you? *Chérie,* I am confused. Perhaps you had best start at the beginning and explain, yes?''

''Yes.'' Miranda's eyes met his. ''Could we go someplace else? I thought it would be easy to talk here, but—''

Jean-Phillipe was already on his feet, draping her coat over her shoulders, pulling back her chair.

''We will go to my apartment,'' he said, and Miranda nodded, let him slip his arm protectively around her waist, and lead her away.

Jean-Phillipe lived in a handsome duplex with a wonderful view of the Luxembourg Gardens. By the time they reached it, Miranda had told him the entire story, not once but twice, and still he wasn't satisfied.

''You should have called the police,'' he said, as he flung their coats onto a curved leather sofa.

''No, I shouldn't,'' she answered wearily. She sank down on the sofa and leaned her head back against the cushions. ''Would you want that kind of publicity? Well, neither do I. And what's the point? Nothing had been stolen. Besides, what could they have done?''

''There might have been clues.''

She sighed, kicked off her boots and put her feet up on the low table that stood in front of the sofa.

''This isn't a movie script, Jean-Phillipe. Nobody left a telltale match book behind. Besides, if they had, O'Neil would have found it.''

"O'Neil," Jean-Phillipe said, and scowled. "The man claimed to be a detective and so you believed him, just like that."

"He showed me identification."

"I carried identification certifying that I was a *gendarme* during my last film. Did that make me one? *Mon Dieu,* did it not occur to you to telephone your mother and inquire about this man?"

"There's no reason to phone Eva." Miranda smiled tightly. "It's not her birthday, or mine."

"That is a poor attempt at humor, *chérie,* considering the situation."

"All right, maybe I should have called her. Maybe O'Neil's not what he claims he is. But he's not the person who ransacked my bedroom, I'm certain of it."

"There can be no mistake about what happened? You could not, perhaps, have left things in disorder?"

Miranda shook her head. "This wasn't disorder. It was mayhem. Whoever did this wanted to be sure I knew it."

Jean-Phillipe came up behind her and lay his hands lightly on her shoulders. Gently, he began kneading the taut muscles.

"I am so sorry, *chérie.* If only I had gone upstairs with you . . ."

"Don't be silly. It wouldn't have changed anything." She let out a deep sigh. "Mmm," she said, letting her head droop forward, "that feels wonderful."

"I cannot imagine who would have done such a thing, or why."

"I know. I thought, at first, it might be some kook."

"*Oui.* A pervert. But this man, O'Neil, thinks otherwise, that whoever broke into your apartment also sent this mysterious note to your mother?"

"He thinks it's possible."

"A note meant to threaten her."

"That's what he says. And he says the note Eva received mentioned me and my . . ." Her mouth twisted. ". . . my elopement."

Jean-Phillipe kissed the top of her head, came around the sofa and sat down next to her.

"It is not logical, *chérie.* Why would someone make such a reference, after all these years?"

"Did I tell you Hoyt—my stepfather—is going to become an ambassador?"

"So?"

Miranda sighed. "So, ambassadors are like Caesar's wife. You know, above reproach."

"Ah, I begin to see. Your Mr. O'Neil thinks someone intends to use this to blackmail your mother and stepfather?"

"I guess."

Jean-Phillipe put his feet up on the table, too, and crossed them at the ankles.

"It is possible, I suppose. Has he spoken with the animal you married?"

"I don't know. When you come right down to it, I don't know anything except that Eva got a note, my apartment got taken apart, and, as always, it's somehow going to end up being all my fault."

"I am going to speak with your Mr. O'Neil, and ask him some questions."

"Jean-Phillipe, please, he is not *my* Mr. O'Neil. And I don't want you to talk to him. I don't want you to get involved in this at all. It's liable to get messy."

"I am not afraid, Miranda."

"I know that," she said gently. She smiled and took his hand in hers. "Don't worry about me. Honestly, I'll be fine."

"You will telephone Eva, and question her? Make certain the man, O'Neil, is who he claims?"

"Yes. I promise."

"It is also time to move from that apartment of yours. I have tried and tried to tell you, the Marais has charm but it can also be dangerous."

It was an old argument, one they'd had many times. When they'd met—when he'd rescued her from a dark Paris street—Jean-Phillipe had lived in a tiny attic apartment in the Marais and she had lived there with him, until she'd begun earning enough money modeling to take a small place of her own.

They had both moved since then, she to a comfortable apartment off the Rue de Rivoli, Jean-Phillipe to this elegant location near the Arc de Triomphe. He kept trying to convince her to move nearby, but Miranda was happy where she was—or she had been, until last night.

And she would be, again. No one was going to force her out of her home.

"I told you, there's a new lock on my door. The Marais isn't dangerous, it's just different."

"Locks do not impress me. As for the Marais, it is unsafe. What happened to you proves it."

"Please, let's not quarrel." Miranda got to her feet and dug her bare toes into the velvety Aubusson carpet that covered the living room floor. "Is this the rug we bought at the flea market last week?"

"You are trying to change the subject!"

"You're darned right I am. I don't want to think about last night anymore, or about Eva or Conor O'Neil." Her smile was quick and beseeching. "Let's talk about something else."

Jean-Phillipe sighed. How could he deny anything to this woman he loved most in the entire world? He got up, ruffled her hair and went to the fireplace where kindling lay neatly on the hearth.

"You know," he said, as he put a match to it, "that is the first thing I remember noticing about you, *chérie,* that despite your perfect schoolgirl French and your even more perfect schoolgirl clothes, you could not wait to walk around barefoot. 'The child is an American barbarian,' I said to myself, 'and her face is dirty but still, she shows promise.' "

Miranda smiled. She bent down, planted a quick kiss on the top of his head, then made her way to the wooden wine-rack built into the half-wall that separated the living room from the kitchen. "Red or white?"

"Red for me, always, but if you prefer . . ."

"Red's fine."

She chose a bottle, deftly uncorked it and poured two glasses. Jean-Phillipe made a face as she handed him a glass and sat down beside him on the carpet.

"This is a vintage bordeaux, Miranda. You are supposed to let it breathe."

"Really?" she said, flashing an impish grin. "Well, what do American barbarians know about letting wine breathe?" She took a slow sip. "Mmm, that's nice."

"Yes." He leaned back and smiled. "The studio sent over a case."

"Ah, the price of fame. Little girls oohing and ahhing, terrific *vin rouge,* an apartment fit for a king . . ."

"A prince, *chérie.* Until I succeed in my first Hollywood movie, I will not be a king."

"It's really that important to you?"

"You think I am silly, yes?"

"No. I'd never think anything about you was silly. I just don't see why it should matter so much."

"Who knows? Perhaps it is simply my actor's ego. Or perhaps I wish to prove that even one such as I can do whatever he sets his mind to."

Miranda put her hand lightly over his. "You mustn't say things like that."

"You are good for me, *chérie.* You always have been."

"As you have been, for me."

Jean-Phillipe smiled. "I think your fondness for me dates back to that long-ago evening when you realized your sacrifice would be unnecessary."

"You know it goes further back than that." Miranda laughed. "Was I that obvious?"

"About offering to martyr yourself by sleeping with me? Oh yes, you were as transparent as glass. Even after eight years, I can clearly recall the look of relief on your face when I turned you down."

She smiled, reached for the bottle of wine and refilled both their glasses.

"I didn't know how else to repay you. If you hadn't rescued me that night . . ."

"Who could have done less? There you stood, a poor waif stranded on the street-corner of life with the rain beating down on your head, soaked to the skin and looking as if you had lost your last friend."

"I'll never forget how I felt when you came up to me and said, 'Here, child, take this money and buy yourself a meal.' " She looked at him. "What made you do that? So many people had just walked by."

"Who knows? Perhaps it was that sad look in your eyes, or the way your shoulders were hunched against the chill." He chuckled. "On the other hand, it may have been that you reminded me of a half-drowned kitten I rescued when I was a boy. I have always been, how do you say, a sucker for orphaned animals."

"That was me, all right." Miranda's voice hardened. "Orphaned."

"You chose not to return home with your mother, *n'est-ce pas?*"

"Sure. The same way you chose to live your life the way you do." Sighing, she reached for his hand. "Never mind all that. I'm just trying to tell you what it meant to me, that you bought me supper, took me home and let me sleep on the sofa."

"*Alors,*" he said, and shuddered, "with the mice that used to steal the stuffing from the cushions to keep you company. That apartment was not like this one, eh?"

Miranda laughed. "No. It was not like this one at all."

"Still, you improved it while you lived with me. I remember coming home to rooms that were clean, to freshly ironed shirts and hot meals."

"I remember shorting out your vacuum cleaner and scorching your shirts. And to this day, I think it's a miracle my cooking didn't kill you!"

He chuckled. "What is it you Americans say, *chérie?* It was the thought that counted."

"I knew it wasn't enough. You'd done so much." She hesitated. "That was why I offered to sleep with you. It was all I had to give."

"*Oui.*" He put down his glass, rolled onto his back and folded his hands under his head. "Truly, it was a generous offer. I was touched."

"But you're right. I was relieved when you turned me down. Very relieved." Miranda put down her wine and stretched out beside him on her belly, her chin propped on her hands. "But it wasn't because of anything about you, Jean-Phillipe. You know that, don't you?"

"Miranda, little one, this was all a long time ago."

"I know, but we've never really talked about it. And I want to be sure you understand. You mean everything to me. I just didn't want to do—to do that with anyone."

"And nothing much has changed in eight years, hmm?"

Miranda sat up again. She picked up her glass and looked down into it. The firelight, reflected in the deep ruby color of the wine, gleamed hot and golden.

"No," she said softly, "it hasn't."

"I have never asked you about it. I always thought, if you wished to discuss it, you would do so. But I knew, in my heart."

"That's okay. I don't mind you asking."

"I shall ask, then. You still feel nothing when you are with a man?"

"I am never with a man." She smiled, but her eyes were dark. "Not the way you mean."

Jean-Phillipe reached up and stroked a strand of hair back from her cheek.

"It is a dangerous game you play, *chérie,*" he said, very softly.

"What game?"

"The one you play with men."

"I do not play games with men."

"You tease, Miranda. You torment. You snap your lashes and say, 'are you man enough to take me' and then, when a man accepts the challenge . . ."

"It's *bat,*" she said sharply.

"Chérie?"

"A woman *bats* her lashes, she doesn't *snap* them. And I can't help it if men come to the wrong conclusions. It only proves that they're all pigs. They deserve learning that not every woman is fool enough to believe their lies."

Jean-Phillipe sat up and looked directly at her. "There is a word in French," he said softly. "It is not a nice word, but it is a word men use to describe a woman who teases. They say she is *une allumeuse.* I do not know how to translate this word into English."

Color burned in Miranda's cheeks. "You don't have to. I'm sure I can figure out the English equivalent." Her chin rose in defiance. "I'm who I am, that's all. If men choose to misinterpret, that's their problem, not mine."

"This man, O'Neil . . ."

"What about him?"

"Does he choose to misinterpret, too?"

Miranda rose to her feet. "I have no idea what you're getting at."

"That performance yesterday, at the Louvre. That was for him, was it not?"

"What performance?"

"Miranda, *chérie* . . ."

"Don't give me that, 'Miranda, *chérie,*' business with the long-suffering sigh and the little smile. It wasn't a performance. I was just glad to see you."

"Of course." Jean-Phillipe narrowed his eyes. "That is why you clung to me like a squid."

"Like an octopus. Dammit, if you're going to speak English, get it right."

"Is not a squid an octopus?"

"No. Yes. I mean . . ." Miranda looked at Jean-Phillipe. His face was a study in innocence but his eyes were filled with laughter. "You're impossible," she said, but the tension had left her and she was smiling, too.

"As are you, Miranda." He stood up. "And now that your

good mood has returned, I shall risk ruining it by asking again that you move to a better neighborhood.''

''No.''

''I am concerned for you, *chérie.*''

''I'm concerned for me, too, but there's nothing to worry about. I told you, O'Neil sent over a guy who installed the kind of lock that would keep a bank safe.''

''And you can truly return to that apartment, after what happened?''

''I can,'' she said, not adding that first she'd throw out the bedding and then she'd scrub the place down with disinfectant. ''And I will.''

Jean-Phillipe put his arm around her and drew her close. ''You are still the most stubborn female a man ever had the misfortune to know.''

His tone was stern but she knew that he was smiling, and he was holding her as gently as if she were the sister he'd never had. Miranda hugged him, then leaned back in his arms.

''I have a wonderful idea.''

''Yes?''

''Let's go shopping. We'll buy a bunch of extravagant, fattening things, come back here and make a wonderful lunch.''

He kissed her forehead. ''Fauchon's?''

''Fauchon's, definitely.''

''We will buy oysters. And *foie gras.* And very ripe brie and champagne,'' he said, draping her coat around her shoulders and grabbing his own. ''Everything that is extravagant and fattening.''

Laughing, they made their way downstairs, to the street. A light snow had begun to fall, adding magic to the boulevard and to the brightly lit Arc de Triomphe just ahead.

''It sounds decadent,'' Miranda said.

''Everything pleasurable in life is decadent. Besides, we are celebrating.''

''We are?''

''Of course. We shall raise our glasses and wish a short and most unhappy future for the *trou de balle* who violated your privacy.''

''The what?'' Miranda said, laughing.

''Ah, even after so many years, your French needs work.'' Jean-Phillipe grinned. ''I called him an asshole. It is not a polite term, in your language or mine. And then, we shall drink to my current film, which wraps by the week's end.''

''That's wonderful!''

''What is wonderful is that everyone predicts it will be a great success.''

''Why is it I can almost hear the word *but* at the end of that sentence?''

''Because you know me well, *chérie*. Yes, there is a *but.* The studio has asked me to make another movie.''

''And that's a *but?* Jean-Phillipe, that's terrific!''

He sighed as they paused on the corner and waited for a break in the traffic.

''It would be better news if I had been asked to make a film in the States.''

''Why? You've got a wonderful career building here.''

''I know that.'' The flow of cars eased. Jean-Phillipe clasped Miranda's hand and they hurried across the road. ''But I want more. I want to be an international star. Or perhaps a director, with an Oscar on the mantel. Who knows? *Merde,* Miranda, don't look at me as if I were crazy.''

''I don't think you're crazy.'' She hesitated. ''I just think you should, you know, consider the ramifications.''

''What ramifications? I am a good actor. You know that.''

''Yes, but Hollywood is different. The press is relentless. They'll want to know everything about you.''

''So?'' His voice swelled with defiance. ''Let them. People should judge me on my talent. Is that too much to ask?''

''No, of course it isn't. Jean-Phillipe, what are you doing?''

It was a silly question because she could see what he was doing. He'd swung out in the path of a woman hurrying towards them, her head and shoulders bent against the wind-driven snow.

"How do you do, madame?" he said, dancing along backwards in front of her. "Do you know me?"

"Jean-Phillipe!"

Miranda tugged at his sleeve but he ignored her. "Do you?" he demanded.

The woman came to a dead stop. Her eyes widened.

"You're that actor," she said. "Oh my goodness! You are, aren't you?"

He grinned, doffed an imaginary hat and made a deep, courtly bow.

"Indeed I am. And I must ask you, madame, would it change your opinion of me if you learned that—"

"Don't," Miranda hissed.

His voice dropped to a conspiratorial whisper.

"My charming friend," he said, "fears that I am about to be indiscreet. She is afraid that if I tell you the truth—"

"Jean-Phillipe, please—"

"—the truth, madame, which is that I am longing to go to America and become a big star, you will no longer go to my films." He smiled. "You do go to see my films, do you not?"

"Yes," the woman said, staring from one of them to the other, "oh yes, all the time."

"Ah. And would you continue to do so, even if you knew that I . . ." He shrugged off Miranda's hand. ". . . that I was not the same old Jean-Phillipe Moreau you've come to know?"

"Of course," she said in bewilderment. "Why wouldn't I?"

"My sentiments, precisely." Jean-Philippe took the woman's hand, lifted it to his lips and kissed it. *"Merci,"* he said, "and be sure to see my latest movie when it opens."

Miranda grabbed his arm and tugged him along the sidewalk, away from the woman who stood staring after them.

"You are a crazy man," she said fiercely. "She'll go around telling everybody that you ought to be in an asylum."

"What did you think? That I was about to make an announcement on the Champs Elysées?"

"The thought occurred to me, yes."

His laugh was quick and sharp.

"Trust me, *chérie*. I know full well that one does not become a Hollywood star by standing on a street in Paris and asking a strange woman for her good wishes." His voice cracked. "I also know that you speak the truth. The more I reach out for my dream, the closer I come to losing it."

"Oh, Jean-Phillipe, I didn't mean . . ."

"It is foolish to deny it." He stopped walking, turned and faced her, and she could see the anguish in his eyes. "You have been wonderful, letting the world think you are my lover."

"Don't make me sound like a saint," she said, smoothing her hands over the lapels of his leather coat. "I've gotten something out of the deal, too."

"*Oui*. Having me hover in the background keeps other men from demanding too much of you."

"Stop fishing for compliments," she said, smiling. "You know I meant that being known as your girlfriend adds luster to my reputation." Her smile tilted. "Besides, I love you. You know that."

"And I love you, *chérie*." Jean-Phillipe clasped Miranda's face. Snowflakes dotted her hair and lashes; he thought that she had never looked more beautiful. "If I were not gay . . ."

"But you are," she said softly, "and someday the world will be ready to accept it."

He kissed her gently on the mouth. Then, hand in hand, they continued towards the Place de la Madeleine.

Chapter Eight

Conor's day had not begun well.

He'd awakened to a pounding headache, a desperate need for a cigarette and the sure knowledge that he'd made an ass of himself last night.

The headache was the kind that made even the thought of lifting his head from the pillow an accomplishment worthy of the Croix de Guerre but finally he'd managed to get up, gulp three aspirin with the steaming cup of *café au lait* the chambermaid delivered to his room, and hope for the best.

The urge for a smoke had been tougher to deal with. He'd told himself that it was a dirty habit, that he never even had a yen for a cigarette except when he was in France where everybody over the age of puberty seemed to be puffing away. He'd reminded himself that not even his daily four-mile run or workouts on the Nautilus in the gym back home could dull the effect of smoking on your lungs. And while he'd told himself all those things, he'd patted down his pockets on the off-chance he'd come up with a stray Gauloise.

After a while, he'd given up. He had as much chance of finding a cigarette as he had of convincing himself he hadn't behaved like a fool with Miranda, meaning the odds on either ranged from zero to none.

With only a cup of coffee to fortify him, he'd phoned Miranda to tell her to expect Cochran to change the lock on her door, and he'd ended up feeling like a damn fool all over again, caught between her obvious irritation at his interference and an erotic image so powerful it had infuriated him.

No, he thought as he opened the door and stepped out on his tiny balcony, none of that had been a good way to start the day.

The air was crisp but the sky was bright. Conor finished what remained of his coffee while he gazed out at the soaring towers of Notre Dame Cathedral and the grey ribbon of the Seine.

Why in God's name had he kissed her last night? She wasn't his type and he'd bet a month's worth of paychecks that he most definitely wasn't hers.

She was beautiful, sure. A man would have to be dead not to admit it. But she was all glitter and flash. Even if you only took a woman to bed, you liked to think there was more to her than just a face and a body.

Besides, he never got personally involved. Never. It was what had made him a good soldier and an effective agent. It had also been his ex-wife's chief complaint.

"Don't you ever feel anything?" Jillian had shrieked, towards the end of the disaster they'd called a marriage.

Conor swallowed another mouthful of coffee. Of course, he felt things. He enjoyed a crimson-and-gold sunset, a good bottle of wine, a concerto that could make your throat constrict and the feel of a woman in his arms.

That hadn't been enough for Jillian.

She'd wanted, she'd said, a man who would "communicate."

God, how he'd come to hate that word.

Share with me, Conor. Tell me what you're thinking, Conor. Let me inside you, Conor.

One day, when he'd had all he could take, he'd said okay,

if she really wanted to know what he was thinking, he'd tell her. What he was thinking, he'd said, was that he wanted her to stop trying to invade his space and his head.

Then he'd flown off on a brief assignment. When he got back, Jillian was gone. All she'd left waiting for him was a polite note, her attorney's phone number and a faint drift of perfume.

Conor had felt some loss but the truth was, he'd known the marriage had been over for a long time. The last months, they'd only been making each other miserable. It wasn't her fault or his; they just weren't right together.

But it had bothered him that, at the end, Jillian had accused him of being just like his father.

He knew better than that.

He was nothing like his old man. Christ, no. He'd lived his whole life making sure of that.

His father was a cop, with a cop's mentality. Things were good or they were bad; there was no in-between. He never smiled, never had a good word for anybody. He didn't read books or listen to music; he'd never been more than a couple of hundred miles from home and his idea of a good time was to sit around the house, drink beer and watch TV.

A cold breeze drifted up from the river. Conor shivered, stepped back into the room and closed the balcony door. He'd made damn certain his world was a hell of a lot bigger than his father's and if Jillian hadn't been able to see that, that was her problem. Anyway, he hadn't been cut out for marriage. There were too many things to do in this world besides tying yourself down to one woman.

As for Miranda Beckman—okay, his gonads had taken over last night, but it wouldn't happen again. A man was nothing, if he didn't have control of his emotions.

He had a job to do, and he'd do it. He needed to figure out what was going on here. Was Eva Winthrop being threatened? Was her daughter? And if so, were the two incidents connected?

First things first. He shot back his sleeve, glanced at his watch. Cochran would be just about finished installing the new lock on Miranda's door. He'd check it out, ask her a few more questions and tell her she was to keep close to home until she heard from him.

Conor smiled. He had the feeling he knew exactly how she was going to take that bit of news.

Whistling softly, he headed out of the hotel.

Cochran had said changing the lock would take thirty, forty minutes. "An hour, max."

Conor had told him to make sure it took an hour. He got to Miranda's with five minutes to spare but either his timing or Cochran's was off. Whichever it was, by the time he got to the apartment building off the Rue de Rivoli, the locksmith was gone—and so was Miranda.

The *concièrge,* who bore more than a passing resemblance to one of the gargoyles that looked down from the roof of Notre Dame, looked at him coldly and said she was sorry but she could tell him nothing of Mademoiselle Beckman's whereabouts. Mademoiselle, she said, looking at him down her classic Gallic nose, was out. No, she did not know where she had gone. No, she had no idea when she would return.

Pressed, she finally agreed that Monsieur might, if he truly wished, leave a note.

Conor truly wished. He scrawled his telephone number on a sheet of paper yanked from his address book, added a terse line which was not quite "Where the hell did you go?" but a close equivalent, tucked it into an envelope Madame ungraciously provided, sealed it and handed it over. Then he went around the corner, found a telephone and put in a call to Cochran.

"Yeah," the redhead said, "I did the babe's locks." He made a wheezing sound Conor figured was supposed to be a "just between us guys" chuckle. "Tell the truth, I'd sooner have done her. Man, that is some piece of ass! You gettin' it on with her or what?"

Conor felt his stomach knot. An image shot into his head, his fist connecting with Pete Cochran's grinning face and turning it into hamburger.

"How's that parole arrangement of yours going?" he asked pleasantly. "The Sûreté still sending reports back to D.C., assuring them you're living a righteous existence?"

"Hey," Cochran said in the tones of a man who's been grievously misjudged, "what'd I say? Since when is it a crime to notice that a babe looks hot?"

Conor shut his eyes and leaned his forehead against the glass wall of the telephone booth.

"It isn't."

"Damn right, it isn't."

"Yeah." Conor took a deep breath, then expelled it. "Sorry. It hasn't been a great morning."

Cochran chuckled. "I have days like that myself, man."

"Listen, I've got to get moving. Thanks for doing the job so quickly."

"No problemo. Maybe we can get together sometime, have a drink?"

"Sure," Conor said, lying through his teeth, and broke the connection.

Moments later, he was on the phone again, talking with a very irritable Eva Winthrop.

"Do you have any idea what time it is here, Mr. O'Neil?" she said, her voice made husky by sleep and annoyance.

"I'm sorry to wake you," Conor said politely, "but I thought you'd want to know that I've seen your daughter."

There was a silence. "And?" Eva said finally.

"I passed myself off as a private detective, working for you and your husband."

"Why?"

"It gives me more latitude. I told her you'd received a threatening note and that there was some reason to think the threat might extend to her."

"You mean, you led her to believe I hired you to check on her welfare?"

"Yes."

"That's a far-fetched proposition, Mr. O'Neil. I'm quite certain Miranda knows I'd do nothing of the sort."

Conor's jaw tightened. "She said as much. But something happened that changed her mind."

Eva sighed. "Are you going to tell me, or am I supposed to guess?"

"It's possible that someone broke into her apartment and went through her things."

"What do you mean, it's possible?"

"It's what your daughter claims, Mrs. Winthrop."

"Miranda has always lied as readily as others breathe. Why would you take her word for such a thing?"

"I saw the apartment. Somebody went through her stuff, all right."

There was a moment's silence. He waited for the questions, for Eva to ask if Miranda had been hurt.

"So? Frankly, Mr. O'Neil, I fail to see what that has to do with my situation."

Conor's hand clenched into a fist. He gave the wall of the booth one quick, hard shot. When he spoke, his voice was calm.

"It's conceivable that the two incidents are related. If someone were trying to threaten you, Mrs. Winthrop, they might feel they could make it even more effective by also threatening your daughter."

"It would be a useless ploy. Miranda lives her life. I live mine. We have nothing in common."

"Nothing but blood," he said, before he could stop himself.

Eva's voice took on a even greater chill.

"Making judgments is not part of your job, Mr. O'Neil. Perhaps I should ask my husband to put in a call to Mr. Thurston and tell him you're overstepping your bounds."

"That's a wonderful idea," Conor said, and slammed down the phone. He counted to ten, then to twenty before picking it up and dialing Harry Thurston's home number.

It was obvious that he woke him, too, but Thurston covered it better.

"What's the good word, Conor?"

Conor brought him up to date.

"Well, now that you've eyeballed the girl, what's your best guess? Could she have sent that note to her mother? Or could it be somebody else? That Frenchman she married, maybe? Or the Frenchman's cousin?"

Conor shifted the phone to his other ear and glanced at his watch.

"I haven't ruled anything out yet, Harry. The embassy dug up some phone numbers and addresses for me. I'm going to pay a couple of visits today, do some sniffing around but I've got to tell you, what I'm figuring is that the note was a one-shot."

Thurston yawned. "And the break-in at the Beckman girl's apartment?"

"Probably another one-shot. I doubt if there's any connection."

"Maybe it wasn't even a break-in. The girl could just be a slob."

Conor laughed. "I'll be in touch," he said, and hung up.

An hour later, he was tooling down a back road southwest of Paris.

It wasn't much of a road, not even by French standards. Barely one-car wide, cut off from the sun by the overgrown branches of the oak trees that grew along either side, it was closer to a dirt track than a road. Unless Conor missed his guess, nobody had bothered to re-grade the surface since the days of the Three Musketeers.

He shot another glance at the directions he'd scrawled during his phone call to Amalie de Lasserre. When you were dealing with a series of lefts and rights marked by signposts like the crumbling walls of an ancient chateau or what remained of an old vineyard, it was hard to tell if you were on track or not.

It wouldn't have surprised him if Miranda's once-upon-a-time roommate had given him instructions that would lead him straight to the middle of a cow pasture. She had sounded politely guarded at first, when he'd identified himself as a journalist, but when he'd mentioned Miranda, her tone had become downright frigid.

"I know nothing about Miranda Beckman," she'd said. Conor had spoken quickly, sensing she was about to hang up. He'd explained that he was a writer doing an article about American models working in Paris and that it was off-the-record background information he was looking for.

"I have not seen Miranda in many years," Amalie had said, but less abruptly, and Conor had assured her that the Miranda he was interested in was the one Amalie had known as a teenager.

"Why?" she'd said, and he'd gone for broke, following his instincts, telling her he wasn't just writing an article, he was writing an exposé about the seamier side of high fashion. Of course, he'd added, he'd pay her for her time. Amalie had asked how much, he'd tossed out a number he figured might raise a couple of eyebrows when the bean counters checked his expense sheet, and now he was bouncing along a road in the middle of nowhere, looking for a grey stone farmhouse with a slate roof and the ruins of a church just behind it.

And there it was. Conor stood on the brakes. And there *she* was, Amalie de Lasserre, standing in the doorway and looking just as he'd pictured her: stout, unwelcoming and unattractive.

There didn't seem to be a driveway so he pulled the car onto the muddy stretch of ground that he assumed had once been a lawn and got out.

"Mr. O'Neil?"

Her English was perfect, better than his French. He smiled and extended his hand.

"Mademoiselle de Lasserre. Thank you for agreeing to see me."

She hesitated, then gave him her hand. It was large and callused. She had, he saw, a faint mustache.

"You said you would have something for me, Mr. O'Neil?"

Conor took a handful of bills from his wallet and dumped them into Amalie's meaty palm.

No dancing around the issues, he thought. Well, that was something to be grateful for.

"We agreed upon twice this amount," she said brusquely, after she'd counted it.

"We did. I'll give you the rest after we've talked."

She looked at him for a long moment. Then she turned and marched into the house with Conor following after her.

"Shut the door, please. I don't want all the heat escaping."

What heat? he wondered. There was a fire glowing on the hearth at one end of the room but the air was cold enough so he could see his breath plume. An old-fashioned, very plain oak table stood to the left of the fireplace. Amalie settled herself into one of the chairs. There was a cup filled with some sort of steaming liquid on the table in front of her. She lifted it to her lips and took a noisy sip.

"Now," she said, plunking down the cup and fixing him with a sharp look, "what do you want to know?"

So much for hospitality. Conor walked to the hearth and held his hands out to the fire.

"I want you to tell me about Miranda Beckman, mademoiselle."

"You can leave off the French terminology, Mr. O'Neil. I speak your language quite well and I am not impressed by your ability to speak mine."

"Of course," he said politely.

"What is it you wish to know about Miranda?"

"Whatever you think will help me get a picture of her as she was in the days you and she roomed together."

Amalie de Lasserre folded her arms over her ample bosom.

"I didn't know her well. We were not friends."

"But you were her roommate."

"So everyone at Miss Cooper's said."

Conor arched his brows. "I'm afraid I don't follow that."

"It's quite simple. I had been at school for three years before

Miranda arrived. She moved into my room, not I into hers, yet no one ever referred to her as *my* roommate.''

He smiled. ''I see your point, Miss de Lasserre.''

''No, you do not. You couldn't possibly see my point. You have never been an overweight seventeen-year old with pimples and stringy hair, called to the headmistress's office one morning to be told that you are about to share your room with a girl who couldn't pass a mirror without looking into it and admiring her reflection.''

Conor kicked a chair out from beneath the table, turned it around and straddled it.

''You didn't hit it off?''

Amalie laughed. ''The understatement of the year, sir. We hated each other on sight. Oh, she put on quite a performance, sweet little Miranda, smiling and simpering when we first met, but I saw what she was.''

''And what was she, Miss de Lasserre?''

Amalie's nostrils flared, as if she'd caught the scent of something unpleasant.

''A rich brat, vain and spoiled, just like her mother.''

''You met Eva Winthrop?''

''Only once, the day she brought Miranda to Miss Cooper's, but it was enough. The woman acted as if she expected me to kneel and kiss her ring.''

Conor smiled. ''So, you didn't like either Eva or Miranda.''

''No intelligent person would.''

''But Miranda tried to be friendly, at the beginning?''

''She put on an act, yes, but I paid no attention. Did she think she could fool me so easily? No one wanted to be my friend,'' Amalie said bluntly. ''I wasn't pretty, I wasn't popular. I knew what she wanted from me.''

''And that was?''

''I was an excellent student. She wanted me to do her homework for her, write her research papers.''

Conor thought back to Miranda's records and all those A's and B's.

''And did you?'' he asked.

"Certainly not. She got nothing from me, I can tell you that!"

"Except an introduction to your cousin," Conor said gently.

Amalie's head snapped up. "What do you mean?"

"Just what I said, Miss de Lasserre. You introduced her to your cousin, Edouard."

"I did." The moon-like face filled with color. "Even though Edouard had come to see me at the request of my dear *maman.*"

"A courtesy call," Conor said, "from cousin to cousin?"

"Edouard is my cousin, but twice removed. And I did not think that he was a fool like all the rest, to be taken in by a pretty face." Her jowls quivered. "He'd stopped in the States, on his way home from checking on some property he owned in the islands, and so he paid me a visit. We got along famously. He was quite taken with my intellect."

"Ah," Conor said softly.

"Ah, indeed. Then he met Miranda and she—she victimized him!"

"She married him, you mean."

Amalie's eyes narrowed. "How do you know of this, Mr. O'Neil?"

"Why? Is it a secret?"

"It is not common knowledge."

Conor shrugged. "I told you, I'm doing research for an article. The information was there. All I did was stumble across it."

"Then I hope you also stumbled across the fact that Miranda seduced poor Edouard."

"You saw her?"

"She flaunted herself before him. And she insinuated herself into every encounter. Edouard was a perfect gentleman. He would come to take me to tea or for a drive and he would ask her if she wished to join us, out of politeness, mind. But Miranda never refused so off we'd go, she sitting in the car between us, laughing and fluttering her lashes." Amalie's mouth tightened into a cramped knot. "How long could he resist such enticement?"

"I don't know," Conor said pleasantly. "How long was it, do you recall?"

"Two months! Eight short weeks and she—she lured him into running off with her. Of course, the marriage did not last long. Miranda decided she'd wearied of the game and left poor Edouard, just like that."

"Didn't he try and stop her?"

"Stop her?"

"Yes. Did he try to talk her out of leaving?"

"Certainly he did, but she would not listen. I don't know all the details, Mr. O'Neil. Edouard and I never speak of it. It is still a very painful memory for him, you understand."

"Did Edouard know Miranda was underage when he eloped with her, Miss de Lasserre?"

"Of course not."

"Did he know her mother and stepfather were wealthy?"

Amalie shot to her feet. "What sort of question is that? What would her family's money matter to Edouard? He has plenty of money of his own." She picked up a poker and stabbed viciously at the burning logs until sparks flew into the air. "You cannot imagine the guilt I feel, sir. If only I had warned him! She was no good, that girl. Everyone knew it."

"What did they know?"

"That she was wild. A common tramp."

"How did everyone know? Did Miranda boast about her behavior?"

"She didn't have to. Just to look at her was enough. All that hair. Those eyes. Besides, there was talk. Girls at Miss Cooper's knew girls at other schools she'd attended. She'd been expelled from dozens of places before she came to us." Amalie turned towards him, her expression fierce. "If Miranda's in trouble now, it's no more than she deserves."

"Trouble?" Conor stood up, his eyes on hers. "Why would you think she was in trouble?"

"Well, she will be, won't she, after you've written your article?"

"Would you like that? For Miranda to be in some sort of trouble?"

Amalie de Lasserre stared at Conor, her breathing labored. Then she went to the door.

"I have work to do, Mr. O'Neil. And I have told you all I can."

"You've told me very little."

"I tried to make it clear that I didn't know much. If you expected more, that's your problem." She held out her hand. "Please pay me what you owe me and leave."

"Just one last question, Miss de Lasserre. Do you live out here all by yourself?"

"I do."

"And how do you support yourself?"

"That is two questions, Mr. O'Neil, but I will give you the answer. My family is rich. As rich as Miranda Beckman's, I assure you." She smiled coldly. "I live here because I prefer my own company to anyone else's, and because my family will not support the charity I began some years ago."

"Charity?"

"Yes. A fund for abused farm animals."

Conor dug the remaining francs from his pocket and dumped them into her palm.

"That's very decent of you," he said.

Amalie smiled again. "Animals are innocent creatures that deserve our help and generosity, Mr. O'Neil. Humans are the only evil in this world."

The door shut in Conor's face. Moments later, he was on his way back to Paris.

Edouard De Lasserre lived on a quiet, tree-lined street in a neighborhood that whispered of wealth, antiquity and proper bloodlines. Depending on your point of view, his home was either gloomy or magnificent. Conor couldn't help thinking it was the kind of place Dr. Frankenstein would have loved.

He'd phoned earlier, and he was expected. A servant bowed

him in, then led him through a series of dark rooms crowded with antiques and smelling of beeswax. They reached a long gallery hung with tapestries and battle flags. Brightly polished suits of armor were mounted in each corner.

He had examined the tapestries and the flags in minute detail by the time de Lasserre finally put in an appearance in the doorway at one end of the gallery.

"Monsieur O'Neil?"

Conor swung around. A handsome man, tanned, fit and in the prime of life, was coming down the three steps that led from the door. He was smiling pleasantly and holding out his hand politely, but Conor felt the hair rise on the back of his neck.

There was something about the Count Edouard de Lasserre he didn't like, and every cell in his body was telegraphing the message.

"Count." He forced himself to smile in return and accept the man's handshake. "It's good of you to see me on such short notice."

"My pleasure, sir. May I offer you something? A drink, perhaps? Some coffee?"

"Thank you, but I'm fine." Conor drew back his hand and fought down the almost overwhelming need to wipe it against his trouser leg. "I promise, I won't take too much of your time."

"That's quite all right, monsieur. My dear cousin, Amalie, telephoned me. She said you'd been to visit her this morning."

Conor smiled. "She warned you about me, hmm?"

De Lasserre laughed. "Well, she did say you were quite persistent, if that is what you mean." He crossed the room to a massive sideboard and opened a paneled door. "Are you certain you won't join me in a drink?"

"Quite certain. But you go right ahead."

"Oh, I will." De Lasserre smiled as he unstoppered a faceted decanter and poured a couple of inches of amber liquid into a delicate snifter. "I am not a believer in self-denial, monsieur. Life is too short for that, don't you agree?"

He lifted his glass in Conor's direction, took a sip of the liquid and smacked his lips.

"Excellent brandy, if I must say so myself. I own a small vineyard. We don't produce anything of the quality of Armagnac, but given time . . ." De Lasserre shook his head. "Listen to me, prattling on and on when here you are to ask me some important questions. Amalie says you are writing an article, yes?"

"On the fashion business. Right."

"About Miranda."

"Among other things."

De Lasserre motioned to a pair of massive, carved wooden chairs. "Shall we sit and be comfortable?"

The chairs didn't look comfortable. They looked like older, man-eating versions of the chair that had threatened to consume Conor's Burberry in the Winthrop foyer. Was there something about the rich that made them fond of carnivorous furniture?

"Handsome chairs," he said politely, as he eased into one.

Edouard de Lasserre smiled. "Indeed. They were commissioned by my ancestor, the fifth Count de Lasserre." His hand slid over the highly-polished arm in a sensual caress. "They have been in this house for centuries, as has almost everything else you see around you."

"Very impressive."

"Ah, it is not meant to be impressive, I assure you. I am simply pleased that history has put so much trust in me. It is an honor to bear the responsibility for all this."

"And an expense."

"Indeed. But a worthwhile one. Now, monsieur, what may I do for you?"

"Well, as I explained to Amalie, anything you can tell me about Miranda would be helpful."

"For this newspaper article you write, yes?"

Conor smiled. "I didn't say it was for a newspaper, Count de Lasserre."

"No? Then, for what magazine do you write, Monsieur O'Neil?"

"I work free-lance. I write for whomever pays me the most money."

"Then, you have not, as yet, a buyer for your article?"

"That's correct."

De Lasserre nodded. "Well," he said, almost gently, "I cannot help you, I am afraid."

"No?"

"I have no, how do you say, grist for the mill." He sighed deeply. "And even if I did, my time with Miranda was precious. I would not wish to say anything untoward about her."

"You loved her, then?"

"I adored her. What man would not?"

"But she left you the day after your wedding."

"You are well-informed, Monsieur O'Neil."

"I pride myself on doing my homework, Count de Lasserre."

"Then you must know that I married Miranda when she was quite young. Too young, I fear, to know her own mind."

"The marriage was your idea?"

De Lasserre rolled his eyes. "I see what has happened, monsieur. My dear cousin said unpleasant things about Miranda, yes? That she lured me into the elopement?"

Conor smiled. "Actually, the word she used was *seduced.*"

"Sweet Amalie. So innocent of the ways of the world. She could not comprehend the passion that so quickly arose between Miranda and me."

"Passion? Not love?"

"Monsieur, I assume that you are a man of some sophistication. Surely you understand the power of a swift, overwhelming sexual attraction." De Lasserre leaned forward, his smile razor-sharp. "I will tell you this much. Miranda and I could not keep our hands off each other. I could have had her within an hour of meeting her, *comprenez-vous?* But I was brought up in the old school, to believe in a woman's honor."

What Edouard de Lasserre was talking about had happened years ago. Besides, what did it matter? Conor wouldn't have cared if Miranda and this man had gone at each other like a couple of stray dogs in the middle of Times Square.

Then, why could he feel his gut knotting? Why should his blood pressure be shooting for the moon? It had to be de Lasserre's manner. The Count's suit was Armani, his shoes were crocodile, his lineage was probably longer and bluer than any entrant's in the Westminster Kennel Club and his smile was strictly high-wattage. And yet, for all of that, there was something about him. Something unpleasant, maybe even sinister.

Or was it only the knowledge that he'd slept with Miranda that made him so easy to dislike?

Conor stuck his hands deep in his pockets, his fists tightly balled. What did it matter? He didn't give a damn who she slept with, now, or in the past, or in the future.

"... you understand, monsieur?"

Conor cleared his throat. "I'm sorry, Count. Would you repeat that?"

"I said, I have never regretted asking Miranda to marry me. I only regret that I had to give her her freedom."

"Why did you, then?"

"I had no choice." De Lasserre rose, walked across the room and took a small marble figure from its place on the shelf of an elaborately carved *étagère.* It was the figure of a girl, nude and very beautiful. He smiled down at it, then ran his thumb slowly over the delicate curves. "Miranda was, as I have told you, very young."

"She was a minor."

De Lasserre looked up. "A detail of which I was not aware at the time," he said pleasantly, but his eyes had gone cold.

"Tell me what happened when Eva showed up."

"Who?"

"Eva Winthrop. Miranda's mother."

"Ah, of course." De Lasserre shrugged. "It was all so long ago." His finger trailed over the small breasts of the marble figure, caressing, rubbing. "Well, Ava was upset."

"Eva," Conor said. He tried to tear his eyes from the Count's hand but it was impossible. The long, slender fingers were moving again, between the legs of the little sculpture. ''Miranda's mother is named Eva.''

''Eva, Ava, what does it matter? All I truly recall is that she appeared on my doorstep, told me Miranda was underage and demanded I grant her her freedom.''

''Was Miranda glad to see her mother?''

De Lasserre smiled and gently placed the marble figure back on its shelf.

''I am afraid she was. The reality of marriage had begun to pall for my bride.''

''So quickly?''

''She was young, as I have told you. Our elopement was very romantic, yes? An older man, a meeting in the dark of night outside the rough walls of her rather Spartan school, a flight to Paris . . .'' He smiled modestly. ''It was all the stuff of girlish dreams, *n'est-ce pas?*''

''You didn't try and convince her to give the marriage a chance?''

''Have you ever loved a woman with all your heart and soul, Monsieur O'Neil?''

The question caught Conor off guard. For the second time that day, he thought about his ex-wife.

''No,'' he said, after a couple of seconds, ''I don't think I have.''

''Well, to love a woman that way is not to wish to give her up. It is also not to wish to keep her caged.'' De Lasserre held out his hands. ''It was what you Americans call a no-win situation, yes?''

''Surely it helped,'' Conor said politely, ''that Eva Winthrop was willing to pay you a lot of money for Miranda's freedom.''

He had waited for just the right moment to drop that bit of information into the conversation. Not that he'd known what to expect. Denial, maybe, or at the very least, surprise. Whatever he might have expected, it wasn't de Lasserre's quick, incredulous stare, which was followed by a roar of laughter.

''*Mon Dieu!* Is that what you believe? That Eva bought me off?''

"I don't know that I'd have put it quite that way but yeah, the thought's crossed my mind."

"Who was it who told you this lie? Eva?"

"One person's lie is another person's truth," Conor said, and smiled.

De Lasserre's eyes narrowed. "You are not researching an article, O'Neil, any more than I worship the memory of my abortive marriage to Miranda."

"Ah," Conor said softly, "now we're down to basics."

"Who do you work for? Your government? Hoyt Winthrop?"

"That's an interesting question. Why would the U.S. government or Hoyt Winthrop send somebody to question you about your marriage to Miranda Beckman?"

"It was a fiasco," De Lasserre snapped, "not a marriage. But everything is of importance when the girl's stepfather awaits a presidential appointment. Did you think we do not read the newspapers over here?"

Conor undid the button of his jacket and tucked his hands into his trouser pockets.

"Go on."

"Let me paint a picture for you, yes? Not a pretty picture but a graphic one. I ask you to visualize a man of some sophistication meeting a beautiful young woman. She flatters his ego, elevates his hunger by bringing him almost to the point of no return many times over, but she will go no further. She is, she insists, pure as the driven snow; she cannot possibly sleep with him." De Lasserre folded his arms and rocked back on his heels. "The young woman tantalizes. She titillates. She lets him touch but not take. The man is crazed with desire. She mentions marriage and he leaps at the idea. He is a more than acceptable suitor; he has a title, land, more money than the girl herself. He says he will ask for her hand but she blanches, weeps, assures him that her wicked mother and stepfather will lock her away forever if he so much as approaches them."

It was a good story and nothing Conor hadn't already thought of by himself. Miranda had seduced de Lasserre, not just with her body but with every emotional trick in the book. Then, why was it so difficult to listen to this cool recitation? Why did he want to wrap his hands around the man's neck and squeeze?

"The man, fool that he is, believes her story. He accedes to her wishes. They elope. He flies her to Paris in a private jet bedecked with white flowers, carries her over the threshold of his ancestral home with love and pride in his heart. His staff greets her with the respect that should be accorded a new Countess. 'All of this is now yours,' the man tells her. He carries her to his rooms, his innocent young bride, and starts to make tender love to her . . . and she laughs in his face and tells him she is not a doll, she is a woman, that his lovemaking bores her and that she has been with boys who have made her feel more than he can ever hope to imagine."

De Lasserre's fists clenched. He trembled with emotion.

"Eva Winthrop appeared at the door the next morning. She was arrogant and rude, she did not even ask to hear my side of the story but immediately informed me that Miranda was a minor and that I had committed a criminal act. Miranda chimed in and said that I was a beast who had tricked her into marriage and forced her into bed. The two of them, mother and daughter, turned on me, called me names I will not, to this day, repeat."

"Are you saying that the money you got from Eva was money you more than deserved?"

"For God's sake, man, use your head! My name, my title, my home and my lands go back to the very beginning of my country. Look around you. Do I look as if I needed Eva's money?"

"I only know what Eva told me," Conor said, his eyes on de Lasserre's face. "She said she bought Miranda's freedom from you."

"That is ridiculous! I gave her the girl and our marriage license, both quite willingly. Oh, she tossed a handful of franc notes on the floor, as if I were a beggar, but—"

"A handful of franc notes?"

"The equivalent of five hundred of your dollars, perhaps. I

didn't stop to count. I gathered it up and ran after her, but she and Miranda were gone."

"Five hundred dollars," Conor said softly. "Well, who could blame you for keeping such a pittance?"

"I did not keep it! I took a taxi to the Gare d'Austerlitz. As always, there were half a dozen young *putains,* just about Miranda's age, plying their trade on the streets. Like an angel of mercy, I dispensed Eva Winthrop's francs into their grubby hands until it was gone." He smiled coldly. "All things considered, it seemed a most appropriate charity."

A muscle knotted and unknotted in Conor's jaw. "You've been very forthcoming, Count."

"I see no reason to deny the truth."

"No. Neither do I. There's just one other thing I wanted to ask you . . ."

"Yes?"

"How do you feel about underwear?"

"What?"

"Underwear. You know, panties. Camisoles. Maybe garter belts." Conor's smile curled at the edges. "Silk stuff, mostly, with a few pieces of lace mixed in."

De Lasserre's face was like a mask. "I have no idea what you are talking about."

"I hope not."

"What are you saying, O'Neil?"

"Let me put it in words you'll understand." Conor's smile fled. "I'm telling you not to fuck with me."

Edouard de Lasserre stiffened. "Get out of my house!"

Conor nodded. "Don't bother seeing me out. I'll just keep going until the air smells clean again."

The Count was still sputtering as Conor slammed the front door behind him.

It was a long drive back to Paris.

The snow had made the traffic heavier than usual and there was a fender-bender just outside the city. Cars and trucks were caught in a snarl so dense it would have done D.C. or even New York proud.

That was fine. It gave Conor plenty of time to think.

Miranda Beckman was a complete enigma.

Had she sent Eva that note? She had reason to want to upset her mother, but so did Edouard de Lasserre. And it was a cinch to make a case for the sad, frumpy Amalie.

Traffic inched forward. A space opened in the next lane and Conor shot into it, ignoring the frantic horn blasts of the car he'd cut off.

Take the initiative, that was the key to survival in Parisian traffic.

In life.

And he was about to do just that.

He'd come to Paris to check out Miranda and he'd done it. Now, he wanted out.

Tonight, he'd order in a sandwich and a couple of bottles of ale—you could find ale at his hotel, it was one of the things that made the place civilized. And then he'd take out his notebook computer, type up his notes, plug in his modem and send everything winging across the Atlantic to Harry Thurston's office.

Let Thurston give the mess to somebody else. The FBI. The CIA. The French police. Hell, Dick Tracy. Whatever, whoever, he didn't care.

He was taking himself out of the loop.

Harry would phone, try to talk him into hanging in. He'd refuse, head for the airport, buy a ticket on the next flight out and go home.

Maybe he'd give Mary Alice a call.

Maybe he'd try somebody new.

A taxi slipped into a space the size of a shoebox in front of him. Conor stood on the brakes and cursed while what sounded like a thousand tinny horns blared in fury.

He loosened his collar and tie.

Yes sir, he was going home.

No more crazy French traffic. No more smarmy French counts. No more death wishes for nicotine and tar.

And no more Miranda, to screw up his head.

He'd see her one last time, tell her to watch herself, that somebody would be in touch soon. Then he'd wave good-bye, and never look back.

It was a great plan.

A hell of a plan.

It held up all the way to Miranda's apartment.

But when she opened the door, raised a tear-stained face to his and sobbed, ''Oh, O'Neil,'' as if his name was a prayer, when his arms closed around her and he felt her tremble as he drew her close . . .

When that happened, Conor knew he wasn't going anywhere until he'd solved a puzzle named Miranda.

Chapter Nine

Conor was here.

He was here, and his arms were around her, and she was safe.

Miranda burrowed against him like a frightened animal, letting his heat, his scent, the hardness of his body encompass her. The coppery taste of fear was still in her mouth but she knew she was safe. Safe, because Conor had come.

It was crazy and she knew it, but it was his name she'd invoked moments ago, when she'd come home and found the horror that awaited her.

"Conor," she'd cried, closing her eyes to the scraps of paper that had fallen to the floor, and then the doorbell had rung and, like the answer to a prayer, he was there.

It made no sense but then, after last night, nothing made sense. An icy chill ran through her blood as she imagined the unknown hands that had gone through her clothes, the unseen head that had left its imprint on her pillow. And now there was this, the hideous picture and the sickening note . . .

A whimper rose in her throat, and Conor's arms tightened around her.

"Miranda, what is it? What's happened?"

She wanted to tell him but she couldn't. Her teeth were chattering and if he let go of her, she knew she would collapse. Her legs felt as if somebody had stripped out the bones and muscle and left behind nothing but jelly. The only thing she was capable of was clinging to him while the breath shuddered in and out of her lungs.

"Talk to me, dammit!"

His voice was rough. He clasped her shoulders, tried to hold her out at arm's length and look at her, but she wouldn't let him. She shook her head, tightened her hold on the lapels of his jacket and dug in harder.

"Hold me," she whispered, "just hold me. Please."

He hesitated, and then his arms folded around her again. She gave a long sigh and slumped against him.

God, what was this all about?

Conor had seen fear before, even terror, but nothing that came close to this. Miranda was shaking from head to toe. Her heart was racing so fast against his it felt as if it might burst from her chest. Her skin was icy cold and her face, in the quick glimpse he'd gotten, was the sickly white that warned of shock.

His jaw clenched. If someone had touched her, if the sick-ass son of a bitch who'd gone through her underwear had so much as laid a finger on her, he'd—he'd—

He blanked his mind to the pictures racing through his head. He had to keep his cool and restore hers before he could figure out what to do next but hell, he'd never known how to deal with crying women. His ex-wife had been a weeper. Every time they'd tried to sort things out, every time the sorting-out had ended in a blank wall, Jillian had wept buckets while she accused him of being heartless but the truth was, her sobbing was beyond him to comprehend.

His mother had never cried. Kathleen Margaret O'Neil had dealt with every emotion, from joy to sorrow, by assuming a stiff-lipped countenance and hurrying off to St. Michael's to light candles to her favorite saints and yet here he stood, his arms filled with a bawling female who wanted his comfort, not her God's, and who was clinging to him as if he was a rock set in the middle of a storm-tossed sea.

Conor shut his eyes. Slowly, his hand lifted. He stroked it down Miranda's hair, then over her shoulder.

"It's okay," he said, "it's all right."

He went on stroking her, whispering to her, saying whatever came into his head, and after a while she wasn't shaking as hard and her heart slowed to something approximating normal. Still, she stayed where she was, in his arms, her face buried in his throat, and it was amazing, how good it felt to have her there.

She must have been out in the snow because her hair was damp and cool. And it smelled of something soft and feminine, violets maybe, or roses. He wasn't very good with flowers and he'd never paid attention to perfume except to know that you could always send a woman a bottle of Chanel if you wanted to say an easy good-bye but, whatever it was Miranda smelled of, was wonderful.

She felt wonderful, too, all warm and soft in his arms. Her breasts were pressed to his chest so that he could feel their rounded firmness. Her impossibly long legs and sweetly rounded hips were snug against his. Her waist, under his hands, was slender. Her back was long and straight and each time he stroked the length of it, he became aware of the almost imperceptible tilt of her pelvis.

Conor shut his eyes. *Damn you, O'Neil, don't get a hard-on now!* But he would. He would, if he held her much longer, if she went on nuzzling his throat, breathing her warm breath against his skin, clinging to him as if he were the only man in the world and she the only woman.

"Shh," he said, "it's all right, baby, it's all right."

Baby? Had he really called her baby?

It was such a silly word, an affectation, really; she'd never liked hearing men call women baby, not even in those old Humphrey Bogart-Lauren Bacall movies Jean-Phillipe was so fond of.

And yet, when Conor said it, it sounded altogether different. It sounded like a word of comfort, a reminder that she was a woman and he was a man and that he would protect her. Which was ridiculous. Stupid, really. She didn't want looking after, didn't need it.

Certainly not.

She shuddered, took a step back, and Conor's hands wrapped around her shoulders. He moved back, too, and looked down at her.

"Better?"

She nodded. "Yes."

"Tell me what happened."

His tone was calm and reassuring, but there was an intensity about him that was almost palpable. His eyes were dark, the pupils so enlarged that for one absurd moment, she wondered if she might fall into them and drown as she almost had last night, in the heat of his kiss.

"Miranda?"

She took a deep breath and returned to reality. "Someone sent me something."

He thought of the note that had been sent to Eva and knew right away that a woman, especially one as strong and determined as Miranda, wouldn't verge on collapse over a cryptic message culled from a half-forgotten philosopher.

"Where is it?"

She shuddered and wrapped her arms around herself. "Over there, on the floor where I dropped it."

He looked past her. A cream-colored envelope lay on the polished wood floor beside a folded sheet of paper and what looked like a page torn from a magazine. He went to where the stuff lay, stooped to pick it up, and felt a red flood of rage surge behind his eyes.

The magazine page was an advertisement. It was a full-length photo of Miranda in what he supposed was classic modeling pose. She stood with her head up, her hands on her hips, her legs slightly apart and a look of sultry sexuality on her face. She wore a skimpy T-shirt that hung to just below her breasts and a pair of skin-tight jeans that rode low on her hips.

Someone had drawn heavy black circles around her breasts, marked the center of each with a red X, and then torn a jagged slit between her navel and the juncture of her thighs that ended in a blob of something crimson.

He couldn't think. Hell, he couldn't breathe. The mutilated photo made him want to kill whoever had sent it, whoever had done this disgusting, terrifying thing to Miranda. He stood almost paralyzed by the emotions coursing through him, telling himself to calm down, that he wouldn't be able to do anything until he got himself under control.

When he felt his breathing begin to return to normal, he opened the folded sheet of notepaper. It was familiar: Eva's note had been written on what was almost certainly the same stuff, and the handwriting and the ink rang bells, too. But the message sure as hell wasn't the same.

It was three lines long, and in French.

As-tu passé une nuit blanche?

J'ai la tringle pour toi.

Je te baiserai et je ne brûle pas les étapes.

Shit. It might as well have been written in Sanskrit. He spoke French pretty well. A couple of semesters of college French, a weekend immersion course sponsored by the Committee and a posting in Paris had done the trick. He could order a meal, deal with the snootiest of *sommeliers,* hold his own with any of the nut-cases who thought Paris was just one long Grand Prix racetrack. But reading this note was something else. He could make out most of the words, all right, but putting them together into something that made sense was another story.

He looked at Miranda. She had stopped shaking but her face was still drained of color. He thought of going to her, taking her back into his arms and kissing the warmth back into her flesh.

Stop it, he told himself fiercely, and forced his attention back to the note.

"Did you spend a white night?" he translated, and frowned. *"I have a something-or-other for you. I'll kiss you and . . .*

"It says, 'Did you have a sleepless night?' " Miranda said.

Conor looked at her. Her voice was calm and color was coming back into her face, but in a way that made her look feverish. She swallowed; he could see her throat working and he knew that whatever was coming next wasn't good.

"It says . . ." Her mouth trembled. "It says, 'I have a hard-on for you. I'm going to f-fuck you, and I won't be in any r-rush . . .' "

Conor crushed the note in his hand. The rage he'd fought against moments ago swept over him like a tidal wave, peaked and receded and left him taut with a deadly purpose. He knew, in that instant, that he would find and destroy whoever had sent this to her.

"So much for your locksmith," Miranda said, and gave what he figured was supposed to be a laugh.

Her words stunned him. He stared at her as she turned away and then he went after her, caught her arm and spun her towards him.

"What?"

"I said—"

"I heard what you said. What the hell's wrong with you, Beckman?" He saw the surprised look on her face, heard the barely controlled fury in his own voice, and welcomed it. That was fine. It was what he needed, something to fix on, something that was a lot safer than whatever it was he'd been feeling from the moment he'd walked in here tonight. "Are you telling me you got home, found the goddamn door was open, and went strutting on through it?"

"Of course not!"

His hand tightened on her arm. He felt the soft, yielding silkiness of her flesh beneath his fingers and in some distant part of his brain he realized he was hurting her, but he didn't give a damn.

"Let me tell you something, lady. Maybe you lead such a jaded existence that you think a little run-in with a fruitcake might be fun but it wouldn't be, I guarantee it."

"Wait a minute, O'Neil."

"No," he snarled, hauling her onto her toes, "no, *you* wait a minute! You come home, find the door standing open, what you do is get your ass out of here. You got that, Beckman? You move as fast as your little feet will go and you scream your fucking lungs out!"

"For God's sake!" Miranda wrenched her arm free, slapped her hands on her hips and glared up at Conor, her face flushed with anger. "I hate to burst your bubble, but I am not the ditz you think I am."

"No?"

"No."

"Listen, baby—"

"And do not call me baby! It's a disgusting term and I don't like it!"

"Yeah. You're right. Stupid is a better name for you. How could you be so dumb?"

"You want to talk about dumb?" Miranda stabbed a finger into his chest. "Dumb is you, going off like an alarm clock before you've got the facts. *I'm* the one that came home to find this—this thing waiting for me."

"The fact is," he said, shoving her hand aside, "the lock Cochran put in couldn't have been opened by anything short of *plastique*. But did that stop you from strolling in here like a sheep to the slaughter when you found the door open?"

"I didn't find it open."

"Hell, no, it did not, you just . . ." He stopped and glared at her. "You said the door was open."

"Try listening instead of lecturing, okay?" Miranda blew a strand of hair out of her eyes. "I came home. I unlocked the door. I found an envelope lying on the floor just past the threshold. All I meant when I said that about the lock was that it had never occurred to me that whoever's paying me these little visits wouldn't be stopped just because he couldn't get past the door."

Her momentary show of bravado slipped. Her voice quavered, and she turned away and snatched up Mia, who'd been weaving between her legs and meowing. Conor felt his anger drain away, too. His hands clenched and he shoved them deep into his trouser pockets, fighting the desire to go to her and try to comfort her again.

"Well," he said gruffly, "that's something, anyway."

She looked at him. "Meaning, I'm not the complete jerk you figured me for?"

"You've got things to learn, Beckman. Coming home after dark, all by yourself, isn't clever."

"Here we go," she said wearily. She put the cat down, made her way into the kitchen and hit the wall switch. Light flooded the room. "We went over this before, remember?"

"Taking off and disappearing without checking with me this morning," Conor said, following after her, "wasn't much better."

Miranda spun towards him, her face a study in disbelief. "Without checking with *you?* You've got to be kidding."

"Do I look as if I'm kidding?"

He didn't. He looked furious but that was fine with her because she was getting angry all over again, and that was a lot better than being scared. Who was Conor O'Neil, to give her orders? Being toyed with by some crazy was bad enough. She certainly didn't need a stranger, bought and paid for by Eva, to watch over her like some kind of unwelcome overseer.

"Let's put it this way, O'Neil." Miranda folded her arms and gave him a look composed of equal parts disdain and dismissal. "It'll be a cold day in hell before I check in and out with you or anybody else."

"How about showing some common sense, then? Or is that too much to ask?"

"How's this for a display of common sense?" Miranda pointed to the door. "Get out."

"You don't order me around, Beckman."

"Who the hell do you think you are, O'Neil?"

She shrank back as he strode towards her but there was no place to go. It was hard not to look cowed when your shoulders were pinned to a wall and a man who was all muscle and anger was towering over you, but she tried.

"Maybe you haven't quite grasped what's happening here, Beckman."

"Maybe you haven't figured out that I want you gone."

A muscle tightened in his jaw. "Listen, baby—"

"I told you not to call me that."

"Yeah, you're right. Pig-headed suits you better." Conor leaned towards her, his eyes flashing. "Five minutes ago, I came through the front door and you threw yourself at me as if I was the last stagecoach out of Deadwood."

"I did not."

"You sure as hell did."

They stood toe-to-toe, glaring at each other, and then, without meaning to, Miranda laughed.

"The last stagecoach out of Deadwood?"

Conor's mouth twitched. "What can I tell you? I've always been a sucker for old Westerns."

"You've got no taste," she said, "you know that?"

But she was smiling, and after a couple of seconds, he smiled, too.

"Listen," he said, "how about we start from the top?"

She nodded. He stepped back, picked up a chair, swung it around and straddled it.

"You left here early this morning."

"Uh-huh," she said. She pulled a chair out from the table and sat down opposite him.

"I came by around nine and you were already gone."

"You came by?"

"Yes."

"What for?"

"To check out the lock. And to lay out some ground rules until I can figure out what's going on here, but I was too late. You'd taken off."

She sighed, propped her elbow on the table and rested her chin on her fist.

"I went out for breakfast."

"Where?"

"I went to . . ." Two spots of pink rose in her cheeks. "To this little place off the Champs Elysées."

"Has it got a name?"

She shrugged. "What's the difference?" What *was* the difference? So what, if she let him know she liked McDonald's? Nobody knew that except Jean-Phillipe, but it wasn't exactly a state secret. "Just a place, that's all."

"That's a long way to go for a *croissant.*"

Miranda shrugged again. She stood up, went to the cabinet above the sink and took down the fixings for coffee.

"I had breakfast with someone."

Conor felt his stomach knot. "The Frenchman," he said tonelessly.

"His name is—"

"I know his name. Jean-Phillipe Moreau. Okay. So, you and he had breakfast together in some trendy little place whose name you can't remember."

"McDonald's." The word blurted from her lips. Damn, she thought, but now that it was out, she looked at him, her chin tilting in defiance. "We had breakfast at McDonald's. And after that, we went to his place."

Nothing about Conor's expression changed, yet she could almost feel the sudden tension in his big body. She knew what he was thinking, but so what? Her reputation—her supposed reputation—didn't embarrass her. On the contrary, it pleased her. She worked hard at maintaining it. Jean-Phillipe, ever the armchair analyst, said she did it to get even with Eva, but Miranda knew better. She just liked having people whisper about her.

Then, why was she having such trouble with this conversation?

"Maybe you want to take notes," she said. "Breakfast, then we went to his place, then—" She looked at him over her shoulder. "You won't really need all the details, will you, O'Neil?"

No, Conor told himself, hell, no, he didn't need the details. His brain was on overload already, grinding out X-rated scenes guaranteed to never make it past any censor.

"How long has the Frenchman been your lover?"

"That's none of your business."

"Is he the only one? Or does he just have the inside track?"

Miranda turned around. "I just told you, my private life is none of your business."

"You just got a note, a charming one, I might add, and written on the same kind of paper as Eva's, in what looks like the same ink and handwriting." His smile was all teeth. "That makes everything my business."

"Was Eva's note . . . was it like mine?"

"Answer my question, Beckman. Is Moreau your only lover?"

"You answer mine first. Was the note Eva got like the one I just found under the door?"

"No," Conor said brusquely, "it wasn't half as creative. Now it's your turn. Does Moreau hold the franchise or doesn't he?"

For the first time in years, the easy answer, the fiction she'd worked so hard to maintain, froze on her lips. She turned her back to him and finished making the coffee.

"We have an unusual relationship."

"Yeah, I'll bet. Well, maybe you'd better tell him that, for a while anyway, it's not going to be enough to take you out for a meal and a tumble in the hay."

"You're crude, O'Neil. Do you know that?"

"I'm also direct and to the point so there can't be any doubt about what I'm telling you. If Moreau gives a damn about your safety, he's going to have to stir his ass, climb out of that pimp-mobile he calls a car, and walk you to your door."

Miranda slammed the cabinet door shut.

"What were you doing the other night, spying on us?"

"You give him the word, or I will."

"For your information," she said, fixing him with a cold look, "Jean-Phillipe wanted to take me home this evening but I wouldn't let him. He took a taxi in one direction and I took one in the other. I came home, unlocked my door, and found that—that message from the funny farm waiting for me."

"Can you think of anybody who'd want to do this to you?"

"Terrify me, you mean?" She laughed, though the sound of it was brittle, and plopped down in the chair again. "Well, I've probably stepped on lots of toes since I broke into modeling, and every now and then, a fan decides I was heaven-sent just for him—but no, I can't come up with a single person who'd do anything like go through my underwear and send me a note and a picture like that." She hesitated. "O'Neil? I'm right, aren't I? You think whoever broke in here was the same person who sent me that—that thing?"

Conor stood up, shoved the chair under the table, and paced across the room. What could he tell her? He didn't know what to think; that was the trouble.

He was supposed to be concentrating on the note sent to Eva Winthrop and her hotshot husband. He was supposed to break his ass to keep the President's nose clean, to figure out who was at the bottom of this mess. The old brain was supposed to be click-clicking away with government-approved, grade A efficiency.

Instead, he'd spent the night thinking about a woman who sure as hell didn't like him and who he didn't much care for either, and now he was standing here with his brain locked on what she'd said about spending the day with the Frenchman. He kept imagining her in Pretty Boy's arms, her hair spread over the pillow, her beautiful face taut with ecstasy.

"O'Neil? Do you think it's the same person?"

Conor looked at her. "It's a good bet," he said, because there was nothing to be gained for either of them by lying.

She took it well, nothing giving away her reaction except for a slight flicker in her eyes.

"And is it good or bad, that it's the same person who's doing these things?"

Bad, he thought, definitely bad. If one person was behind everything, then that person was at the very least dangerous and, at the very worst, the kind of lunatic who'd long ago lost touch with reality.

"Good," he said, this time opting for whatever lie would work. "If I'm right, then we can devote all our resources to locating one individual."

"How will we do that?"

So much for his clever response. Damn, but she was full of good questions he couldn't answer but he wasn't going to tell her that, not when she was back to looking at him the way she had when he'd first come through the door, as if he was John Wayne riding a white horse.

"By doing the job I'm trained to do," he said, wondering what Harry Thurston would say if he could hear this crap. "Tracking down leads, asking questions . . . which reminds me, what's the dragon lady's name?"

"Who?"

"The *concièrge.* Does she have a name, or just a number?"

Miranda smiled. "Madame Delain, you mean. She's not as bad as she looks."

"Yeah, and *Mein Kampf* was only a wish list." Conor went to the door and opened it. "You stay put. I'll only be a minute."

Miranda stood up and went after him. Last night, she'd obeyed his command to stay like a well-trained spaniel, but not this time.

"Forget it, O'Neil." She plucked her coat from the chair and drew it around her shoulders. "Whither thou goest," she said, "I trail along."

Conor took one look at the determined tilt to her jaw and decided not to argue.

Madame Delain not only insisted she had not permitted any strangers to enter the building, she grew indignant at Conor's even raising the question.

"I grant access to no one without the knowledge and permission of our tenants,'' she said, drawing herself up until her ample bosom rested under her chin. ''Surely, Mademoiselle Beckman is aware of this.''

''Oh, of course, madame,'' Miranda said quickly. ''It's just that someone—''

''Someone slipped something under Mademoiselle Beckman's door,'' Conor said, his voice sliding over hers. ''And she just wondered if you knew who it was.''

''I do not know because no one did such a thing,'' madame said, her words dipped in ice.

''Were you at your desk all day, madame?''

''*Certainement.*''

''No lunch break?''

''I had lunch here. It is my custom.''

''No breaks to visit the bathroom?''

Madame Delain gave Conor a look that suggested only mortals were in need of such things.

''None.''

''Miss Beckman received no deliveries?''

''If she had, the package would have been left with me.''

''What about workmen? Did anybody come by to fix something?''

The *concièrge* started to shake her head, then changed her mind.

''Well, yes, early this afternoon, but I can assure you, he went nowhere near Mademoiselle's apartment.'' Madame sniffed. ''An annoying little man he was, too.''

''What did he come to fix?''

''Oh, it was nonsense. Pure nonsense. We have all these rules and codes now. Paris has survived for centuries but lately there is always some fool stopping by to peer into the chimneys or tug at the wiring and tell me I must spend more money to meet some foolish new law.''

''Did something like that happen today?''

''A man came, to check the elevator.'' Madame Delain sighed deeply. ''I told him that there was nothing to check, that it was inspected two months ago, but he would not listen. Well, bureaucrats never do, do they? I told him to wait, that I would escort him to the elevator but he said, why did I need to bother when anyone with two eyes could see it stood right over there?''

''And?'' Conor prompted.

''And,'' she said, with a shrug, ''he rode down, he rode up, he made a pest of himself. He vanished for a while on the upper floor.''

''My floor,'' Miranda said softly, and Conor's hand closed on hers in warning.

Madame Delain's brows arched. ''He said it was to check the cables but I know how these fools do things.'' She leaned across her desk, her lips pursed like a prune. ''He was hoping I would get nervous and offer him a few francs to give me a good report. Well, I did not do it. The elevator is fine, and so are the cables. This is a well-run building. Anyone can tell you that.''

''What did he look like?'' Conor said.

''Who?''

The temptation to seize madame, drag her out of her chair and hang her up by her heels, was close to overpowering.

Conor smiled. ''The elevator inspector,'' he said politely.

''Who would notice such a thing? A civil servant is a civil servant. They all look the same.''

Conor opened his mouth, felt the swift squeeze of Miranda's fingers against his, and cleared his throat.

''Of course,'' he said.

''You think this man left this thing under mademoiselle's door?''

He nodded. ''It's possible.''

''*Mon Dieu,* such nerve!'' The *concièrge* looked at Miranda, eyes bright with curiosity. ''What was it?''

Miranda hesitated. ''Oh, you know.'' She smiled. ''It was a nothing, just a message from a devoted fan.''

* * *

"Well," she said to Conor, as they sat across from each other in a crowded *café* a little while later, "it might have been."

"Have you ever had gotten anything even close to that from a fan?"

"No, thank goodness. But I've heard about some weird stuff. You'd be amazed at the things people send to celebrities. Well, to people they think are celebrities."

"Weird, huh?"

"Weird is putting it nicely. I knew this British model once who got a letter that gave a whole new meaning to the words *rubber room.*"

Conor laughed. A long walk in what had turned into a cool, clear night and a couple of drinks had taken the edge off the ugliness of what had happened.

He knew what he had to do, that it was important to concentrate on getting answers so he could begin to piece the puzzle together. He had some answers already. Not enough, but some.

Miranda, for instance, was off his suspect list. Her panic last night had seemed genuine. As for today's envelopeful of goodies . . . Even if she'd been capable of putting together a package like that, she couldn't have timed her hysteria to coincide with his arrival.

Still, the big questions remained. Who was behind this? And what did he—or she—want? To thwart Hoyt Winthrop's appointment? Or was some nut really leading up to hurting Eva Winthrop and her daughter? And what was Eva hiding? Something, Conor was sure of it. Despite her seeming willingness to confide in him, her apparent bewilderment at what was happening, there was something else there that he had yet to figure out.

Until he knew the answers, all he could do was keep digging and do whatever he could to keep mother and daughter safe.

Eva, with her socially correct existence, would be a cinch. The powers-that-be could add half a dozen bodyguards to her retinue of servants and she'd never complain. She might even bask in her newly acquired status.

Miranda . . . ah, Miranda was a different story altogether.

He looked at her, seated across from him, her face lit by the soft glow of the recessed lights. He could just see how she'd react if he told her he was going to arrange for protection for her, three shifts a day of guys with bulging muscles that would hang on her every move.

She'd laugh in his face, that was what she'd do, and set out to lose every last one of them.

He doubted if he could ever convince her to keep a low profile, either. Not that it would help. There was nothing outrageous in the way she was dressed this evening. She had on a white sweater, angora maybe, something soft and fuzzy, and a pair of black wool slacks. Her camel-colored coat was draped on the chair behind her; her hair, that ebony cloud of silk, was pulled back from her face and secured with a barrette. She wasn't wearing any makeup, not that he could tell, anyway, or any jewelry except for a pair of little gold hoops in her ears.

And yet, every man in the place was aware of her. He'd felt the stir that had gone through the room the minute they'd walked in.

It didn't surprise him. A man would have to be dead not to be aware of Miranda, not to want her soft mouth under his, her warm breath on his skin . . .

". . . didn't come to anything, though, except to give us a good laugh."

Conor shifted in his chair.

"Sorry," he said. "I was, ah, my mind was wandering. I didn't get that."

She smiled, shrugged her shoulders and took a sip of her Campari and soda.

"I was talking about a note Nita once got, a real winner from a fan."

"Nita. The girl you were with yesterday?"

She nodded. "Yes. Nita Carrington. She's my best friend."

"You've known her for a long time?"

Miranda shrugged. She touched the tip of her finger to the rim of her glass and ran it along the edge.

"For years. We started modeling around the same time."

"She's American, isn't she?"

She smiled. "Atlanta born and bred."

"And you're close?"

"Well, we've got lots in common. We started out together, we're both from the States, and neither of us has any family."

"You have family, Miranda. A mother and a stepfather."

Her smile tilted. "Eva gave birth to me." she said, the same way she might have offered a weather report. "That's the extent of our relationship."

"And Hoyt? He told me that you and he were very close, when you were little."

She plucked the twist of lemon from her Campari and dumped it into the ashtray, her smile gone.

"I'm not going to discuss my family with you, O'Neil."

"Why not?"

"What are you, a shrink?" She looked at him, her eyes suddenly cool. "You're here to do a job, not to analyze me."

"My job is to find out who's behind these threats. Until I do, everybody's a suspect."

"Including me?"

Conor sat back and watched her face. "What about Nita?"

"What about her?"

"Does she have any reason to want to frighten you?"

"Nita?" she said incredulously, and laughed. "I'd trust Nita with my life."

"I suppose you'd trust your Frenchman, too."

Her eyes flashed fire. "You're damn right I would."

Conor felt as if a knot were forming in his gut again. The image was back, the one that had plagued him earlier. Miranda in Moreau's arms, his hands on her body . . .

"Can you think of anybody who'd have something to gain by terrorizing you and Eva?"

"Nobody."

''What about your ex-husband? Do you think he'd have something to gain by doing something like this?''

''Edouard's not my ex anything. We weren't married long enough for me to think of him like—'' Her breath hitched. He'd caught her off guard; he could see it. ''My, but you've been doing lots of digging.''

''Just part of the job.''

''How'd you find out that I'd been—about Edouard?''

''Your mother told me.''

''Good old Mother.'' Miranda gave a bitter laugh. ''What'd she tell you?''

''What do you think she told me?''

''What is wrong with you, O'Neil? Is it impossible for you to make a statement? I ask you a question, you respond with a question. It's annoying as hell.''

''Your once-upon-a-time hubby doesn't seem too fond of you,'' Conor said, ignoring the outburst.

Miranda leaned forward, her hands folded on the table top. He tried not to notice how the action made her breasts push together under the soft wool of her sweater.

''Have you ever been married?''

''What's that got to do with anything?''

''Just do us both a favor, okay? Answer the question.''

''Yes,'' he said, with a little shrug, ''I was married, once.''

She smiled sweetly. ''If I went to see your former wife, would she seem fond of you?''

He had to laugh. ''Point taken.''

Miranda took a sip of her drink, put it down and sat back, her eyes on his.

''So, when did you go to see Edouard?''

''Today.''

''How'd you know where to find him?''

''Friends in high places.''

''Boy, that embassy is just a fount of information, isn't it? Locksmiths, ex-husbands . . . Why'd you go to see him? Do you suspect him of being involved in this?''

''Do you?''

"There you go again. Is that what they teach you in detective school? To avoid answers whenever possible?"

Conor lifted his beer to his lips and took a long drink. It was German, and dark, but it was cold and bitter and it suited his mood.

"He could be involved," he said, putting the bottle down, "but I doubt it. He's got a line of blue-blooded ancestors running all the way to Cro-Magnon man."

"You really think people with pedigrees don't do awful things?" Miranda laughed. "Oh, have you got a lot to learn!"

"What I'm saying is that the simplest motive behind what's happening is blackmail. A couple of nasty tricks and then *the* note, the one addressed to Eva that says, pay up or else. I can't imagine a man risking everything for a payoff he doesn't need. It's obvious de Lasserre has money."

"He didn't have any, when he married me."

"No?"

"No. Why do you sound so surprised?"

"So," Conor said, ignoring the question, "what's he been doing the last few years, do you know?"

"He got married, two or three times, the last time out to an English girl, I think, an heiress. They're divorced now but she's supposed to have settled a hefty amount on him."

"And you didn't?"

"Me?" Miranda laughed. "I was living on a starvation allowance. Come on, who are you kidding? Eva wouldn't have missed the chance to tell you how much she paid to buy my freedom. It's one of her favorite tales. The whole thing, from start to finish. How I seduced Edouard, how she had to rush to my rescue when I decided I wanted out . . ."

"When good old Edouard didn't live up to expectations, you mean." He looked across the table at her, waiting for her to say something, but she didn't. That taunting, Mona Lisa smile crept across her lips and he thought about what de Lasserre had told him, how she'd turned on him when he hadn't pleased her in bed.

The knot in his belly tightened. I could please her, he thought,

I could make her forget Moreau and de Lasserre and God only knows how many others.

"Eva told me everything," he said softly. "So did good old Edouard. He says you didn't like his bedroom technique."

Miranda reached back and drew her coat around her.

"Good night, O'Neil," she said briskly. "Thanks for the drink."

He reached across the table and caught hold of her wrist. "No comment?"

"It was a long time ago. I don't really remember."

"And a lot of guys ago, too, I'll bet." She tried to push back from the table but he wouldn't let her; his fingers dug into her flesh. "Maybe we should put our heads together, try and work up a list. A suspect list, you know? Men you've fucked and forgotten."

He wanted to call back the words as soon as they'd left his mouth, but it was too late. Her face went white; her chair tipped over as she pulled her hand from his and got to her feet.

"Miranda? Miranda, dammit, wait."

She could hear him calling after her as she flew towards the door but she didn't stop, didn't pause, didn't look back. Faces turned up to her in surprise; she wondered if they knew who she was or what she was running from.

The truth was, she wasn't sure what she was running from. When you came down to it, what had Conor said that she hadn't encouraged him and everybody else to say or, at least to think? Why should she care that he'd looked at her as if she were beneath his contempt?

The cold night air stung her flushed face as she ran out into the street. O'Neil was nothing to her. He was less than nothing. She moved in a world that had no connection to his pathetic ideas about morality.

Dammit, where were all the taxis? There was never a taxi around when you needed one. It didn't matter. Her apartment was only a couple of blocks away. She yanked up the collar of her coat, stuffed her hands into her pockets and started walking.

What a fool she'd been tonight. Rushing into his arms, feeling safe, sitting opposite him in that smoky bar, laughing and talking and forgetting, just for a little while, the real reason he was with her. It was all a lie, what she'd felt—what she'd thought she'd felt—last night, when he'd kissed her and then tonight, when she'd ached for him.

Conor's hand clamped around her elbow.

"Where do you think you're going?" he growled as he swung her towards him.

"Let go of me!"

"Can't you ever manage to think further than the end of your nose? It's dark, it's late, for all you know there's a welcoming committee waiting for you at your apartment. You cannot go home alone."

"Don't give me orders, you bastard! Let go!"

He cursed and his hand locked around her elbow. She yelped but he didn't give a damn, he just lifted her to her toes and quick-marched her into the darkened doorway of a nearby shop. She balled her hand into a fist and swung it towards him but he was expecting it and he caught both her hands in his and locked them against his chest.

"Listen to me, dammit."

"There's nothing you could say I'd want to hear."

"I'm sorry I hurt you. I didn't mean—"

"Save the apology, O'Neil. Just let go."

"When I'm good and ready."

God, how she despised this man! He was a solid wall of muscle, crowding her back against the locked door of the shop. His strength was overpowering and it frightened her.

"Don't manhandle me, you oaf! I don't like it."

"That's no surprise. You don't like much of anything I do," he said, "except for this," and he bent his head and kissed her.

His mouth was hot and hard, and terror swept through her like a flood tide.

"Don't," she said, against his lips, and even though he was almost beyond control, he heard the fear in her voice. The anger, whatever in hell had been driving him, fell away. In its place, he felt a yearning so vast and deep it made him shudder.

"Miranda." She whimpered and tried to twist her face away from his. He caught her face between his hands, his fingers spreading over her cheeks. "Don't be afraid, baby," he whispered. "I won't hurt you. I'd never hurt you."

He kissed her temple, her hair, the soft curve of her cheek. She was trembling; there were tears on her lashes and he tasted their salt as he kissed her closed eyes.

"Miranda," he said, and he put his lips against hers.

She went still in his arms. Then, just when he thought he would have to let her go, she gave a soft cry he knew he would never forget. Her arms slipped around his neck, her lips parted like the petals of a flower and she gave herself up to the kiss.

She tasted warm and sweet, of tears and of Campari, but most of all she tasted of herself, of woman and, then, so quickly that it stunned him, she tasted of hot, urgent desire.

He felt his body tighten, his penis thicken and rise, pressing against the softness of her belly. It happened with a swiftness that shocked him. He groaned, knowing he was at the edge of reason, knowing, too, that he couldn't let go of her.

He slid his hands down her back and cupped her bottom, lifting her into him, wanting her to feel him, to know how primitive and urgent was his need. He wanted her, needed her, needed everything she was and everything she could be. He thrust his tongue into her mouth, deepening the kiss, and then he slid his hands under her coat, up over her skin, so hot and silky, and cupped her breasts . . .

She went rigid in his arms. He felt the change in her even before she jammed her hands against his chest and began to struggle against him.

"No," he said, "Miranda."

But it was over. A sob of such awful desperation burst from her throat that he felt its impact in the marrow of his bones, and she twisted out of his embrace and slipped past him, fleeing into the night.

He stood looking after her, a man lost in a dream of what

had almost been. At last, sanity returned. He drew a long breath, pulling the knife-sharp air deep into his lungs. Then he turned up his collar and set out after her, his pace steady, fast enough so he never lost sight of her, slow enough so there was no possibility he'd overtake her.

He stood in the shadows while she unlocked the gate in the courtyard of her apartment building but as she started towards the front door, he came up behind her. She swung towards him, her eyes as bright and wide as a cat's.

"Get away from me, O'Neil." Her voice was steady and cold. "Or I'll kick you where it hurts."

He smiled at that. He'd almost forgotten all the fancy moves she'd laid on him the other night.

"You won't have to," he said. "I'm just going to see you upstairs, to your door."

"Not in this lifetime."

She meant every word, he was sure of it. After a minute, he nodded.

"We'll compromise," he said. "You give me your keys, wait in the lobby while I check out your apartment."

Her chin lifted. In the faint light cast by the street lamp, he thought he saw a faint glitter of moisture in her eyes.

"You really expect me to trust you?"

Her words dripped contempt and he knew he deserved every bit of it, but he showed nothing.

"I'm all you've got," he said.

He saw her mouth tremble. Then she unlocked the door that led into the lobby. They stepped inside. Wordlessly, she dropped her keys into his outstretched hand.

Moments later, he rode down in the elevator.

"Everything's fine," he said. "I turned on a lamp in the living room. Switch it off, then on again once you've locked the door after you."

Miranda took her keys from him and got into the elevator. He waited until he heard the ancient mechanism groan to a stop. Then he went out to the street and looked up at her windows.

The light he'd left burning went out, then came back on. She was safe. He had done his job.

Conor turned his back on the lamp's glow and walked off into the night.

Chapter Ten

Nita Carrington tucked back one corner of the crimson velvet drapes that covered the windows of her *salon* and peeked out at the street.

What a strange winter this was turning out to be. It hardly ever snowed in Paris, but a light snow was falling again tonight, etching the winter-bare branches of the Tuileries Gardens with lace.

And, as she'd half-expected, there was Conor O'Neil's car, just pulling up across the way. The car, and the man, had become equally recognizable over the last few days.

He was persistent, she had to give him that. It was sure going to be interesting, seeing Miranda's reaction when she discovered him waiting out there.

Right now, Miranda was still in the bathroom, getting dressed. The two of them had come here after the Thierry Mugler showing, Miranda hoping O'Neil would lose her trail so that she'd be able to shake him for the evening.

Uh-uh, Nita thought. "No such luck, girlfriend," she said softly.

Miranda was going to be royally pissed off but that wouldn't be anything new. She'd been hissing like a cat for days, ever since Mr. Conor O'Neil had come strutting onto the scene. Darned if *she* would hiss, if O'Neil turned his attention to her. Not that she had any hopes, even if he knew she was between men. O'Neil was single-minded; he had eyes for nobody but Miranda, although Miranda insisted it was all business.

Sighing, Nita let the drapes fall back into place. Maybe she'd meet somebody tonight, at the party. Lord knew she was ready, not just for a new lover but for something different. Everything seemed boring lately. Paris, the showings, even this room.

It was a stunner, especially if you were into gilt cherubs and red velvet, which she had been a couple of years ago. The pansy who'd designed it for her had kissed his fingertips and pronounced it the best thing he'd ever done. Nita had figured the best thing he'd ever done was probably some leather-freak with a shaved skull but she got the general message. And he'd been one hundred percent right.

The room was spectacular, kind of over-the-top rococo meets braggadocio baroque with maybe some high-priced brothel tossed in for good measure. Her Georgia ancestors would spin in their graves, if they'd seen it, but Marie Antoinette would have been thrilled. Nita had been, too, but now the look was wearing thin.

Oh yes, she thought, plucking a pair of ruby earrings the size of hummingbird eggs from the table and screwing them into her ear lobes, it was definitely time for something new. Something along the lines of what Miranda had done with her place, all whites and beiges and blacks, lots of indirect lighting and simple lines.

Nita fastened a ruby choker around her long, *café au lait* neck and slipped a matching bracelet on her wrist. She could still remember the first time she'd seen Miranda's apartment, how surprised she'd been by the laid-back, almost Spartan design which just didn't suit Miranda's party-girl image. But as the friendship had grown, she'd begun to think that maybe the décor wasn't so out of sync, after all.

Crazy as it seemed, she suspected the inner Miranda might not have a whole lot in common with the outer one.

A pair of red sequined sandals with skinny four-inch heels sat on top of a scarlet-covered chair. Nita tried not to wobble as she stepped into them.

How could you be friends with somebody all this time and still have the weird feeling that you didn't really know her? This thing Miranda had going with Jean-Phillipe, for instance. Nita walked to a smoky, gilt-framed mirror on the far wall, her steps tiny and mincing to accommodate the figure-hugging lines of her ankle-length, red jersey gown. He was always sending Miranda flowers and hugging her and she was always hanging on to him and sighing, but for all of that, there was something missing. Nita couldn't put her finger on it but she'd sensed it right away, from the time so long ago when the friendship between Miranda and Jean-Phillipe had suddenly seemed to turn into a hot-ticket item.

"You really gettin' it on with the Frenchman?" Nita had asked, deliberately couching the question in her phoniest down-home drawl.

Miranda had laughed and said yes, of course she was—but there'd been a couple of seconds when her eyes had said something else.

Now, with Conor O'Neil in the picture, Nita was more puzzled than ever. Miranda was blunt about disliking the guy, but anybody with a functioning brain could tell that the temperature went up a couple of hundred degrees whenever he came near her. He was an investigator, Miranda had said, making a face; she said there'd been some trouble at her apartment and some similar stuff involving her mother in New York, that her mother had bought and paid for O'Neil to play bodyguard until it was cleared up and that he was about as welcome in her life as the plague.

"Mmm-mmm-mmm," Nita had said with a sexy grin, "that man can guard my body any time he wants."

Miranda hadn't even cracked a smile.

"That's only because you haven't had to deal with him.

O'Neil is a thickheaded, chauvinistic,egotistical, judgmental—''

"Sounds good so far,'' Nita had answered, batting her lashes.

"He's a bully with an over-active libido,'' Miranda had snapped, "and the quicker he's out of my life, the better.''

Miranda had spent the last few days trying to lose him, but O'Neil stuck like Crazy Glue.

Sooner or later, you just knew there were going to be old-fashioned, Fourth of July fireworks between those two.

"Nita?'' Miranda's voice floated out from the bathroom. "Is our cab here yet?''

Nita went to the window again. The snow had stopped and a full, perfect moon had risen. A cab was just pulling up to the door . . . and there, across the road, Conor stood leaning against his car, arms folded.

She whistled soundlessly through her teeth. What a gorgeous man he was, with that tough-but-beautiful face and that terrific body. He was all gussied up, too, in a black tuxedo that showed off all his assets—the wide shoulders, the broad chest, the narrow waist and hips and those long, very masculine legs.

"Well? Is it here?''

Nita cleared her throat.

"Yeah. It is. You ready?''

Miranda stepped into the room. One look, and Nita knew that she'd definitely had it with crimson and gilt.

Miranda was a study in simplicity. Her gown was a long, demure column of heavy white silk but Nita had seen her model it at the Chanel showing; she knew that its innocent appearance was an illusion. The silk would take on the warmth of Miranda's body and, as she walked, it would cling to her breasts, her hips, her legs. Even the neckline wasn't what it at first seemed; it was high in the front but it dipped almost to the base of her spine in the back. Her hair was loose, drawn back from her face with a pair of antique silver combs. The only other pieces of jewelry she wore were the silver slave bracelets that adorned her wrists.

"How do I look?'' she asked.

Nita smiled. "Like the Fourth of July."

"Huh?"

Nita strutted across the room and plucked her sable cape from where it lay across a red velvet chair.

"Trust me," she said. "It's gonna be an interesting evening."

The party, given by a Prince Something of Somewhere in celebration of Fashion Week, was in one of Paris's most elegant hotels. Everyone who'd been invited had accepted, for this was *the* party to attend, and virtually each guest had brought along others who had not been asked. There was a certain cachet in making it look as if you were such a close friend of the prince's that you could simply invite your house guests or visiting business associates to his party.

The prince didn't mind. Tomorrow, society column headlines in the tabloids on several continents would mention his name and that of his latest trophy wife, a woman half his age who had made her name as Miss October in *Penthouse* magazine.

The hotel minded, but only a little. Things were crowded, it was true, and the head chef was screaming at the sous-chefs, who were frantically redoubling everything they'd prepared for the buffet tables, but tomorrow the hotel's name and photographs of the glittering ballroom would appear everywhere.

Miranda, trapped by the fast-talking owner of a big-time New York modeling agency, had just about decided she was the only person in the entire place who was not having a wonderful time.

". . . marvelous opportunities for your career, dear girl. If I could just have a few minutes of your time . . ."

Even Nita, who'd agreed the much-ballyhooed party would probably be boring, boring, boring, had deserted her.

"You remember some old song about seein' your true love across a crowded room?" she'd said under her breath and headed, straight as an arrow, for a tall, skinny guy who looked as if he'd staked out a permanent location near one of the buffet tables.

". . . is right for this absolutely incredible career move. And you have my assurance . . ."

The noise level was awful, an inevitable result of the conversational buzz of several hundred people vying for contention with the shrieks of the latest heavy metal group blasting over the sound system.

". . . do you think? Or perhaps you have some questions you'd like me to answer?"

Miranda blinked, looked at the man who'd been talking her ear off, and tried to figure out what, precisely, he'd been saying.

"No," she said, "I, ah, I can't think of any."

"I assure you, Miss Beckman, this is the perfect time for you to take your career to the States."

"The States? Is that what . . ." She smiled politely. "I'm sorry, but I'm not interested in working in the States, Mr.— Mr. . . .?"

"Stone. Brian Stone. Call me Brian, please. And I do wish you'd reconsider."

"Brian, I really don't want to talk business tonight. Why don't you give me your card and I'll be in touch."

"Well, of course, but I do want to make a couple of points. As I was saying, you have my assurance . . ."

Miranda felt her smile stretching her lips. The only assurance she wanted right now was that she could get out of here, and soon.

Nita had said tonight was going to be interesting and she'd hoped that would turn out to be true. Maybe a splashy party with too much champagne and too many people would improve her mood.

Not so far, it hadn't.

She was bored. No, it was more than that. She was . . . what was the word? Disconnected, as if she were watching everything going on around her from a distance.

Nita, who'd inched by a couple of minutes ago with the intense-looking stranger in tow, had picked up on it right away.

"Smile, girlfriend," she'd whispered. "You look like Dr. Ruth taking notes at a clerics' convention."

That was a perfect description of how she felt. She was observing, not participating, and the things she saw and heard struck her as dull and pointless and even silly.

Darling, you look fabulous. You've gained a little weight, haven't you, but it's so becoming!

Did you see Lana? Such a stunning woman. I wonder, who's her plastic surgeon?

I couldn't decide between the Bulgari and the Cartier, so Teddy bought them both. A woman can never have too many diamond necklaces, I always say.

Silly. And boring, especially in a world so filled with disaster and trouble. it was how she'd felt years ago, when she'd first gained admission to this much-vaunted circle. What had happened? How could she have forgotten?

If only Jean-Phillipe were here. She could say anything to him, that the blonde in silver sequins looked as if she'd had cantaloupes implanted in her breasts, that the fat German playwright over near the bar seemed to have put his hairpiece on backwards. But Jean-Phillipe was on the Côte d'Azur. He'd been there all week. His movie had wrapped, as expected, but the director had decided he needed to re-shoot the ending.

"I am sorry, *chérie,*" he'd said, "but it cannot be helped, *tu comprends?*"

Of course, she understood. And there was no good reason he had to be here with her. She knew practically everybody in the crowd and the ones she didn't know would inevitably trip over themselves to impress her, like Brian what's-his-name, who'd managed to box her neatly into a corner.

What was it, then? What was getting her down? Because something certainly was. She couldn't relax and just have a good time.

Conor O'Neil, she thought suddenly, that's what it was. She hadn't spotted him yet; she might even have escaped him by dressing at Nita's but it didn't matter because here she was, on edge anyway, looking around and knowing, just knowing, that he was going to appear any minute and put a damper on things.

That's what a week's worth of having him hovering over her had accomplished.

She'd phoned Eva, as she'd promised she'd do, and they'd had a stilted, five-minute conversation during which Eva had assured her that O'Neil was, indeed, in her employ.

"Accept his presence, Miranda," Eva had said coldly.

She had, the way you accept a necessary evil, but after a couple of days, the awful impact of the note and the picture had begun to fade. She'd thought back to the stuff she'd heard over the years, the weird notes and gifts that some of the other girls had received. Yes, what had been tucked beneath her door had been nasty but it hadn't been lethal.

Besides, she'd grown tired of having O'Neil around. He made her feel uncomfortable. She couldn't lead any kind of life with a silent but glowering stranger following at her heels like a suspicious rottweiler.

A couple of mornings ago, she'd sailed out of her apartment building and gone straight to where he stood waiting for her across the street.

"Don't you have anything better to do than follow me around?"

He hadn't answered or even acknowledged her presence, which had only made her angrier.

"Go home, O'Neil," she said, "and tell Eva thanks but no thanks. I don't want your services."

She'd headed for the Rue de Rivoli and he, damn him, had fallen in behind her.

She tried losing him on the Métro, waiting till the last second to open the subway car door, then racing for the exit—but he made it out the door and after her, just in time. She took a taxi to Versailles, stuffed herself into a huge group of American tourists—and found O'Neil wandering alongside. She strolled into her favorite *bistro,* dashed madly through the kitchen and exited by the rear door—and found him leaning against a wall in the alley.

He was like the poem Hoyt used to read her when she was little, the one about having a shadow that followed you about.

No matter what she did, where she went, Conor was always there. And even when he wasn't, like right now, he occupied her thoughts so that she had no idea what in heaven's name the man from the modeling agency had just finished telling her. Whatever it was, he was waiting for her response.

"So, what do you think?" he said. "Sounds like a good deal, doesn't it?"

Miranda cleared her throat. "Well, Brian, I don't really know what to say."

"Just say yes. I don't want to be pushy but hey, we both know you've got to make the jump soon or forget about it." He smiled, his teeth an artificial flash of fish-belly white against his sunlamp tan. "We don't want to lose our chance at the Big Apple, do we? Trust me, dear, I know what I'm talking about. Not to be immodest, but I only book for the top girls."

The crowded room was warm. Brian's smile was unctuous and made her skin crawl, and her twitching nostrils told her he must have dumped half a bottle of Joop! over his head before coming here tonight.

Help, Miranda thought desperately, and at that moment, a hand closed around her arm. Her skin tingled, and she looked up.

"Conor," she started to say . . .

But it wasn't Conor who'd come to her rescue, it was—it was . . .

"How lovely you look tonight, Miranda."

It was the man she'd met at the party after the Diderot showing. What was his name?

"Hello," she said, and gave him a glowing smile. "How are you?"

"Miranda." The man from the agency frowned and dipped his head to hers. "I was hoping we could go someplace quiet and talk. A late supper, maybe, or a drink."

"Thank you, Brian, but really—"

"I'm sure we can work out mutually satisfying terms."

"I'm sure we could, but . . ." Miranda shot a desperate look at the man who'd just joined them. "But—"

"But Miss Beckman is with me," her savior said. He slipped his arm lightly around her waist and smiled pleasantly. "And I'm afraid I have no intention of sharing her. Now, Miranda, let me get you some champagne and then we'll find ourselves a quiet corner."

Brian Stone looked wounded but not defeated. Miranda offered an apology, tucked his business card into the tiny silver purse that hung from her shoulder and let herself be led through the crowd. Champagne flute in hand, she smiled up at her rescuer.

"I can't thank you enough for saving me, Mr. . . .? I'm sorry, I've forgotten your name."

"Moratelli. Vince Moratelli. Call me Vince, please. And it was my pleasure."

"Well, thank you again, Vince. I was desperate."

Moratelli chuckled. "I could see that you were."

"Really?" She blushed. "Oh, that's awful. I didn't mean it to show. It's just that I hate when people corner me and insist on talking shop."

"I agree. On a night like this, matters of a more intimate nature should be the only topics for discussion."

Miranda's smile flickered. Moratelli spoke politely and what he'd said wasn't even much of a come-on, not in this crowd, but a whisper of unease drifted over her skin as she looked into his overly handsome face.

"Well," she said, "if I can ever return the favor—"

"Ah, darling, such a quick brush-off. I'm disappointed."

"It's not a brush-off at all. I just—"

His hand closed around her wrist. His fingers were firm and cool and reminded her of marble.

"I lied for you, Miranda."

"Let go of me, please."

"Aren't you the least bit curious? About my turning up here tonight, I mean."

"No. Why should I be? I just assumed—"

"I came to see you."

"Me? But why?"

Moratelli smiled slyly. "Well," he said, "I thought we could take up where we left off the other evening."

"We didn't leave off anywhere, Mr. Moratelli. Please let go of my wrist."

Didn't you like my little present, Miranda?"

"I don't know what you're talking about."

"I'm disappointed. I went to such trouble, finding just the right picture and then adding my own special touches to it."

"What picture? You didn't send me any . . ." An image of the magazine ad flashed into her head, and she felt the blood drain from her face. "Oh God," she whispered, and Moratelli laughed. His hand tightened on hers and he pulled her close against him, so that his breath washed over her face.

"Did it excite you, darling? I hoped it might. I want you to be hot and wet and ready for me when I fuck you."

The champagne glass slipped from her hand and shattered against the floor.

"Darling, what's wrong? Didn't you like your champagne? I can get you something else. Campari, perhaps. Or would you prefer some chocolate? I know all your favorite things, Miranda."

His hand fell from her wrist. Miranda spun away; she could hear him laughing behind her. She wanted to scream, but her throat had closed up. She wanted to run, but there were people jammed in all around her. Desperate little sounds rose in her throat as she fought her way across the room while she prayed that Moratelli wouldn't follow her . . .

"Miranda?"

She did scream this time, as a man's hands closed on her shoulders, but the sound was lost in the noises blasting from the band.

"No," she said, struggling fiercely against the hard press of those hands, "don't—"

"Baby, what is it?"

She looked up, and saw Conor.

His arms folded around her. For long seconds they stood that way, while her heart raced so hard she could hear its pounding beat in her ears, and then Conor drew back just enough so he could look down into her face.

Something had damn near scared the life out of her.

A familiar rage rose inside him. If only she hadn't been so determined to blow him off. He'd have been here, watching over her . . .

Hell, who was he kidding? It was his fault, not hers. She'd tried to lose him but, in the end, it was he who'd lost her. First the rental car had broken down and then an army of taxis had flashed by, their drivers oblivious to his waving arms. When he'd reached the point of desperation, he'd stepped out in front of one, ordered its occupants out, flashed his ID at the driver as if this were the States and he had the right to commandeer a cab in the first place. Then he'd ordered the frightened driver to take him here, pronto.

By the time he'd finally reached the hotel, you couldn't have fit another person into the ballroom with a shoehorn but he'd forced his way into the mob and set out to locate Miranda.

Just when he'd decided she'd managed to give him the slip, he'd spotted Nita hanging on to some guy. There was no point in playing cat and mouse. Nita knew he was tailing Miranda; he'd even seen her watching him from the window tonight. So he'd clapped his hand on her shoulder, turned her towards him and asked, without any preliminaries, where in hell Miranda was spending the evening if not at this godforsaken party.

"Don't be silly, handsome," Nita had purred. "She's here."

"Where?" he'd growled, and Nita had given a throaty laugh and said why, the last she'd seen, Miranda had been right over there, in that corner.

He'd caught a quick glimpse, just enough to know Nita was pointing him in the right direction, and he'd set out towards her. But some jerk had blocked his view and his path and the next thing he'd known, Miranda had been clawing her way through the mob, her beautiful face white with fear, her eyes shining with it, and now she was here, in his arms, and dammit to hell, he would kill whatever son of a bitch it was who'd put that look of terror into her eyes.

"Conor," she whispered, "oh, Conor!"

He slid his arm around her shoulders and brought her close against his body.

"Let's get out of here," he said, and she nodded.

He led her to the door, shouldering his way through the mob, ignoring the protests of those he shoved out of his way. At last, they broke free and reached the comparative quiet of the lobby. He clasped her shoulders, his eyes hard and questioning as they locked on hers.

"What happened?"

She put her hand to her heart. She could feel its fluttering beat hammering beneath her fingers.

"There was a man."

"What man?"

She stared at him blankly, her eyes glassy. Conor's fingers bit into her flesh.

"Answer me, dammit!"

"A—a man came up to me."

"Who was it? Did you know him?"

"I met him last week. At—at the party Jean-Phillipe took me to." She shuddered and Conor drew her against him again, stroking her hair until he felt the tremors stop. "I was talking to someone, you see, and I was going crazy, trying to figure out a way to get rid of him, and . . ." She swallowed hard. "And this man suddenly came up to me. He said hello and I said hello, and then he acted as if we'd arranged to meet here."

"Had you?"

"No. I didn't even remember his name until he told it to me."

"What was it?"

"Moratelli. Vince Moratelli. He was very pleasant and he seemed to have figured out that I was trying to get away from this other person, so when he made it sound as if he'd been looking for me, I went along with it. He asked me if I'd like some champagne and I said I would and he took me over there and we started to talk and, oh God, Conor, he said—he said, did I like the little present he'd sent me?''

''What present? Miranda, you've got to . . .'' Conor's face went white. ''The picture?''

''Yes,'' she whispered. ''He asked me if—if it had excited me. He said he hoped it would, that he wanted me ready before he—before he—''

Her voice broke. Conor cursed and drew her close against him. He was offering comfort, but she could feel the anger vibrating through his body. When he finally pulled back and held her at arm's length, what she saw on his face was terrifying.

''What does he look like?''

''I don't remember.''

''Think, Miranda. What does Vince Moratelli look like?''

''He's tall,'' she said slowly, ''but not as tall as you. Five ten, five eleven, maybe. I'm not sure. Average build. Dark hair and eyes. A pleasant face, nothing unusual.''

''Stay here.''

''No!''

''I've got to find this bastard, Miranda.''

''You'll never find him,'' she said, her hand clutching his sleeve. ''Not in that mob. And I don't want to stay here by myself.''

He knew she was right. He'd never find the son of a bitch, not this way. How could you search for one man in a room packed with hundreds? Her description wasn't enough to go on and besides, she was right about something else, too. He couldn't leave her alone. He wouldn't, not for any reason.

''Conor?'' She looked up at him, and he had all he could do to keep from taking her in his arms. ''Please,'' she whispered, ''get me out of here''

He nodded. ''Where's your coat?''

''I checked it.'' She opened the silver purse and dug out the claims ticket. ''Here. It's black velvet, with a hood and a silver trim.''

''I know what it looks like.''

''You do?''

"I saw you and Nita going out tonight."

"Then, where . . ." She flushed. Where were you? she'd almost said, why did it take you so long to come to me?

"The damn car quit," he said, his eyes on hers. "And then I couldn't get a mothering taxi or I'd have been right behind you."

She tried to smile. "I'm just glad you showed up when you did."

Conor cleared his throat. "Okay," he said gruffly, "you wait right here."

"No."

"I'm just going to get your coat." He looked at her, saw the determined tilt to her chin, and gave up the fight. "Fine," he said, and held out his hand. "We'll get it together."

There was a line of taxis waiting outside the hotel but Miranda said she didn't want to go home and be alone, not just yet.

Conor started to reply but thought better of it. She wasn't going to be alone, not tonight, but there was no sense in telling her that and getting into a quarrel before she'd calmed down.

"Let's walk for a while," she said. "Okay?"

Hell, he'd have danced their way back, if she'd asked, anything to bring some color back to her face. He nodded, took her hand, and they started slowly towards the Place de l'Opéra.

"Why would that man have sent me that—that stuff anonymously and then go out of his way to identify himself?" she asked, after a while.

Because there's more to his plan. Because he got a kick out of seeing your terror.

"I don't know," Conor said.

"And why pick that party to tell me about it? I could have screamed."

He was willing to bet you'd be too stunned to say a word.

"Good point."

She looked up at him. "Maybe—maybe that's the end of it. Maybe that's all he wanted, to see my reaction."

No. Hell, no, this prick wants more than that.

"Maybe."

"He must have known I'd run away from him."

Conor could hear the rising hope in her voice and the desire to kill the son of a bitch who'd done this to her intensified because he knew, he *knew,* that this was just the beginning of whatever the guy was planning.

"I mean, if he'd really intended to—to do anything, he'd have chosen another place to confront me, wouldn't he?"

What was one more lie, if it calmed her? Conor squeezed her hand.

"Sure."

She sighed. "I just don't understand any of it. Why would someone do something so sick?"

At least, this time, he could give her a truthful answer.

"I don't know, but I'm sure as hell going to find out." She was trembling again, even though the night had turned soft and still, with the snow giving it a magical quality. Conor put his arm around her and drew her into his warmth. "I'll do some checking in the morning. Until then, I want you to put him out of your mind."

"Believe me, I'd like to, but I don't see how."

"Think about something else."

"What?" She gave a little laugh. "My brain feels like a hamster on one of those wheels. It just keeps chasing around and around and around."

"How long have you lived in Paris?"

"Come on, you know how long."

"Tell me."

Miranda sighed. "Eight years."

"Do you like living here?"

"Conor, I know what you're doing, you're trying to change the subject but it won't—"

"What's your favorite color?"

"Don't be silly."

"Red? I'll bet it's red. Bright, shiny red."

Miranda looked at him. "I hate red."

"Puce, then."

"Puce?" She smiled, just slightly, but it was an improvement. "I'll bet you don't even know what color puce is."

"You're right," he said solemnly, as they waited at the corner for the light to change to green. "To tell the truth, I don't want to know. Anything with a name like that can't be good."

"That's such a male attitude, O'Neil," she said, still smiling. "For your information, puce is just a shade of purple."

"Yuck."

"Yuck? Did you really say yuck?"

"It's better than admitting the truth."

"Which is?"

"I'm color-disadvantaged."

Miranda laughed. It was a soft, lovely sound and it made him smile just to hear it.

"What's that supposed to mean?"

"It's the politically correct way of saying I really don't give a damn for any color you can't find in a dollar box of Crayolas."

"Well, then," she said, "it's a good thing you decided to wear a tux tonight."

"I didn't think you'd noticed."

"I'd have noticed if you hadn't. After all, tuxedos were the uniform of the evening." *But not every man who'd been at the party had looked the way Conor did, in his tux. So handsome, so magnificently male.* A light rush of pink beat up into her cheeks and she moved, putting a little distance between them. "You were right," she said briskly. "I feel much better now."

"Good." His arm tightened around her, bringing her back where she belonged. "All you need now is something to eat."

"No. Oh, no. Thank you, but—"

Protest was useless. He was already leading her under a minuscule awning and through a doorway.

"Ah, Monsieur O'Neil, how good to see you again."

A round little man with a bristling mustache bustled up. Conor was known here; that was obvious. He rated everything but a kiss on each cheek which, Miranda thought with a smile, was probably a good thing.

The *bistro* was tiny, perhaps a dozen tables, all of them filled. The air was redolent with the earthy scent of garlic and good wine. Guitar music, bluesy and soft, drifted through the room. She knew in a heartbeat that the food, the service, and the ambience would all be wonderful.

Paris was crowded with little places like this; how could she have forgotten? The French took great joy in searching out the next candidate for a Michelin star. Once upon a time, she had, too.

It was one more thing that had changed about her, but when?

"Miranda?"

She looked up at Conor, who smiled.

"This is Maurice. He commands the best kitchen in all of Paris."

Maurice grinned. "Well, perhaps Taillevent is the best, *n'est-ce pas,* but who knows?" He took Miranda's hand and brought it to his lips. If her face was familiar, he didn't let on; he simply made some gallant, and Gallic, remark about her beauty before he led them down a narrow, twisting staircase which opened onto a handsome room with old brick walls and a scarred wooden floor. Small round tables, dressed in heavy white linen napery, bore centerpieces of flowers and candles. In a tucked-away corner, a man sat on a high stool, softly strumming a guitar.

"Everything's delicious," Conor said, as he and Miranda sat down at a table set for two. "The *pot au feu,* the *coq au vin,* the *saucisson* . . ." He smiled. "But if you want to win Maurice's heart, let him order for us."

"Really, I'm not terribly hungry."

"Tell that to Maurice."

Miranda looked at the little man standing beside the table, his face wreathed in lines of smiling anticipation, and she sighed.

"I'm in his hands," she said.

Conor grinned. "There's no safer place to be."

* * *

Maurice served their meal himself. Onion soup came first, covered with a thick cheese crust.

Miranda apologized again, as she picked up her spoon.

"I never eat much after seven in the evening," she said, "it's become habit, since I started modeling. It's bad for my weight."

"A couple of pounds more would do you good."

"The camera doesn't agree, but I'll try to eat a little of everything—to please Maurice."

Four courses later, as the busboy whisked away yet another empty plate, she sat back and groaned.

"I'll never forgive you for this, O'Neil. I have two showings tomorrow and I won't be able to fit into anything."

Conor's grin was smugly male. "Great stuff, huh?"

"Stuffed's what I am, right to the gills. I cannot believe I ate all that!"

"Maurice and I are proud of you."

"Tell that to the dressers tomorrow, when they're trying to shoehorn me into those size sixes."

"Exercise, that's what you need."

"Too late. Not even walking all the way home will help me now."

"A few turns around the dance floor might."

Miranda laughed. "What dance floor?"

"Well, there's a couple of feet of empty space right over there. See?"

Some of the tables had emptied and they'd been pushed against the wall, their chairs stacked on top of them. A handful of couples were swaying to the plaintive sigh of the guitar in the center of something only a philatelist would have called a dance floor.

Miranda looked at the dancers, at how close they were in each other's arms.

"No." She heard the sudden breathlessness in her voice, swallowed hard and forced herself to smile. "I mean, it's really getting terribly late. I have an early call in the morning and I can't afford to look tired."

"No excuses, Beckman," Conor said sternly. He took her hand and tugged her gently to her feet. "Have I mentioned the strain you're putting on the seams of that gown?"

She laughed. "That's not fair," she said, as she went into his arms—and in that heart-stopping moment, everything changed.

The postage-stamp bit of space that Conor had called a dance floor, the music, the soft clink of cutlery and glasses faded away. She felt as she had years before, when she'd been walking a craggy beach in Maine and a storm had swept in from the sea.

The air had thickened, and jagged fingers of lightning had sizzled against the rapidly darkening sky. The ocean, moments before a gentle swell of grey, had turned into a white-frothed behemoth that threatened to consume her. It had been a moment filled with heart-stopping danger. She'd known that she should run for safety, but what was safety, compared to the excitement and power of the storm?

Conor's arms tightened around her. He said her name and when she looked into his eyes, she knew that whatever was happening to her was happening to him, too.

Her pulse quickened. Run, she told herself, run and don't look back.

But she couldn't run. She couldn't move, except to slide her hands up Conor's chest and link them behind his neck.

One of his hands cupped her head, his fingers threading into her hair as he brought it to his chest, while the other slid down her back, hot against her naked skin, and drew her hips against his.

Miranda closed her eyes. She was adrift in sensation, the steady beat of Conor's heart, the silken brush of his fingers, the warmth of his breath against her temple.

It was as if they were alone in the universe, floating on the soft whisper of the guitar. Conor began moving, swaying to the magic of the music, and she melted into his embrace, every inch of her body sensitized to his. She sighed with pleasure and he drew her even closer, so that they were almost moving and breathing as one.

"Conor," she said unsteadily.

"Hush," he whispered, "it's all right, baby, I understand."

He couldn't. He didn't. There was no way he could understand because she didn't understand. Something was happening, and it was all wrong. Reality had been turned upside down.

She wasn't the one who should be breathing erratically, whose legs threatened to give way and whose heart was racing like a runaway train. That was supposed to be him. She was always in control with men. Always. That was the pleasure of it, the knowledge that she set the rules and the pace, that she had the power to turn it all off any time she wanted.

And she hadn't lost that power. Why would she? It was Conor's fault this was happening. She'd had a scare, he'd sensed her vulnerability and now he was making the most of it.

She stiffened and put her hands against his chest.

"That's enough," she said.

His hand closed over hers. "You know it isn't." His voice was soft, as warm and thick as honey. "Come back into my arms and let me hold you."

She wanted to, oh yes, she wanted to . . .

"No," she said sharply.

"Baby—"

"I'm not your baby. I'm not your anything. You're here at Eva's request and on my sufferance, and you'd better not forget it."

She saw the stunned look on his face, then the flash of something, anger, maybe even hurt, in his eyes.

She spun away from him, moving quickly, snatching up her coat and flying up the stairs, through the restaurant and out the door.

Conor caught up to her at the curb, just as she was hailing a cab, and swung her towards him. The smokiness was gone from his eyes. Now, they blazed with tightly repressed anger.

"What the hell is the matter with you?"

"Let go of my arm, please."

A muscle flexed in his jaw. He reached past her and yanked open the taxi door.

"Get in," he growled, and when she didn't move fast enough, he propelled her inside the cab. Then he climbed in after her and gave the driver her address.

She expected—what? Anger? Recriminations? A speech? But they made the ride to her apartment in silence. The taxi pulled up outside the gated courtyard and she flung open the door and got out.

Conor was right behind her.

"Keys," he said, and held out his hand.

She opened her mouth to protest, but decided against it. Arguing with him was useless, and she knew it. Besides, the thought of crossing the dark courtyard alone tonight wasn't pleasant. Eva was undoubtedly paying him well for his time. He might as well do his job.

She handed the keys to him, waited while he paid the driver. He reached for her arm but she shrugged off his hand.

"Have it your way," he muttered, and they marched through the gate, then through the heavy front door and to Madame Delain's vacant desk. Miranda turned around.

"Thank you for the guard service." Her tone was polite but removed. "I'll switch the light on and off in the living room, the way I did last night."

Conor yanked open the elevator door and pushed her inside. "Last night," he said grimly, "you hadn't had your little chat with Vince Moratelli."

Her skin prickled as she remembered the threat. The elevator lurched to life, rose slowly, then groaned to a stop.

"Out," Conor growled and she obeyed. He unlocked the door to her apartment. When it swung open, she held out her hand for her key.

"Good night, O'Neil."

He took her arm, prodded her inside, then closed and locked the door. Miranda's stomach lurched, with a combination of fear and something else.

"What do you think you're doing?"

"What does it look like I'm doing?" He tossed her keys on the table, unbuttoned the jacket of his tuxedo and slipped it off.

Mia came hurrying into the foyer, meowing plaintively, and wound around Miranda's ankles. She bent down, scooped the cat into her arms and faced Conor with defiant calm.

"If you think that little dance rates you a berth for the night, think again."

"Sorry, Beckman. I know it'll disappoint you to hear this, but I'm just not into babes who get their kicks out of games like yours." He took the studs out of his cuffs, dropped them beside the keys, and rolled up his sleeves. "I'm staying the night, but it's strictly business."

"You are not staying the night!"

"Is that sofa as uncomfortable as it looks?"

"Maybe you didn't hear what I said. You are not . . . Where are you going?"

"I'm going to get myself a blanket and a pillow. Is that a linen closet?"

"Damn you, O'Neil!"

"Don't argue with me, Beckman." He turned and looked at her, and her breath caught at what she saw in his eyes. "If we play any more games tonight, we'll play them by my rules."

Color washed into her face. She put down the Siamese, marched past him, pulled open the door to the linen closet and hurled a blanket, pillow and bedding in his direction.

"Ever the gracious hostess," he said wryly.

"Ever the unwanted guest. Just so you know, the sofa sags and your feet are going to hang off the end. Oh, and the temperature in the living room bottoms out sometime around dawn."

"Thanks for the warning."

"Warning?" She folded her arms and flashed a smile that reminded him that the cat at her feet wasn't the only creature here with sharp claws. "I'm simply making sure you know in advance that you're in for a long and miserable night. Which reminds me . . . if I even think I hear you outside my bedroom door, I'll scream the house down.''

''I told you, Beckman, you're not my type.'' Conor gave her a chilly smile across the armful of bedding. ''But for the record, the only screaming my women do is when they beg for more.''

''In your dreams, O'Neil.''

She could still hear the sound of his soft laughter after she'd stalked into her bedroom and slammed the door behind her.

Chapter Eleven

Conor lay on the too-narrow, too-short, lumpy-as-cold-oatmeal sofa, glowering into the darkness.

He'd certainly made an ass of himself tonight.

His scowl deepened.

The truth was, he'd been working overtime at making an ass out of himself ever since his size elevens had touched down on the soil of *la belle France.*

What was it about Miranda Beckman that turned him into such a jerk? He'd made enough mistakes in his personal life to fill a bank vault but one thing had always been certain: he was good at his job. He had been, from the day he'd walked away from his father, trading the old man's iron-fisted, because-I-said-so version of law and order for the clearly defined rules of first the army and then the Committee.

You had an assignment, you did it. And by the book. No bull, no second-guessing, no useless expending of emotional energy. You went in, you did what you were supposed to do, and you got out. You didn't get involved.

So what in hell had he been doing, coming on to Miranda?

"Making an ass of yourself, O'Neil," he muttered, "that's what."

He rolled onto his back, almost tumbling off the damn sofa in the process, and linked his hands beneath his head.

Every instinct he possessed told him it was time to terminate this assignment. Telephone Harry, bring him up to date on the stuff that had been tucked under Miranda's door—and then make it clear he was coming home.

He'd done the preliminaries. Let somebody else take it from here.

It was just that he'd never walked out in the middle of an assignment before.

Give it a break, O'Neil.

This wasn't the Boy Scouts. He wasn't going to earn a merit badge for hanging in. He wanted out, and out he'd go.

"Mrrow?"

A hot, furry weight, its paws tipped with what felt like a hundred razor-sharp talons, landed on his chest. Conor shot upright, dumping the Siamese into his lap.

"God almighty, cat," he said, "you like to live dangerously."

What was the animal doing here, anyway? He'd have figured Miranda would have kept it in the bedroom with her, and the bedroom door would sure as hell be locked tighter than a nun's knees.

"Don't get yourself comfortable," he said to the cat, but it was too late. Mia had already settled in on his lap, purring like a demented motorboat.

Conor sighed. Why not? One of them might as well get some rest. He certainly wasn't going to, not on a sofa where he had a choice between letting his legs hang over the arm or tucking his knees under his chin. It was cold as Siberia in here, too. Miranda had said the temperature would drop off at dawn but it was only . . . He squinted at his watch. It was only 3:05 and he was already raising a crop of goose bumps. It didn't help that he'd stripped off his shirt and pants before trying to fit himself onto a piece of furniture designed for midgets but then again, his charming hostess could have managed to provide him with more than one blanket.

Another couple of hours, he'd be frozen so stiff they'd have to chip him out of the ice before hauling him to a chiropractor.

What was the cat doing here, anyway?

Conor tucked his chin in and glared down at Mia.

"What are you doing here, cat?" he said.

The cat didn't answer. It was falling asleep while he froze to death.

Enough was enough.

"Alley-oop," Conor muttered.

He scooped Mia out of his lap and deposited her on the sofa. The Siamese shot him a malevolent look from a pair of satanic red eyes and made a sound midway between a purr and a growl.

"Yeah? Well, the same to you."

Damn, it was cold! Conor felt around for his shirt, couldn't find it, and gave up looking. He knew where the linen closet was, at least. There had to be a couple of more blankets on the shelves.

The old floorboards creaked lightly under his bare feet as he made his way into the foyer and down the hall. Halfway there, Mia decided to come after him and do an allemande-left-and-right through his ankles.

"Dammit," he hissed, and scooped the animal into his arms. The cat purred, butted his chin with her wedge-shaped head and settled in like a baby with her butt in the crook of his arm and her front paws dangling over his shoulder. "Cute," he muttered, "but it won't work with me. I'm not as easy a mark as the lady who owns you."

The cat purred harder and licked his chin with a tongue that felt like sandpaper.

"Okay, okay, we'll go find the blankets together. How's that sound?"

Absently, he stroked his hand down the animal's fur. It was soft as velvet and cool to the touch, though the little body pressed to his was warm. The cat was like Miranda, cold on the outside but with a core of simmering heat deep inside, its beauty a disguise that concealed claws that could gut a man with a swipe—if a man was stupid enough to let it happen.

Frowning, Conor put the Siamese down, determinedly ignoring its soft cries of protest. The linen closet had to be just about here. Yes, there it was. Just turn the knob, nice and easy, slide the door open . . .

Mia made a sound that would have awakened the dead.

"Cat," Conor muttered, "so help me, if you wake that woman up, I'll turn you into a fur piece. The last thing I need is another verbal go-round with . . ."

What in hell was that?

A sound. Not an animal sound but one that made the hair rise on the nape of his neck. He froze, waiting for it to be repeated, wishing he weren't standing here like an idiot in nothing but a pair of boxer shorts.

The sound came again and now he recognized it.

It was the sound of a woman, softly weeping.

He looked down the hall, to where a faint light seeped from under the closed bedroom door.

So what? Miranda was crying. It wasn't his problem. He was here to make sure nobody tried to pay her a nighttime visit, not to worry about . . .

Could somebody have slipped past him? Was that why she was crying, because there was someone in that room with her? Conor stiffened. It didn't seem possible but he'd lived long enough to know that impossible things happened with amazing frequency.

Moving cautiously now, holding his breath, he made his way forward. He could see that the bedroom door was ajar as soon as he reached it. It was open just enough for the cat to have slipped out.

Had it been open all along, or had it been opened by an intruder?

Conor put his hand on the door, eased it open.

A night lamp glowed in the corner, casting shadows along the walls. By its faint light, he could see that there was no one in the room, except for Miranda. She was lying in the center of the bed, on her back, with the blankets pulled up to her chin.

Beckman, the night lamp type? Even after what she'd endured the last few days, it surprised him.

"Miranda?" he whispered. There was no answer. Conor hesitated. Then he took a couple of steps forward. "Hey," he said, "Beckman?"

She murmured something and rolled onto her side. The crying turned into soft, sad whimpers.

She was dreaming, that was all. There was no intruder and he had no further business here. Miranda's nightmares were her affair, not his—but he'd had enough bad dreams to know what it was like to fight demons in the dark. What the hell, it wouldn't take anything from him to wake her.

"Wake up, Beckman," he said briskly, as he strode to the bed. "Come on, open your eyes."

Miranda moaned. She thrashed onto her back and flung her arms over her head. She was wearing some kind of old-fashioned granny gown, flannel, maybe, with little sprigs of pink roses all over it. Her hair was loose and ebony-dark against the high collar of the gown; her face was painfully pale. Tears glittered in her dark lashes.

What could make a woman cry so deeply, in a dream?

She moaned, and a deep furrow appeared between her brows.

"Beckman?" Conor sat down on the edge of the bed. "Miranda," he said, and gently clasped her shoulders, "come on, wake up."

"Nooo!" Her scream filled the room. Her eyes flew open and she stared at him through blind, terror-filled eyes. "Don't, oh please, don't, don't, don't . . ."

"Miranda." Conor lifted her towards him, his hands and voice firm. "Wake up! Do you hear me? You're dreaming."

Ever so slowly, the fear receded from her eyes and was replaced by the light of reason.

"Conor?"

Here it comes, he thought, a speech about the sanctity of a

closed bedroom door or maybe even a right cross, straight to the jaw.

"Conor," she said again, and before he could say a word, explain that she'd been dreaming, that he'd only come into her room to wake her, she launched herself at him, not to slug him but to wrap her arms around him, bury her damp face against his bare skin and weep.

His spine became rigid as a steel bar. Don't, he told himself, O'Neil, you damn fool, don't . . .

A groan burst from his throat and his arms closed tightly around her.

"It's all right," he whispered, "it's all right."

She held on, just as she had the other night, trembling in his arms as if he were all that stood between her and the hounds of hell.

"Conor," she said again, and her teeth chattered, "oh God, Conor."

"What?" She was cold, so cold. Her skin was icy to the touch. "What, baby?" he whispered, holding her close, letting his warmth penetrate the chill that he suspected had penetrated to the marrow of her bones. "What did you dream?"

"I dreamed—I dreamed . . ." The deep, rasping breath she took tore at his heart. She shook her head, so that her tousled hair moved like silk against his cheek. "I had a nightmare." She shuddered. "It was horrible."

Horrible was probably an understatement. No surprises there. She'd gone through hell the past couple of days and what had he done tonight but add to it by being so hard on her, saying ugly things he hadn't really meant.

"Hold me," she said, "just for a little while."

Don't do it, the voice inside him said again. Tell her you'll get her some warm milk. Some tea. Tell her anything but don't be a fool, O'Neil. The last thing you want to do is sit here in the middle of the night with Miranda in your arms.

"Hush," he said, and drew her even closer.

He stroked her hair and her back. He rocked her gently in

his arms. He whispered softly to her and finally, she stopped trembling.

"Better?" he said.

She nodded.

God, she felt so good in his arms. Another couple of minutes, she'd be okay. He'd hold her a little bit longer, for her sake, not his, just to make sure she was really over the dream. Conor closed his eyes and laid his cheek against her hair. The flower-like, feminine smell of her was dazzling.

"You okay?" he whispered.

She gave a deep, shuddering sigh. "Yes."

"Can I get you anything?"

She shook her head. "No."

"Warm milk? A drink of water?"

She shook her head again. "No," she whispered, but she made no effort to move out of his arms.

Why would she, when she felt so safe? When Conor's skin was so hot against hers? He was shirtless; she hadn't realized that, not at first, but now that the dream was mercifully fading, she was becoming aware of everything about him. The strength of his arms, holding her. The heat of his skin, and the soft tickle of the hair on his chest against her cheek. The scent of him, warm and male and clean.

"Miranda?" he said, and she heard the huskiness in his voice and for the first time in more years than seemed humanly possible, she felt a sudden fluidity in her bones.

Her heart thudded. Nothing more had to happen. She could stop now, before it was too late.

Instead, she lifted her face to his.

"Conor," she said unsteadily, and it was all he needed her to say.

It was all there, in her eyes, desire and surrender and a slow-burning passion that needed only his kiss to set it blazing. A saint might have resisted, but Conor had never made any pretense to sainthood. He was a man, with all a man's desires, and the woman in his arms had been in his thoughts for what might have been forever.

He said her name again, bent his head kissed her. Her lips parted beneath his, and they fell back against the pillows.

God, how sweet she tasted. Her kiss whispered of flower-filled meadows and summer breezes, of moon-washed nights and boyhood dreams lost in the harsh reality of manhood.

Slowly, he told himself, there's all the time in the world.

He slid his hands into her hair, cupping her face, holding her a willing prisoner under the plunder of his mouth, while an electric pleasure sizzled through his blood. His thumbs followed the arcs of her cheekbones, then glided the length of her throat to rest for a heartbeat in the shadowed hollow. His mouth took the path his hands had taken; he pressed his lips to where her pulse raced beneath her skin and he felt her tremble beneath his kiss.

"Conor," she whispered, "I'm not . . ."

"Hush," he said, and slid his tongue between her lips.

She made a soft little sound in the back of her throat and her hands fisted in his hair, tugging him down to her, deepening the intensity of his kiss. The tip of her tongue curled against his in a sweet, silken caress. The feel of it made his blood leap. There had been so many women. A lifetime of women—and never a moment like this.

He drew back, holding her to him, and traced the features of her face with a fingertip.

"You are so beautiful," he whispered.

She smiled and set her hand over his where it rested against her cheek. Men had told her how beautiful she was for years but, deep in her soul, she could never bring herself to believe them, especially not when she saw her own face staring back at her from the newsstands. Her face was like an artist's canvas, her image upon it sketched by paints and pencils.

Besides, how could someone like her be beautiful?

But there was something in the way Conor said the words that made them real. She wanted to tell him so, but he was touching her now, his hand moving over her body, cupping her breasts through the flannel of her nightgown, tracing the line of her hip and thigh. His touch was soft, butterfly light, but the heat of his fingers burned through to the marrow of her bones.

His hand slid under the gown. She gasped as he stroked her ankle, her calf; his fingers moved up and up, along the warm, silken flesh, then whispered across the soft curls that covered the delta between her thighs.

Miranda cried out his name and arched like a bow in his arms. He rolled her beneath him and his fingers went to the buttons at her throat.

The buttons were so small, his hands so clumsy. They trembled as he slowly bared her skin to the cool night air, and, at last, to the adoration of his touch.

She gave a keening moan as he bent his head and kissed her, nuzzling the gown away from her throat. His kisses burned against her flesh; his teeth nipped her skin and left the sweetest of wounds.

''Conor,'' she said, sighing his name on one long exhalation of pleasure. She reached up to him and he turned his head and kissed her palms, first one and then the other.

''Look at you,'' he said softly, as he drew the gown from her shoulders, ''ah, sweetheart, look at how perfect you are.''

''I'm not,'' she said quickly, ''not perfect, Conor, never perf . . .''

His kiss silenced her. Her head fell back and his lips moved down her throat, to the curve of her breast.

''Perfect,'' he whispered, his mouth against her skin, ''and so sweet.''

Gently, he eased the gown from her body. And she, who had so often shed her clothing in full view of half a dozen people, felt a flush of embarrassment creep along her skin. Instinctively, she reached for the gown and tried to pull it around her, but he wouldn't let her. He caught her wrists and held them at her sides.

''You can't hide from me any longer,'' he said softly.

It was a lover's whisper, nothing more. She knew he had no way of knowing what far deeper meaning those words held.

Miranda took a deep, unsteady breath. "There's so much you don't understand."

"I understand this," he said, bending to her and kissing her mouth. His head dipped lower; she felt the warmth of his breath against her breast. "And this."

His lips closed around her nipple and she was undone. Something gave way, at last, deep within her. He was right; she couldn't hide, didn't want to hide. Not from him.

"Yes," she said, "Conor, yes, yes . . ."

He touched her, kissed her everywhere, his lips warm against her skin. He moved down the bed, took her foot gently in his hand and kissed her instep and then her ankle; he licked the soft skin behind her knee. She made incoherent little sounds as he moved up the length of her body, his middle-of-the-night beard rough and exciting against the tender flesh of her thighs, and then his mouth was at the center of her and she dug her hands into his hair and writhed against the hot pleasure of his tongue and his lips.

"Please," she said brokenly, "oh please . . ."

Conor drew back and tore off his shorts and then he was kneeling between her thighs, kissing her, whispering to her. Her arms tightened around him; she drew him down to her so that her skin burned against his, matching him kiss for kiss, her hands moving over him in a frenzy, learning the straightness of his spine, the faint indentation at its base. Miranda was moaning, making sounds of need and desire that were rocketing him ever faster towards the zenith of pleasure that awaited him.

Slow down, man, he told himself, slow down.

But he couldn't. He couldn't. He was desperate to be inside her. With a groan of desperation, he slid his hands under her hips, lifted her to him . . . and held back, torturing them both, slipping just the tip of his penis into her silken heat.

"Conor," she sobbed, "Conor . . ."

Oh God, she was coming apart! Something was giving way deep inside her. It was a terrifying feeling, like standing on the highest level of the Eiffel Tower with the wind rushing through your hair and all of Paris spread out beneath you and letting yourself wonder what would happen if you just stepped out into space.

Frantic with sudden fear, she shoved against Conor's chest. "No," she said, "no, I can't!"

He moved, plunging into her deep and hard, and she climaxed instantly, her body contracting around him as a wild cry burst from her throat. Her nails raked his back; she sobbed his name and his mouth dropped to hers and he kissed her, knowing even as he did that he had to be hurting her, that he could taste the tang of blood on his tongue but God, he couldn't stop, couldn't pull back, and now he was coming, coming, he was going to break apart and lose himself forever.

Conor threw back his head and gave himself up to the whirlwind.

He fell asleep, holding her in his arms. And for one long, breathless moment, Miranda drifted, suspended in space.

And then Mia meowed, someplace in the darkness of the apartment, and reality returned.

Conor's arms were warm, but the room was cold. The blankets had fallen to the foot of the bed, and the chill of the night raised goose bumps on her skin. The sheet beneath her was cold and wet; there was an unpleasant stickiness on her thighs.

Carefully, she moved away from Conor, rolled to the side of the bed and sat up. Her discarded nightgown lay on the floor beside the bed. She reached for it and pulled it on, then made her way into the bathroom, shut the door and turned on the light.

A stranger with tousled hair, wide eyes and a swollen mouth stared at her from the mirror. Her hand shook as she lifted it and touched her throat. There was a tiny bruise there, made by Conor's teeth.

She closed her eyes and tried to call back what she'd felt in his arms, the sense of belonging, of fulfillment—even of love.

Her eyes opened and she looked at herself again.

Lies, all of it.

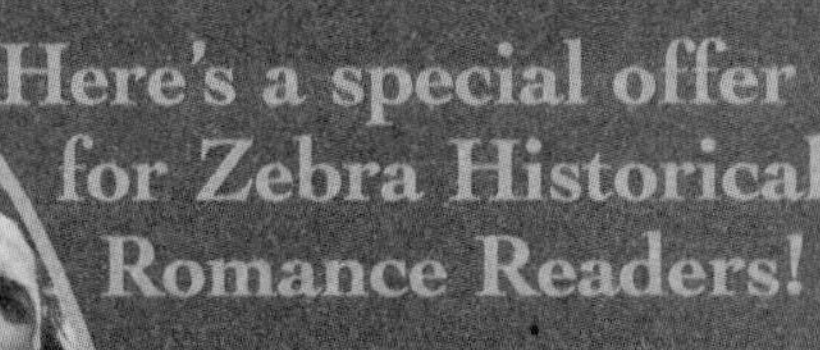

Here's a special offer for Zebra Historical Romance Readers!

GET 4 FREE HISTORICAL ROMANCE NOVELS

A $19.96 Value!

Passion, adventure and hours of pleasure delivered right to your doorstep!

HERE'S A SPECIAL INVITATION TO ENJOY TODAY'S FINEST HISTORICAL ROMANCES— ABSOLUTELY FREE! *(a $19.96 value)*

Now you can enjoy the latest Zebra Lovegram Historical Romances without even leaving your home with our convenient Zebra Home Subscription Service. Zebra Home Subscription Service offers you the following benefits that you don't want to miss:

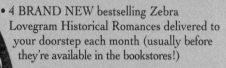

- 4 BRAND NEW bestselling Zebra Lovegram Historical Romances delivered to your doorstep each month (usually before they're available in the bookstores!)
- 20% off each title or a savings of almost $4.00 each month
- FREE home delivery
- A FREE monthly newsletter, *Zebra/Pinnacle Romance News* that features author profiles, contests, special member benefits, book previews and more
- No risks or obligations...in other words you can cancel whenever you wish with no questions asked

So join hundreds of thousands of readers who already belong to Zebra Home Subscription Service and enjoy the very best Historical Romances That Burn With The Fire of History!

And remember....there is no minimum purchase required. After you've enjoyed your initial FREE package of 4 books, you'll begin to receive monthly shipments of new Zebra titles. Each shipment will be yours to examine for 10 days and then if you decide to keep the books, you'll pay the preferred subscriber's price of just $4.00 per title. That's $16 for all 4 books with FREE home delivery! And if you want us to stop sending books, just say the word....it's that simple.

It's a no-lose proposition, so send for your 4 FREE books today!

4 FREE BOOKS

These books worth almost $20, are yours without cost or obligation when you fill out and mail this certificate.

(If the certificate is missing below, write to: Zebra Home Subscription Service, Inc., 120 Brighton Road, P.O. Box 5214, Clifton, New Jersey 07015-5214)

Complete and mail this card to receive 4 Free books!

YES! Please send me 4 Zebra Lovegram Historical Romances without cost or obligation. I understand that each month thereafter I will be able to preview 4 new Zebra Lovegram Historical Romances FREE for 10 days. Then if I decide to keep them, I will pay the money-saving preferred publisher's price of just $4.00 each...a total of $16. That's almost $4 less than the regular publisher's price, and there is never any additional charge for shipping and handling. I may return any shipment within 10 days and owe nothing, and I may cancel this subscription at any time. The 4 FREE books will be mine to keep in any case.

Name ______________________________

Address ______________________ Apt. ________

City ________________ State ________ Zip ________

Telephone ( ) ______________________

Signature ______________________

(If under 18, parent or guardian must sign.)

LF0397

Terms, offer and prices subject to change without notice. Subscription subject to acceptance by Zebra Home Subscription Service, Inc.. Zebra Home Subscription Service, Inc. reserves the right to reject any order or cancel any subscription.

4 BOOKS FREE!

A $19.96 value.... absolutely FREE with no obligation to buy anything, ever!

AFFIX
STAMP
HERE

ZEBRA HOME SUBSCRIPTION SERVICE, INC.
120 BRIGHTON ROAD
P.O. BOX 5214
CLIFTON, NEW JERSEY 07015-5214

Her mouth tightened, and she clutched the edge of the sink.

She had let it happen but it was his fault. It was all his fault.

Everything had been so simple until the day he'd shown up at the Louvre. She had her career, she had friends. Things had been in perfect balance.

And Conor had ruined it.

Conor, bought and paid for by Eva, sent to solve Eva's problems, to do Eva's bidding.

If he destroyed her, and the life she'd created in the process, so what?

Miranda shuddered. And if he could get laid while he did it, so much the better.

Except, it had been more than that. *He'd* been more than that. He'd been passionate and tender, and in his arms, she'd almost become someone else . . .

"Miranda?"

She whirled around, her heart banging in her chest.

"Baby?" The door knob rattled. "Are you all right?"

Easy, Miranda. Take a deep breath. Good. That's the ticket.

She stole another glance at the mirror. Then she ran her fingers through her hair, smoothing it back from her face; she licked her lips, sent her thoughts into the same cool, blank place that was always her refuge just before she went on the catwalk, and opened the door.

"Sorry," she said pleasantly. "Did you want the bathroom?"

Conor smiled at her. He hadn't bothered to hide his nudity. God, he was so—so disgustingly male, so patently sure she'd give him what he wanted.

She could. Oh, she could. She could go to him, clasp his face between her hands, press her mouth to his . . .

And then he smiled, a sexy little lift of the mouth that told her exactly what he was thinking.

"I don't want the bathroom," he said. He held out his hand. "I want you."

Miranda smiled, too, the way she'd learned to do years before she'd needed that mysterious curve of the lips for the crowds or the photographers.

"I'm going to take a shower."

His smile grew even sexier. "Later, baby. We'll shower together."

"Conor, I've asked you before, don't call me baby. I don't like it."

She could see that it was an effort for him to hold his smile but she had to give him credit; he was managing.

"Okay, if it really bothers you. Now, come back to bed."

"I told you, I'm going to take a shower." She reached into the tub and turned on the spray. "That was fun, I have to admit, and probably just what I needed."

"Just what you needed?" he said, and there was a dangerous undercurrent in his tone.

"Well, you know, to get a good night's sleep." She flashed the smile again. "But I never vary the ground rules."

He was looking at her as if she were something nasty that had just crept in out of the night. A sharp pain lanced through her—but then she thought of Eva, and Hoyt, and Edouard, and the pain faded to a dull ache.

"What ground rules?" he said, through his teeth.

"Well, there's only one, really." *Another deep breath, Miranda, and then spit it out.* "No matter how terrific the fuck, I never let a man spend the night in my bed."

His face paled; every bone seemed to stand out so that his blue eyes burned like fire. She thought of the time Jean-Phillipe had convinced her to fly to Vegas with him to see a much-lauded championship boxing match. She'd hated it, the blood and the sweat and the knowledge that a human being should want to pound at another like the most primitive of animals, and Jean-Phillipe had laughed at her.

"Ah, *chérie,*" he'd said, "you do not comprehend the needs of the male animal."

Well, she comprehended those needs now. Conor's eyes glittered with the hunger to beat her senseless.

"Is that what I was?" he said in an ominously soft voice, "A good fuck?"

"You do understand that I meant it as a compliment," she said in her kindest tone.

"Oh, yeah." He smiled tightly. "Yeah, I understand. And I guess it really is a compliment, coming from a connoisseur, like you."

The words were blows that hammered at her soul, but she knew better than to let the pain show.

"There's no need to get nasty, Conor. I'm sorry if you've got some kind of old-fashioned sentimentality about sex, but—"

"Hey," he said, and now his smile was swift and very wolf-like, "trust me, lady. I've got no sentimentality about anything. I just figured, what the hell, this was fun for the both of us, so—"

"So, why not do it again?" Miranda sighed and shook her head. "A lovely thought but I'm afraid I've got a shoot in the morning. The camera picks up every under-eye shadow." She smiled, reached out and gently patted his cheek. "You know how it is."

Conor's fingers closed, hard, around her wrist, and he pushed her hand away.

"Oh yeah," he said softly, "I know exactly how it is. You have an itch, you scratch it. That's the story of your life, isn't that right, Beckman?"

He didn't wait for her to answer, which was good because she wasn't sure she could have managed to come up with one, not while her throat was constricting.

With studied nonchalance, he sauntered back into the bedroom and collected his clothes. She waited until he'd strolled into the hallway and shut the door behind him; then she stepped into the shower, turned the faucet to hot and grabbed the soap.

How long would she have to scrub, before she felt clean again?

It was bitter cold, and the streets were deserted.

Conor blew on his hands and stamped his feet as he stood

in the phone booth at the corner and waited for his call to go through.

"Come on, Harry," he muttered, "what the hell's taking so long?"

It was, what, almost midnight in the States. Thurston had to be home; he had to hear his damn telephone ringing.

"Hello?"

"It's me, Harry."

"Conor, where in blazes are you? I've been trying your hotel for hours."

"Yeah, well, I wasn't there."

"Do tell. Listen, my boy—"

"No, Harry, old pal, *you* listen. I'm out of here."

"I beg your pardon?"

A truck rumbled by. Conor waited until he saw it turn the corner before he spoke again.

"I said, I'm signing off the Winthrop thing."

"Conor, don't be hasty."

"Hasty, my ass. I'm done. Finished. I'm out of here. I'm coming back to the good old U.S. of A., pronto."

"What's happened?"

"Nothing's happened. Enough is enough, that's all."

"But why?"

"Don't push it, Harry."

"Conor," Harry said, his voice growing soft and persuasive, "I can tell you're upset."

"I'm not upset. And don't bother trying to sweet-talk me. Just find yourself another patsy."

Harry's sigh wheezed over the satellite connection as clearly as if he were in the next room.

"Simmer down, my boy, simmer down. You've never been a patsy, you're the Committee's main man, doing a vital job."

"That's a wonderful line, Harry. Did you lift it from an employee motivational seminar or did it just spring into your head?"

"Conor." Thurston's voice was filled with distress. If Conor hadn't known him better, he might have believed it was real. "What have I done to deserve such a display of animosity?"

"It's not animosity. And you haven't done a thing—except ask me to play at being a bodyguard to a woman who doesn't want one."

"You're not playing at any such thing. You're conducting an investigation."

"I'm stumbling around on foreign soil with about as much clout as an ant at an aardvark's picnic."

Thurston chuckled. "What a charming picture."

"Well, it's a charming situation, which is why I'm dealing myself out."

"Difficult cases were always your specialty."

"You're wasting your time. Flattery won't get you anywhere."

"I just don't understand the problem. You say you're on foreign soil without any clear authority but let's be honest; that never stopped you in the past."

"Harry, you're not listening."

"And it isn't as if you've never offered protection to a client before."

"No, it isn't. But our client is Eva Winthrop, not her daughter. And I didn't come over here to offer protection to anybody,remember? I came to get facts."

"This just doesn't sound like you, Conor."

"You know what they say, Harry. The times, they are a-changin'."

"Is that a quotation from some modern French philosopher? I'm afraid I'm not familiar with it."

"Listen, just so you know I'm not being unreasonable about this, I'll give you a couple of days to line up somebody else to take over."

"Suppose you update me. What's the latest situation there?"

The latest situation? Hell, I slept with Miranda Beckman and got exactly what I deserved.

Conor sighed and pinched the bridge of his nose between the thumb and forefinger of his left hand.

"I'll e-mail you as soon as I get back to my hotel."

"You know how I feel about computers. Humor me. Bring me up to date the old-fashioned way. The Beckman girl's apartment was rifled but I take it there's been more."

"There's been more, all right. Somebody slipped a little gift under her door. His name is Moratelli. Vince Moratelli."

"An Italian?"

"An American, I think. Run his name, see what you can find."

"What was the gift this Moratelli sent Miss Beckman?"

Conor hesitated. All he had to do was shut his eyes and he knew he'd be able to see the ugly piece of garbage that had been inside that envelope.

"A picture. And a note. I'll run them over to the embassy and put them in the diplomatic pouch."

"Fine."

"Test for the usual stuff. Prints, ink, paper, and blood."

"Blood?"

"Animal, probably. Look, I'd rather not describe this over the phone. I'll ask the embassy to put it through ASAP."

"Was the note like the one sent to Eva?"

"Not the message, but yes, the paper and ink look like a match."

Harry made a humming sound. Long experience told Conor what was happening. Thurston would have turned his gaze to the ceiling. There'd be a seemingly casual expression on his face. It was all deception. Thurston was about as casual as a fox assessing a hen-house. Something was clicking away in his brain and when he was good and ready, he'd spring it.

"You said you were going to interview Miss Beckman's former husband and his cousin. Have you done so?"

Conor sighed. "Look, I am standing out here in the cold, freezing my tail off. What about saving the debriefing until I'm back in D.C.?"

"I take it you spoke with them."

"Dammit, Harry! Yes, I did."

"Could either one be responsible for these events?"

''It's possible, but I've got my doubts.''

''Which are?''

''The ex is a slime ball, but why would he pull crap like this?''

''Blackmail?''

''I doubt it. He seems to have plenty of money. Besides, he's not a fool. He knows that even if his marriage to the girl isn't exactly public knowledge, it's not the sort of secret that's worth a lot of dough.''

''Are you sure? Hoyt is up for that appointment, after all.''

''So what? We're talking about old news, Harry. Very old news. Besides, turn on Oprah or a dozen other talk shows and you'll see people sitting around discussing things you and I would probably sooner die than admit to a priest.''

''Well, perhaps the gentleman hasn't figured that out.''

''He's been around. He knows there's nothing in the story.''

''What about his cousin?''

''She says she's got money. I'll check it out—I mean, whoever you hand this over to should check it out, but I'd rule out blackmail. On the other hand, she hates Miranda. Eva, too. Maybe she's just been looking for the chance to put in the knife.''

''Who else was on your list?''

Conor's stomach roiled. ''Jean-Phillipe Moreau. Miranda's lover.''

''Have you spoken with him?''

''No. That'll be something else for the new guy to deal with.''

''Anybody else who might want to hurt the girl?''

Yes, Conor thought coldly, me.

''Nobody I can come up with. Listen, Harry, it's late and I'm bushed. I'll phone you when I hit D.C.''

''I was your idea to go to Paris, Conor.''

''I know that.''

''And now, you want me to hand this off to someone else?''

Conor's mouth narrowed. ''That's right.''

''I've never known you to leave an assignment unfinished,

my boy. You admit, you've yet to question Moreau or to check Amalie de Lasserre's motives more deeply, and you've asked me to check out one Vincent Moratelli."

"Isn't it good to know that I'm leaving something for the next guy to do? Listen, I didn't phone to ask permission, I phoned to tell you I was signing off."

"May I ask the reason?"

"I told you, I don't like playing bodyguard, especially where I've got no authority."

"Foreign soil, and all that."

"Now you've got it."

"Well, I can't disagree with you, Conor. It's just that the second note puts a new twist on things."

"Not in any ways that affect me."

"I'm not talking about the note Miss Beckman received." Thurston paused, long enough to highlight the drama of the moment. "A second note was delivered to Eva, just today."

"I still don't see how that changes things," Conor said, but a warning buzz was already tingling down his spine.

"The note was on the same paper as before. Same ink, looks to be the same handwriting."

"I still don't see—"

"It was written in French and it says . . ." Conor could hear the faint rustle of paper. "It says, and I know you'll forgive my accent . . ."

"Just read the damned note, Harry, okay?"

"It says, *C'est de la foutaise, ta fille. C'est une allumeuse et bientôt, elle sera morte.*"

Conor felt his heart begin to swell, until it seemed lodged in the middle of his throat.

"I suppose you had that translated?"

"Please, credit me with some competence. Of course I had it translated. It means . . ." Again, there was the rustle of paper. "It means, 'Your daughter is garbage. She is . . .'" Harry cleared his throat. "'She is a cock-teaser and soon, she will be dead.'" Silence hummed along the line and then he cleared his throat again. "So, what do you think?"

Conor closed his eyes. Thurston, the son of a bitch, knew exactly what he thought.

The notes to Eva, the vile message sent to Miranda and the trashing of her bedroom, were definitely connected. To hell with Hoyt's appointment; that wasn't the issue here. What was happening was about Miranda and had been, right from the start.

"Conor?"

"Yeah," he said brusquely. "I'll call you back in ten minutes."

He dropped the phone back into its cradle, turned up his collar and leaned against the wall of the booth. The lights were still on in Miranda's apartment. He thought of her, lying in the warm, wide bed and then he thought of what she'd said to him and the cold, deliberate way she'd said it.

The bitch.

He owed her nothing. He never even wanted to see her again—but, God help him, there wasn't a way in the world he was going to turn this fucking case over to anybody else. He stood there, shivering in the cold, thinking and planning, and then he picked up the telephone and dialed Thurston's home again.

At two A.M. New York time, the telephone beside Eva Beckman Winthrop's bed began to ring.

Eva sat up, turned on her reading lamp, and reached for it.

"Hello?" she said.

"Mrs. Winthrop? It's Harry Thurston. I'm sorry to bother you at this hour, but—"

"Do you have any idea what time it is, Mr. Thurston?"

"As I said, I'm sorry, but this is important."

"It had better be," Eva said sharply.

Harry Thurston cleared his throat. "Actually, I'd like to speak with Hoyt. If you'd put him on the phone, please . . . ?"

As if on cue, the door connecting the Winthrop's bedrooms

opened. Hoyt stood in the doorway, blinking in the glare of the light.

"Darling?" he said. "Is something wrong?"

"Hold on," Eva snapped into the phone. She put her hand over the receiver. "Go back to sleep, Hoyt."

"Who's that on the phone?"

"It's one of my West coast distributors," she said, forcing a smile. "There's a problem with a shipment. Los Angeles was expecting Swallowtail Red lipstick and they've received Monarch Pink instead."

"And they called you?" Hoyt said indignantly. "Do they know the time?"

Eva nodded, determinedly ignoring Harry Thurston's voice in her ear.

"Apparently, they forget the time change. It's ridiculous, I know, but as long as they've called, I might as well sort the problem out."

"Shall I get you something, my dear? Do you need a notepad, perhaps?"

"No," Eva said. She took a deep breath and smiled again. "No, thank you, Hoyt. You go on back to bed."

"Well, if you insist . . ."

"I do. Just shut the door after you, please." She laughed gaily. "I may have to raise my voice to these people, and I wouldn't want to keep you awake."

Hoyt smiled, turned, and shut the door behind him. Eva waited a few seconds, and then the smile fell from her lips.

"Now," she said into the telephone, "what is the reason for this call, Mr. Thurston? Does it have to do with the note I received today?"

Harry Thurston hesitated. "Perhaps you didn't understand me, Mrs. Winthrop. I should like to speak with your husband."

"Hoyt is asleep," Eva said briskly. "How may I help you?"

"Mrs. Winthrop, I really think I should talk with Hoyt."

"I don't agree. The note in question, both notes, in point of fact, were addressed to me."

Harry sighed. Conor O'Neil and Eva Winthrop, all in one day. How lucky could one man get?

"Very well," he said. "I'll get straight to the point."

"Please do."

"Your daughter has also received a note."

"What kind of note?"

Harry sighed again. It would have been so much simpler to discuss this with Hoyt.

"An unsavory one. Look, I wouldn't ask you to disturb Hoyt if it weren't important—"

"Was it about Miranda or about me?"

"It was about your daughter."

"Then I'm afraid I don't quite see why you're calling me."

Harry rubbed his hand over the top of his head. Eva Winthrop's tone was frigid, though polite. He knew she and the girl were estranged but he had a daughter, too, and he couldn't imagine not worrying about her, no matter what the situation between them.

"Not that I'm not concerned for my daughter's welfare," Eva said, as smoothly as if she'd read his mind, "but I'm certain you and Mr. O'Neil can look out for her. In the meantime, I should think the president's advisors would be pleased to hear from you."

"To hear what, Mrs. Winthrop?" Harry tried, but he couldn't keep an edge from his voice.

"Why, to hear that while this business is most unfortunate, it has nothing to do with Hoyt, or with me, and that the White House can go ahead with Hoyt's appointment."

"I'm sorry, but I can't do that."

"Why not?"

"Because, at this point, I don't know enough about these threats or what repercussions they might have."

"But you just said—"

"Why would someone send notes to you, if these threats were directed only at Miranda?"

"I have no idea, Mr. Thurston. You are in charge of this investigation, not I."

"Can you think of anyone who might wish to harm either you or your daughter? Perhaps you can think of an acquaintance of your daughter's who—"

"I do not know my daughter's acquaintances," Eva said coldly, "and I much prefer it that way but, considering what I know of the life she leads, I would not be surprised if an number of them are unsavory individuals."

"You may be right. We're checking."

"We?"

"Mr. O'Neil. He's still in Paris."

"And has he made any progress?" Eva switched the phone to her other ear. "Or has Miranda succeeding in making him let his hormones do his thinking for him?"

Harry gave an inward groan. He hadn't expected such a blunt question, especially since it was the same one, though not as politely phrased, he'd been asking himself ever since he'd talked with Conor.

"Mr. O'Neil is eminently qualified," he said. "If anyone can get to the bottom of this, he can."

"*If?*" Eva's voice turned even frostier. "Perhaps you've forgotten that my husband is a personal friend of the President's, and that we have both made significant contributions to his campaign. We expect this mess to be dealt with, and quickly."

"It will be—with your help."

"What kind of help are you asking for, Mr. Thurston?"

"Thus far, O'Neil's been acting on his own authority. He has no official status as a representative of the American government and he's in a foreign country."

"Get to the point, please."

"Miranda is not being cooperative. She doesn't seem to understand the importance of keeping a low profile until this situation is cleared up."

"If you're asking me to have a talk with her, you can save your breath. She doesn't take orders or advice from anyone, most especially not from me."

Harry sighed. He had a feeling the hard part was yet to come.

"Mr. O'Neil and I agree that if we're to get to the bottom of this, we need to bring your daughter home."

"Home?" Eva said, as if she'd never heard the word before.

"Yes. To the States. To New York, where we can keep her safe with far more ease and conduct an investigation that—"

"I don't agree. Miranda lives in Paris. If someone she knows is sending these notes, wouldn't it be reasonable to assume that person is French? For that matter, wouldn't you want my daughter to stay in France, rather than run the risk that her pursuer, or whatever you wish to call him, might follow her to the States and present a direct problem for Hoyt and me?"

For the first time in his sixty-odd years, Harry Thurston had to fight the almost overwhelming desire to tell a woman to perform an impossible anatomical act upon herself.

"Let me spell this out for you, Mrs. Winthrop," he said coldly. "It may be that you don't give a damn if your daughter ends up raped or dead but it will matter to the president, I promise you, madam, that if something happens to the girl and you could have helped us prevent it from happening but chose not to, you can kiss Hoyt's appointment good-bye."

Eva threw back the blankets and shot to her feet, her face livid. "How dare you speak to me that way?"

"Miranda isn't about to return to New York because we ask her," he said, ignoring the outburst. "But you are her mother. I'm certain you can think of some reason she will accept."

"Don't be ridiculous!"

"You're right when you say we need to conclude this investigation as quickly as possibly. To do that, we need her on American soil. And before you tell me that you can't, or won't, help bring her here, I'd suggest you consider that it's still possible you're the target and your daughter is simply the means to an end."

Eva licked her lips. The old fool was right. And if she weren't careful, everything she'd worked so hard for would be ripped from her hands.

"Mrs. Winthrop? Have you heard anything I said?"

Eva inhaled, then let out a long, sighing breath.

"You've made your point. I'll discuss this with my husband. I'm sure we can think up some scheme that will bring Miranda home."

"Thank you," Harry said, and then he slammed down the telephone, swiveled his chair towards his study window and stared out into the darkness.

Maybe he'd take the day off tomorrow, and go fishing.

In his line of work, the company of trout was often far more pleasurable than the company of people.

Chapter Twelve

Conor was waiting for her at the gate the next morning. Miranda spotted him as she came out the front door, and her spine stiffened.

What was he doing here? She was done with tolerating his intrusion in her life. Hadn't he gotten the message? She'd figured he had, when she'd heard him leave the apartment hours before.

Their eyes met but his were unreadable. Well, she thought as she crossed the courtyard, she hoped he could read everything in hers.

You are out of my life, Mr. O'Neil. More to the point, I am out of yours.

''Good morning, Miranda.''

She dipped her head in brief acknowledgment as she passed him but she didn't reply.

He fell in beside her as she set off briskly towards the Rue Rivoli.

''We need to talk.''

The light at the corner was just changing to red. She shot a quick look at the traffic, which was revving up the way it always did, and she stepped off the curb anyway.

"Go away," she said, when she reached the other side of the street.

He caught her arm as she stepped up on the sidewalk. "Eva got another note."

"So?"

"So, we need to discuss it."

Her chin notched up in an attitude of defiance. She pulled away from his hand and marched on.

"There isn't a thing in the world we need to discuss. You'd better phone Eva and tell her to take you off the payroll."

"Don't be an ass, Beckman."

"I know this is going to come as an awful shock to you and to my dear mother, but I'm not really interested in her or her mail. Tell her that, too, when you report in."

Conor grabbed her arm and swung her towards him. "Don't push it," he growled.

"Get out of my way, O'Neil."

"For starters, I do not report in."

"For starters, *I* don't like being ordered around. Or having my intelligence questioned." Her eyes fixed coldly on his. "We both know that Eva bought you, just the way she buys everything else."

A dark flush rose in his cheeks. "Is that what you think last night was all about? That what happened between us will go down on my expense account? That it's part of a plot, engineered by your mother?"

"I haven't thought about last night at all. Now, if you'll excuse me, I have an appointment."

Conor's expression hardened. "Yeah," he said grimly, "with me."

He looked around him. They'd come to a stop in the middle of the sidewalk. It was crowded but they were being ignored, just as they'd have been in New York or D.C. Still, this wasn't something he felt like discussing in a public place, especially knowing how Miranda would react when he got to the nitty-gritty.

There was a small *pâtisserie* just ahead. Customers were

hurrying in and out, clutching their morning coffee in white Styrofoam cups, but he could see a cluster of small tables through the steamy window.

"In there," he said.

"In where? Dammit, I'm not going anywhere with you!"

She tried to pull away but he tightened his hold on her arm, quick-marching her to the bakery, through the door and to a table as far from the others as he could manage. She sputtered and threatened him with mayhem but he ignored her, shoved her into a chair and leaned over her, his hands flat on the tabletop, his body blocking her escape.

"Here's the deal," he said, his eyes level with hers and his voice so quiet she had to lean towards him to hear it. "We do this the easy way, meaning coffee and a few of minutes of civilized conversation, or the hard way, where I toss you over my shoulder, take you someplace quiet and hold you down until you listen."

He'd do it, too, she knew; she could see it in his face. God, he was crazy!

"You're crazy," she said, "you know that?"

He smiled thinly. "An astute observation, maybe, but hardly original. Now, what it going to be? Coffee, or a quick round of 'I'm bigger and meaner than you are?' "

"You're a nasty son of a bitch, too," Miranda said, her voice quavering with barely suppressed fury, "but I'm sure that's not original, either."

"It's all part of my boyish charm, Beckman. You want something with your coffee?"

"Yes. Strychnine, to put into yours."

She sat stiffly, watching as he made his way to the counter at the front of the shop. What did he want from her now? Whatever it was, he had five minutes. After that, let him try carrying her off. She'd sink her teeth into him and bite down until she drew blood.

And probably end up with rabies.

The thought made her smile.

Conor plunked two cups of *café au lait* on the table.

"What's so funny?" he said, slipping into the chair opposite hers.

"Listen, O'Neil, let's get something straight. I'm a big girl. Just because you work for my mother doesn't mean I'm going to let you push me around."

Conor thought of telling her he wouldn't work for Eva if his life depended on it and that he'd do more than push her around if she didn't shut up, behave herself and pay attention. He'd put in a long, miserable night, first the call to Harry Thurston, then a call from Harry to him to tell him he'd spoken with Eva, and that he'd checked out Moratelli, who'd come up on the computer as a small-time hood with nothing on his record that would even suggest he'd get into something like this.

And then there'd been more calls, to Hoyt Winthrop and to Eva, to God only knew how many other people, until he'd finally ended up with what just might be a workable plan—assuming he had to put it in motion, assuming Miranda would refuse to do the logical thing he was going to ask her to do.

Of course, she'd refuse. He looked at her as he took a fortifying swallow of his coffee. She was just what Eva had said she was, a stubborn, spoiled, self-involved brat—but there was no denying that she was the most beautiful woman he'd ever seen. The face of an angel, he thought, with the morals of a hooker, although there'd been a time last night, when she'd been in his arms that he'd thought—that he'd almost thought . . .

"Did you hear me, O'Neil? I'm not going to let you bully me."

Conor nodded. He put his cup on the table, folded his hands around it, and leaned forward.

"You're right," he said pleasantly, "you don't have to let me do anything, not even save your ass. Still, I'm going to do my best to try. Now, do you want me to tell you what was in Eva's note or do you want to go on detailing the flaws in my personality?"

Miranda glared at him. There was no winning an argument with a man like this.

"I left one out," she said coldly. She pushed her cup of

coffee to the center of the table. "You're arrogant. Did it ever occur to you to ask me how I take my morning coffee?"

"This is France." Conor tore open two packets of brown sugar and dumped the contents into his cup. "It's unpatriotic not to drink hot milk in your coffee in the morning."

"You forget, I'm not French."

"You're the next best thing, Beckman. You live here, you work for a bunch of pansy European designers, you sleep with an ooh-la-la movie star." He shrugged his shoulders. "I figured you'd forgotten that you started life as an all-American girl."

"Is that why you shanghaied me this morning? So you could run up the stars and stripes and check to see if my passport still says 'born in the USA?' "

Conor gave her a cat-that-ate-the-canary smile.

"Your work permit says it, too."

"What?"

"I said—"

"I know what you said." *Why was he smiling?* "What does my work permit have to do with this conversation?"

He shrugged again, lifted his cup and took a mouthful of the steaming liquid.

"Maybe nothing," he said, and looked at her. "Do you do it often?"

"Do I do what often? O'Neil, if you're going to talk in riddles . . ."

"Sleep with other men instead of Frenchy. I meant to ask last night but I just never got around to it."

"That's none of your business."

"It's very much my business. I'll need a list of your lovers, so I can check them out."

"For what?" she said. She smiled, but her eyes looked like chips of ice. "I'm a big girl. Trust me, I'm perfectly healthy. I do my own checking."

"Do you," he said sarcastically.

She lifted her chin defiantly. "Yes."

Yes, he thought, dammit to hell, yes. She just sat there, watching him with those big, innocent eyes, giving him that little Mona Lisa smile, acting as if they were discussing a walk in the country, for God's sake, instead of her sex life.

Conor felt his muscles tense. He wanted to grab her, shake her until her teeth rattled and she gave up that cool, "who I sleep with is my business" attitude.

She hadn't been so cool-looking last night, in his arms.

Hell, he thought furiously, last night didn't have a fucking thing to do with this. *Keep your mind on business, man, where it belongs.*

"In that case," he said, his tone as cool as hers, "you'd know if one of the men you've played games with would be likely to call you a tease."

"A tease?"

"Yeah. Come on, Beckman, don't give me that innocent look." Conor lowered his voice. "The note to Eva was in French. It said you were *une allumeuse.* Do I have to put that in gutter English, or can you do the translating for yourself?"

Miranda blinked. Then she gave a strangled laugh, reached out and wrapped her hands around her coffee cup. The bone-white of her knuckles stood out in stark relief against the white of the cup. "Jean-Phillipe was right."

Conor's eyes narrowed. "Moreau called you that?"

"No, of course not. He said—he said, it was what I was *being* called."

Her eyes met Conor's. What he thought of her was right there, in his face. The need to reach over, put her hand on top of his and say, "You're wrong, O'Neil, I'm not like that at all," was, for a moment, as strong as her need to draw breath. But the only thing she did was lift her cup and force a swallow of the rapidly cooling coffee down her throat.

"I'm sure Eva was thrilled," she said. "Was there more?"

"Yes." A muscle ticked in his cheek. There was no easy way to deliver the rest of it, especially if he had any hope of getting her to cooperate. "Whoever wrote it said you were going to die."

Coffee sloshed over her fingers. She set the cup down on the table, carefully wiped her hands with a paper napkin, then crumpled it and put it aside. He watched her face as she fought for equilibrium, found it and finally managed a faint smile.

"I suppose I should be flattered. Being threatened on two continents, you know? I'll bet that doesn't happen to everybody."

"No," Conor said flatly, "it sure as shit doesn't."

She nodded. The tip of her tongue snaked out and she moistened her lips.

"Moratelli's doing this?"

"That's my best guess"

"I—I don't suppose you've, uh, you've figured out the reason?"

He shook his head. Her tone was cocky but there was fear in her eyes. Why in hell hadn't he done what he'd promised himself he'd do, bought some cigarettes and tucked them into his pocket? He needed something to do with his hands so that he didn't end up doing a stupid thing like reaching out, hauling her into his arms and telling her he'd protect her.

"Because it doesn't make sense." Her words were rushed. "I mean, who is he? What would he gain from threatening me? And why involve Eva?"

"Blackmail," he said flatly. "Nothing else makes sense."

"To keep Hoyt from getting his appointment?" Miranda shook her head. Her hair slipped across one high cheekbone like dark water over a perfect arch of stone. "But why? I just can't imagine all this over something like a silly ambassadorship."

"Neither can I." Conor looked at her. "I'm talking about old-fashioned, I-know-your-secret blackmail, the kind people do for money."

"What secret? You mean, that I was once married to Edouard de Lasserre?"

"I doubt it." He could be honest about this much, anyway. "Besides, Moratelli's just a front man for somebody else."

"How do you know that?"

He shrugged. "I just do, that's all. And if I'm right about them wanting money, it's Eva's they're after, not yours."

"You mean, this person figures Eva will pay to keep them from doing something to me?" Miranda gave a forced laugh. "Wow. Talk about errors in judgment!"

Here we go, Conor thought.

"Trust me on this, O'Neil. Expecting Eva to worry about me is like asking a shark to become a vegetarian."

"She's concerned about you."

"Right, and I'm the man in the moon." Miranda took a deep breath, then exhaled on a gusty sigh. "Thanks for the update," she said, pushing back her chair. "I'll keep it in mind."

"Sit down, Miranda."

"O'Neil, I am late. I work for my living, in case you'd forgotten, and I have a shoot at the Jeu de Paume. If I don't get moving now—"

"Eva wants you to come home."

Miranda laughed. "Goodbye, O'Neil."

Conor caught hold of her wrist. "She says Papillon's been searching for a model to advertise a new line of cosmetics and you've got the look her people want."

"I'll bet."

"Dammit, what's the matter with you? You go back to New York, you get an exclusive contract with Papillon and for all you know, you and Eva might find some neutral ground."

"What you mean is, Eva's worried about me meeting a nasty end in Paris. That wouldn't suit Hoyt's image, or Papillon's, either."

Hell, Conor thought, trying not to wince. The words were different but the sentiment was damn near the one Eva had expressed when he'd talked to her a couple of hours ago.

"I have decided," she'd said, "albeit with the greatest reluctance, to accede to Mr. Thurston's request."

"It's the right thing to do," Conor had begun, but Eva had interrupted him.

"Both my husband and I are people of some standing, Mr. O'Neil. I will not risk having our good names sullied by some ugly public revelation. If it's necessary to find a way to convince

Miranda to return home so we can put an end to this business and ensure her safety, then I shall do so."

Miranda, watching Conor's face, smiled tightly.

"I'm right, aren't I? She wants me home about as much as I want to go there."

Dammit, he thought, looking into her knowing eyes, what was the sense in pretending?

"She wasn't eager for it," he said, "but once I convinced her it was necessary, she agreed to cooperate."

"Which is why she's offered me the Papillon job. Sort of a bonus. A little tidbit to make me want to roll over like a good little puppy."

Conor shrugged his shoulders. "You could put it that way."

Miranda nodded. "Thanks for being honest." Her eyes were shiny and she brushed the back of her hand across them. "It's too damned warm in here," she said brusquely, and made for the door.

Conor didn't speak until they'd reached the street. Then he took her arm and gently turned her to face him.

"I'm glad you're taking this intelligently."

"I've been taking my mother's feelings for me intelligently all my life. She doesn't like me but that's okay." Her smile was as false as it was bright. "There's no law that says mothers and daughters have to love each other."

"I meant, the part about you going home."

"Going home?"

"To New York." He smiled. This had all gone so much easier than he'd expected. He thought of all the stuff he'd worked his butt off to line up, the arms he'd had to twist, the favors called in by Harry, all of it done because he'd figured he'd have to force her to agree to return to the States. His smile broadened. "Who knows? You might even find you're tired of being an expatriate."

Miranda looked at him as if he'd lost his mind. "Are you crazy? I'm not going to New York."

"But you just said—"

"I said, I knew what Eva's motives were in asking me to

come home.'' She turned up her coat collar; the wind was picking up and there was a faint promise of snow in the air again. ''But that doesn't mean I'm going to oblige her.''

''Dammit, Beckman! Are you naturally stupid or just pretending to be an idiot? Don't you understand what's happening?''

''Someone's threatened to hurt me. Of course I understand.''

''*Hurt* isn't the word I'd use to describe our friend's intentions,'' Conor said sharply. ''Whoever this is wants to do more than that.''

''There are lots of crazies in this world, O'Neil. If everybody jumped each time one of them said boo—''

''Let me lay this out for you, lady. There's a lunatic walking around who's pulling Moratelli's strings. He wants to off you but first he figures on some fun and games. A little torture, maybe, a little rape—''

She flinched under the impact of his words. Good, he thought fiercely, let her flinch, if it means she'll finally accept how serious this is.

''Must you be so descriptive?''

''I can be a lot more descriptive, if I have to. He knows where you live. Either he or Moratelli, maybe both of them, have been inside your apartment. And I don't have a clue as to who this bastard is or why he's after you.''

''So, what are you saying? That you can play detective better in the States?''

''Yes, dammit, I can! My hands are tied here. I'm not a French citizen, I don't have access to—to the things I need.''

''No.''

''Have you heard anything I said?''

''Yes, I heard you and no, I'm not going home.'' Miranda's eyes met his. ''Maybe *I* should lay this out for *you,* O'Neil. I am home. I've got a life here. I have a home, a career, and friends.''

''You have an apartment, a job you could do anywhere, a girlfriend who's idea of permanency is the latest man in her life and a lover who's so busy trying to turn himself into an international movie star that he's barely got time to fit you in.''

Miranda stiffened. ''My,'' she said frigidly, ''you have been a busy little Boy Scout, haven't you!''

''Miranda, use your head! Call Eva, tell her you're coming home.''

''You do the phoning, Mr. O'Neil. Call your employer, tell her what she can do with her heartwarming invitation, and tell her, too, that I'll do my very best to keep from becoming the sort of headline that might make her cringe.''

Her eyes were shiny again; her lashes glistened with tears. One last phony smile, and then she turned and walked briskly away.

Conor jammed his hands into his pockets, looked across the street and jerked his chin towards Miranda. A tall, skinny man with red hair moved out from a doorway, dodged into the gutter and trotted towards him.

''Don't let her out of your sight,'' Conor said. ''If you see trouble coming—''

''Hit my beeper. I know, I know.''

Conor waited until Cochran had fallen in behind Miranda. Then he headed for the nearest telephone.

They'd have to do it the hard way, after all.

Two days later, Miranda stood in front of the ticket booth at the Eiffel Tower, looking towards the Champ de Mars, checking the faces of people as they approached and tapping her toes with impatience.

Where was Nita? She was always late, but today she was setting an all-time record.

And why were they meeting here? The Tower was the heart of Paris and magnificent to see, but they'd both been here before, on their own as tourists and at least two or three times for fashion shoots. Still, Nita had been adamant about meeting here today.

"We have to go up in the Tower," she'd said mysteriously. "There's something I want you to see."

They weren't going to see anything if Nita didn't get here soon. Miranda glanced at the sky. Clouds were rolling in over the city. Visibility wouldn't be good.

"There you are!"

Miranda turned and saw Nita hurrying towards her, tall and striking in a hot pink cape that went clear down to her ankles.

"There *I* am?" Miranda said, offering her face for an exchange of quick cheek-to-cheek air kisses. "I don't want to upset you, my friend, but *I* have been here for half an hour."

"Did you buy our tickets?"

Miranda waved the two *billets* in the air. "Yes. Now, are you going to tell me what we're doing here?"

Nita grinned, looped her arm through Miranda's and hurried her to the stairs.

"Be patient, girlfriend. You'll find out, in a few minutes."

"Wait a minute. You're going to pass up the elevator?" Miranda stared at Nita. "I don't believe it. What's going on?"

"We're only going to the second level and I'm too excited to wait for the elevator. Come on, come on—if I can do it, so can you."

It was windy, and cool, and they were the only two people taking the stairs. Nita groaned when they reached the first level.

"High heels weren't made for climbing," she said. "Just give me a minute."

"Nita," Miranda said, "this had better be good."

"It is. It's wonderful."

"Uh-huh."

"Go on, don't believe me. I promise, this is going to be something very, very special."

"What? Stop being so mysterious."

"I'm not being mysterious, I'm being dramatic." Nita huffed as they began climbing the stairs again. "Nothing wrong with a little drama, is there?"

"There is, when I've had a long and trying day."

"Poor darlin'. Your friend, the gorgeous American hunk, givin' you trouble again?"

"He's not my friend and he's not, as you so subtly put it, a hunk. He's a pain in the *derrière.*"

"I think you've got the man wrong, girlfriend. He seemed really nice the other day, when he came to see . . . Oops!"

"O'Neil went to see you?"

"Damn! I knew you'd be pissed. Look, he just asked me a few simple questions."

"About me," Miranda said coldly.

"Yeah. Well, about us. When we met, how long we know each other . . . stuff like that."

"Did it ever occur to you I wouldn't like the idea of you talking to that man behind my back?"

"Oh, give me a break! It's not like we discussed your bra size! The whole thing took five minutes. I told him that you were my best friend in the whole wide world and that was it."

"I still don't like it."

"Well, that makes two of us." The women reached the second level of the Tower. Nita breathed a sigh of relief, took Miranda's arm, and drew her to the railing. "I get the feeling you haven't told me everything, you know? Trouble, you said, but I figure it must be pretty bad trouble hangin' over your head if O'Neil's still around."

"It has nothing to do with me," Miranda said, wishing she believed it. "It's this ambassadorship my stepfather's up for."

"Yeah, that's what your Mr. O'Neil told me. Said there were problems and that he's just doing his job, looking out for your interests and keeping you safe."

"Safe?" Miranda laughed. The wind snatched at her hair and she scooped it back behind her ear. "You want to hear his idea of safe? The jerk wants me to pick up and run. Go back to the States, he says."

"Go back to the States?" Nita squealed with delight and threw her arms around Miranda. "Oh, that's wonderful news, girlfriend, wonderful! I am so glad to hear it!"

"Don't be silly! I'm not—"

"And we'll be friends forever, right? No matter where you or I live."

"Nita, you're not listening to me. I never said—"

"Look, there it is!" Nita's voice rose excitedly. She grabbed Miranda's sleeve, tugged at it and pointed west. "Look!"

"Look at what?"

"Way over there, see? That grey building? The one with the black roof and the chimney pots?"

"All the buildings in Paris are grey, with black roofs and chimney pots," Miranda said, making a face. "Which one am I supposed to be looking at?"

"*That* one. With the red flowers in the window box."

"Red flowers?" Miranda shielded her eyes with her hands. "How can there be flowers in the window box? It's the middle of winter!"

"They're not real flowers, silly, they're artificial." Nita sighed, flipped up the hood of her hot pink cape and snuggled into it. "Carlos says it's up to the artist to create his own environment."

"Carlos?" Miranda looked at her friend. "Who's Carlos?"

"You see how out of touch you are? Carlos just happens to be the love of my life. I met him at that party we went to last week." Nita smiled slyly. "I'd have introduced you, but you cut out early and went off with the guy you keep insisting isn't a hunk."

"He isn't, and I didn't . . ." Miranda blew out her breath. "Never mind," she said. "Just tell me about Carlos."

"What's to tell?" Nita said dreamily, and launched into a five-minute description that covered everything from Carlos's brown eyes to the way he wanted to paint her, naked and smiling on the beach in Tahiti. "I am," she sighed, "head over heels in love!"

Miranda grinned and tucked a strand of hair behind her ear. "Uh-huh."

"Go on, scoff. Carlos is the man I've been looking for my entire life."

"Sure he is."

"You don't believe me?"

"I'd love to believe you, but I've heard the story a thousand times before. Well, with bits and pieces changed." Miranda smiled. "I don't think you've ever had a guy wanted to paint you on the beach at Tahiti."

"Not just wants to," Nita said, her voice rising with excitement. "Is!"

"Is what?"

"Carlos is taking me to Tahiti! Isn't that wonderful?"

"Well, sure. A couple of weeks in the sun, while the rest of us shiver in the cold . . ."

"No, no, you don't understand. We're going to live there."

Miranda stared at Nita. "Live there?" she said, bewildered. "You? And Carlos?"

"Isn't it wonderful? Oh, wait until you meet him! This is the most terrific man in the world! We clicked, just like that, and the very first night, after we'd . . ." Nita blushed with unaccustomed modesty. "Well, after we'd done it, we were talking and Carlos said, what's your deepest, most secret, wish? And I said, no, you have to tell me yours first, and he said, well, he'd always wanted to go to the South Pacific and do the Gauguin thing." She giggled. "So then I said, wasn't it amazing but my deepest, most secret wish had always been to fall crazy in love and set up housekeeping on an island in the South Pacific!"

"I thought your deepest, most secret wish was to marry the Sheik of some oil-rich kingdom and bathe in a tub full of L'Air du Temps," Miranda said dryly.

Nita nudged her in the ribs with her elbow. "You aren't listenin', girlfriend. I am in love. L-O-V-E. Do you understand?" She took a breath. "It was all just talk, anyway. Carlos said he was the same as all artists. Lots of dreams but no money, and I said, well, that was okay, because I was worried about leaving you. I mean, we've been friends for such a long time, and now you're having all this trouble—whatever *that* means."

"Nita, slow down. If he's broke, how's he taking you on vacation to Tahiti?"

"Well, that's the miracle. He's not broke anymore. Carlos got this letter from some *mucho mysterioso* bunch of folks that gives out grants to artists, telling him he'd won a humongous grant!"

"But—but what about your work?"

"What about it? Listen, I'm damn near a living fossil, same as you. I've got, what, maybe another year or two left?"

"You're sure?" Miranda said slowly, staring at Nita, trying to feel happy for her instead of feeling what she did feel, a selfish, awful sense of loss. "That you love this guy?"

"I sewed a button on his shirt last night," Nita said with a soft smile. "Tonight, I'm gonna cook him dinner."

Miranda smiled back at her. "Well, I have to admit, that does sound serious." Her smile tilted. "And the money? I mean, he's not planning on doing a trip on you, is he?"

"My God, this girl is such a cynic! It's absolutely light. I saw the letter he got, telling him he'd won this grant. It came hot on the heels of my chat with your Mr. O'Neil." Nita threw her arms into the air. "Oh, Miranda, I just can't believe everything came together like this, you deciding to go home, then Carlos getting this money . . . Isn't it all just wonderful?"

"Wonderful," Miranda said, and blanked her mind to the sudden, absolutely ridiculous thought that Conor was somehow, someway, involved in this.

It was worse than ridiculous.

It was insane.

At ten that night, Miranda was curled up on the sofa with Mia in her lap.

She was watching TV or trying to, anyway, when the telephone rang.

The noise made Mia jump. Miranda jumped, too. Who would phone her so late? Jean-Phillipe, maybe. She hadn't heard from him in a couple of days, except for a hard-to-hear message he'd left on her answering machine yesterday, something about suddenly being called to the Côte d'Azur. That was what she thought he'd said, anyway; there'd been too much background noise to be certain.

She sat still, letting her machine screen the call, something she'd never done until lately.

It was Madame Delain phoning, which was a surprise. The *concièrge* never called. If she had something to say, she came to the door. Miranda picked up the phone.

"Yes, Madame Delain," she said, "what is it?"

Madame, never one to be flustered by anything, was obviously flustered now.

"Mademoiselle," she said, "I am afraid I do not know how to approach this."

Had there been another visit from the elevator inspector? Miranda sat up straight. "What's wrong?"

"Your apartment, mademoiselle."

"Yes? What about it?"

"You must vacate it before the month is out."

Mia offered a loud, Siamese complaint as Miranda pushed her from her lap and shot to her feet.

"Are you crazy? Why would I do that?"

"The owner of your rooms wants them back."

"Madame, what are you talking about? *I'm* the owner! I have a lease."

"You are the renter. Perhaps you forget that I explained, when you signed the lease, that the apartment was owned by a bank."

"Perhaps *you* forget that you also told me I could rent it for as long as I wished and even buy it, when I was ready."

"It would seem that things have changed. I am afraid you must leave. It is unfortunate, but I hope mademoiselle understands."

No, Miranda thought as she slammed down the telephone, mademoiselle did not understand. Conor O'Neil wanted her out of Paris and all of a sudden, her best friend was moving halfway across the world, she was losing her home . . .

The phone rang again. "Listen, madame," Miranda said as she snatched it up, "I refuse to believe—"

"Ah, *chérie,*" Jean-Phillipe said, laughing, "how can you refuse to believe my good fortune when I have yet to share it with you?"

"Jean-Phillipe." Miranda sighed with relief and sank down onto the sofa. "You can't imagine how glad I am to hear your voice. I've had the most impossible day."

"No more notes, surely?"

"No, no more notes."

"*Bien.* I did not think there would be any, not with your Monsieur O'Neil hovering over you like a guardian angel."

"He's not *my* Mr. O'Neil and he sure as hell isn't a guardian angel."

Jean-Phillipe chuckled. "You might be quicker to agree if you had heard the questions he asked of me."

"What?" Miranda stood up. "The bastard! When did he talk to you? And why did you let him?"

"Now, Miranda, you must not think ill of a man who is concerned with your welfare."

"He's nothing but a stooge, hired by my mother!"

"He is a man with a job to do, *chérie,*" Jean-Phillipe said patiently, "and he asked me nothing I would not have asked myself of a man who knows you well." He paused, and when he spoke again, there was the hint of a smile in his voice. "Though I will admit, his questions did grow somewhat personal."

"Personal? What do you mean, personal?"

"He wanted to know how long we had known each other, if it bothered me to know there were other men in your life from time to time, that sort of thing. I had the feeling he would like to have made our talk a bit more man-to-man." He laughed softly. "Perhaps I should say, *mano a mano.* I do not think he likes the idea of you belonging to anyone else."

"I don't give a damn what he thinks. And you're probably right—he's just the type who would settle a dispute with his fists."

"Miranda? Has your relationship with O'Neil taken a more intimate turn?" His voice softened. "I was tempted to tell him the truth, *chérie,* that you and I have never been more than good friends."

"But you didn't," Miranda said quickly.

"I would not do such a thing, without consulting you first. But I felt much empathy with him. I sense that he feels as protective of you as I."

"He isn't protective, he's a bully."

"His job is to watch over you, and he does."

"Not anymore. I showed him the door days ago."

"His interview with me took place the day before yesterday, *chérie.* It would seem your protector is still there."

"And still unwanted," she said grimly. "The man is as hard to get rid of as the flu."

He laughed and she smiled a little. It had been an awful day but things would look up, now that Jean-Phillipe was back. He was, wasn't he? Or was he phoning from the Côte d'Azur? Mia leaped into her lap, purred and settled down for some petting.

"Enough about O'Neil," Miranda said. "What's the good news you were going to tell me? Does it have something to do with your trip to the Côte d'Azur?"

"The Côte d'Azur? Why would you think that?"

"Well, your message. You said you were flying to the Côte."

"No, no." Jean-Phillipe laughed. "Those airport telephones can be so noisy, can they not? I left word that I was flying to the *coast.*"

"The coast?" Miranda frowned. "What coast?"

"Yours, of course. The West Coast. I am in Hollywood, *chérie.* Isn't that exciting?"

Miranda sat back. "Yes," she said slowly. She did her best to put some enthusiasm in her voice but it wasn't easy. "It's very exciting. How come?"

"Do you recall my saying plans for my next film were all set? That it would be made in France?" His voice quickened. "Well, that has changed. I met someone at the Cannes festival last year. Harlan Williams, an American film producer. I must have mentioned him to you, no?''

''You and Nita.'' Miranda said. ''Love must be in the air.''

''No, no, this is business.'' He chuckled. ''Well, it is business now, but who knows? At any rate, Harlan phoned me last week. In Cannes, he had told me of a film he wished to make, here in California. Oh, it sounded wonderful, and with a part for me. Not a starring role, *tu comprends,* but one which—how do you say?—one which pivots. But he could not raise the money he needed. The script was too *artistique, n'est-ce pas?''*

''Don't tell me,'' she said softly. ''The money suddenly turned up.''

Jean-Phillipe laughed delightedly. ''How did you know?''

Miranda's head drooped back against the sofa. ''Oh, just a lucky guess.''

''My only concern is you, *chérie.* I do not like to leave you alone in Paris with all that has been happening. But with your Mr. O'Neil to watch over you, what is there to worry about?''

''What, indeed?'' she said, wished him luck, and gently hung up the phone.

Sometime during the night, it occurred to her that Liliane, who'd handled her bookings for years, had not called with any assignments in the past few days.

A gust of wind hit the window and fluttered the bedroom drapes. Goose bumps rose on her skin.

Coincidence, nothing more. It was all coincidence, Nita and Jean-Phillipe and the loss of her apartment . . .

At seven, Miranda showered, dressed, and phoned for a taxi.

Things were going at the usual frenzied pace at the agency. The waiting room was packed with hopefuls, young and not-so-young, the unknowns and the once-knowns all vying for work. Miranda said a couple of quick hellos, waved at the receptionist, and hurried down the hall to Liliane's cluttered office.

The booker was on the phone when Miranda knocked on the half-open door. She rolled her eyes skyward, pointed at the phone and made a retching motion.

Miranda laughed. "My very sentiments."

Liliane jerked her chin towards a chair. "Sit," she hissed, with her hand over the mouthpiece. A couple of minutes later, she said a sweet *adieu,* followed by a not-so-sweet *merde* as she slammed down the receiver.

"What a pig," she said, and smiled beatifically. "*Ma petite,* I was just about to ring you."

Miranda sighed dramatically and put her hand to her heart. "What a relief! Considering the way things have been going in my life lately, I was half-convinced I was never going to hear from you again."

Liliane smiled nervously. "There is no need to concern yourself with that. You are much in demand."

But? Miranda waited. The word, unspoken, hung in the air.

"But . . ." The booker smoothed her hands over her skirt as she stood up and came out from behind her desk. "We had a visit from some man from the government yesterday."

Miranda tried to smile. "He wasn't an elevator inspector, was he?"

Lilian frowned. "No, of course not. Why would you think that?"

"Just a bad joke, sorry. Go on, tell me. What did he want?"

"He said—I know it is a mistake, Miranda, I said so at once." Liliane frowned. "He said that your work permit is no longer valid."

Miranda bolted from her chair. "What? Liliane, don't be silly! My papers are fine!"

"I said as much to him, of course, but I am afraid I can give you no assignments until the matter is clarified." Liliane put her arm around Miranda's waist and walked her to the door. "You must take this up with your embassy. Surely, they can sort it out."

* * *

Surely, they could not.

A round-faced woman whose desk plate identified her as Mrs. Tully assured Miranda in the most pleasant way that her permit had not expired.

"Your modeling agency misunderstood," she said. "The problem is with your visa."

"My visa?"

"I'm afraid so."

"What's wrong with it?"

"I don't know, exactly."

Miranda's eyes narrowed. "Then, send me on to someone who *does* know, exactly."

Mrs. Tully smiled again. Dammit, was she paid to smile or to solve problems for Americans in France?

"We can't do a thing on this end. I'm afraid you'll have to return to the States and reapply."

"Reapply?" Miranda said in disbelief.

"It shouldn't take more than a few weeks to sort things out."

"You're telling me I have to return to America and reapply for a visa that's been perfectly acceptable for years?" Miranda glared at the woman. "That's the stupidest thing I ever heard!"

So much for Mrs. Tully's professional smile. It vanished, as did her unctuous tone.

"The embassy suggests you make arrangements to leave France immediately, Miss Beckman."

"And if I don't?"

"Rules are rules," the woman said stiffly. "I don't make them, I only follow them."

Miranda took a deep breath.

"Where is he?" she demanded.

"Where is who?" Mrs. Tully pushed back her chair an inch or two.

"You know who! Where's Conor O'Neil, that no-good, fast-talking, sneaky son of a bitch!"

"Miss Beckman, I must ask you to calm down or I shall be forced to call Security."

"You're all in this together," Miranda said furiously. She leaned over Mrs. Tully's desk. "Well, you can just tell O'Neil that it isn't going to work!"

"Security?" Mrs. Tully said in a quavering voice. She picked up her telephone. "Security," she said again, and hit a button, but Miranda was already marching out the door of her office and towards the exit.

"O'Neil," she muttered, and punched open the door, "O'Neil, you bastard!"

A couple walking past the embassy looked at her in surprise as she came down the steps.

"Mademoiselle?"

"You heard me," Miranda said. "Conor O'Neil is a sleazy bastard!"

The man and woman looked at each other.

"L'Américaine, elle est folle," the man murmured, his eyebrows lifting.

"I'm not crazy," Miranda shouted to their rapidly retreating backs.

An angry sob caught in her throat. She wasn't. It was Conor who was crazy, thinking he could pull this stuff and get away with it . . .

Her shoulders slumped. "Damn you, O'Neil," she whispered.

Eight years ago, she had taken a vow. Now, she had no choice but to break it.

Like it or not, she was going home.

Chapter Thirteen

Blue Ridge Mountains, Virginia, spring, 1996

Tucked back against a stand of old-growth oaks, the log cabin sat snugly protected from the late March wind that swooped and whistled just outside.

Harry Thurston, who was seated at one end of the rough pine table that marked the boundary of what he called the kitchen, looked up from the brook trout he was filleting and smiled.

''Weather can't make up its mind,'' he said.

Conor, who was trying to scale their catch without also removing all the skin from his hands, nodded in agreement. ''Spring in the East, One minute it rains, the next the sun's out.''

''We had snow in these mountains, about this time last year.''

''You better hope history doesn't repeat itself,'' Conor said wryly. ''A day's fishing is one thing, Harry, but a snowbound weekend with you doesn't exactly turn me on.''

Harry chuckled. ''Relax, my boy. They're predicting clear skies right through tomorrow. We'll fry our trout, open a couple of those beers you so thoughtfully provided, sit around the fire and relax, then head back to town. You done with that fish?''

Conor nodded and shoved the trout towards the older man. Then he bundled up the newspaper that held the messy results of the past hour's work, dumped it into a bag of trash, wiped his hands with a couple of paper towels and leaned back against the wall, arms folded, watching as Harry deftly filleted the last of their afternoon's catch.

''There,'' Harry said, ''that'll do it. Now we're ready for some of Thurston's Magic Dust.''

''Magic Dust, huh?'' Conor grinned. ''Sounds like something left over from the sixties.''

Harry laughed as he began taking canisters from the shelf behind him.

''There's nothing hallucinogenic about this recipe, though I do guarantee the end result will make your head spin. Open that ice chest, will you? There should be a container of cream inside. Get out the bacon and eggs, too. Good. Now, pay attention, please. There are fishermen who'd kill for the Thurston recipe.''

''From the looks of it, the recipe would kill them first. You've got to be kidding. Cream? Eggs? Bacon?'' Conor shook his head. ''Why don't we skip the preliminaries, just mainline the stuff straight into our arteries and get it over with?''

''I'm surprised at you, Conor, worrying about such things at your age.'' Harry broke three eggs into a chipped enamel bowl, poured in the cream and began whipping the mixture to a froth. ''Besides, risk puts the spice in life. Isn't that what you always say?''

Conor's brows lifted. ''Is it?''

''Well, maybe you don't say it but it's the message you always seem to send.''

''Amazing,'' Conor said with a little smile. ''Here I've been all these years, doing the job I was paid to do, while you were doing armchair psychoanalysis.''

''We all like a little element of danger, or we wouldn't have gone into our particular line of work.'' Harry set the bowl aside, pulled another one towards him, and began opening the canisters. "Lay half a dozen slices of bacon in that cast-iron skillet and set it in the embers on the hearth, please. Just make sure there's no flame underneath." He dumped cornmeal and flour into the fresh bowl, then reached for an array of spice jars. "Am I right?"

Conor, kneeling before the stone fireplace, looked up.

"I wouldn't know," he said with a lazy smile. "This is your recipe, remember? Not mine."

"I'm talking about risk. Danger. The stuff that gets the adrenaline pumping."

"My adrenaline's pumping just fine." Conor got to his feet and dusted his hands on the seat of his jeans. "And so will yours be, once you finally get around to telling me what we're doing here today."

The older man looked up, his expression one of total innocence. "You know what we're doing. I told you, I thought it was time I introduced you to the peaceful joys of fishing."

"Fishing for what? And please, don't tell me the answer is trout."

Harry Thurston dipped the last filet in the batter, rolled it carefully through the cornmeal and flour mixture, then wiped his hands on a towel.

"Such distrust, Conor."

"Such subterfuge, Harry. Come on, let's have it. Why'd you ask me to come up here?"

Thurston looked at him. Then he plucked two bottles from the case Conor had placed against the wall and handed one over.

"Let's sit down, have a beer, and talk."

"It's ale," Conor said with a little smile. Harry eased into a maple rocker that stood facing the fireplace; Conor sat down on the edge of the hearth. "Calling what's in this bottle beer is about the same as calling a trout a sunfish."

Harry shuddered. "Point taken." He twisted the cap from the bottle, lifted the bottle to his lips and took a long swallow.

"An excellent brew. And you were right, room temperature's best. Is it always, or is it just this particular brand?"

Conor put down his ale. He leaned back, his hands on the hearth behind him, stretched out his legs and crossed them at the ankles.

"Harry," he said softly, "we have discussed the best way to catch trout and to clean them. We've discussed how to cook the fillets and how to serve them. If you really think that now I'm going to get sidetracked into discussing the relative merits of chilled ale versus ale at room temperature, you're crazy. I want to know why we're here."

The older man sighed. "All right, I admit, I did have an ulterior motive in asking you up here today."

"Which was?"

Harry's eyes locked onto Conor's.

"Miranda Beckman."

The name, unspoken between them for weeks, seemed to echo through the little cabin.

"I'm finished with that assignment," Conor said coolly. "Had you forgotten? I turned in all my reports and handed the file off to Bill Breverman, as per your orders."

"You gave me little choice in the matter. You brought the girl home and announced that you were signing off."

"I didn't bring her home," Conor said, even more coolly, "I set it up so she had no choice but to decide to go home."

"Look, if you want to split hairs—"

"I'm not splitting hairs, I'm simply being accurate." Conor got to his feet, crossed the room and exchanged his empty ale bottle for a full one. "And," he said, wrenching off the cap, "there's nothing about Miranda Beckman for us to talk about."

Harry cleared his throat. "I'm afraid there is."

Something in Thurston's voice made the hair lift on the back of Conor's neck. He swung around, his face suddenly pale.

"Has something happened to her? Goddammit, Harry—"

"No, no, it's nothing like that. The girl is fine . . . so far."

"So far?" Conor stomped towards the older man and glared

down at him. "What the hell's that supposed to mean? Cut to the chase, Harry, or I'll find out for myself."

"Take it easy, please."

"Take it easy? You shanghai me, drag me to the middle of nowhere—"

"I did no such thing," Thurston said with righteous indignation. "I invited you to learn about the fine art of angling, and this is hardly the middle of nowhere."

"Save that crap for somebody else, dammit! Tell me what's going down and what it's got to do with me."

"This is—was—your assignment, Conor."

"Yeah. It was. That's past tense, in case you hadn't noticed. I haven't so much as thought of the Beckman broad since I got back from Paris."

There was a hiss from the fireplace. Thurston turned, saw flames dancing beneath the skillet, and muttered something under his breath. He plucked the skillet from the embers, picked up a spatula and began rearranging the fillets.

Conor watched him, his eyes and mouth hard.

What was this shit? Whatever was going on with Miranda, it didn't have a thing to do with him. As he'd just told the old man, he hadn't even thought of her since . . .

Oh, what a liar you are, O'Neil.

Hadn't thought of her? Hell, he hadn't been able to *stop* thinking of her. Day after day, night after night, Miranda was in his head. He couldn't get her face, with its mysterious smile, out of his mind. Not that she'd been smiling the last time he'd seen her, when she'd confronted him at his hotel in Paris.

"I hate you, O'Neil," she'd said, her eyes flashing fire. "And if I ever see you anywhere near me again, I swear to God, I'll kill you! You got that?"

Yeah. Oh yeah, he'd gotten that. And he didn't much care. She wanted no part of him; he wanted no part of her. End of story. What had happened in her bedroom that night hadn't meant a thing to either of them, it had been nothing but what she'd called it, a good fuck . . .

"Conor?"

. . . and there wasn't a damn thing extraordinary in that. The world was full of women who felt right in a man's arms, whose kisses tasted of honey, who could sigh his name in a way that made him feel, if just for a second, that he was the only man who'd ever mattered.

"Conor?"

Conor looked up. Harry was standing beside the table, the skillet in his hand. The fish were done to a soft, golden hue; the air in the cabin smelled delicately of spices and frying bacon—and crackled with electricity.

"The girl is a problem, Conor."

"Tell me something new," Conor said coldly.

"She's modeling for her mother's cosmetics firm—"

"How nice for them both."

"—but other than that, she's leading a life much like the one she led in Paris."

Conor's jaw tightened. "She's over eighteen."

"She goes to those clubs that spring up overnight in lower Manhattan and she's with a different man each night."

"Sleeping around isn't against the law," Conor said, though the words all but stuck in his throat.

"I don't know that she's sleeping with anyone." Harry set the skillet in the center of the table. "Breverman says she always comes home alone."

It was stupid to feel a sense of relief but that was exactly what Conor felt. He covered it with a careless shrug.

"How touching. Maybe she's being faithful to Moreau. Hell, stranger things have happened."

"Stranger things, indeed," Harry said. He drew a chair to the table and motioned Conor to do the same. "We did some deeper checking on Moreau, as you'd requested."

Conor reached for the skillet and dumped a couple of fillets on his plate.

"Looks good," he said. "Pass the salt, will you?"

"Taste it first."

"Harry . . ."

"As I was saying, we dug around a little, as you'd asked."

"I asked when I was still interested. Now, the only thing I'm interested in is the salt."

"Aren't you the least bit curious to know what we came up with?"

Conor sighed, put down his fork and leaned his forearms on the table.

"Tell me," he said, "because I can see, if you don't, I'm not going to be allowed to eat my meal in peace."

Harry Thurston took a mouthful of fish. "Mmm. Delicious."

"Harry, goddammit . . ."

"He's gay."

"Who's gay?"

The older man smiled. "Miss Beckman's lover. Her supposed lover. Jean-Phillipe Moreau."

Conor stared at Thurston. "You're crazy," he said flatly.

"He's been very, very discreet. And extraordinarily cautious. But there's no doubt about it. The man is a gender-bender."

"He can't be. I saw him with Miranda. I saw . . ."

What? What had he seen, really? Miranda clinging to Moreau like a honeysuckle vine to a fence post, that was all. But it had been enough. More than enough. She'd said—she'd made it clear . . .

"We checked thoroughly, Conor." Thurston forked more fish into his mouth. "In fact, you know that producer he's working with, out in Los Angeles?"

"Harlan Williams," Conor said wryly. "How could I forget that name? The guy's probably still trying to figure out how five million bucks suddenly dropped into his lap so he could ask Moreau to make that movie."

"Well, Williams and Moreau have taken up housekeeping. Cautiously, of course."

"Suppose I buy Moreau being gay. Why would Miranda lie about their relationship? It doesn't make sense."

"Indeed it does. She's provided the cover Moreau needs."

"And what does she get out of it?"

"She's a beautiful, much-desired woman. Being thought of as Moreau's lover would be an enhancement to her career."

Thurston frowned and pointed his fork at Conor's plate. "You want to dig into that while it's hot. The coating loses its crispness as it cools."

"Try again, Harry. She doesn't need to enhance her career."

"Well, perhaps it's the other way around. Perhaps she enhances his. Conor, I do wish you'd eat."

Conor picked up his fork and glared across the table.

"You're turning into an old woman, you know that, Harry?" He stabbed his fish, then shoved a forkful of it into his mouth. "Delicious," he said, and let the fork clatter against his plate again. "Did you ever consider that whoever got this information made a mistake?"

Thurston gave a long, sorrowful sigh. He rose from the table, retrieved two bottles of ale, set one in front of Conor and sat down again.

"There's no mistake. And before you ask, no, Moreau is not bisexual. He goes one way and one way only. He likes men."

Conor let out a soundless whistle.

"Unbelievable," he said softly.

"Eva and Hoyt are concerned."

"You told them about Moreau?"

Harry laughed. "Of course not. They're worried about how casually Miranda's been dealing with the situation."

"Which situation? Dammit, Harry . . ."

"That first note to Eva, the threats the girl received, in Paris. They find her rather relaxed attitude disturbing."

Conor smiled grimly. "Eva's exhibiting maternal instincts, is she?"

Harry shook his head. If Eva had any maternal instincts, he'd yet to notice.

"The Winthrops are simply waiting for the other shoe to drop. For that matter, so am I. It would be irresponsible to assume the worst is over. And then there's Hoyt's appointment. The President can't keep it on hold much longer."

"Poor Hoyt."

"You can take as sarcastic a tone as you like, Conor. The fact remains that there is cause for concern.

Conor shoved back his chair and stood up. "Okay, let's stop jerking each other around. What do you want from me? You've got Breverman on this, and he's been around long enough to know what he's doing."

A muscle flexed in Harry Thurston's jaw.

"By the time he does," he said quietly, "it may be too late."

Conor's eyes locked on Thurston's face. "Have there been more notes?"

"No."

"What, then? Has somebody tried a break-in at the Winthrop place?"

"No. Not there, or at the duplex the girl's taken on the East Side."

"Maybe I'm missing something here. She's not getting any more notes, there's been no break-in . . ." His eyes darkened. "Has she been hurt?"

"She's fine. Breverman's been keeping tabs on her—when he can."

"What do you mean, when he can?"

Harry sighed. "I mean just that. The Beckman girl manages to disappear on him whenever it suits her fancy."

"She . . . " Conor laughed and sat down again. "Are you telling me that a babe who knows more about shadowing her eyelids than shadowing someone has figured out a way to lose Breverman?"

"That's what I said. She's completely uncooperative. He wants to talk to her, you know, ask some questions, she won't let him. He wants to go inside, check out her apartment, she won't permit it. It's as if she's playing a game where she gets points for being stupid."

"She isn't stupid," Conor said sharply.

"I didn't say she was stupid, I said she was *being* stupid. There's a difference."

Conor thought of how he'd let himself get carried away, that last night he'd spent with Miranda. Tell me about being stupid, he thought, and he kicked back his chair, picked up his plate and carried it to the trash can.

"I still fail to see what any of this has to do with me," he said, scraping his meal into the garbage.

Thurston rose, too. "Did you have a relationship with her?"

Conor's fork clattered to the floor. He bent down and picked it up.

"If you mean, did she show as much contempt for me as she's showing for Breverman—"

"I mean just what I said." There was nothing friendly or casual in Thurston's voice or face. "Did you have a relationship with Miranda Beckman?"

Conor turned and faced him. "What the fuck is that supposed to mean?"

"You slept with her. Or you wanted to sleep with her. I don't know which, O'Neil, but sure as God grows little green apples, something happened between the two of you, in Paris."

Conor's smile seemed pasted to his face as he strode to the cabin door.

"Good-bye, Harry," he said, reaching for the denim jacket he'd left hanging on a wall peg. "Thanks for the fishing and the recipe."

"I'm right," Thurston said, his voice rising, "something did happen, something you can use to work your way into her life again, that will get you close enough to her to keep her alive."

"Shove it, Harry." Conor reached for the door. "You and I both know you're full of—"

"Breverman intercepted a package sent to her yesterday. It was a carton. A small one. Came sealed, delivered by messenger."

Conor stopped, his hand on the doorknob. Don't ask any questions, he told himself fiercely, for God's sake, don't!

"You want to know what was in that box, O'Neil?"

Conor turned slowly, his eyes meeting Thurston's.

"A pair of very dead cats," the older man said softly. "One was a Siamese, like the girl's. The other had coal-black fur and green eyes.'' His mouth twisted. ''You'll forgive me if I leave the details until after I've digested my lunch.''

Conor nodded. It was bad, but it wasn't over yet; he could see it in Thurston's eyes.

''And?''

''And, there was a note in the box.'' Thurston reached into his shirt pocket and drew out a folded piece of paper. ''Perhaps you should read it for yourself.''

Conor stared at his boss's outstretched hand. Slowly, he reached for the note. His brain registered that it was different from the others. This wasn't handwritten. The words were made up of letters that had been clipped from newspapers, then pasted on a sheet of plain white paper so that they looked lopsided and seemed, at first, to make no sense . . . and then, all at once, they did.

Miranda, darling Miranda, the note said. *Soon you'll agree that a dead pussy is the only kind that's worth fucking.*

Conor heard a roaring in his ears. He forced himself to take a deep, deep breath. Then he read the note again.

''Well?'' Thurston asked, when the men's eyes met.

''I'm going to kill the piece of shit who wrote this,'' Conor said. His voice was calm, as if they were discussing nothing more urgent than the weather, but a vein had risen in his forehead and pulsed visibly just beneath his skin.

Thurston's lips curved in what might have been a smile.

''I take it you're back on board, then?''

''Call Langley. I want a plane waiting at Charlottesville, to fly me to New York.''

Thurston pulled a cellular phone from his pocket. ''Done. What else?''

''I get *carte blanche.* No idiocy with filling out forms in triplicate, no wasting time getting court orders if I need to do something that's not quite kosher.''

''Of course.''

''And you'd better make sure the Committee understands, I'll do whatever it takes to protect the girl, even if it means the President ends up with dirt on his shoes.''

"My dear boy, presidents never end up with dirt on anything."

"Nixon did."

Thurston's smile flickered on again. "Ah, but Nixon didn't have the Committee. Do whatever you must. Just clean up this mess, once and for all."

Conor pulled on his jacket. "You're all heart, Harry, did anybody ever tell you that?"

"Having a heart never meant a thing in this business, O'Neil. When you come down to it, having one's a liability. You, of all people, should know that."

Conor nodded. He had not only known it, he had lived by it. And he would, again, when this was over.

Boring, Miranda thought, bor-ing!

Why had she let herself be talked into attending this party?

Eva had told her it was a charity function. Papillon, she'd said, believed in supporting good works. What she'd neglected to mention was that the purpose of this particular good work was to raise monies to provide works of art for homeless shelters around the city.

Art? For people who needed roofs over their heads and, probably, food in their bellies?

It was a concept that was totally Eva. There she was now, holding court across the room, her hairdo impeccable, her makeup perfect, her gown the latest creation from Bill Blass. Hoyt was beside her, resplendent in his tuxedo, looking for all the world like the perfect ambassador, though he wasn't an ambassador. Not yet.

To hear Eva tell it, that was her fault.

"Those dreadful notes surely originated with someone of your acquaintance," she'd said at dinner the first night Miranda had been back in the States. "Please be sure you keep better friends, so long as you remain in this city—which we shall help you do, by having you live here, with us."

Miranda had sat there, smiling politely. The next morning,

she'd gone apartment-hunting, subletting the first place that was acceptable. Then she'd made some phone calls, to people she knew. Hi, she'd said, wasn't it cool? She was in town and hey, where did people go to have fun?

The next day, she was living in her new apartment and the day after that, she'd made both *The News* and *The Post,* her name splashed in heavy black print beneath photos of her snapped on the dance floor at a hot little club off Ninth Avenue where she'd probably been the only person in the place who didn't have a tongue full of gold studs.

Eva had phoned, voice icy with disapproval.

"The Papillon image is not well-served by such publicity," she'd snapped, and Miranda had said that if Eva preferred, she could find someone else to be the Chrysalis girl.

Eva had made it clear that personal preference had little to do with the situation. Using Miranda as the Chrysalis model was the story she and Hoyt had concocted to explain her return. Miranda had almost laughed. She'd thought of pointing out that people who knew them also knew that mother and daughter had barely spoken to each other in the past eight years, but she hadn't. She'd simply repeated, politely, that the choice was Eva's. As for her, she would conduct her personal life as she saw fit.

"As you always have," Eva had snarled, and hung up.

A couple of hours later Hoyt had called and asked, pleasantly enough, if Miranda could please try to keep a low profile until things calmed down.

"Meaning what?" Miranda had asked, just as pleasantly. "Meaning, stay low until Eva sells a billion new lipsticks? Or until you get your precious appointment?"

Why, until it was certain no harm would come to her. Or to Eva, Hoyt had said in a wounded tone.

"I've never wanted anything but the best for you both, Miranda," he'd said. "You know that."

Hoyt, still standing at his wife's side, seemed to hear Miranda's thoughts. He looked around, caught her eye, and smiled. Miranda didn't smile back. His charm was wasted on her. She didn't like him. She never had, though Eva insisted that wasn't true, that she'd adored him, when she was little . . .

"Miss Beckman?"

A tall, skinny man with a bristling mustache and a shiny bald head had appeared at her elbow.

"It is such a pleasure to have you here, Miss Beckman."

Miranda smiled dutifully. "It's a pleasure to be here."

"Such a fine, charitable event, don't you think?"

What she thought was that the event was stupid and anybody who didn't realize that was even stupider. Not that she was much better. Here she was, back where she'd sworn she'd never be, at Eva's beck and call.

At least she'd had the sense to look up Brian Stone and ask him to represent her.

". . . so many organizations raising money for food and clothing and shelter that we asked ourselves, why should we duplicate . . ."

Brian hadn't turned a hair at the thought of getting as much money as possible out of Miranda's own flesh and blood. Thanks to him, Papillon was paying a fortune so it could plaster her face everywhere. Even Jean-Phillipe was impressed. Nita was, too. The last time they'd spoken on the phone, she'd laughed and gone straight to the nitty-gritty.

"This is so great, girlfriend! That mama of yours, paying through the nose to have you in her ads, after she once dumped you like a load of dirty laundry!"

Trust Nita to put the right spin on things. Viewed that way, being in New York wasn't so bad. Eva was eating crow, Miranda was getting terrific exposure, the notes had stopped coming—and Conor, the meddling son of a bitch, was out of her life.

But the news wasn't all good. O'Neil had been replaced by a jerk named Breverman. He'd come straight to her door, rung the bell and introduced himself.

"How do you do, Miss Beckman," he'd said. "My name is Robert Breverman but please, call me Bob." Then he'd flashed a government ID at her.

The government! A private detective peering over her shoulder had been bad enough, but to have Big Brother breathing down her neck was ridiculous, especially since the nut who'd sent the awful notes and the picture had faded back into the woodwork.

She'd asked Eva to call the guy off but Eva had shrugged her shoulders and said it wasn't up to her, that the government was doing what it had to do to safeguard Hoyt. So Miranda had swallowed her pride and asked Hoyt to see about getting rid of Breverman but Hoyt had only given her that phony, elder-statesman smile and launched into a speech about the importance of patience and tolerance.

Finally, she'd taken things into her own hands and figured out ways to give Call-Me-Bob the slip. It was almost painfully easy, considering that she could pick him out of a crowd at a hundred yards. Hadn't ever occurred to him that not that many guys hung around the Papillon offices on Fifth Avenue, or the building on Madison, where Brian Stone had his agency, wearing black suits that had a shine and black wing-tips that didn't?

If it had been O'Neil watching over her, she'd never have gotten away with it. He'd have stuck like glue, just the way he had in Paris. If she'd tried to evade him, he'd have shouldered his way into her apartment, demanded to know what in hell she thought she was doing and after they'd yelled at each other maybe, just maybe, he'd have gathered her into his arms and kissed her until nothing mattered but the taste and the feel of him, though why she should even think such a thing was beyond her comprehension.

Miranda gave herself a little shake. This was what came of standing around and being bored out of your mind. You got maudlin and stupid, you began to think about things that had no meaning. Enough, she thought, and she turned to the man standing beside her, gave him a dazzling smile, and interrupted him in midsentence.

"I'm sure Art for the Homeless is a wonderful cause," she said earnestly, "and I'm very grateful to you for explaining it to me."

"You're more than welcome, Miss Beckman." He cleared his throat and edged closer. "Perhaps you'd like to have a late supper with me. I'd love to fill you in on some of our future plans."

"Another time," Miranda said, her smile even more brilliant. "Unfortunately, it's quite late."

"Late?" His gaze shot to the Rolex on his pale, hairless wrist. "But it's barely nine-thirty."

"Ah, but I have to face the cameras in the morning. You wouldn't want me to look anything less than my best, would you?"

She patted his arm before he could come up with an answer and made her way to the table where she'd left the pale grey suede coat that matched her dress.

Eva caught up to her as she was halfway to the door.

"The party's not over," she said coldly.

"I know, but I have an early shoot tomorrow."

"This is an important event. Papillon is one of the sponsors and Chrysalis should be properly represented."

"Don't worry, Mother. I shook all the right hands and smiled at all the right people."

Eva's lips thinned with contempt. "I suppose you have a late date."

"That's none of your business."

"Nothing is different," Eva said in a low, razor-sharp voice. "You still have no sense of morality or obligation."

"Isn't it nice to know some things never change?" Miranda said, her smile unwavering. "Good night, Mother."

It was cool out, but not unpleasantly so. She could even smell the green fragrance of spring on the sighing breath of a light breeze. The only thing that spoiled the evening was a quick glimpse of Bob Breverman, lurking just a few yards past the hotel.

The doorman started to whistle for a cab but Miranda waved it away. It was only a short walk to the apartment she was renting and besides, she needed the exercise. Paris was a city of walkers; New York was a place where you took a taxi, even if you were only going half a dozen blocks. Maybe she'd join a gym. Or take up running. Something. Anything. She didn't want to put on weight.

Didn't want time to hang heavy on her hands because when it did, she ended up thinking.

About Conor, and what he'd done to her, taking away her friends, her home, all the things that had been her life.

About how it had been between them, that night. That one fantastic night, when almost anything had seemed possible.

That awful night, when she'd come painfully close to making a complete fool of herself.

A horn blared, and she almost jumped out of her skin as a taxi squealed to a halt only a couple of feet away. The driver leaned out his window, cursing her in some language she'd never heard before. Other horns blared as she zigzagged through the traffic.

Terrific. If she wasn't careful, she'd end up not on the society pages tomorrow, or even on the gossip pages, but as a front page headline.

Famous Model Finds Fate on Fifth.

Eva would probably love the publicity.

Miranda stepped up on the curb and made her way to the entrance to her apartment building. At the last second, she came to a dead stop. Call-Me-Bob Breverman was right on schedule, following her so closely that he almost crashed into her as she turned and confronted him.

"Good evening, Mr. Breverman," she said politely. "Lovely night for walking, isn't it?"

Breverman flushed. "This is a foolish game, Miss Beckman."

"Perhaps. But it's my game, and I enjoy playing it. You can go home and get some rest, Mr. Breverman. I promise, I'm not going out anymore tonight. I'll be locked up, safe and snug, until nine tomorrow morning."

One last smile, and then she walked briskly to the entrance.

The doorman touched his cap in greeting, the door swung open, and Miranda stepped inside the lobby.

Conor, watching from the shadows, cursed under his breath.

He waited until the door closed after her. Then he strolled across the street, to Bob Breverman's side.

"She made you," he said conversationally.

Breverman's flush deepened. "Yeah, but then, she almost always does."

Conor nodded and dug his hands deeper into the pockets of his leather flight jacket.

"She's a winner, all right."

"She's a bitch," Breverman said, "and she's all yours, O'Neil."

Conor watched as Breverman strode away. No, he thought, and his gut tightened, she isn't mine.

But God, how he wished she were.

Chapter Fourteen

Miranda had no idea he was watching her.

Conor dogged her footsteps for the rest of the week but he might as well have been invisible.

She never caught a glimpse of him. He was certain of that, although a couple of times she'd hesitated as she'd stepped out onto the street in the morning, her head lifted, her nostrils delicately flaring, and he'd remembered a filly he'd seen once, during a stint in Saudi Arabia, and the way she'd come out into the meadow, tossing her head and seeking the scent of the stallion that was waiting for her.

It was a fanciful, pointless thought and he'd have laughed at it and at himself if he'd had the time, but he was too busy making sure he kept out of the way so she didn't spot him.

He knew she was wondering what had happened to Bob Breverman. He could tell by the way she glanced around, as if she were a kid playing a game of hide-and-seek. That pissed him off. He wanted to step out of the shadows, grab her and shake her and say, dammit, lady, haven't you figured out yet that this isn't a game an amateur stands a chance of winning?

Breverman had given him a rundown on her schedule. Out

the door at eight; coffee, wheat toast and half a grapefruit at a little place a couple of blocks over, then a brisk walk to the office or a taxi ride to wherever the cameras might be filming that day. She had lunch—a container of yogurt, fruit and a small bottle of Perrier—on the set, if she was being photographed. If she was in the office Eva had assigned her at Papillon, she ate on a bench in the atrium of a skyscraper a couple of blocks away. She never lunched at Papillon itself, where there was an executive dining room.

Eva took that as an indication of her daughter's intransigent behavior.

"My daughter prefers to go her own way," she'd said with a chill smile, when Conor paid her a quick visit, told her not to mention his presence in the city to Miranda, and asked her to provide him with Miranda's weekly schedule in advance. "Following her, when she's on her own time, should prove interesting, Mr. O'Neil. Heaven only knows where she goes, or what she does, even on her lunch hour."

Or who she does it with. The unspoken words had seemed to hang in the air between them.

Conor wondered what Eva would say if he told her that so far, Miranda's lunchtime assignations were with a bunch of cooing pigeons that had already figured out she was an easy mark. But he didn't answer; he just kept quiet and nodded wisely, as if he were taking it all in.

In the afternoons, Miranda invariably went out to promote Papillon's new cosmetic line. Eva's people had arranged appearances for her all over Manhattan and in half a dozen other major markets. She taxied to Bloomingdale's and Barney's; she was greeted with glitzy excitement at Saks, Henri Bendel's and the other Fifth Avenue stores.

A week after Conor took over, she began going out of town to tout Chrysalis. She flew to Dallas and Miami, Phoenix and San Francisco and Conor flew with her, in the same plane, folding his long legs into his coach class seat because there was no way he could sit in business class, or first, without her seeing him.

She flew to Los Angeles, too, and scooted off to a handsome house high in the hills for a couple of hours to visit with Jean-Phillipe Moreau. The house was damn near all windows, which made Conor nervous, but at least it gave him an easy view of things, enough to see the easy familiarity between Moreau and Harlan Williams, and to know that you couldn't call the kisses and hugs Miranda shared with the Frenchman anything but brotherly.

In the evenings, she went out. To the clubs, as Thurston had said, and always with a group of people, the women fashion-model gorgeous, the men successful-looking and handsome. She wore outrageous outfits, body-hugging dresses that came to mid-thigh, with her hair hanging loose down her back and a smile he knew was phony painted across her face, and she shimmered like heat-lightning on the dance floor. Watching her turned his body hard and his temper mean; it was all he could do sometimes to keep from marching onto the floor, tossing her over his shoulder and carrying her off.

She had the same effect on every other man who watched her and he could tell that she knew it. She flirted like crazy, damn her, batted her lashes and pouted and purred until half the guys in the place were panting to have her. And then she went home.

Alone.

Conor couldn't figure it out. He'd seen her with Moreau in L.A.; he knew that what Thurston had said about the man's sexuality was true. So, if she wasn't being faithful to the Frenchman, why was she sleeping by herself?

And through it all, she never had a clue that he was watching. Breverman, the poor sap, had slunk around dressed like a G-12 clerk. Conor knew better. He hadn't given a damn about blending into the background in Paris. If anything, he'd worn his Harris tweed jackets, his cords and his sweaters as a not terribly original way of distancing himself from the smarmy fashion scene, but here he knew he had to fade into the woodwork.

He'd moved into a sublet two blocks from Miranda's place,

courtesy of his expense account, and the only things he hung in the closet were his Burberry and his tux. Everything else was Manhattan casual: a couple of pair of snug, faded Levi 501's, his ancient denim jacket that had once been a rite of passage, a leather flight jacket he'd had, and cherished, for more than a decade. He took himself over to Ralph Lauren's, bought some cashmere sweaters, a couple of sports jackets, pants, and a handful of shirts. Then he thought, what-the-hell, ducked into a nearby shop and picked up a pair of leather boots, although he spent half an hour scuffing the boots with sandpaper so he wouldn't come off looking like some midnight cowboy and end up having to defend his honor. A pair of dark shades, and that was it.

He was in business.

Now he could bide his time, hang back and wait. Sooner or later, something was bound to happen. It was just that when something finally did, it wasn't what he'd expected.

Friday afternoon, Miranda was heading for her apartment. She was walking, taking her time, looking into shop windows, when she suddenly veered into a place called The Milepost. Conor tucked his hands into the pockets of his jeans, sauntered to the window, and looked in.

The shop was crammed with running gear. Sneakers, shorts, tops, warm-up suits—a sea of Spandex and Polartec flowed in all directions. From where he stood, he could see Miranda making her way down one aisle and up the other, taking stuff from the racks and finally toting it to the counter.

Had she taken up running? Had she joined a gym? One or the other seemed likely, but he had no idea which it was.

He knew she got a late start on Friday nights. He had plenty of time to go home, dress for an evening of club-hopping, then return and stake the place out.

Logic told him that, but instinct told him something else.

He trotted the couple of blocks to his apartment but instead of putting on one of his Polo jackets, he pulled on a pair of sweats, added his old Columbia sweatshirt with the hole in the sleeve, and laced up his Adidas. A little past six, he took up station outside Miranda's apartment building.

Somewhere between seven and seven-thirty, she came out the door.

She was wearing stuff he'd seen her buy that afternoon, no-nonsense grey sweats and white running shoes. Her hair was pulled back in a French braid and her face was shiny, scrubbed and makeup-free. She looked up at the sky, checking the weather. He wanted to cross the street, tell her that what she should be checking was her head.

You didn't go running at night, not in this city.

She did a couple of quick stretches and he figured she was about to get on her way when she stopped, cocked her head in his direction and got that funny "Is somebody there?" look on her face. And she smiled.

The skin on the back of Conor's neck prickled. He knew that she couldn't see him. This side of the street was in shadow and he was standing far back in a doorway. Still, he had the damnedest feeling, not that she suspected he was there but that she hoped he was.

A middle-aged woman crossed from his side of the street to Miranda's. She was holding a leash and at the end of it, a silver grey Yorkie wearing a bright red bow in its top-knot hurried along as fast as its short legs would carry it. Miranda grinned, bent down and rubbed the dog's ears as it trotted past. Then she did another couple of stretches, adjusted her laces and set off at an easy lope towards Central Park.

Conor let out his breath.

It was going to be tough to figure which of them was the bigger jerk.

He counted to thirty, then set off after her.

Miranda puffed a little as she headed into the park.

What was the matter with her this evening?

Aside from being out of shape, that was, because she certainly was that, otherwise she wouldn't be breathing so hard.

What on earth had made her think of O'Neil just now?

Not that it was the first time. It had been happening with regularity, ever since that fool, Call-Me-Bob, had mercifully been pulled out of her life.

For reasons she couldn't figure at all, she'd come out of her building the morning after the Art for the Homeless thing and stopped dead in her tracks, her heart doing a fluttery two step. She'd had the eerie sensation that Conor was somewhere close by.

He hadn't been, of course. He was wherever he'd been before Eva had hired him, doing whatever it was private investigators did. Spying on somebody else, probably, making some other poor soul's life a misery.

Damn, when was the last time she'd done any running? Nita had always said they ought to get into it but Nita didn't really need the exercise. She could stuff her face from morning until night and never gain an ounce.

Miranda smiled, thinking of the letter she'd gotten from Nita the other day. "I am too happy for words," she'd written, and tucked inside the brief but telling note had been a photo of her, wearing a yellow sarong and with a big pink flower tucked behind her ear. Her arms were locked around the neck of a skinny guy sporting a smile as big as Nita's. "Me and Carlos," she'd scribbled on the back of the picture. "Isn't he gorgeous?"

That was what love was all about, Miranda thought, picking up her pace a little. It was getting easier to breathe, now that she was getting into the rhythm of the run. You met a man, he made you smile, not just with your lips but with your heart, and if he asked you to follow him to the ends of the earth, you paused only long enough to pack your toothbrush.

It wasn't like what she'd felt for Conor, anger so fierce she wanted to hurt him where he lived one minute and a need so powerful she ached to be in his arms the next. Whenever *he'd* asked her to do something, she'd been torn between doing it and breaking something over his head.

Why was she even thinking about him? Dredging up all those memories would only spoil the run. The park was all hers, and the solitude was wonderful after the noise of the city streets. She'd been hesitant about running tonight, wondering if it might not be a better idea to roll out of bed early and hit the park then, but she'd been eager to give it a try and besides, it was still fairly light out.

Plenty of time to enjoy finding her stride.

Plenty of time to think about Conor.

Maybe she hadn't hated him. Hate was an awfully strong word. What had she felt, then? Dislike? No, dislike didn't make it. Dislike was how she felt about brussel sprouts or cold oatmeal, the lumpy stuff she'd always thought of as Boarding School Breakfast. Dislike had nothing to do with emotions so powerful they made you feel as if you'd been turned inside out.

Damn, what was she doing? Only a lunatic would waste time, trying to categorize her feelings for a man who meant nothing to her. Less than nothing, to be accurate. And there it was, that weird sensation again, that if she could only turn around quickly enough she'd spot him watching her. Following her.

"Stop it," she said impatiently, under her breath.

The path jigged just ahead, cut into a stand of forsythia that was just coming into bloom. Miranda got her knees up a little, tucked in her elbows and picked up her pace.

No more thinking about Conor O'Neil. From this second on, he was history.

She ran well, he had to give her that.

And she looked good, too. Those long legs, that nicely rounded bottom . . . Coasting along a couple of dozen yards behind Miranda was turning out to be a very pleasant way to end the day—even if Central Park at dusk wasn't the place he'd have chosen.

Running wasn't a bad idea, either. He was holding back so he wouldn't get too close to her but still, he was working up a light sweat, feeling a nice stretch in his muscles. That was always good but after days of mostly standing around with his thumb up his butt, just watching and waiting, a little workout was just what he needed. It was good for his body, and for his brain. There was nothing like some physical stuff to clear out the cobwebs and God knew, he'd picked up more than his fair share the past weeks.

Was that what his thoughts about Miranda were? Cobwebs? Meaningless debris, lodged in his mind?

Not that it mattered. This assignment would be done soon—he could feel it in his gut. And once it was, it would be goodbye, *au revoir, adios, auf wiedersehn* to her and everything about her . . .

What was that?

Up ahead, Miranda had just gone around a curve and disappeared into a sea of yellow forsythia. He couldn't see her, but he *could* see the four big, burly teenaged boys who'd slipped out of the shrubs behind her. The boys were moving fast and running close together and as they vanished from sight, he remembered a film he'd once seen on cable about a pack of wolves on the trail of a deer.

Conor put his head down and really began to run.

The feeling was back, that somebody was on her tail.

Only the feeling wasn't the same as before. She knew, without hesitation, that it wasn't Conor coming up behind her. It wasn't even Bob Breverman.

It was somebody—several somebodies—that meant her harm. Every urban survival instinct told her so.

Miranda lengthened her stride.

Behind her, somebody laughed.

"Laaydee . . ."

The voice was young, male and deceptively soft. It was a voice that was rich with the promise of pleasures yet to come . . . pleasures that would surely not be hers.

She began to run flat-out, her feet pounding the path, her arms swinging. She could hear the footsteps quicken behind her, and the laughter. The urge to turn around and see who was coming after her was overwhelming but she knew better than to give in. She'd lose precious time—and God only knew what she'd see.

Who she'd see.

Somebody who wants to hurt you, Miranda. Somebody who sent you that awful picture and that terrible, bone-chilling note.

"Hey, laaydee . . ."

A hand brushed her shoulder, another cupped her ass. She cried out and twisted away but fingers clamped around her arm and spun her around. She had a quick glimpse of four laughing faces and then a fist landed in the middle of her chest. The air whooshed from her lungs; she fell to her knees.

"Son of a bitch!"

Like an avenging angel, Conor burst upon her attackers. There was a thud, a muffled grunt, the sound of bone cracking against flesh. A high-pitched scream pierced the air and one of the boys went down, his left arm clutching his right, which hung uselessly at his side.

"Conor," Miranda wept, "oh God, Conor!"

"Kohnuh," a voice mimicked cruelly, "oh God, Kon—"

Conor moved again, fast as lightning. The second assailant went down, his mouth opening and closing as he gasped for air, his arms wrapped around his jackknifed body.

Conor laughed. He was on the balls of his feet as if he were dancing, his body loose, his arms out and his hands open. There was a smile on his face and a terrible coldness in his eyes and Miranda could smell base, animal rage in his sweat.

"Okay," he was saying to the third of her attackers, his voice very soft, "okay, shit-head, come and get me."

The boy's eyes shifted from side to side. Something glinted in his hand.

"He's got a knife," Miranda screamed.

The boy moved fast, the knife coming in gut-low. But Conor moved faster. There was a scream. The knife went flying and then Conor was standing behind the boy, who must have outweighed him by fifty pounds, with his right arm wrapped tightly around the kid's neck.

The fourth assailant turned and ran.

"Don't, man," pleaded the one in the armlock.

Conor yanked back, hard. "Give me a good reason why I shouldn't."

The boy rose on his toes. "We was only funnin', man."

"The truth or you're dead, scumbag."

The boy grabbed Conor's arm and hung on, trying to ease the choke hold that was cutting off his breath.

"Please, man, let go!"

"Who set this up? You?"

"It was just some fun, is all. A little fun with the lady."

"I asked who set it up."

"James did."

"James?"

"The guy who bugged out."

"Why?"

"I told you, man, it was for fun."

"You've had fun like this before?"

Conor jerked back and the boy lifted on his toes.

"On my mother, man," he babbled, "we never did! Hey, the lady shouldn't have been runnin' on our turf, you understand what I'm sayin'? You can't let people dis you, man, so we was just gonna, you know, teach her a little somethin', have some fun."

Conor flung the boy from him. His pals scrambled to their feet and the three of them stood huddled together.

"If I ever see you again," he snapped, "the rats will be eating your eyeballs. You got that? Now, get the hell out of here before I change my mind."

The trio turned and ran.

Conor swung towards Miranda. She was still on her knees. There was dirt on her face and terror in her eyes and all he could think about was how close he'd come to losing her. If he hadn't taken over from that idiot, Breverman, if he hadn't followed his instincts and been waiting for her when she'd come out the door tonight . . .

An image flashed through his head. He saw Miranda lying crumpled in among the forsythia, raped or worse, and what he'd thought and what he felt terrified him so completely that he reacted the only way he dared.

"Goddamn you, Beckman," he roared, "you are one dumb broad!"

She stared at him for a long, long minute. Then she took a deep, shuddering breath and got to her feet, ignoring the hand he extended, making it on her own even though her legs were so watery they didn't feel as if they belonged to her.

"You're right," she said. Tears of anger glinted in her eyes and she brushed them away. "I *am* stupid, because just for a minute there, I was going to say—I was going to say . . ."

She swung away from him, head bowed so that her braid swung forward, revealing the tender nape of her neck, and Conor cursed himself for a fool and reached for her.

"They could have killed you," he said harshly.

She stiffened as his hands closed on her shoulders and then a sound, terrible in its anguish, burst from her throat and she turned and went into his arms. He held her while the moments ticked away, his arms hard around her, his heart thudding against hers, telling himself it was best not to think about anything, certainly not to try and figure out what he was feeling, knowing only that holding her close was the best thing that had ever happened to him, that he was never going to let her go again, and then she stiffened and pulled back in his arms.

The shock that had turned her eyes dark was fading. In its place was confusion, anger and distrust.

"At the risk of sounding like somebody in a bad movie, O'Neil, what's a man like you doing in a place like this?"

Shit. It was the million-dollar question, and he hadn't an answer. What could he tell her, that wouldn't infuriate her? The truth, that he worked for the Committee, that he'd worked for it all along, would only prove him a liar. On the other hand, pretending he was working for Eva again would probably only earn him a sock in the jaw.

"I asked you a question." Her eyes locked on his. "Why were you following me?"

Think, he told himself, dammit, think! What he needed was a simple answer, one that wouldn't enrage her or dig him in any deeper.

She took his silence as all the answer she needed.

"Damn you," she whispered. Anger flashed in her eyes, anger and—and what? Disappointment? He didn't know, didn't have time to try and figure it out. All he could do now was talk his way into her life because that was where he knew he had to be, to keep her safe. "Good old Eva. She's got you back on the payroll."

"You're wrong," he said vehemently, "I'm not working for Eva."

"Please, O'Neil, don't insult my intelligence." Briskly, she brushed the dirt from her shorts. "Well, when you report in, tell her you scored ten points today but that it's not enough to guarantee your job security."

"Listen, Beckman—"

"Because if I look around and find you following me again, so help me, I'll head for the nearest cop and swear you're molesting me." She took a step back, folded her arms over her chest and glowered up at him. "You got that?"

His smile was chilly. "What's the world coming to, I wonder? Here I saved the lady's ass and now she wants me busted. Funny way to say thanks."

"You were doing your job, mister. Forgive me if I can't get excited about it."

"I told you, I don't work for Eva."

"Right." She leaned over and brushed off her bare legs. They were grimy and blood was oozing from a cut in her left knee.

"You're bleeding," he said.

"Isn't that wonderful?" she said sweetly. "You're not just a mass of overblown muscle, you're observant, too."

His lips hardened into a thin line. ''You've got a smart mouth on you, lady.''

''Just remember what I said. If I spot you anywhere near me, I'll have you arrested.''

''For what? Stupidity, for thinking I might deserve even a grudging thank-you?''

''Thank you? *Thank you?*'' Her chin lifted in anger and defiance. ''What am I supposed to thank you for, exactly? Getting me evicted from my apartment? Getting me tossed out of France? Getting Jean-Phillipe shipped off in one direction and Nita in the another?''

''Wow.'' Conor folded his arms and rocked back on his heels. ''Did I do all that?''

''Good-bye, O'Neil. And remember what I said. You so much as breathe in my direction, I'll have you locked up.''

''For what?''

''I'll think of something.''

She turned away and started to walk off, back straight, shoulders square. He gave her a couple of seconds lead time and then he caught up to her.

''You know, Beckman, everybody's wrong about you. You're not just a spoiled brat, you're a dumb one.''

''I beg your pardon?''

''Why would I be working for Eva again?''

''Because the money's good,'' she said briskly, picking up her pace.

Conor grasped her shoulder and swung her towards him.

''Try using your brain instead of your mouth for a change. Do you really think I'd put myself in a position where I had to deal with you again?'' He smiled tightly. ''There's not enough money in the world to make me do that.''

For the first time, he saw doubt cloud her eyes. She put her hands on her hips, considering, and he plunged ahead before he lost momentum.

''Besides, why would she want me to tail you? Are you saying there have been more notes?''

Her hair was coming loose from the braid. She put a hand to her forehead and scraped the strands back.

"Well, no."

"Listen," he said, keeping his voice brusque, letting her feel his impatience, "I had a job to do in Paris and I did it. Eva wanted you watched, then she wanted you back home. I took care of both items. End of job, end of paychecks. Understand?"

Her teeth fastened lightly on her bottom lip. He held his breath, waiting, trying to read her face as she assessed the situation, and then she gave a barely perceptible shrug.

"But if you weren't following me . . ."

"Hell," he said, rolling his eyes, "are we back to that?" He reached into the pocket of his shorts, dug around for a quarter. "Here," he said, shoving it at her, "go ahead. Phone Eva. Ask her if I'm back on the clock."

Her gaze flew to the coin in his outstretched hand, then to his face, and he worked at keeping his own gaze open and level. It wasn't difficult. After all, he was telling her the truth, as far as it went. Plus, he was one hell of a liar. Lying was a way of life, in his business. Disinformation, Thurston and the Committee called it, but the down and dirty reality was that whether you called it disinformation or just evading the truth, he could do it with the best of them.

It was an art he'd developed early, at St. Vincent's, where telling the good sisters the truth usually earned you a crack across the knuckles, and at home, where it might result in a whacking that could make you very careful about sitting down for a couple of days. By the time he'd gotten to Special Forces and then the Committee, he was more than ready to be turned into an expert. Oh yeah. He could widen his baby blues, swear on everything holy that what he was saying was the truth, the whole truth, the only truth.

"So, what are you saying? You weren't following me? You just happened to be in New York, in this park, on this path when those—those animals jumped me?"

"Yahoos," he said, with a little smile.

"What?"

"Swift," he said, "*Gulliver's Travels,* remember? They're yahoos. Hell, I like animals. They don't rape, they don't murder, they don't steal."

"They don't lie."

"And I'm not lying, either. I don't work for your mother or your stepfather."

"Then why—"

"Beckman, what's with you? You think you're the only person lives in this town? I have an apartment ten minutes from here. And I run. I have, for years, whenever I can." That, at least, was true. The Nautilus, lap pools, stationery bikes were all okay but there was something about running he'd always liked, the sense that you were doing something real, not just pitting yourself against a machine.

"And I'm supposed to believe that you just happened to pick this particular time and place to run?"

"Believe it or not, it's the truth, and I must be as dumb as you are, to hit the park at this hour."

She blinked, puzzled, and he knew he'd figured this right. All she needed was a little shove.

"Listen," he said, "I'm tired of defending myself. You want to go around thinking I'm working for Eva, tailing you, well, be my guest." He gave her a chilly smile. "Good-bye, lady, and I promise, if I have the misfortune to run into you again, *I'll* be the one calls the cops."

He turned sharply and trotted off, just fast enough to put some distance between them, feeling that prickling sensation between his shoulder blades that told him Miranda was watching, wondering if he'd overplayed his hand and knowing there wasn't much he could do about it now.

"O'Neil!"

He thought about turning around, thought again, and didn't do it. Come on, he said to himself, come on.

"O'Neil?" Her footsteps sounded on the path behind him and then she danced around him and held up her hand. Her face, that beautiful face that haunted his dreams, was flushed.

"Listen," she said, "if I was wrong . . ."

"If?" Conor made a face, detoured around her and kept going.

"Okay," she said breathlessly, dancing past him again, this time putting out both hands and pressing them lightly against his chest. "Okay. Maybe I—maybe I over-reacted."

He stood still, folded his arms, and gave her a stony glare. "Damn right, you over-reacted."

"But I'm sure you can see why I'd think . . ." She hesitated, then ran the tip of her tongue over her lips. "I mean, it just looked . . ."

She hadn't bought it all yet, not one hundred percent. But she would.

"Take my advice, Beckman. Pick a better time to run."

"Well, I thought seven o'clock was—"

"No time at night's okay. Morning's the time. Lots of people pack it through here then, but hey, come to think of it, you might end up seeing me and we wouldn't want that to happen."

"If you run in the morning," she said, looking confused, "then, what were you doing here tonight?"

Okay, O'Neil, let's hear you get out of this one.

"I never got the chance, today. The guy upstairs had a racket last night, went on until dawn so by the time I finally hit the sack, I overslept."

"So, you just happened to decide you'd take your run at night?"

She'd gone from looking confused to dubious, and who could blame her? He was doing the telling, and he was having trouble swallowing the story.

"Well," he said, with a smile he hoped was disarming, "it's one thing to give good advice and another to take it." He worked the smile up to a grin. "Besides, I'm a guy. I figure I can take care of myself."

She smiled back at him and he thought he'd done it. But then her smile disappeared, she didn't say anything, and he figured it was time to go for broke.

"Anyway, do yourself a favor. From now on, run when the

sun's out.'' He nodded, touched his hand to his forehead in a quick salute. ''Good-bye, Beckman. Nice seeing you again.

He turned and walked away.

But she didn't call after him. What was the matter with her? By now, she was supposed to be properly and thoroughly chastised, supposed to say, hey, O'Neil, wait a minute . . .

''O'Neil? Wait a minute.''

Conor closed his eyes, stopped walking and offered a silent thank-you to whatever gods might be looking down as he turned towards her.

''What?''

She came towards him slowly. She wasn't smiling, not exactly, but she wasn't looking at him as if he were the last man on earth she wanted to see, either.

''I guess I should thank you. If you hadn't come along—''

''Don't be modest. If I hadn't shown up, you'd have gone into your best Steven Seagal crouch, whirled around and done a karate move on that wolf pack.''

''Yahoos,'' she said, and now she *was* smiling, even if you had to work hard to see it. ''You're right. I've got nothing against animals, either.''

Conor grinned. ''There you go. At long last, we agree on something.''

She stood there, her big eyes on his, and then, very slowly, she held out her hand.

''Thank you, O'Neil.''

His hand folded around hers. She tried not to notice the warmth and the strength of it, and the way it made her pulse quicken. She tried not to think about how many times she'd dreamed of this moment, of seeing him again, even though those dreams had all ended with her kicking this man in the shins, well, except for a couple of dreams that had ended differently, with her in his arms and his kisses hot on her lips.

''Are you okay?'' he said. ''Your face is all flushed.''

She took her hand back, dug it into the pockets of her shorts. ''I'm, uh, I'm fine. I'm just—I'm just . . .''

''Thirsty? Exhausted?''

"Yes," she admitted, smiling up at him, trying not to notice how his sweat-stained shirt was molded to his body, how wonderful he looked.

"Yeah, I feel the same way. First the running, then all that adrenaline pumping . . . You need liquids, after something like that, maybe even some food. Have you had supper yet?"

"Uh-uh. I didn't want to run on a full stomach."

"Well, after what just happened, you need to chow down some calories. We both do. A steak,maybe a baked potato, a salad . . ."

Miranda laughed. "Scrambled eggs and toast is more my speed."

"Done," he said. "Your place, or mine?"

She blinked. "I didn't mean—"

"I'd suggest a coffee shop but in a minute or two, we're both going to start feeling the cold."

"What cold? It isn't—"

"We're both sweated up, Beckman. When the rush wears off, you'll start feeling it. Besides . . ." He jerked his chin at her leg. "You need to clean that cut."

She glanced down. Blood was oozing from the knee and now that she thought about it, her leg was beginning to feel stiff. She was beginning to feel chilly, too, just as he'd said she would.

"I could use some first aid myself." Conor rolled his shoulder, not lying, exactly; he'd dislocated it, a couple of years before, and it still hurt from time to time, especially if he took a whack in one spot—which he apparently had, he thought in surprise, his breath catching at the sharp jolt that shot through him when he tried a cautious twist.

"Conor?" Miranda put her hand on his arm. It felt cool and soft against his skin and for one crazy minute, he almost did what what he'd seen her Siamese do, shut his eyes and give himself up to that gentle touch. "Are you in pain?"

Oh yes. He was in pain, all right, he was hurting for the feel of her in his arms, for the way it had almost been.

"It's nothing," he said, biting back a groan, "Just my shoulder."

Her hand swept up his arm, leaving behind a trail of goose bumps. "I don't see anything."

"It's an old dislocation, acts up once in a while. I must have pulled it, dealing with those—"

"Yahoos," she said, grinning.

"Yeah," he said, smiling back at her.

Miranda hesitated. Every bone in her body was telling her it was a mistake to even stand here and talk to this man. Remember what happened, she told herself, remember how he made you feel, how dangerous it was.

"The walking wounded," he said, still smiling. "You need to get that knee cleaned up and I need to down a couple of aspirin."

She nodded, and her heart banged up into her throat.

"I have some stuff in my medicine cabinet," she said.

"Yeah?"

"And if you were serious about making a meal of scrambled eggs and toast—"

"No bacon?"

Miranda laughed. "Bacon's bad for you, O'Neil, haven't you heard?"

His eyes, as blue as the sea, met hers.

"Risk is what puts the spice in life," he said softly.

She nodded. "I know." A long time seemed to pass, and then she took a deep breath. "I haven't got any bacon," she said, "but I've got bagels in the freezer, and even some cream cheese."

He smiled, and her heart soared.

"You talked me into it," he said, and as they turned and headed out of the park, she had the feeling her life would never be the same again.

Chapter Fifteen

"Nice place," Conor said, as the door to Miranda's apartment closed behind him.

"It's okay," she said, switching on the lights, "or it will be, if I ever get around to fixing it up."

Fixing what up? Things looked pretty good, to him. The living room was enormous, twice the size of the one she'd had in Paris and maybe three times the size of the one in his place, back in Arlington. A staircase rose to the second floor, where he figured the bedroom to be.

Her bedroom in Paris had had a wonderful view, out over the Marais. This one would look out over the park, but it would still carry the scent of her perfume, the way it had in Paris.

Dammit, O'Neil, forget about Paris and her bedroom! This is a job. A job, you got that? Keep your mind on work.

"It came furnished," she said over her shoulder, as she headed for the kitchen.

Mia came strutting from the bedroom, her Siamese tail held high, and Miranda bent down and scooped the cat into her arms, grateful for something to hang on to. What was the matter with her? Why was she so nervous? Conor had saved her life, saved her from something nasty, anyway. The least she could do was give him something to eat.

"Yeah. So did my place."

It wasn't a lie. The apartment he was bunking in belonged to a guy he'd known at Columbia, a million years ago. Jack was a partner at a megabucks Wall Street law firm, doing the kind of clean-hands, deep pockets work Conor had once thought he'd be doing, too. They saw each other maybe once a year for a drink and a round of "remember when" and the last time, six weeks ago, Jack had mentioned he'd be working in Singapore for a few months.

"You know anybody wants to sublease the perfect bachelor pad," Jack had said with a grin, "you let me know."

"Sure," Conor had said, grinning back at him, never figuring that the "somebody" would turn out to be the Committee, which had agreed to pay the hefty rent on the place without blinking.

". . . really don't love living in a space that's got somebody else's fingerprints all over it, do you?"

Conor shrugged his shoulders. "It doesn't bother me," he said truthfully. "I've never been much for home and hearth, that kind of thing. What's that old song? 'Anywhere I hang my hat . . . ' "

"Not me. I like having my own things around me." Miranda put the cat down, opened the cupboard and took down a can of Friskies. "All my stuff's in storage. When I go back to Paris and find a new apartment—"

"You're going back?" he said, lounging in the doorway, arms folded, feet crossed.

She turned and looked at him in surprise.

"Yes, of course. There's nothing for me, in the States."

Stupid, the way her answer made him feel. Angry, and maybe even a little bit . . . a little bit . . .

"What?" she said.

"What, what?"

"I don't know. You've got a weird look on your face."

Conor cleared his throat. "Nothing. I mean, I was just wondering—I thought you said we'd have scrambled eggs and bagels."

"So?"

"So," he said, nodding at the can of cat food, "that doesn't look much like an egg to me."

Miranda laughed. "Relax, O'Neil. Mia gets fed first, or she'll yowl." She scooped the cat's food into a dish, then reached for the coffee pot. "Then it's our turn."

"You left a step out."

"I did?"

"Well, you're all sweated up. And dirty."

Miranda's eyebrows shot up. "You're just full of compliments, aren't you?"

"Don't argue, Beckman. You take a hot shower and I'll start the meal."

"Don't be silly. I'm fine."

"You're not fine. You're starting to shiver. And that cut on your knee still needs to be cleaned."

"Do you ever lose an argument?"

He grinned. "Not that I can recall. I'll give it some thought, while you're in the shower."

He could see the narrowing of her green eyes that told him she wasn't pleased. That's it, he told himself, keep this up, she'll be sorry she asked you here. Not that it mattered. He was already sorry he'd come. Why should he want to stand so close to her that he could smell her incredibly sexy combination of sweet woman and honest sweat? Why should he want to see how her damp shirt clung to her breasts, with her nipples standing hard and firm under the cotton, just waiting for the touch of his fingers?

Dammit, he thought, and he stepped back, far enough away so he couldn't be tempted to reach out and skim his hands up under her shirt.

"Get going," he said, his irritation with himself turning his voice gruff, "or I'll dump you under the shower myself."

Miranda glared at him. "Your wish is my command, *mein*

Führer,'' she said, rammed the coffee pot into his middle, and marched out of the room.

Safely inside the bathroom, she clutched the rim of the sink and flinched at the sight of her flushed face in the mirror.

So much for owing her rescuer a cup of coffee, a couple of eggs and a bit of polite conversation.

She yanked off her sweat-soaked, dirt-encrusted shorts and shirt, kicked off her muddy sneakers and tossed the entire mess into the corner. Then she turned the shower to hot and stepped under the spray.

The polite thing to do was to show O'Neil some appreciation for his help, but he didn't make it easy. He was still the same arrogant male he'd always been.

On the other hand, it was probably just as well he'd reverted to type and started barking out orders because a minute before that, she'd looked into his blue eyes and felt the world tilt beneath her feet. And that was ridiculous. He'd saved her butt but that didn't change things.

He was still Conor O'Neil, and she wanted nothing to do with him.

Miranda dumped a handful of shampoo into her hair and worked it through.

When she was done showering, she'd get dressed, go straight back to the kitchen and tell him, politely, that she was really very thankful he'd come along but that, on second thought, she wasn't much in the mood for company. He could have a cup of coffee, since he'd probably have it made by then, and then she'd walk him to the door, shake his hand and say good-bye.

Unless he took matters into his own hands, before she got that chance. Unless he opened the bathroom door, came walking in, stripped off his clothes, stepped under the water with her and took her in his arms.

Miranda's heart began to race. There was no point in pretending, not to herself. If he came for her, she wouldn't stop him. Standing in that kitchen, it had been all she could do to keep from reaching out and putting her arms around his neck, from rising on her toes and fitting her mouth to his.

She reached out and twisted the mixing knob to cold. The water sluiced down like liquid ice, rinsing away the soapy lather on her hair and skin. She gasped at the shock but she didn't turn the water off until her teeth were chattering and the pictures in her head were gone.

By the time she'd dried her hair, pulled on a pair of loose, white cotton drawstring pants and a long-sleeved white cotton T-shirt, she was fine—right up until the moment she entered the kitchen and saw Conor.

He didn't know she was there. Her entrance had been noiseless, partly because she'd padded down the hall in her bare feet but mostly because he'd turned on the radio and was humming along with it. He'd dialed past her usual station so that what drifted in the air was vintage McCartney instead of Mendelssohn.

He'd not only made coffee, he'd set the table, poured the orange juice, found the bagels and sliced them so they were ready for the toaster. By the looks of the pile of eggshells stacked up on the counter, he'd cracked open the entire dozen and now he was beating them into a frothy mass, wielding the fork in time with the music, his body moving with the beat.

The sight of him stirred not just her passion but her heart. He was so beautiful, but how could that be? Men weren't beautiful, not inside or out. And yet, Conor made her feel—made her feel . . .

Her breath caught and he must have heard it, because he glanced over his shoulder and shot her a grin.

"There you are, Beckman. And just in time, too." He gave the eggs one last stir, then dumped the fork into the sink and wiped his hands on the seat of his shorts. "Your turn at K.P., and let's just remember that I did the hard stuff."

Her turn at K.P.? His turn at the shower, was what he meant, and then she'd be expected to sit at the table across from him, trying not to touch his hand or smile at his jokes, most of all, trying not to think about that night in Paris, when they'd made love.

She had to get him out of here, and fast.

''O'Neil,'' she said briskly, ''I'm really terribly sorry but—''

She jumped as he strolled past her and swatted her lightly on the backside.

''It's okay, Beckman, you don't have to apologize. Women always use up all the hot water. It's the lot of the male of the species to shower and shiver at the same time.''

What he really meant, he thought as he headed for the bathroom, was that he wasn't going to let her throw him out. That sure as hell was what she'd intended to do. It had been written all over her face.

Someplace between the shower and the kitchen, Miranda had changed her mind. She wanted him gone but he wasn't going anywhere. He was here to do a job and he would do it, and if the shower was cold, so much the better.

He was too old to let a thing like a hard-on come between him and duty, he thought, trying to laugh at the bad pun and succeeding only in making a sound that was closer to a groan as he stepped into the still-warm bathroom and smelled Miranda's scent on the air.

Her damp towel was draped across the rod. He had to grit his teeth to keep from grabbing it and burying his face in its folds.

Jesus, he was in bad shape!

If he could just get through the next hour, he'd be fine.

Ten minutes later, he was positive he not only could, he would.

Cold showers were truly wonderful things. So was perspective. He'd had the one, gained the other, and life was back on track.

Music drifted faintly through the closed door. McCartney

had given way to something else. Mozart? Mendelssohn? It didn't matter. He liked both.

Whistling softly, he toweled off with a bath sheet he found shelved opposite the tub. Then he pulled on his running shorts. Except for a little tear and a faint smudge of dirt, they were okay. His shirt, however, was a write-off. Conor picked it up, made a face at the smears, the smell and what looked suspiciously like a bloodstain.

The only place the shirt was going was the incinerator. He balled it up, dropped it into the wastebasket. Okay, he thought, and he glanced in the mirror, ran his fingers through his towel-dried hair, and headed for the kitchen.

Miranda was at the stove, her back to him, scrambling eggs in a skillet. His throat tightened as he imagined coming up behind her, slipping his arms around her and nuzzling the hair away from her throat.

Stop it, O'Neil!

"That was great," he said briskly. "Makes me feel almost human again."

"Good," she said. "I was afraid maybe you were right, that I hadn't left you enough . . ." She swung towards him, and the rush of words stopped. Her eyes widened as she looked at him. ". . . that maybe I hadn't left you enough—"

Her voice cracked. She was looking at him as if she'd seen a ghost, her green gaze skittering first over his dark, wet hair, then dropping to his shoulders and chest before retiring to his face.

For the first time in his life, Conor blushed.

"What's the matter?"

"Nothing," she said. "It's just—you're not wearing a shirt."

"I know. My shirt was a mess. I couldn't bring myself to put it back on."

It was a perfectly reasonable answer. Miranda told herself that a couple of times before she tried speaking again.

"How do you—how do you like your eggs?"

"Listen, if my being shirtless bothers you . . ."

"No." Of course it didn't bother her, the sight of Conor,

half naked in her kitchen, his broad shoulders taking up the doorway. Why should it bother her?

"You sure?"

"I said it didn't." She cleared her throat. "But if you'd asked . . ."

"Asked?"

"For—for something to wear." God, her mouth was going dry. She had slept with this man but this was the first time she'd really had the chance to take a long, slow look at him without his clothes on. Well, almost without his clothes on. Those shoulders. That washboard abdomen. The dark hair on his chest.

The color of his skin.

It was golden, like honey, but that wasn't how it tasted. She could remember his taste so clearly, the clean, faint salt tang. And the heat of him; she remembered that, too, and the comforting weight of him as he rose above her and thrust into her . . .

The fork fell from her hand. She snatched it up, tossed it into the sink, pulled out the drawer and took out a long-handled spoon.

"I'd have given you something, if you'd asked," she said, her voice cold, her blood hot, her heart pounding in her ears. She swung away from him and gave the eggs a vicious stir before dumping them on two waiting plates. "It's really inappropriate to walk around half naked, O'Neil. Even a barbarian like you should know that."

"I should have known the truce wouldn't last," he said, watching that proud, straight back, recognizing the anger etched in her stance, growing angry himself though he wasn't sure why he should.

"And I should have known you'd have difficulty behaving as if you were civilized."

"Listen, Beckman, I'm sorry if the sight of me turns your stomach but it never occurred to me you'd have anything that would fit me."

"Well, I do." She spun around, her hands on her hips, her chin tilted in that defiant way that drove him crazy. "I've got sweatshirts,'' she said, forcing herself to concentrate on whatever oversized clothing she owned and not on him, not on all that naked male flesh, ''and I've got some denim work shirts.''

An image rose up before him, crowding out her angry, haughty face. He saw men, a long line of them, marching in and out of her life here as they had in Paris, and the anger he'd been holding tightly in check burst into his heart.

''Yeah,'' he said, moving towards her, ''I'll just bet you have. Hell, I probably could have had my choice of color and size.''

She flew at him, her hand upraised, and cracked it against his face. The blow was hard and unexpected and it sent him staggering back against the counter.

''You bastard,'' she cried, ''you no-good, dirty-minded son of a—''

The air rushed from her lungs as he caught hold of her.

''This makes two times you've slugged me, baby. Don't even think about trying for three.''

''Let go!'' She struggled against him, not strong enough to break his hold but furious enough to make him think it might be easier to try and hang onto a rattlesnake. Her foot shot out and connected with his shin. It wasn't much of a blow but it put him off balance, just enough so that his hold loosened. She got one hand free, doubled it into a fist, and drove it into his solar plexus.

''Damn you, Beckman,'' he gasped.

She pulled back her arm and aimed at him again but he was ready for her. He clamped his arms around her and lifted her from the floor, spinning around as he did so that their positions were reversed and she was pinned against the counter by the weight of his body.

''Bitch,'' he snarled, ''crazy bitch!''

''Bastard,'' she panted, ''miserable, arrogant bast—''

Damn her to hell! There was only one way to keep her quiet, and Conor took it. He kissed her, and it was like that night in

Paris all over again. As soon as his mouth found hers, the world ceased to exist.

Miranda's arms wound around his neck.

"Conor," she whispered, "oh God, Conor . . ."

He was trembling, with desire and with a far stronger emotion but there was no time to think, to do anything but bury himself within her soul. It was what she wanted, too. Her hands were at his shorts, tugging them down his legs as he stripped away her pants. He tried to pull her shirt over her head but as simple as the act should have been, it defied him. With a strangled oath, he seized the neckline and ripped the shirt to the hem.

And all the time, the kiss went on and on, as if their very existence depended on their lips never parting.

Miranda whispered his name and he answered her in kind, murmuring hers as if it were a mantra that had been his from the first time he'd held her in his arms.

He told himself to take control, slow down and prolong the ecstasy of what lay ahead, but she was touching him, her hands moving over him, cupping him, exploring his erection, testing the power of it. He groaned and lifted her onto the counter, pressed his mouth to her throat, then bent his head until her breast was against his lips. She cried out as he drew her hardened nipple into his mouth. Her hands tunneled through his hair; she dragged his face up to hers and kissed him, her mouth open and hot on his.

"Now," she sobbed, "Conor, now, please."

"Yes," he said, "yes, baby, yes."

He moved between her thighs, opening her to him. His thumb slid over the engorged bud of her clitoris; his fingers sank into her slick heat. She cried out and he knew he couldn't hold back, that he had to have her now. Her legs closed around his waist as he moved against her and she shuddered at the touch of his swollen penis against that most sensitive part of her body.

"Miranda," he whispered, and he moved, entering her on one long, heart-stopping thrust, feeling the contractions begin deep within her as he did.

"Conor? Conor, oh Conor . . ."

She was breathless, sobbing his name, rocking against him as she came and while she was still wild in his arms, he lifted her from the counter, backed her against the wall and drove into her, again and again and again until he felt the uncontrollable spasms of her climax begin once more. Then, at last, his head fell back and he went with her into the stars that exploded across the blackness of the sky.

Somehow, a long time later, they found themselves in the bedroom.

The bed was wide and soft, but nothing was as soft as the feel of Miranda in his arms.

"Miranda," he whispered, holding her against his thudding heart, "my God, Miranda."

"Oh yes," she breathed, and he knew she was smiling, just as he was.

He rolled to his side, his arm still thrown across her, his hand lightly cupping the gentle rise of her breast. Her face, bare of makeup, was the loveliest he'd ever seen.

"My beautiful Miranda," he murmured, and her lips, still softly swollen from his kisses, turned up in a tender smile.

"That was," she said, "it was . . ."

His heart clenched as he remembered the ugly words she'd used to describe this act the last time.

"It was wonderful," she sighed. "I've never—I've never felt—"

He caught her to him and kissed her until she was clinging to him. Then he drew back and looked down into her eyes.

"Baby," he said huskily, "we have to talk."

It wasn't what he'd planned to say at all. But it was right; he knew it as soon as the words left his mouth. He didn't know what he felt for her, couldn't name it and wasn't ready to examine it closely. He only knew that whatever it was, he wasn't going to walk away from it, which meant that it was time to tell her the truth. About himself, who he really was and who he worked for, how he'd come into her life in Paris and even that she was right, he was guilty of getting rid of her friends, of getting her tossed out of her home and her job . . .

That he hadn't come across her accidentally today.

Except for tonight and that night in Paris, every step of their relationship had been a part of someone else's script, and she had to know it.

Wanting Miranda, needing her, had nothing to do with his job and everything to do with his life. He needed her the way the evening sky needs a sunset, the way a flower needs the rain, and all at once he knew what he felt for her. Hell, he'd always known, he just hadn't been ready to admit it.

He loved her, and he would not build that love on lies.

"Miranda. I want you to hear me out before you say—"

She laid her fingers lightly against his mouth.

"It's my turn, first."

Conor caught her hand in his and pressed his lips to the palm.

"Baby . . ."

She silenced him again, this time with a kiss.

"Please," she said, and the desperation in the word made him nod his head in agreement.

She took a shaky breath and sat up. It was time to tell him everything and she needed to do it quickly, before she lost courage, because there was no way of knowing how he'd react.

Years ago, Jean-Phillipe had tried to warn her. Someday, he'd insisted, she would meet a man and fall in love.

You'll want him to know the truth, chérie, he'd said gently, *but you will have to be very, very sure of what he feels for you because any man who is not a fool will understand that in offering him your secret, you are also offering him your heart.*

Now, she knew that Jean-Phillipe had been right. She didn't know what Conor felt for her; the only certainty was that she wanted him to know the truth about her. If he couldn't accept it, it would be better to know it now.

"Before," she began, "when—when I said I could have lent you something to wear?"

"I was an asshole," he said bluntly. "Sweetheart, I've never been a saint. I don't care that you haven't been, either." He hesitated, searching for the right words. "That's what I want to explain, Miranda. The past doesn't matter, not to us."

"But it does matter," she said quickly. "Because—because I lied to you, Conor." She swallowed. He could see her throat work as she did. "I don't—I don't have a past."

A puzzled smile arced across his mouth.

"I don't understand."

"It's really very simple. I don't have a past. Not the kind you suppose. I've let everyone—let you—think that I've been with lots of men, but—"

"Miranda, I just told you, that doesn't matter."

"But it does. It matters a lot because—because the truth is, there hasn't been anybody. Not since Edouard, and that was—"

Conor shot up against the pillows. "What?"

She nodded. The tip of her tongue crept out from between her lips, then swept over them in a nervous gesture.

"I only—Edouard was the only man who . . ." She cleared her throat and looked into his eyes. "Even Jean-Phillipe. He was—he is—my friend. But I never slept with him, never with anybody, after Edouard. I never wanted to . . . until you."

Conor stared at her. He thought of the things the headmistress of Miss Cooper's had said about her; of what Eva and Hoyt had said. He thought about her reputation . . .

"I know it's hard to believe."

But it wasn't, that was the damndest part. He'd deliberately blanked that night in Paris out of his head, because it hurt too much to remember, but the evidence had been there, all the time, taking niggling little pokes at his subconscious.

How she'd seemed hesitant, about touching him. How her eyes had widened into pools of shocked darkness, at the intimacy of his caresses. How she'd tried to hold back, at the last moment, just before she'd shattered in his arms.

"Conor?"

He looked at her. Her face was pale; her mouth was trembling.

"Conor, I'm only telling you this because—because . . ." She caught her bottom lip between her teeth. "I'm not trying to put any kind of pressure on you. I mean, I don't want you to feel—to feel any obligation." Her chin lifted. "Damn you, O'Neil, will you please say something? If you're angry, admit it."

"Angry?" he said, his tone giving nothing away. "Angry, to find out I'm the first man you've slept with since that son of a bitch, de Lasserre? Angry, to learn that your reputation is a P.R. lie?"

"P.R.? You mean, public relations? Oh no. It's not that at all. I just—I didn't want men coming around, you see, and—and when I tried to think of a way to stop them . . . I mean, in my business, men are an occupational hazard."

Conor reached out and hauled her into his arms.

"Beckman," he said, "you are, without a doubt, the most exasperating, impossible, incredible woman."

Miranda blinked back her tears.

"Does that mean you're not angry at me?"

Conor took an unsteady breath.

"It means," he said, cupping her face in his hands, "that I'm crazy about you. And that you've just given me the greatest gift imaginable."

"Oh, Conor." She laughed, threw her arms around him and kissed him. "I didn't know how you'd take it. Jean-Phillipe said—he told me that this would happen, someday, you know, that I'd fall in love and . . ." Her eyes widened and scarlet flooded her face. "Oh, hell. Hell! I didn't mean—I shouldn't have said—"

"Yes, you should have." He kissed her, with a tenderness that was new to him. "I love you, Miranda. I have, since the time I first saw your picture."

Happiness shone in her eyes. She gave a soft laugh and leaned her forehead against his.

"Don't tell me you're one of those guys who buys the hype in magazine ads!"

Conor's smile faded. It was the perfect lead-in. *Take a deep breath, pal, and go for it.*

"I'm talking about the painting of you that hangs in the foyer at the Winthrop house."

Miranda stiffened in his arms and a wintery stillness came over her.

"Is that still there?"

"All it took was one look, and I was lost."

"It's a horrible painting. I'd hoped they'd taken it down by now."

"Well," Conor said, smiling as he touched the tip of his finger to the end of her nose, "it's not exactly a work of art, no, but considering that it was painted by an amateur like Hoyt—"

"Conor." Miranda lay back against the pillows and looped her arms around his neck. "I don't want to talk about Hoyt now."

"No, neither do I. I want to talk about us."

"Us," she said, and smiled. "What a lovely word."

"Miranda, sweetheart—about the way we met . . ."

"Mmm." She laughed softly as she trailed her hands down his shoulders, to his chest. "You didn't just 'happen' to be on that running path this evening, did you?"

Conor felt his muscles tense. *Here we go.*

"No, baby, I didn't."

"I thought so." Her fingers swept into the dark hair that covered his chest, exploring its texture and the play of firm muscle beneath. "Did you come looking for me?"

"Yes. Yes, I did, and before you get ticked off—"

"I knew it, as soon as I saw you." She smiled again, though it was a different smile now, as her hand danced lower. "Are all private detectives as efficient as you, O'Neil?"

"Miranda." Conor reached between them and caught hold of her hand. "Don't—don't do that. You're distracting me, and I'm trying to tell you something."

"There's no need. I told you, I know you sought me out. And I'm glad you did. When I saw you today . . . oh Conor, I kept telling myself I hated you but the truth was that I couldn't stop thinking about you, and missing you.'' She laughed softly. ''I even missed your pig-headed interference in my life.''

''Sweetheart, listen to me for a minute. I need to tell you about Eva. About what I told you, that she hired me—''

''But that doesn't matter now. Don't you see? I'm not angry about that anymore. Bringing you into my life, was the first—the only—good thing my mother ever did for me.''

How could he get her to listen? For that matter, how could he think, with her lying close to him and touching him? Her hands felt like silk, smooth and warm, against his body.

''Miranda, you don't understand.''

She clasped his face and brought his mouth to hers. She kissed him, her mouth open and soft against his.

''All of them—first Eva, then Hoyt, and finally Edouard . . . all of them used me, all of them wanted something from me. But you,'' she whispered fiercely, ''you wanted only me. Just me. You didn't lie, you didn't use me.''

She kissed him again, and he told himself not to respond, to pull back and say the things that had to be said.

But he couldn't. There was no way to resist her sighs and her kisses, and no way to tell her the truth, not without the risk of losing her, and that was a risk he couldn't take.

So he told her the one true thing that mattered.

''I love you,'' he said, and then, with a groan born of despair and desire, he buried himself in her heat.

Chapter Sixteen

Spring had truly arrived.

Golden daffodils and red and white tulips, blooming in chic wooden tubs, brightened the grey canyons of the city. Tables and chairs crowded the sidewalks outside trendy cafés. Lovers strolled through Central Park, hand in hand.

It was—Conor thought as he lay sprawled in the grass in the Sheep Meadow, his head pillowed on his arms and his gaze fixed on Miranda's face—a wonderful time to be alive.

A week had passed, and in all those days and nights, they'd only been apart for a handful of hours. She was between photo shoots; he told her he was between assignments.

There was no reason to do anything except be together.

Sometimes, he even forgot reality. Keeping her safe wasn't an assignment, it was a commitment. Staying close to her wasn't part of the job; it was a function as necessary as breathing.

He wanted Miranda in his life forever.

He'd never known a woman like her. She was funny, she was serious; she could discuss politics and Plato, then pick up the Sunday paper and giggle over the comics. She understood the things that really mattered. For instance, runny eggs weren't civilized. Rare steak was. And she didn't even mind when he forgot, on occasion, and left the seat up in the john.

But sometimes, when the nights were too dark and long for sleeping, worries crept into the corners of the bedroom. He thought about what would happen, when he finally had to tell her the truth, not just about who he was and how he'd come into her life this second time but that whoever wanted to hurt her was still out there.

She was convinced the nightmare was all over. She'd told him that and smiled, explained her belief that the notes and picture had been the work of some kook who'd moved on to other interests, now that she'd left France. Somehow, he'd managed to look convinced. She'd told him about Bob Brever-man, too, and it had been no trouble at all to laugh when she'd described him as a jerk.

She was a good storyteller, with a nice flair for the dramatic. Right now, she was telling him about her very first roommate at her very first boarding school, and what they'd done to get back at the headmistress for the awful food the girls were served.

"Beryl wanted to dump the sugar out of the bowls in the cafeteria and fill them with salt instead but I said, heck, we'd get caught whatever we did so we might as well do something interesting."

She'd been twelve then, she said, and he could just imagine her, sitting cross-legged on her narrow bed, dressed in a flannel nightgown and with her hair in braids and a sprinkling of freckles on her nose, whispering and giggling in the dark with another poor little rich girl every bit as homesick as she was.

". . . and I said, 'Beryl, did you ever notice, Miss Blakely'—she was the headmistress at the Jefferson Academy, did I tell you that?—'Miss Blakely never eats at the faculty table in the dining room, she just sits there and goes through the motions?' "

He was going through the motions, too. He was too damn distracted to keep his mind on the story but even a Martian would have responded to Miranda's shining eyes and mischievous smile, to the animation in her voice and the feel of her hand as it touched his for emphasis.

"... and that was when I said, I'll bet Blakely dines on lobster and pâté in the privacy of her rooms." She frowned and shot him a mock glare. "Are you paying attention to this, O'Neil? There's gonna be a quiz, you know."

"Of course I am. You guys were being served stale bread and gruel but you figured Madam Ogre was chowing down lobster and pâté." He grinned. "Lobster and pâté, huh? Pretty sophisticated thinking for a gawky kid."

Miranda gave him an indignant look before grinning back at him.

"I was not gawky. Skinny as a stringbean, maybe, and convinced I was never going to stop growing until my head hit the ceiling, but not gawky. Miss Blakely wouldn't have allowed it."

"I see. A dead ringer for Michael Jordan, but with a classy palate."

"Give me a break, O'Neil! My idea of gustatory paradise—"

"Gustatory paradise?" Conor said, laughing as he sat up.

"If you can think of a better way to describe peanut butter, onions and sardines on whole wheat bread, let me know."

"You're joking."

"Cross my heart and hope to die. It was the midnight dorm rage that entire semester."

Conor shuddered. "What they say is true. There are inconceivable differences between little girls and little boys."

Miranda's smile grew wicked. "Are you only just figuring that out?"

Their eyes met. After a minute, Conor cleared his throat.

"Go on with that story," he said softly, "or I'm liable to show you that I know the difference, right here and now."

Miranda reached out, put her hands against his shoulders, and he let her tumble him backwards into the grass.

"How?" she whispered, scooting into the curve of his outstretched arm.

"Behave yourself, Beckman, and finish your story. You were about to corrupt poor Beryl."

"Right. She wanted to do the salt-for-sugar thing but I said, if we're gonna go, let's go big time." Miranda rolled onto her belly, plucked a blade of grass and ran it down Conor's nose. "Did you break this?"

"You mean, you can tell?" He smiled up at her. "Heck, Dr. Strangelove promised no one would ever know."

"Well, I really wouldn't, except one time I had this roommate who broke her nose playing field hockey and after it was set, it healed just fine except it had this ever-so-slight tilt to the left."

"Beryl?"

Miranda sighed and fell back again, this time with her head cradled on his shoulder.

"I don't know if poor Beryl ever got around to playing hockey or anything else, for that matter. She was pretty much in purgatory, after we did our thing."

"Which was?"

"Well, you have to keep in mind, I'd organized this very polite petition drive, asking for a review of the food they served us. I even went to the Student Council for their support."

"And?"

"And, the council was scared of getting in trouble. Everybody agreed we were getting screwed but nobody wanted to confront Blakely. I didn't blame them. I didn't want to march into her office, hold out my dinner bowl and say, 'More, please,' either."

"So you came up with another plan, one that got Beryl tossed out?"

"She didn't. Get tossed out, I mean. Her parents decided to move her to another school." Her voice changed, lost just a bit of color. "Even after the school made it clear they intended to expel me, Beryl's father said that any school that permitted someone like me to slip through their admissions screening in the first place wasn't the right place for his daughter."

Conor felt his belly knot. He wanted to turn back the clock, seek out Beryl Whatsis's old man and punch out his lights—after he put old Blakely on a bread and water diet.

"Hey," Miranda said softly, "don't look like that. It was a long time ago—and when you hear what I did, you might not feel so sorry for me."

She gave him a self-satisfied little grin that eased away his anger. He grinned in return, rolled over, and looked down at her.

"Come on, Beckman, can the suspense! What'd you do?"

"I sneaked into Blakely's rooms one night, after dinner. I hid in a closet."

"Ah ha," Conor said. "A covert operation."

"And you'd know all about those, of course."

For just an instant, his heart skipped a beat. But she was still smiling, and finally he realized that she'd been referring to the job he'd told her he held, as a private detective.

"Sure," he said casually, chiding himself for having tossed out such a dumb, off-hand remark. "A pamphlet on covert operations comes packed inside each Handy Dandy Junior Detective kit."

Miranda smiled and linked her arms loosely around his neck.

"So I hid in the closet and sure enough, in just a little while, Blakely came in and sat herself down at her desk. A couple of minutes later, one of the monitors who worked in the kitchen came trundling up the stairs, carrying a tray. She set it down in front of Blakely, who whipped off the cover, and there it was."

"Lobster and pâté?"

"Better than that. Steak and a baked potato, oozing with butter. Oh, I still drool when I think of it! The closest we'd come to meat in weeks was some slimy grey stuff."

"Mystery meat," Conor said, "yeah, we had that in the army."

"Is that where you broke your nose? In the army?"

Damn, what was the matter with him? He never so much as hinted at anything in his background to anybody. It was right up there on his How to Survive list, not just professionally but personally. You didn't give pieces of yourself away; what was the point? Nobody gave a damn about anybody in this world, not really. Nobody cared what was your favorite color, or what kinds of books you preferred. He'd always known that; it was one of the things Jillian had thrown at him, when they'd split up, that he'd never let her in, and now here he was, dropping bits and pieces of information like a flower girl going up the aisle with a basket of rose petals on her arm, not just wanting to know everything there was to know about Miranda but, dammit, wanting her to know about him . . .

Wanting her to know the truth, that he'd lied to her from Day One, that he wished to God he hadn't, that she was becoming a part of his life he didn't want to think about ever losing . . .

"Conor?"

He blinked, forced himself to focus on her slightly puzzled smile.

"Yes," he said, catching a strand of her hair, letting it slip like silk through his fingers, "I was in the army. But it isn't where I broke my nose."

"I'll bet it was playing football, in high school."

He laughed. "Football heroes don't break their noses."

"Is that what you were?" Miranda planted a gentle kiss on his slightly bent nose. "A football hero?"

"Well, I would have been," he said modestly, "but I broke my leg, taking a joyride on a Harley, and that was the end of me and football."

"Joyriding? As in borrowing?"

"Joyriding, as in borrowing without permission. Are you horrified?"

She laughed. "When you hear what I did to Blakely, you'll be sorry you asked that question. So, what was it? A sudden yen? A boyish prank?" She grasped the open collar of his shirt and tugged on it. "A fit of youthful rebellion?"

"All of that, I guess. The bike belonged to the guy who lived downstairs. He'd let me ride it a couple of times; I figured I'd take it out for half an hour, bring it back, and nobody'd be the wiser."

"But?"

"But, my old man caught me. He said what I'd done was a sure sign I was destined for a dissolute life."

Miranda's brows lifted. "You sure your father and my mother never met?"

Conor chuckled. "Not unless Eva put in some time down around the Magnificent Seventh."

"The Magnificent Seventh? What's that?"

"My old man's police precinct. He was a cop."

"A law-and-order type, hmm?"

Conor's smile tilted. "Yeah, you might say that."

He stood up, drew Miranda to her feet and put his arm around her. They strolled along a path bordered by bright yellow daffodils.

"Just look at the flowers," she said." Her smile lit his heart. "Aren't they beautiful?"

"Beautiful," Conor agreed, watching her.

She bent down to the daffodils and reached out, as if to touch one, but her fingers never quite reached the golden petals. Suddenly, Conor thought of the photo tucked inside his wallet, the one of Miranda sitting under a dogwood tree, smiling with the innocence of youth and holding a flower in her hand.

That's the sort of girl she was, Agnes Foster had said coldly, *sitting on the grass when she knew it was forbidden, plucking blossoms. She would have been reprimanded for that.*

He reached down, plucked a daff from the sea of gold and handed it to Miranda.

"It's okay," he said solemnly. "There's an old Irish proverb says you have to pick the first daffodil of the season or they won't bloom the next year."

A smile curved over her mouth. "You made that up."

"Yeah." He smiled, too, as he took the flower from her and tucked it into her hair. "But you have to admit, it's a nice thought."

He slipped his arm around her again and they headed into the leafy coolness of the Ramble. "So," he said, clearing his throat, "you were telling me about the scam you pulled on old lady Blakely. Why'd you want to swap places with the kid on K.P. duty?''

Miranda laughed softly and ducked her head against his shoulder.

''Well, how else could I switch Blakely's dinner plate for one containing a dead mouse?''

Conor burst out laughing. Ahead, the graceful grey stone of Bow Bridge arched across Central Park lake.

''You didn't.''

''I did. Poor little guy met his end in a trap in the stable, but I gave him the closest thing I could to a big send-off. Oh, it was wonderful! Blakely whisked off the cover and there was Mickey, lying on a bed of watercress with his little feet pointing straight up.''

The bridge was deserted, and lit by the sun. When they reached the center of the span, Conor leaned back against the warm stone and put his arms around Miranda. She was still smiling, but darkness was stealing into her eyes.

''Blakely knew, right away, that I'd done it. So she sent for Eva, told her what I'd done, and said I was unfit to continue at the school.''

''Did you tell Eva about the rotten food and that you'd tried to have it changed?''

''Remember your father's little speech to you? Eva's was pretty much the same. She said I'd been nothing but trouble all my life and that the next school she sent me to would know how to deal with 'problem girls' like me.'' She gave a soft, sad little laugh. ''And I was on my way.''

Conor took her face in his hands and kissed her.

''Nobody's allowed to feel sad on the first really nice spring day.''

She smiled and lay her palms against his chest.

''That's a rule, huh?''

''Absolutely. Besides, you haven't finished your story. What part did poor Beryl What's-Her-Name get to play in all this?''

''Beryl Goodman. Poor Beryl, is right. All she'd done was watch the door while I made the switch, but Blakely chewed her out and sent for her parents. Beryl cried and cried. I felt awful about it, but . . .'' She made a face. ''Come on, O'Neil, that's enough about me. You haven't finished your story, either. Was that how you broke your nose? In the motorcycle accident?''

''Actually,'' he said, with a little smile, ''my old man did it.''

Her face paled. ''What?''

''He beat the crap out of me, for taking the bike. Hey, I had it coming.''

''Nobody has that coming,'' Miranda said furiously. ''What kind of a man would do such a thing to his son?''

''He was a hard-liner, I guess. You know, spare the rod, spoil the child, that kind of stuff.'' Conor took her hand and brought it to his mouth. ''If it makes you feel any better, I hated him for it for a long, long time.''

''It doesn't make me feel a bit better, O'Neil, and don't you patronize me!''

''Whoa, take it easy. I'm not trying to—''

''A boy shouldn't have to hate his father, dammit. No child should have to hate a parent.'' Her voice broke as Conor gathered her against him. ''I'm sorry,'' she whispered. ''I don't usually waste time feeling sorry for myself. It's just that I've never been able to figure out why a child wouldn't be loved.''

''Maybe there is no why,'' he said softly, stroking her hair. ''Nobody ever said life was perfect.''

Miranda smiled, framed his face with her hands and brought his mouth to hers.

''Until now,'' she said, kissing him, and the knowledge that he was deceiving her rose within him until it felt as if it might stop his breath.

He told himself he wasn't violating her confidence, that he was only doing his job when he telephoned Thurston.

''Check out a Beryl Goodman for me, Harry. She attended

a place called the Jefferson Academy with Miranda fourteen, fifteen years ago.''

''A kook?''

''Probably not. Look, just check, okay? It's not much, but it's something.''

Harry told him the lab people had finished going over every inch of the box Bob Breverman had intercepted, as well as its ghoulish contents.

''Nothing,'' Harry said glumly. ''Not a print, not a smudge, not a clue. Any leads on your end?''

''No.''

''Nobody with reason to come after the girl?''

Conor rubbed his forehead. ''Not as far as I know. Any more notes delivered to Eva?''

''No. Eva's not the key to this, Conor, I'm certain of it. The Beckman girl is. Find out what you can about her, anything she's kept hidden in her past.''

''I'm here to protect her,'' Conor said angrily.

''You're there to do a job,'' Thurston said, and broke the connection.

Conor told himself not to think about the deception.

There was no reason to think about it. He could protect Miranda and love her at the same time. He didn't have to let his thoughts revolve around what a conniving bastard he was. As for learning about her past . . . she was more than willing to talk about herself, and he loved to listen.

It was easy to let himself think they were like any other couple, exploring the city while spring overtook the grey canyons. They did the things lovers do, strolling through the South Street Seaport, riding the elevator to the top of the Empire State Building, dining on pushcart hot dogs or in pricey restaurants as the spirit moved them.

Early one evening, they sat at a table at Windows on the World, she sipping a glass of white wine and he drinking an ale, with the city and the harbor far below.

"We could have dinner here," Conor said.

"Or?"

He smiled. "How'd you know there was an *or?*"

Miranda grinned, put her elbows on the table and propped her chin in her hands.

"Innate genius," she said. "So, what's the *or?*"

"We could go to this place I know in Chinatown."

"That sounds good. I like Chinese food."

"Szechuan?"

"Is it really, really hot?"

"Guaranteed to make your eyes water and your ears turn red."

"In that case, what are we waiting for?"

"You had me worried there, Beckman. That was a test and for a couple of seconds, I wasn't sure you were going to pass."

"And?" She smiled. "If I hadn't?"

"If you'd turned up your nose at Szechuan, you mean?" He shook his head. "I guess I'd have been forced into rethinking this whole arrangement."

Miranda looked at him over the rim of the glass, her smile suddenly soft and vulnerable.

"Is that what we have?" she asked. "An arrangement?"

It was such a cool, businesslike term but the way she said it, and the way she looked at him, made it anything but cool or businesslike.

"Yeah," he said gruffly, and reached for her hand, "I think we do. Is that okay with you?"

Her eyes glowed.

"It's wonderful with me," she said.

Conor leaned across the table and kissed her.

They took a taxi to the restaurant. Conor asked for a corner booth and ordered for both of them.

It had always bothered her, the easy way some men had of taking over, as if the female of the species were incapable of making decisions, but it was different with Conor. He made her feel safe, in a way she never had before, not just from physical danger but from the things she'd feared for as long as she could remember. Love, and desire, and most of all, trust.

Sometimes, in the middle of the night, she awakened in his arms and wondered how such a miracle could have happened. Nita had once called her a cynic where men were concerned, but she wasn't, she was just a pragmatist and anyway, despite their closeness, there were things about her Nita didn't know, things she'd never told anyone, not even Jean-Phillipe.

Things that might change the way Conor felt about her.

"Miranda?"

She started. Conor was watching her, a puzzled smile on his face.

"Don't you like the hot and sour soup?"

She looked down at the table. A bowl of steaming soup had appeared before her but she had no idea when.

"Because if you don't, that's okay. We can order something else."

"Conor." Miranda folded her hands in her lap. "You've never asked me—you've never asked me why I married Edouard."

Conor put down his spoon. "No," he said carefully, "I didn't. You married him and that's that. You don't owe me any explanations."

"I know that. But I want you to know. There are things about me . . ."

Pieces of her past, she meant. And he realized he ought to encourage her to share them. For all he knew, they'd shed light on why someone had targeted her.

For all he knew, de Lasserre, that pompous son of a bitch, had been the love of her life. And if that was true, he didn't want to hear it.

"I married him because I was lonely."

Conor looked across the table at her. "Did you love him?"

"I thought I did. You have to remember, I was seventeen years old. I had no real friends; I never stayed in one school long enough to make any. My mother and I didn't—we didn't get along. And suddenly this man came into my life. He was older, and kind. He was handsome, too, and sophisticated—a teenaged girl's dream, you know? And he told me all the things a lonely kid dreams of hearing, that I was beautiful and desirable and that he'd take care of me forever."

"And you believed him."

"Sure. Why wouldn't I? Edouard was very polished and I was this dumb kid." She drew a deep breath. "I met him through my roommate, Amalie, did I ever tell you about her?"

Conor cleared his throat. "No. No, you didn't."

"Amalie hated me on sight. I tried everything I could think of to make friends with her. I let her copy my homework, I coached her in the subjects she was failing . . . God, I must have seemed so pathetic! But it didn't matter. For some reason, she flat-out disliked me from the start, and when Edouard—he was her cousin—when Edouard started paying her visits, taking her out to lunch and inviting me along . . ."

Conor reached for her hand across the table. "Amalie was pissed," he said, with a little smile.

Miranda laughed. "Exactly. I knew it upset her and honestly, I didn't want that, but I was so flattered by Edouard's attention, so—what's the word?—so infatuated . . ." She let out a long sigh. "Anyway, he proposed. He loved me, he said, and by then I was convinced I loved him, too. I told him my mother would never give permission, she'd say I was too young, and he said we didn't need her permission, that we'd elope." Her eyes met Conor's. "He thought I was eighteen. I let him think it. I'd been afraid that if he knew the truth, he wouldn't bother with me."

"Miranda." Conor's hand tightened almost painfully on hers. "You don't have to say any more. Look, we all make mistakes. Hell, I was married, once, too, but it didn't work out. And I didn't have the excuse of being a lonely, mixed-up seventeen-year-old kid."

"I'm not apologizing for what I did, Conor, I'm just trying to explain why—why I never . . ." She swallowed dryly. "By the time we reached Paris, I knew I'd made a terrible mistake.

I tried to tell that to Edouard. I said I wanted to go home. And he laughed.'' Her voice dipped; Conor had to lean forward to hear her. ''He said nothing would part us, after he'd—after he'd . . .''

''Baby, don't. It isn't important, not anymore.''

''He raped me,'' she said, with sudden, awful ferocity. Her head came up, all the pain of so long ago blazing in her eyes. ''When it was over, he said I was pathetic, that I'd have to learn to make believe I was a real woman if I didn't want him to teach me a lesson I'd never forget. Then he locked the door and left.''

Conor felt the rage twisting inside him like a snake.

''Eva turned up the next morning. Oh, I was so happy to see her! I was sure she'd come to take me home.'' Her eyes went flat. ''But it wasn't like that. She said I was no better than a whore.''

''Jesus Christ, your own mother?''

''She said she'd take care of Edouard, and that when she and I got back to the States, I'd be going to a special school for girls who were bad, like me.'' Her voice quavered. ''I knew the place—we used to joke about it, at Miss Cooper's, we'd say, well, this place isn't the end of the line anymore, now there's the Newton Academy, where they lock you in your room and pump you full of dope if you don't behave.'' She took a deep breath. ''I begged Eva not to do it. I said I'd rather stay in Paris than be locked away like that and she said, then stay. The next thing I knew, I was standing in the street, watching her taxi drive away.''

He was almost afraid to speak, because of the rage he felt.

''Let me get this straight,'' he said carefully. ''Eva drove off and left you?''

''Yes.''

''Just left you?''

''We didn't see each other again, or even speak to each other, for years,'' Miranda said in a shaky voice.

Conor's eyes narrowed. ''Surely, she sent you money to live on,'' he said, remembering what Eva had told him.

"No. But that was okay," she added with a touch of defiance. "I wouldn't have accepted it, even if she had. Anyway, I was lucky. Jean-Phillipe found me, standing on the street corner where Eva had left me. It had started to rain and he took pity on me." She gave a little laugh. "It's not a very pretty story, is it?"

"Dammit, how could Eva have done such a thing? Kids get into trouble, it happens all the time, but to turn her back on her own daughter, to abandon her for an elopement and a few indiscretions—"

"There were no indiscretions!" Miranda hunched forward. "I'd done some dumb things. Drinking beer. Breaking curfew. Smoking a joint one time."

"And inhaling," Conor said, trying to bring a smile to her face, telling himself that he was a civilized man and that there were laws that said he couldn't rip out Eva Winthrop's throat or fly back to France and beat Edouard de Lasserre to a bloody pulp.

"And inhaling," Miranda said, with a little smile, "and then getting sick enough to never want to do it again." She hesitated, and he knew that whatever she was about to say was the thing that she'd been heading for from the start of her unexpected confession. "But when it came to boys—to sex . . ." Her hand suddenly trembled within his. "Edouard had always been so gentle, until that night. He hardly touched me and when he kissed me, it was like being brushed by a butterfly's wing. I wouldn't let him do more than that. Something had happened, you see, years before . . . What I'm trying to tell you is that I was a virgin when I married Edouard, and terrified of sex."

The restaurant was a quiet one; it was one of the reasons Conor had chosen it. Hardly any sounds penetrated to this dimly lit corner. Now, suddenly, a vertiginous roaring filled Conor's ears.

"Are you telling me that son of a bitch took your virginity?"

She nodded.

"And that was it? That one ugly experience was all you had, until—"

"Until you."

She was trying to smile, but tears rose in her eyes. She began weeping, as if her heart were going to break.

Conor got to his feet, dug out his wallet and tossed a handful of bills on the table. Then he drew her from her seat, put his arm around her, and took her home.

He awoke abruptly, in the middle of the night. Something had awakened him, but what? Miranda lay in the curve of his arm, her head pillowed on his shoulder.

Conor's muscles tensed.

She'd been telling him about de Lasserre, who had raped her. She'd been a virgin, she'd said, and terrified of sex.

Something had happened. That was what she'd said. *Something had happened, years before.*

Miranda stirred beside him. "Conor?"

He shifted to his side and drew her closer, so they were lying breath to breath.

"Yes, baby. I'm sorry if I woke you."

"No, that's okay. I wasn't sleeping anyway." Her hand cupped his face. "I'm sorry about what happened in the restaurant." She kissed him, and he felt her lips curve in a smile. "Such terrific shrimp and because of me, we didn't get to finish it."

Conor laughed softly, though his nerve ends were humming. "I don't know how you stay so skinny, Beckman."

"I'm not skinny at all. Manuel says I've put on weight."

"Manuel?"

"The guy who's doing the Chrysalis ads."

"Yeah, well, what does he know? He's probably got a boyfriend." Conor hesitated. "Miranda? When you were telling me about de Lasserre—you said something had happened, years before."

"Did I?"

Conor felt her sudden tension. He had the feeling she was on the verge of shoving him away and fleeing.

"What happened, Miranda?"

"Nothing."

"Sweetheart, if somebody hurt you . . ."

She pushed free of his arms, just as he'd expected, and rolled onto her back.

"It isn't worth talking about, Conor. It was so long ago."

He felt the coldness growing inside him. He sat up and switched on the light.

"Who was it?" he said. "What did he do?"

Miranda turned away from him and dragged the blanket almost over her head.

"I don't want to talk about it," she whispered. "Please, it doesn't matter anymore."

In that instant, he knew.

"Hoyt," he said softly, and the sound that burst from Miranda's throat gave him all the confirmation he needed.

Conor closed his eyes. He could see Hoyt's patrician face, hear that oh-so-cultured voice explaining how close he and Miranda had once been, how he'd painted the portrait of her, the one with that sad, haunted smile . . .

"Son of a bitch!"

"Conor, don't."

"That goddamn son of a—" Conor roared with pain and rage. He flung back the covers, shot to his feet, and smashed his fist into the wall. "That fucking piece of shit! I'll kill him. I'll beat the crap out of him first and then I'll put my hands around his throat and—"

"No!" Miranda flung herself at him and wrapped her arms around his waist. "I beg you, don't do anything."

"Goddammit, Miranda!"

"Listen to me. Please. Sit down and just listen."

He felt like a coiled spring, tightened to the breaking point, needing to release all the energy stored inside him before it exploded. But this had been her pain, long before it had been his, so he sucked in a couple of lungfuls of air, let her take his hand and tug him down to the edge of the mattress beside her.

"He never really—really did anything to me. He looked at

me. Touched me, but he didn't actually . . ." She licked her lips. "I was too young to understand what was happening but I knew it wasn't right. I told him that, and he said that he was my daddy now, and that he loved me."

"Miranda, dammit, I know you want me to be calm and hear you out, but don't you see? I *have* to kill him. He deserves killing."

"I was going to tell Eva. But I didn't have to, because Eva—because my mother—"

"Because she what?" Miranda bowed her head, and Conor felt as if he were going crazy. "Are you telling me she knew?"

She nodded, and then she looked at him and her chin took on that defiant tilt that struck him now as the saddest thing he'd ever seen.

"I told Eva I didn't want Hoyt to tuck me in at night anymore. She said that was nonsense. She said I was an ungrateful brat, that every little girl in the world wanted a stepfather as kind and generous as Hoyt."

"Damn her," Conor whispered.

"She said she'd punish me, if I didn't behave. I tried. God, I tried . . . but then one night, when he came to my room, he started to—to touch me differently, and I screamed."

Conor looked at the woman he loved. She wasn't weeping; she wasn't trembling. He had the strange feeling she wasn't even in the room with him. Her thoughts and memories had gone back to a night he knew had changed her life forever.

"Eva came bursting into the room," she said softly. "And she saw what he was doing. There was this one awful minute where everybody froze and then she pointed to the door and Hoyt skulked off, like a dog that's been caught doing something it shouldn't. Then she closed the door, yanked me out of the bed, and told me that I was no good. She said I was evil, that I was just what she'd expected I'd be, and that she was going to send me away."

Conor nodded. He'd retreated into a detached coolness so he could listen without interrupting because he understood that what Miranda needed now was his love and support, not his rage, but God must have made women from different stuff than men because he knew he'd never be able to set aside what had happened to her until he destroyed Hoyt Winthrop, utterly and completely.

For now, though, he could only take Miranda in his arms and feel her tears hot against his face. He held her, and rocked her, and whispered that he loved her until, at last, the first rosy glow of dawn streaked the sky.

Chapter Seventeen

Watching Miranda pose for the camera was heaven and hell combined.

She had a shoot a couple of days later, at a loft in lower Manhattan, and Conor went along with her. He was still between assignments, he told her, and he wanted to see what fashion photography was all about.

"You'll make me self-conscious," she said, but she was smiling.

"You won't even know I'm there," he promised.

She gave him a coffee-flavored kiss.

"You're not exactly the inconspicuous type, O'Neil. But the truth is, I'd love to have you come with me. I'm sure Manuel won't mind."

Manuel, who turned out to be a little guy with a sad face, a lisp and an unusual, if interesting, devotion to leather, didn't mind at all. He eyed Conor up and down, told Miranda she had excellent taste, and got to work.

"Your lady has a special relationship with the camera," he said, as Miranda sailed out of the dressing room in a shimmery column of white silk trimmed in gold.

Conor took only a few minutes to decide he understood what Manuel meant. He also decided that if he ever sensed electricity flowing between Miranda and another man the way it flowed between her and the camera, there'd be a classic tragedy in the making.

She smiled.

She pouted.

She teased.

And the camera loved it all.

"Yesss," Manuel kept saying, as he shot off photos from every imaginable angle and some Conor figured only a tightrope walker would have attempted, "oh yes, darling girl, you are superb!"

Every now and then, Miranda glanced over, caught Conor's eye, and winked.

"Having fun?" she whispered once, when she rushed past him to make a costume change.

He smiled and assured her that he was. And he probably would have been, if he could have turned off the thoughts racing through his brain.

Every person Miranda had loved had lied to her, and that included him. Would she forgive him, when he could finally tell her the truth?

He had to go on telling himself that she would, just as he had to tell himself he could hang on and not wring Hoyt's neck, or de Lasserre's, until the time was right. And Eva's, too. Hell, he was a firm believer in equality of the sexes.

How could Eva have done such things to her daughter?

He had long ago reached the point where there was little that could surprise him. It was one of the things that happened, in his line of work. You discovered a basic truth about the human race and you learned to accept it.

Some people, most people, would do anything—anything—for a buck, if they thought they could get away with it. But not even that explained Eva's behavior. By the time she'd married Hoyt, she'd made her first million at Papillon, and probably her second and third. If she didn't need Hoyt's dough, what had stopped her from tossing him out on his ass? Not love. Whatever Eva and Hoyt Winthrop felt for each other, it wasn't the kind of passion that would make a woman blind to a man's faults.

And, dammit, they weren't dealing with small potatoes here, they were dealing with child molestation. With a grown man putting his hands on a defenseless little girl, and the little girl's mother finding out and blaming her . . .

"Conor?"

It took a couple of seconds to bring himself back. When he did, he found Miranda standing over him, wearing a dress the same color as her eyes.

"Sweetheart," he said, "are you done?"

"Yes." She smiled, bent down and kissed him. "And you're ringing."

Damn. She was right. His cell phone was shrilling. Conor smiled sheepishly, took the phone from his pocket and flipped it open.

"Hello?"

"Can you talk, my boy?"

Miranda kissed his cheek. "It'll take me five minutes to change," she whispered. He nodded, jerked his chin towards the door, and stepped outside.

"Conor? Can you talk, or do you want to phone me back?"

"I can talk, Harry." Conor said quietly. "You sure took your time, getting back to me."

"You phoned at seven this morning. It's not even noon."

"Listen, I'm not interested in hearing how overworked you are. Hang onto what you've got." Conor shot back his sleeve. "I'll call you in half an hour, from a secure telephone."

"There's no need. I don't have anything to tell you."

Conor's eyes narrowed. When he'd spoken with Thurston's secretary, she'd told him Beryl Goodman had come up clean. He'd said he'd expected as much, and then he'd made it clear that he wanted in-depth, heavy-duty background checks on Hoyt and Eva Winthrop.

"We must have our wires crossed, Harry. I told Sybil—"

"I know what you told her. And now I'm telling you that the examinations on those, ah, items, were completed weeks ago. Perhaps you've forgotten that it was you who carried word of the final check to our client."

"I've forgotten nothing, and you know it. Those examinations were standard. What I'm asking for now is cabinet-level."

"You want us to dig deeper and look for bodies."

"Yes."

"Such a thing will stir things up. If our primary client finds out, he will not be thrilled."

Your primary client would be even less thrilled, Conor thought grimly, if he knew his ambassadorial candidate has a thing for little girls.

"Remember our agreement, Harry? I get *carte blanche,* whatever I want, and no questions asked."

"Conor, my boy, this is an unreasonable request."

"Do it, and get the results to me quickly, or I'm done with this assignment. I'm not fooling around, Harry. You got that?"

Harry Thurston's tone grew cool. "I seem to have no choice in the matter. Is there anything else, while we're at it?"

The door opened, and Miranda stepped into the hall. Conor reached out and clasped her hand.

"Yes," he said pleasantly. "Stop calling me 'my boy.' "

They headed uptown, holding hands and walking because it was, Miranda said, an absolutely beautiful day.

"So," she said, glancing at him, "who was that on the phone?"

"A client," Conor said, hating himself for how easily the lie came to his lips. "Well, a possible client. He wanted to set up an appointment for next week."

She smiled. "Ah."

"Ah?"

"Ah, as in ah, the man really does work for a living."

Conor laughed and tugged her closer as they reached the corner.

"Give me a break, Beckman. Nobody's ever accused me of being independently wealthy."

"No, but you're pretty independent, nonetheless. Here you are, sashaying around the city with me instead of keeping your nose to the grindstone."

"You complaining?" he said with a mock growl.

"And I heard what you said to that man on the telephone."

Conor's smile faded. "What did you hear?"

"Oh, you know. 'Don't call me "my boy,"'" she said, dropping her chin to her chest and her voice to her shoes. She smiled. "Do you always treat prospective clients that way?"

Conor laughed. "Listen, kid," he said, in his best Humphrey Bogart imitation, "you stick with mugging for the camera and I'll stick with playing gumshoe."

"How does somebody become a detective, anyway?"

"I told you. You buy this Handy Dandy kit . . ."

Miranda poked him in the ribs. "Come on, be serious. I mean, is that what you wanted to be, when you were growing up? A detective?"

He looked at her, his smile fading. Okay, this could be a start. He could begin the long process of telling her the truth about himself, not all of it, but at least enough so that when the time came, he could make her see that not everything had been a fabrication.

"No," he said, "not exactly. What I wanted to be was a cop, like my old man."

"That's right. You said your father's a policeman."

"Was. Detective-Sergeant John O'Neil, NYPD retired."

"And your mother? What did she do?"

"Whatever the old man told her to do." Conor smiled, trying to take the edge off but doubting he was succeeding. He wasn't very good at this. Talking about himself had never been his thing, and his ex had never let him forget it—but then, she'd never studied his face while he spoke, hanging on to his every word as if each one was special. "My mother was the quintessential mom, a 1950s leftover, I guess. She cooked, she cleaned, she ironed his shirts and polished his shoes . . ."

"You speak of her in the past tense," Miranda said softly.

"Yeah." Conor cleared his throat. "She died when I was fourteen."

"I'm sorry, Conor, I shouldn't have—"

"No, it's okay. Hey, it was a long time ago." He cleared his throat again.

"The thing was, I blamed her, for a while."

"For dying and leaving you?"

"For letting the old man do her in. Oh, not really," he said quickly, when Miranda turned a stunned face up to his. "What I mean is, he wore her down. Hell, he wore everybody down."

"I'll bet he did," she said. There was a sharpness to her words and he knew she was remembering what he'd told her, about the beating the old man had given him after he'd taken the motorcycle for a joyride.

"Anyway, when I said I wanted to become a cop, he almost went crazy. He said he hadn't worked his tail off so I could clean up the garbage in the streets, the way he had. Nope, not the son of John O'Neil. I was gonna go to college, get a law degree, hang out my shingle and make him proud."

"And, naturally, you decided you wanted no part of college, or of law, or of making him proud."

Conor sighed. "Am I really that easy to read?"

"It takes a rebel to know a rebel," Miranda said lightly. "So, what did you do? Join the force anyway?"

"I wasn't that dumb. The old man would have sabotaged me."

"Sabotaged you?"

"Sure. I don't know how, exactly. Maybe he'd have seen to it I flunked the exam or that I didn't make it out of the Academy, or if he couldn't manage that, he'd have gotten me appointed to a shit detail."

"The South Bronx?"

Conor laughed. "The Internal Affairs Division." He took her hand, drew her towards a cluster of tables sheltered under a striped awning outside a neighborhood bar. "It isn't the Champs Élysées but how about we sit down and have lunch?"

''I'd like that.''

''I think you have to go inside and place your order. What would you like?''

''A salad or a sandwich. Whatever you have. And some iced tea, please.''

''Payment up front,'' Conor said, and he dipped his head and kissed her.

Miranda sat back, smiling to herself as he strolled inside the bar. He was right, this wasn't Paris, not by a long shot. It was a grey, slightly grungy street in New York—but she was happier than she'd ever been in Paris, happier than she'd ever been in her entire life, now that she'd fallen in love with . . .

God, what was that?

Her heart gave an unsteady leap. She sat forward, trying to see through a snarl of traffic to the other side of the street. For a minute, she'd thought she'd seen—

''Here we go, mademoiselle. Two iced teas, one ham on rye, one turkey on white. Mademoiselle gets her choice of . . .'' Conor got a look at Miranda's bloodless face and set the tray down with a clatter. ''What's the matter?''

She looked up at him. I just saw that man, she wanted to say, I saw Vince Moratelli.

But she hadn't seen him. There was nobody on the opposite sidewalk, nobody in the street at all that bore more than a passing resemblance in height and weight to Moratelli. It had only been a horrible illusion and to talk about it would be to give life to an ugly memory.

''Nothing's the matter.'' Conor looked unconvinced, so she shot a look at the turkey-on-white, gave an exaggerated shudder, and lapsed into an overdone French accent. ''On second thought, monsieur, perhaps somesing iz zee mattaire. Do zee Americans truly call zat white stuff 'bread'?''

Just as she'd hoped, the put-on eased the tension and made Conor laugh. He sat down, shoved the ham-on-rye towards her and bit into the turkey-on-white.

''You just don't know what's good. This is gourmet fare.

Spongy bread, lots of mayo . . . Are you laughing at me, Beckman?''

''I am indeed, O'Neil.'' Miranda took a bite of her sandwich. ''And I'm waiting to hear the end of your story. What happened after you decided you were going to spite your father by not studying law?''

Conor swallowed, wiped his mouth with a paper napkin, and took a drink of iced tea.

''I enlisted.''

''In the army?''

''I know you'd prefer the French Foreign Legion but yes, in the army.''

''And?''

''And, I hated it. The orders. The jerks giving the orders. The whole bit.''

Miranda grinned. ''Just like home, huh?''

''Exactly like home—except, after a while, I saw that it wasn't. The rules made sense, for a change.'' Conor moved his glass of iced tea idly over the table top, leaving a pattern of rings within rings. ''I ended up in Special Forces.''

''The guys who wear those sexy berets?''

He looked at her and chuckled. ''Amazing, how all you broads think alike.''

''Conor O'Neil, you're impossible.''

''But sexy. Remember that.''

''I could never forget it,'' she said softly.

Their gazes met and held. Conor smiled and reached for her hand.

''So,'' he said, ''here we sit, just a pair of overgrown delinquents.''

''Well, not anymore. We've both got completely respectable jobs.'' Miranda straightened in her seat, tossed her head and gave him the kind of smoldering look she'd given Manuel's camera. ''I,'' she said in tones of deepest drama, ''am a famous model. And you are an internationally recognized private investigator.''

A muscle knotted in Conor's jaw. ''Yeah,'' he said, after the slightest hesitation, ''that's me, all right.''

''Were you an investigator when you met your wife?''

''Ex-wife,'' he said, his fingers lacing through hers. ''No, I was in college when—''

''College?'' She thought back to the evening in the park, and the frayed Columbia sweatshirt he'd been wearing, and she began to smile. ''Don't tell me. Boy enlists in army rather than follow orders and go to law school, boy survives army and grows up in the process, boy gets his discharge, enrolls in school—''

''And gets his law degree.'' Conor laughed. ''Some rebellion, huh?''

''Absolutely. You got the degree because you wanted it, not because your father wanted it. But how come you aren't practicing?''

Because Harry Thurston, that smooth-talking bastard, got hold of me and convinced me I'd be doing the honorable thing for God and country if I went to work for the Committee instead.

''My ex used to ask me the same thing.'' He shrugged his shoulders, let go of Miranda's hand, picked up the remaining half of his sandwich and then put it down and pushed the plate aside. ''I don't know. Law seemed too tame, after Special Forces.''

''Is that why you got divorced? Because your ex wanted you to be a lawyer instead of a detective?''

Conor looked at Miranda. He could almost see the lies he'd told her stacked up between them, pulsing with the glow of their duplicity.

''I'm sorry,'' she said quickly, ''I don't know what's gotten into me. It's none of my business. I never ask anybody so many ques—''

''It's very much your business,'' he said, clasping her hand again as he leaned towards her. ''I want everything about me to be your business. It's just that—that . . .'' Anger knotted in his gut. ''Dammit to hell, why couldn't we have met like anybody else? Over a bowl of pretzels, at a party, or on a plane."

Miranda's face went white. Her hand shot out, as if she were warding something off, and her glass of iced tea toppled over.

"Oh God," she said, "I knew it! It's him!"

"Who?" Conor was already on his feet, swinging around and scanning the street.

"Moratelli."

The name thrummed through Conor's blood. He took a step forward, all his senses fixed on the street that stretched before him, but he saw nothing, no one that could be the man who had terrorized Miranda.

"Where?"

"He's gone, but he was there a second ago, I swear it, just beside that lamppost. I thought I saw him before, when you were getting our lunch."

"Dammit," Conor growled, spinning towards her, "why didn't you tell me?"

"Because I was sure I'd imagined it. Because I didn't want to bring back all the awful stuff that happened in Paris . . . God, what does he want?"

The million dollar question, Conor thought grimly, and he still had no answer.

"I don't know, but I'm sure as hell going to find out. Listen to me, Miranda. I want you to sit right where you are while I—"

"No!" She reached out and grabbed his hand. "Don't leave me here!"

There was terror in her eyes, and in her voice. Hell, he couldn't leave her, not when she was so frightened, and anyway, that might be just what Moratelli wanted, to lure him off and leave Miranda unprotected.

He held out his hand and drew her to her feet.

"It's okay, baby," he said softly, "it's okay."

She shuddered and burrowed into his enfolding arms.

"Conor," she whispered, "please, let's go home."

* * *

He phoned Thurston on his cell phone from the taxi that took them back to her apartment.

''Vince Moratelli's in town, Harry.''

''How do you know that?''

''Miranda saw him, that's how.'' He could hear the barely controlled rage in his own voice, feel it in the tightness of his muscles. ''I want to know why, and when he arrived. I want everything you can dig up on this guy, and never mind telling me that he's just a small-time hood.''

''I can't help it if that's what he is.''

''Don't hand me that crap, dammit! Go deeper. I want to know everything he's ever done, starting in the sandbox. You understand me?''

''Are you all right, Conor? You don't sound well.''

''Just get me the information, and fast.''

''Conor? Where are you calling from?''

Conor looked at Miranda. Her face was still pale; she was huddled in the corner of the taxi, her eyes glued to his face.

''I'm in a taxi,'' he said coldly, ''just turning onto Fifth Avenue. Miranda Beckman is with me.''

''Are you insane?'' Harry's voice turned sharp. ''You're going to blow the whole thing, O'Neil. Have you forgotten who you are?''

''I'm only just starting to remember,'' Conor said, and flipped the phone shut.

''Who was that?'' Miranda asked. ''Somebody who works for you?''

Conor reached for her. Trembling, she went into his arms.

''A business acquaintance.'' He drew her closer still, until his face was buried in her hair. ''But I don't think we're going to be working together, not for much longer.''

* * *

Thurston rang at six.

"Call me back on a secure telephone," he said, and hung up.

Conor flipped his phone shut. He was sitting on the sofa in the living room, with Miranda's head in his lap. She was sleeping, after he'd finally convinced her to let him pour her a double brandy. He'd been watching the news on TV, but with the sound turned off.

Gently, he eased her head onto a throw pillow. He pressed his lips to her forehead, drew the light afghan further over her shoulder, and made his way to the bedroom.

Harry picked up on the first ring.

"Okay," Conor said, "what have you got?"

"Not much more than I had the first time."

"And for that, we're playing spy games?"

"We're exercising appropriate caution, something you seem to have decided to ignore."

"Skip the lectures, Harry. Just tell me what we know now that we didn't know before."

Thurston sighed with impatience. "Nothing vital, I assure you. I can tell you where Moratelli was born."

"Don't you mean where he was hatched?"

"At Bellevue Hospital," Harry said, in the tones of a man whose feelings have been deeply wounded.

"Great. At least now we know that he had a mother. What else?"

"He was raised on Anton Street. That's down around—"

"I know where it is," Conor said. He sure as hell did. Anton Street was in the middle of his father's old precinct. "What else?"

"Nothing else. I kicked over every rock I could find. There's nothing on the man. Nothing official, anyway. You need more, you'll have to turn it up yourself."

"Okay, I'll see what I can do. Meanwhile, do some digging on the Winthrops."

"Are we back to that? I'll remind you again, they've *been* checked out. You told them so."

Conor smiled coldly into the telephone.

"You have a conveniently short memory, Harry. I also told them I'd check out the note Eva had received." He turned his back to the door and let his voice drop to a whisper. "That's what you want me to keep on doing, isn't it?"

There was a short silence and then Harry Thurston sighed.

"You know, O'Neil, you're one of the few people I know who can say the words, 'or else,' without speaking them."

"Do some digging on the Winthrops. There's something that one or the both of them isn't telling us, and I need to know what it is."

"What about you? Have you come up with anything new?"

"Nothing."

"I see you've insinuated yourself appropriately into the Beckman girl's life."

Conor's jaw tightened. "Meaning what?"

"Meaning, you've managed to get into her bed—not that I'm chiding you for it, mind. Living with her, sleeping with her, may be the only way to keep her alive until we find out what's spooking the Winthrops."

"I don't give a flying fuck about the Winthrops," Conor said furiously. "You got that, Thurston? If they get through this, it'll only be because Miranda makes it. And what I'm doing or not doing with her isn't any of your goddamn business."

"Temper, temper, my boy."

"I told you not to call me that."

"You told me a lot of things, Conor. Perhaps you've forgotten who's in charge here."

"You want your pal's nose kept clean or not?"

"You've made your point," Thurston said coldly. "Anything else?"

"I assume you've put a tap on this line?"

"I'm not a fool. Certainly, it's tapped."

"What about the Winthrop phone? Are you on that?"

"Well, no. I suggested it but Hoyt didn't feel—"

"To hell with Hoyt's feelings. Tap their lines. All of them."

"Are we finished?"

Conor reached for Miranda's appointment calendar and leafed through it. She was going to be at the Papillon offices the next day for a business luncheon.

"Miranda has a meeting at Papillon tomorrow, with a bunch of fashion magazine editors. She'll be tied up from one o'clock until three."

"How interesting for you," Harry said dryly. "Perhaps they'll be good enough to offer you suggestions on how to spruce up your wardrobe."

"I'm going to be elsewhere while the meeting's going on," Conor said, ignoring the remark. "Have somebody cover for me. Make certain they understand that things may be heating up. They need to be prepared for any eventuality. And for crissakes, don't send that ass, Breverman. Get Sorenson to do it, or Hank Levy."

"Certainly, Mr. O'Neil, sir. May I be of any further help?"

"Conor?"

Conor turned around. Miranda was standing in the doorway, barefoot and looking sleepy and rumpled in her pale yellow robe. He smiled and held out his hand, and she smiled back and came towards him.

"No," he said into the telephone, "but when I think of something, I'll let you know."

He hung up the phone while Harry was still sputtering, and Miranda stepped into his arms.

"Hi," he said softly. "How do you feel?"

"Much, much better."

It was true, she did. Perhaps she'd imagined seeing Moratelli and even if she hadn't, this was a free country. The man had a right to walk the streets of New York, and she just wouldn't think about anything else. Whatever that had been about, the notes, the picture, the break-in, she'd left it all behind, in France. She was here now, with Conor, and it was as if her life had begun all over again.

She smiled and looped her arms around his neck.

"Honestly, I feel fine."

"Good." He stroked a skein of silken hair back from her cheek. "How about some supper?"

Her stomach gave a ladylike growl, as if in response, and they both laughed.

"I'll make us something," Conor said.

"I'll do it."

"No, you won't. You'll sit down, take it easy, and watch me scramble some eggs."

"I told you, I'm fine." She kissed his chin. "There's a couple of steaks in the freezer. I'll broil them and make a salad."

"What's the matter, Beckman? Don't you trust my cooking? I'll do the steaks. I'll even whip up my very own version of *sauce béarnaise.* How's that sound?"

"Too good to be true. What's your version of *sauce béarnaise?*"

"Well," he said, straight-faced, "you start with a couple of tablespoons of mayonnaise . . ."

Miranda laughed. She leaned back in his arms and spread her hands over his chest. He felt so warm and solid; the steady thump-thump of his heart seemed to seep through her palms and into her own blood. Sometimes, in the middle of the night, she came abruptly awake, trembling in the dark from dreams she couldn't quite remember, and put her head on his chest so she could heart the beat of his heart and let it comfort her.

"Okay," he said, his smile tilting in the way she loved, "so it's not what you'd find in *The Joy of Cooking*. But it's good."

God, how she loved him! Her body sang with it, and her soul.

"What're you smiling at, Beckman. You think just because I'm male and you're female—"

"Good grief, O'Neil, is that right? By golly, I knew there was some kind of difference between us but I just wasn't sure what it was."

His smile tilted even more. "Really."

"Uh-huh."

"And just when did this occur to you, hmm?"

"Well, the other morning, I was watching you shave."

"Were you, now."

"Mmm." She lifted one hand lazily, brought it to his face and rubbed her fingertips lightly over the late-day stubble that had begun to shadow his jaw. The faint abrasiveness sent a shudder of delight along her skin. "It's very sexy, watching a guy shave."

"Yeah?"

"Yeah. Especially a guy who shaves in his shorts. Where on earth did you get all those muscles, O'Neil?"

"Clean living, Beckman."

Miranda laughed throatily. She undid the first few buttons on his shirt and slid her hands inside the parted cotton. His skin felt hot under her fingers.

"We're very conscious of things like that in my profession, you know."

"Things like what?" Conor said, biting back a groan as her hands stroked over his shoulders and across his chest.

"Oh, you know. Musculature. Body development." Her tone was serious, almost earnest. How long could she keep it that way, she wondered, as heat spread through her blood? "These muscles here, for instance." Her fingers danced. "What do you call these?"

Conor swallowed convulsively. "Pectorals."

"That's it. Pectorals." Gently, she tugged his shirt off his shoulders and eased it back until it dropped to the floor. "And these." He caught his breath as her hands moved downward. "The ones that feel like the ridges on a washboard."

"Miranda . . ."

"Abdominals? Is that what you call them?"

"Miranda, if you don't stop . . ."

She undid his belt and the button at the top of his fly.

"And then there's this," she said, her voice soft as darkness. His zipper hissed as she drew down the tab. "This wonderful, uniquely masculine part of you."

"Miranda." His voice was choked. "Miranda, I'm warning you . . ."

She dropped to her knees before him and took him in her hands.

"I love you," she said, "do you know that, Conor?"

"Baby," he whispered, "Miranda . . ."

She brought him to her lips.

The warmth and heat of her mouth enclosed him. He moaned softly and his head fell back.

"Miranda," he said, "sweetheart . . ."

When he could take no more, he drew her to her feet, undid her robe and fell back with her onto the bed.

"I love you," he said, as he parted her thighs. His voice shook with emotion, then turned fierce. "Will you remember that? Promise me, Miranda. Say you'll never forget that I love you."

"Never," she whispered.

She arched and took him deep inside her, where he exploded and burned with the shattering force of a thousand shooting stars.

He awoke hours later, in the dark, with Miranda cradled in his arms. Her hair was spread over his chest; her hand lay curled on his chest.

Christ, how he loved her!

He wasn't a sentimental man and he didn't think of himself as an especially romantic one, but he'd read his fair share of poets and poetry. He knew all about love, and the power it was supposed to have to transform lives, but knowing and believing were not the same thing.

He had never counted himself among the believers, until now.

Miranda sighed in her sleep. She shifted in his arms and her hand rose and flattened against his heart.

Despite all the odds stacked against him in this random, unfeeling universe, he had found this woman and he had been healed by her innocence and by her adoration.

Conor put his hand over hers.

He had done a lot of things in his life, and he'd truly believed some of them to be important for his country. Now, he knew that nothing he'd ever done, in the name of survival or patriotism, had been worth a damn compared to what lay ahead.

Miranda was a pawn in someone's game. He had to keep her safe from the horror snapping at her heels, and he had to tell her the truth about himself without losing her.

And if he failed at either, his life would be meaniningless.

Chapter Eighteen

John O'Neil, Detective-Sergeant, NYPD, Retired, sat in his high-backed chair and watched the flickering shadows on the screen of his television set.

The set was a Sony, a new one, and he'd paid a lot of money for it, but the reception was piss-poor. He'd called Crazy Howie's, down on 34th and 6th, where he'd bought it, and after a lot of back-and-forth they'd finally sent over somebody to take a look. The guy had poked, and prodded, and taken a shit-load of readings with an Ohm meter as if he was a doctor taking its temperature, and then he'd shrugged and said there wasn't a thing wrong with it that moving it away from the window wouldn't cure.

''Too much light on the screen,'' the guy had said, and put his ropy arms around the Sony, and John had said, what do you think you're doing? ''Movin' it over there, back against that wall,'' the guy said, as if he was doing him a favor, and John told him to leave the damn thing alone, that he was perfectly capable of moving the TV himself, if he wanted to, which he didn't.

''Yahoos,'' Detective-Sergeant John O'Neil, NYPD, Retired, muttered as he changed channels.

Every TV he'd ever owned in this apartment, forty years worth of them, had stood over there, against the wall. What was wrong with a little change, every now and then?

''Not a thing,'' he said, answering his own question, ''not a damn thing.''

This way, with the set and his chair beside the window, he could catch a breeze as the weather grew warmer. He could see down to the street, too, if he wanted, watch the kids playing stickball or whatever it was kids played today, see the young mothers sitting on the stoops, warming their bellies and their babies under the spring sun.

Not that he watched what was going on for pleasure. No way. The street had changed, most of the Kellys and O'Briens and Guardinos gone now, giving way to names like Cruz and Rodriguez. Well, he was staying. He'd lived here the better part of his life and he'd be damned if he'd leave.

It was still okay here, safe enough and not even much graffiti. Al Brady, who lived in 2G, said it was because people on the block were working to keep it that way but that was just because he was pushing what he called the Block Association. Truth was, John O'Neil was the reason things were all right on this street. Everybody knew he'd been a cop, knew he still gave a damn about doing things right. It was one of the reasons he'd moved his chair here, by the window.

''Nice to look out and see folks,'' Brady had said, when he'd come knocking on the door, looking for a contribution to the Block Association.

John grimaced. Did Brady take him for a fool? He hadn't been dumb enough to give the man money but he'd set him straight, made sure he understood that he didn't give a crap what ''folks'' were doing and never had. He wasn't sitting at the window for the scenery. It was so he could keep an eye on things. He was a man who believed in law and order. People knew that, and respected it.

He leaned forward, narrowing his eyes. Was that the boy from 4D? What was the kid's name? Juan, probably, hell, they were all named Juan. Kid was lounging against the doorway across the street, eyeing the girls, looking for trouble. Well, why not? Kid didn't have any rules to live by, none of 'em did anymore. No wonder everything was coming apart.

You had to raise your kids to know right from wrong, paddle them on the tail when they needed it, tell 'em what to do and how to do it, if you wanted 'em to grow up right. Even then, there were no guarantees. Just look at what had happened with his very own flesh and blood.

Not that it was his fault. Conor had been born late in their lives and his wife, God rest her soul, had spoiled him rotten.

"Can't you be gentle, John?" she'd say, when the kid would fuck up and need a lick or two with the belt. "Show the boy you care for him."

"I know what I'm doing, Kathleen," he'd tell her.

But it hadn't mattered. The boy was defiant, even more so after Kathleen, God rest her soul, had passed on. He'd done what he could, tried to teach the kid to be obedient and God-fearing, but the more he'd tried, the worse things had gotten. Conor had run wild, got himself into one scrape after another, done his own thing and ignored his father's good advice. Finally, he'd announced he wanted to go on the job.

On the job, hell, John had said. He hadn't raised the boy to walk a beat. He'd put his foot down and said that would happen only over his dead body, so the kid ran off and joined the fuckin' army, for crissakes, instead of going to college and becoming a lawyer, the way he was supposed to.

John O'Neil rose to his feet and went into the kitchen. The water in the kettle was still hot enough, and there was another dunk or two left in the tea bag from breakfast. He refilled his cup and went back to his chair, slurping down the lukewarm tea, watching as the kid—Carlos, that was his name—leaned away from the building and swaggered towards some pretty little thing with tits just starting to fill out her blouse.

It had damn near killed him, his very own son, Jesus, Mary and Joseph, such a fuck-up. In and out of trouble while he was growing up, then the army and a failed marriage to some la-de-dah bitch, and even after the boy had finally come to his senses and gotten himself a law degree—and not at City College, either, oh no, that wasn't good enough—even after he had the degree, what had he done with it?

''Not a thing,'' John O'Neil said aloud, ''not one damn thing!''

Was Conor an attorney, making a good living at insurance like the Murphy boy, or raking in money doing accident claims, like the Donelli kid? Hell, no. Conor still hadn't grown up. He was running around playing spy games for some fancy government agency . . .

What the hell?

The tea sloshed over the rim of the cup and onto his fingers.

Was that Conor, coming up the block?

It couldn't be. They saw each other two, three times a year, plenty for the both of them, talked on the phone from time to time . . .

By God, it *was* Conor, come to pay his old man a visit.

It was a long time since he'd seen his son at a distance. He was tall, was Conor. Good-looking, too, like his mother, and he walked as if he owned the world.

John O'Neil felt an unaccustomed warmth rise within his chest.

Who was that, coming down the steps of the next building? Annie Genovese, that old gossip. She said something to Conor, who paused and stopped at the bottom of the stoop.

John's gaze flickered over Conor again, and his expression soured.

Annie Genovese was always boasting about her sons, all three of 'em. The doctor. The accountant. The college professor.

What did he have to boast about? Not his son, the junior G-man, dressed like a bum in dungarees, leather jacket and a pair of boots.

Boots?

''Mother of God,'' John O'Neil said, and he drew back from the window, folded his arms, and waited.

* * *

''It's lovely to see you, Conor,'' Mrs. Genovese said. ''It's been a long time.''

Conor smiled. ''Good to see you again, too, Mrs. Genovese.''

''So,'' she said, ''what are you doing with yourself these days?''

Ah, he knew this game. It was called, Can You Top This? And he never could, because it would have been rude as hell to have said, listen, Mrs. Genovese, if your sons are happy, living their lives in their safe little ruts, that's okay with me but I need more than that. I always did.

''Oh, this and that,'' he said pleasantly.

''That's nice.'' Annie Genovese's plump chest seemed to expand. ''I'll be sure and tell my boys I saw you, Conor.''

''You do that.''

''Joey's teaching at Cornell. I suppose you've heard of it?''

Conor smiled. ''I think so,'' he said. ''Well, it's been nice talking with you—''

''Danny's opening his own business, did your father tell you?''

''No, no he didn't.''

''You know how it is. Why should a CPA work for anybody else?''

''Right,'' Conor said. ''Well, you take care, Mrs.—''

''And Frank's a partner in a practice up on Pelham Parkway. Of course, he could have gone anywhere, bein' he's such a wonderful doctor.''

''Optometrist,'' Conor said politely.

Mrs. Genovese flushed. ''It's the same thing.''

''Sure. You tell your boys I said hello, will you?''

''Certainly,'' Mrs. Genovese said, and looked coldly away.

Amazing. He'd managed to silence the old biddy. Conor whistled softly as he headed up the steps of the next building, the one where he'd lived until he turned eighteen.

Some things never changed.

Mrs. Genovese, for example, with her incessant boasting.

Her boys, too. He grinned as he pushed open the door and stepped inside the vestibule of the six-story walk-up. He'd bet his last dollar that Joey was still a nice guy, happier talking Shakespeare than baseball, that Danny could still add up ten numbers in his head before you could blink, and that Frank was still called, by those who knew him and detested him, A Four-Eyed Little Fuck.

The street hadn't changed much, either. In his time, it had been mostly Irish and Italian; now, it was mostly Puerto Rican, but the Irish and the Italians were still hanging in. It made for an interesting mix, typically New York, though he suspected his father didn't think so.

His father.

Conor stared at the brass panel on the vestibule wall. There were twenty-five buttons on it, one for each apartment and one for the super, all neatly labeled. You had to ring to be buzzed past the locked inner door but his father didn't even know he was coming. He hadn't phoned to tell him. That would have made it seem too much like a real visit, and he hadn't visited the old man in, what, maybe two years.

The vestibule door swung open. A couple of kids came out, carrying bats and gloves. Conor scooted inside before the door could close and started up the stairs.

They spoke on the telephone, he and his father, every couple of months or so. And last winter—or was it last fall?—they'd met for supper at a cop bar in the Forties, the kind of place where everybody except the waitresses carried a shield and a gun. His father had come as close to having a good time as Conor had ever seen him, though it had had nothing to do with him. It had been being back among men who were still on the job that had made the old man smile.

Conor hadn't been to the apartment in a long time. There was no reason to come. His father never invited him and he had no wish to drop by. There was nothing here, not a memory worth keeping or a feeling worth cherishing. There were only old hurts and old angers, and the knowledge that they'd never go away.

He reached the fourth floor landing. His father's health was good but a man his age would surely feel this climb. Well, that was the old man's problem, not his. He'd mentioned it, the last time he'd come by, and gotten his head bitten off for his trouble. He'd mentioned, as well, that most of the people his father had known had moved away.

''Maybe you ought to look for another apartment, Dad,'' he'd said.

John O'Neil had fixed him with a look Conor knew from his childhood and said that this apartment and this street suited him just fine.

''Despite what you may think,'' he'd snapped, ''I'm not ready for a rocking chair at some old folks' home.''

Conor had started to say that he hadn't been thinking of that at all, he'd only meant that just because a person had lived in one place most of his life didn't mean he had to stay in that place forever. And then he'd realized that for somebody like John O'Neil, it meant exactly that.

Change was too difficult. It made for too many uncertainties. His father would stay until either he or the building gave out, and Conor's money was on the building.

It was a tired old tenement, the sort that you found everywhere in the city, and over the past few years it had lost most of its middle-class pretensions. The stairway walls had been dabbed with graffiti, not anywhere near the amount you'd find in one of the city's slums but enough to make it clear that the residents were fighting a battle they'd probably end up losing. There was even some graffiti on the apartment doors, though there was none on the one marked 4E. Had his father cleaned it off, or were the spray-can *artistes* afraid to screw around with him?

Conor smiled, knew what the answer had to be, and jabbed the doorbell.

To his surprise, the door opened almost immediately. His father was always cautious. City people were, by habit. Cops were, by nature.

"Well, don't stand there," the older man said sharply. "Come in."

Conor stepped inside the narrow entry hall and the door swung shut after him.

"Dad, you know, you shouldn't open the door without asking—"

"Of course, I know. Do you think I'm senile? I saw you, coming up the block."

Conor looked past his father into the living room. It was caught in a sixties time warp, exactly the same as it had been when he was growing up, the orange sofa, the matching club chair, the brown shag rug with a clear plastic runner covering the area you walked on to get through the room to the rest of the apartment. But the high-backed chair that was his father's, the one that had stood before the TV for as long as Conor could remember, had been moved closer to the window. The TV had been moved, too.

His father saw him looking.

"I like to be able to see out," he said. "Keeps 'em on their toes, down in the street, knowing there's somebody that don't take any crap watchin' 'em."

Conor nodded. Had there been a whisper of defensiveness in his father's voice? John O'Neil was still tall and unstooped, with that same look of whipcord strength he'd always possessed, but his hair had gone completely white and there was a prominence to the bones in his face, as if his skin had become too tight.

"It's good to see you again, Dad."

"You should have called before you came by." John looked at his watch. "I have an appointment in a little over an hour."

Conor smiled. There was nothing like a warm greeting to make a man feel welcome.

"I won't be long," he said, deciding to return tit for tat. "Something came up, and I want to check it out with you."

His father's brows lifted. "With me?"

"Yeah. If you've got a minute, that is."

John nodded, turned and marched into the kitchen. Conor

followed. His father was filling the kettle with water. Tea, Conor thought, repressing a shudder. God, he hated the stuff, had hated it ever since he could remember, but it didn't matter. His father didn't keep coffee in the house. It wasn't good for you, he said, something about the caffeine, and there'd been no convincing him there was just as much caffeine in tea, nor even in getting him to give over a bit of kitchen space to a percolator and a can of coffee, as Conor had once foolishly suggested.

Rules were rules, in this house, and John O'Neil made them all.

"Sit down."

Conor pulled a chair out from the red Formica table, force of habit making him choose the one where he'd eaten three times a day until he'd turned eighteen. His father dumped tea bags into two thick china mugs, plunked both down on the table, then settled himself across from Conor.

"So," he said, "what is it that's brought you here?"

"How've you been, Dad?"

"I have good days and bad." His father looked him over. "I see you've gained some weight."

"No, I don't think—"

"Have to watch that, once you get past thirty."

"Yeah, well—"

"What kind of jacket is that? Some fancy new style?"

Conor glanced down at himself. He was wearing his leather jacket, which was about as stylish as his well-worn jeans.

"No," he said, "it's not any kind of style. It's just a flight jacket. A bomber jacket, I think they used to be called."

John O'Neil took a noisy sip of tea.

"In my time, a man went to work, he put on a suit and a tie."

Dammit, here we go!

"Listen, Dad, I know you said you've got an appointment, so why don't I tell you—"

"Of course, I keep forgetting. Yours isn't that sort of job.

You don't report to an office each morning, sit down behind a desk and get ready to face the day."

"Dad—"

"But then, you aren't practicing the law, even though you've the right to do so. I've never understood how you could do it, ignore your true profession and dabble in such nonsense instead."

Conor clenched his jaw. Sidestepping this topic was like trying to sidestep a charging elephant. It was useless, even to try.

"We've talked about this," he said with deliberate calm, "and you know that's not true. I don't dabble in nonsense. I work for the federal government. And one of the reasons I qualified for this job was because I've got a law degree."

"Edgar Murphy's boy. Kevin, his name is. You remember him? He took the Bar before you, of course, went straight into college from high school, the way you should have done instead of running off and enlisting."

"Dad," Conor said, "I didn't come here to—"

"Kevin's just been made a full partner in a firm specializes in insurance claims."

"That's nice."

"Bought himself a fine house in Glen Cove."

"Yeah, terrific. Dad, listen—"

"You're letting everybody move ahead of you."

Conor could feel his patience stretching to the breaking point. "Look," he said, "I didn't come here to argue."

"I'm not arguing, I'm merely stating facts. You're not a kid anymore. It's time you got a real job."

"Dammit, I have a real job."

"You play cloak-and-dagger games with a group of little boys who don't want to grow up."

"Jesus Christ—"

"And watch your mouth!"

Conor slammed his fist on the table, shoved his chair back and stalked into the living room. What in hell had he been thinking of, coming here? He and his father had never managed five minutes without an argument in their lives; why would he have thought today would be different? As far as the old man was concerned, he was still a kid to be ordered around.

To ask the man for help was crazy.

Yes, but what choice did he have? If there was even a chance the old man could tell him something about Vince Moratelli, it was worth eating all the humble pie he could dish out.

Conor ran his hands through his hair, squared his shoulders and returned to the kitchen. His father was still sitting at the table, stony-faced.

"I'm sorry if my language offended you," Conor said stiffly.

"You're a grown man," his father said, just as stiffly. "I've no right to censor your speech but this is my home and I expect you—"

"—to adhere to your rules." Growing wings and flying would have been easier than mustering up a smile, but Conor managed to produce one. "Yes, sir. I remember."

"Rules are the basis of a civilized society, Conor. I tried to teach you that."

"That's one of the reasons I'm here today, because someone's breaking those rules." *Go for it, O'Neil, even if it hurts.* "And I'm hoping you can help me stop him." He paused. "I'm on an assignment, Dad. An important one."

"My son, James Bond," John O'Neil said, and snorted.

Conor started to speak, then thought better of it. He sat down instead and folded his hands on the table.

"I'm trying to get information on somebody. A man named Moratelli."

"Yes?" his father said, politely.

"My sources haven't been able to come up with anything."

"Wonderful. My tax dollar at work."

"I thought you might have heard of him," Conor said, refusing to be baited.

"Why? Do I look as if I have more resources than your pals in Washington?"

"Moratelli grew up in the Seventh."

"So?"

Was he going to have to beg?

"So," Conor said, fighting to keep his tone even, "I figured maybe you knew him."

John O'Neil took a drink of tea.

"Moratelli . . . I can't say that the name rings any bells."

"It's important," Conor said carefully.

"Well, I'm sure it is, if you had to come to me."

Conor studied his father's stern face for a moment. Then he got to his feet, walked to the window and sat down on the sill.

"I met a woman during my current assignment. She's become very special to me."

"A mistake. A man should keep a professional distance."

"I agree. And I tried to keep it that way, but it didn't work."

"So?"

"So, I've reason to believe that this man's going to try and hurt her."

His father looked at him. "Stop him, then."

Conor's smile was mirthless. "I've thought about it. I'd love to kill the bastard. But it isn't that simple. I'm convinced he's just the muscle in this deal."

"You don't know who he's working for?"

"No. And until I do, the woman would still be at risk."

His father nodded. "That's probably true."

"There are other ramifications, too. My assignment involves people in sensitive positions."

"Politicians," his father said, with a smirk.

"Believe me, I don't think much more of them than you do, but—"

"But, you've learned to kiss ass."

Conor stared at his father. Then he kicked back his chair and marched out of the kitchen.

"Conor?"

Conor strode to the front door and yanked it open.

"Conor! You come back here!"

He spun around, white-faced with anger. His father was hard on his heels, his face flushed.

"Don't you dare walk out on me, boy."

"I'm not a boy. And I don't take orders from you."

"Conor, you shut that door and sit down."

"What for? So you can insult me some more? Listen here, old man—"

"Who are you calling an old man?"

"I took your bullying and your yelling for years, but I don't have to take them anymore."

"I'm your father!"

"I'm sorry I bothered you. I'm even sorrier I was fool enough to think you'd help me."

John O'Neil watched his son turn away. To hell with the boy, he thought. Who needs him?

He reached out, started to slap the door closed—and caught a glimpse of himself in the entry mirror.

His face was flushed, the bones pronounced. His hair was white, and thin. He'd been in his prime, the first time he'd driven his son from this house, wanting only the best for this child born so late in his life. You'll drive him away, with your rules and your pride, Kathleen had said, when Conor was small, but he was a cop, he'd seen what happened when people laughed at the law. And then, to make matters worse, the boy had said he wanted to become a cop, too, waste his fine mind and quick wit in a useless fight against the slime of the city.

John O'Neil looked deep into the mirror and saw the ghosts of all the years wasted and gone. He flung the door wide and stepped into the hall.

"Conor," he bellowed.

Halfway down the steps, Conor paused, his hand on the bannister, and looked up.

"Nobody knows the Seventh like I do. I've still got friends there, who'll be glad to answer some questions for me." John cleared his throat. "To tell you the truth, Conor, you'll be doing me a favor, handing me something to do. I'm as bored with watching that street outside as I am with watching the tube."

It was as close to an apology as John O'Neil had ever come,

and Conor knew it. He stared up at the older man, and then he made his way back up the stairs.

"Now then," his father said briskly, as if nothing had happened. He shut the door and led his son into the living room. "Tell me what you need."

Miranda was waiting for him in the marble and glass lobby at Papillon, as they'd agreed she would.

She was sitting on the raised wall surrounding a small reflecting pool, along with half a dozen women. They were, he suspected, the editors with whom she'd met for lunch. Each woman was the height of style and elegance. Miranda, simply dressed, stood out among them like a glittering jewel.

She stood up when she saw him, her face lighting with pleasure, said something to the other women and then hurried towards him.

"Hello," she said softly.

Conor was not a man given to public displays, by nature or by vocation, but when he saw the way she was looking at him, his heart swelled.

"Hello, yourself," he said, and took her in his arms and kissed her.

Miranda gave a breathless little laugh.

"We're being watched," she whispered.

"I don't care." He smiled, tilted her chin up and kissed her again. "Do you?"

"Not a bit."

"I missed you."

"Not half as much as I missed you." She linked her arm through his as they strolled to the exit. "And that's not just sloppy sentimentality, either, O'Neil, so don't let it go to your head." She smiled up at him as the automatic doors slid open and they stepped out onto the street. "Or have you forgotten that while you were out, doing whatever manly thing it is you were doing, I was trapped in a room full of frills and froufrou?"

"With the harpies back there?"

"Uh-huh." She shuddered. "Heaven save me from ending up that way."

"What way?"

"They're nice women, but scary. All of them afraid to eat an extra lettuce leaf, exchanging the addresses of their latest plastic surgeons . . ."

"You don't want to end up the next Helen Gurley Brown, hmm?"

"God, no! Do you think we could get something to eat? I'm starved!"

"Sure. But I thought you just had lunch."

"We had something the menu called a Spring Surprise." She giggled. "The surprise was that nobody could get a fork in it long enough to hold it still and saw off a piece."

Conor laughed. "How does a hamburger sound?"

"With onion?"

"Raw or fried?"

"Raw," Miranda said indignantly. "Only the potatoes on the side should be fried."

"Beckman, you're a woman after my own heart."

"I don't suppose I could get a malted with my burger and fries?"

"Even a pickle," Conor said.

Miranda grinned. "You're on."

He took her to a place he knew on Tenth Avenue.

It was a diner, a glittering chrome palace of a place, complete with a jukebox stocked with records from the sixties. Elvis sang about the Heartbreak Hotel while they attacked their hamburgers, which Miranda pronounced perfect.

"I have," she sighed, "died and gone to heaven."

"What happened to that finely educated French palate?" Conor said, smiling as he watched her pluck a French fry from her plate with her fingers.

"O'Neil, I'm not a dope." She dunked the fry into a glob

of ketchup, then popped it into her mouth. ''There are some things only the French do well, like champagne or *crême brûlée,* but when it comes to hamburgers, pickles and greasy French fries, only the Americans know their stuff.''

''You have ketchup on your mouth.''

''Where?''

Conor leaned over and kissed her.

''There,'' he said softly. ''And there. And . . .''

His cell phone shrilled.

''Dammit,'' he said, and yanked it from his pocket. ''Hello?''

''Conor, it's Harry.''

''Yes?''

''I don't want to talk on an unsecured line.''

Conor shot a glance towards the rear of the diner. There were two public telephones on the wall, both of them in use.

''I can call you back in five or ten minutes,'' he said.

''No. This is important.'' Harry took a breath. ''The information you requested? About the couple we've been dealing with?''

Conor sat up straighter.

''Yes?''

''It's come in.''

''Something on him?''

''No. Not on him.''

''On the woman, then?''

''Yes.'' Thurston paused. ''The point of origin we'd learned, Conor, do you remember it?''

''Point of—''

''Conor?''

Conor looked across the table at Miranda. She wasn't smiling anymore.

''Conor, what's the matter?''

''Hold it a second,'' he said into the phone, and put his hand over the mouthpiece. ''Nothing, sweetheart. This is just, ah, it's just the same guy I called yesterday, remember? He promised to get back to me with some information.''

''About Moratelli?'' she whispered.

"Miranda, just let me finish this call, okay?"

She nodded and pushed aside her plate, her eyes gone as bleak and dark as they had yesterday.

Conor turned away from her, the phone still pressed to his ear.

"All right," he said very softly, "let's have the rest of it."

"The woman's point of origin is not Argentina. It's Colombia."

"She lied?"

"Conor, I am not going to discuss this over this phone. Call me back."

Conor winced as Harry slammed down the receiver on his end. He flipped the phone closed and looked at Miranda.

"I forgot," she said. "For a little while, I forgot all about everything."

Conor nodded. For a little while, he'd forgotten, too.

Eva had been born in a little town in Colombia, not in Argentina.

But the rest of her story was true enough. She'd met a marine named James Beckman, who'd been stationed at the American Embassy in Bogotá, and married him. He'd brought her to the States and they'd had a baby they'd named Miranda. Beckman died in an auto accident when the child was still a toddler, and Eva started selling a lotion she'd brewed up in her kitchen, door-to-door. Five years later, she'd hocked everything she owned to open the first Papillon factory.

Conor sat back on the sofa in Miranda's living room, put his feet on the coffee table, and crossed them at the ankles.

Okay, so she'd lied. So she'd bought herself a phony Argentinean birth certificate.

So what?

That still didn't explain why somebody had zeroed in on her and it sure as hell didn't explain why they'd zeroed in on Miranda.

Miranda.

He sighed and scrubbed his hands over his eyes.

Nothing had been the same since that phone call in the diner, and it went beyond the fact that the call had tossed both of them back into harsh reality.

''There's something you're not telling me,'' she'd said, when they'd gotten back to her apartment. ''Conor, what are you holding back?''

Everything, he'd thought.

''Nothing,'' he'd said, and the look on her face, that said he was lying and she knew it, had been as sharp as a knife to his heart. ''Miranda,'' he'd said, reaching out for her, but she'd brushed past him.

''I'm going to take a shower,'' she'd said, ''and then I'm going to lie down for a while.''

He'd known better than to argue with her, or to take her into his arms and make love to her. Don't touch me, her eyes had warned, so he'd just stood there, feeling angry, stupid and helpless, watching as she scooped up Mia, went into the bedroom and closed the door.

Then he'd called Harry and gotten the details about Eva—which brought him back to the beginning.

Eva had lied, she'd been born in Colombia, not Argentina, but so what?

''Dammit,'' Conor whispered, ''dammit to hell!''

His phone rang. He snatched it from the coffee table and jammed it to his ear.

''What else have you got for me, Harry?''

''Conor,'' John O'Neil said, ''I've got some information on—''

''I'll call you back.''

He went into the foyer, dialed his father's number on Miranda's phone. His father picked up on the first ring.

''I'm sorry if I called at an inopportune time,'' he said stiffly.

Conor sighed. ''It isn't that. I didn't want to talk on my cellular phone. They're too easy to monitor.''

''Why have one, then?''

Conor laughed. ''You're right. I'd be better off with a pager.''

"I checked on—the individual we discussed."

"Moratelli. It's okay to use his name. This phone is safe."

"I'm afraid your people were right, Conor. There's nothing on the man."

Conor rubbed his hand over the back of his neck.

"Shit."

"Not that he's clean, mind. My sources say he's a gonzo of the first order, that he's a strong-arm pimp with pretensions of grandeur who ran a couple of girls until he beat his number one lady so bad she talked the rest into hustling for somebody else. The other guy put the word out on the street and Vince had to quit the game."

Conor nodded. "Nice guy. Well, listen, Dad, I appreciate your trying."

"There is one thing. I'm not sure if it's going to help you or not."

"What is it?"

"There's a rumor he's involved in something big-time. The word is, he's working for some foreigner and that he's about to come into a lot of money."

"A foreigner?" Conor's eyes narrowed. "What's that mean, exactly?"

"I don't know."

"Somebody here? Or somebody overseas?"

"I'm telling you, I don't know."

"Well, find out." Conor ran his tongue across his lips. "Can you do that?"

"I'll try."

Conor gave his father Miranda's number, then hung up the phone. He told himself to take it easy, not to get too excited. He'd been in this business long enough to know that two and two didn't always add up to four. Still, things did seem to be falling into place. It took no great leap of the imagination to figure that the foreigner Vince Moratelli was working for was Edouard de Lasserre. Or his cousin, Amalie.

But if this was a blackmail scam, as he'd suspected all along, why was it moving so slowly?

"Conor?"

He turned at the soft sound of Miranda's voice. She'd scrubbed off her makeup and brushed out her hair. She was wearing her pale yellow robe. He could see her bare toes peeping out from under the hem. She looked innocent, and vulnerable, and he knew he loved her more than he'd ever dreamed he could ever love anyone.

"Miranda," he said.

Miranda's throat constricted when she saw the way he was looking at her. She had hurt him before, she knew. Now, she longed to run to him, go into his arms and tell him that she loved him with all her heart.

But she couldn't.

It wasn't that she didn't love him. God, she did. She'd never imagined loving anybody the way she loved Conor.

But something was wrong between them.

She knew he was a man who kept things to himself, that he'd opened up to her more than he'd ever opened up to anyone, even his ex-wife. Still, there was a dark secret in his eyes, and it had to do with her. The realization terrified her.

Other people had lied to her and she'd survived. She'd even grown stronger as a result of those lies. But if Conor had lied, if he'd deliberately set out to use her . . .

Did he know what power he held, that only he could wound her so deeply that she might never recover?

She couldn't go to him. Not yet. Instead, she walked to a chair, sat down and folded her hands in her lap.

"I've been doing a lot of thinking," she said.

"And?"

She swallowed. "And," she said softly, "I need to know the truth."

What truth? he almost said. But he couldn't lie to her, not anymore. She wanted the truth and he'd tell it to her. He had to tell it to her, everything, from the real reason he'd sought her out that day at the Louvre to the hellish package that had brought him back into her life. She had to understand why he'd deceived her, understand, and forgive him.

''Conor? You didn't just happen to bump into me in Central Park that evening, did you?''

He sat down opposite her, on the sofa. ''No.''

''You came looking for me.''

''Yes.''

''Because you're still working for Eva,'' she said, her voice trembling just a little.

''No! I don't work for Eva. Nothing I've done has been for—''

The doorbell rang. Miranda shot to her feet, her face gone white.

''Conor?'' she whispered.

Conor held up his hand. ''Stay put.''

He moved past her, and opened the door.

Chapter Nineteen

It was the porter, standing in the hall with a manila envelope in his hand.

It had been delivered by private messenger, he said, for Miss Beckman.

Conor let out his breath, dug in his pocket and pulled out a bill.

"Yeah," he said, stuffing it into the man's hand, "thanks."

He shut the door and turned to Miranda. The color had come back into her face.

"For me?" she asked.

Conor thought of the package that had been delivered to her the last time, the one she knew nothing about.

"Let me open it," he said.

She shook her head as she rose to her feet. "I'll do it," she said, and held out her hand.

He gave the envelope to her and watched as she tore the flap. A puzzled look spread over her face.

"Pictures," she said, pulling three eight-by-ten black and white photos from the envelope.

Conor's first instinct was to rip them out of her hand. He

still remembered, all too clearly, the picture Moratelli had sent her, in Paris. But these photographs, whatever they were, hadn't upset her. She looked puzzled, even baffled. Nothing more.

"I don't understand," she said finally. "Why would somebody send these to me?"

He took the pictures from her and stared at the first one.

It was a snapshot of an intersection of a road. No. No, it wasn't. It was a photo of a sign at the intersection of a road. It said, Avinida Rio Azul.

The second photo, taken from a slightly different angle, still showed the intersection and the sign but now you could also see a street corner and a street sign that said, Calle La Perla.

He flipped to the final picture. The intersection and the street corner were still visible but whoever had taken the shot had moved further back. A building showed in the photo now, a narrow, three-story structure that bore a small sign over the door.

"El Gato Negro," he murmured. "The Black Cat."

"Why would someone send these pictures to me?" Miranda said. "What do they mean?"

Conor looked up. "Damned if I know."

"Maybe it's a mistake."

He wanted to tell her she was right, that the envelope had somehow been misaddressed, but he couldn't do it. The pictures had been meant for her, all right, but why?

"Conor—there's something written on the back of that photograph."

He turned the picture over. Every muscle in his body tensed. Something was, indeed, written on the reverse side and if he'd been a betting man, he'd have put his money on the ink and the handwriting being identical to the ink and handwriting in the first notes that had been sent to Eva, and to Miranda.

Miranda had seen the message, too. She moved closer and read it aloud.

"Dile a tu madre que divulgue su secreto," she said, and looked at him. "Why would someone send me a message in Spanish?"

Conor frowned. "I don't know. Can you translate it?"

"I'm not sure." Miranda chewed on her lip. "I can pick out some of the words. *Madre* means mother, and the last part sounds like 'reveal the secret'—"

The phone rang. Conor moved quickly, grabbed the receiver and barked, "Hello."

"Conor?" His father's voice was alive with excitement. "I've got something for you."

"What is it?"

"The name of the guy Moratelli's supposed to be working for. French, it's supposed to be, but it doesn't sound it."

Conor's hand tightened on the telephone.

"Tell me," he said.

"Dee Lassiter. Does that mean anything to you?"

De Lasserre. The name screamed inside Conor's head.

"Conor? You still there?"

"Yes," he said hoarsely, "yes, I'm here."

But he wasn't. He was back inside that moldy pile of stone that was the home of Edouard de Lasserre, hearing the Count talk about Miranda as if she were little better than a whore.

Miranda was staring at him, her eyes wide and shiny. He knew she was reading his face, that now she was fighting hard not to be afraid. He knew what he wanted to do. Drop the phone, go to her, take her in his arms and kiss her and tell her everything would be fine, it would be fine . . .

He tried what he hoped was a reassuring smile, turned his back and walked into the next room, as far as the telephone cord would stretch.

"The name isn't Dee Lassiter," he said softly to his father. "It's de Lasserre."

"Now, that sounds right." John O'Neil chuckled. "Fella I talked to didn't have much of a French accent, if you get my drift. So, you know this guy?"

Images crowded in. De Lasserre's arrogant face and cruel smile, and what Miranda had told him of her wedding night in that medieval fortress.

"Son? Does it help?"

Conor cleared his throat. ''Yes, yes, it does. Thanks, Dad.''

''No problem. To tell the truth, it felt good, poking my nose into things again. If there's anything else . . . ?''

''Actually, there is.'' Conor looked at the photo in his hand. Sometime during the last few minutes, he'd crushed it in his fist. Now he tucked the phone in the crook of his shoulder and smoothed the creases out of the picture as best he could. ''Some of your neighbors read Spanish, right?

His father laughed. ''Is the Pope Catholic?''

''You think one of them would translate something for me?''

''Well, I guess. Let me grab a pencil here . . . Okay. What've you got?''

''Dile a tu madre que divulgue su secreto,'' Conor said slowly, then spelled it out. ''I know it's something about your mother and revealing the secret but—''

''It means, 'Tell your mother to let the cat out of the bag.' ''

Conor's eyebrows shot up. ''How'd you know that?''

''You can't work in Nuevo York as long as I did without learning something.''

''In that case,'' Conor said, fanning through the photos, ''maybe you can help me with something else. I've got some pictures here. That message was written on the back of one of them.''

''Uh-huh.''

''There are some signs in the pictures, in Spanish. I figure they must have some connection to the message.''

''What do the signs say?''

''The first says Avenida Rio Azul.''

Conor could hear the sharp intake of his father's breath over the phone.

''Avenida Rio Azul?''

''Yeah. Does that mean something to you?''

''Tell me what the other signs say, Conor.''

''There's a second sign that says Calle La Perla. And then there's a sign on a building. It says—''

''El Gato Negro.''

Conor frowned. ''That's right. You know this place?''

"Damn right, I know it. Where'd you get those pictures, son?"

"It's too complicated to go into now. Just tell me what the hell I'm looking at here."

"There was a big drug bust a few years back, some yahoos from Medellín got taken down by the DEA."

Conor felt the hair rise on the nape of his neck.

"Medillín? Colombia?"

"Yes. They were running high-octane coke right through the heart of the Seventh. I ended up working with the DEA guys. They had lots of surveillance photos."

"Like these?"

"Exactly like those."

"So, what am I looking at, then? A Colombian drug factory?"

"El Gato Negro, at the intersection of Calle La Perla and Avenida Rio Azul wasn't a drug factory."

"Conor?"

Conor turned around. Miranda had moved close to where he stood. Her face was pale and puzzled.

"Who are you talking to?"

He tried for a smile and forced his attention away from Miranda and back to the telephone.

"If it wasn't a drug factory, what was it?"

"It was the favorite meeting place for every fat cat who dealt dope in that part of Colombia."

"Why?"

"Because El Gato Negro was the best whorehouse in town."

"I don't understand why I can't go with you."

Conor slipped into his leather jacket. He and Miranda had been at this for almost twenty minutes, her insisting on going with him, him coming up with what he hoped sounded like logical reasons for her to stay right here. Well, she wasn't going with him, that was for sure, not if he had to lock her inside this damn apartment and throw away the keys.

No matter what Miranda's relationship was with her mother, he wasn't going to have her standing there while he told Eva he knew she'd lied about her place of birth, then shoved a picture of a whorehouse under her nose and asked her what in hell she knew about it.

"Damn you, O'Neil, don't you dare ignore me!" Miranda grabbed his arm and stepped between him and the door. "Why won't you take me with you?"

"Sweetheart . . ."

"Don't sweetheart me. I want an answer."

"I've given you my answer, half a dozen times." He smiled, but she wasn't buying it. Her eyes still flashed defiance. Conor sighed. "Okay, I'll try again. I want to check out a lead."

"About these photos," she said, and he nodded. "I have the right to know why, Conor. They were sent to me."

"I know that."

"And you won't tell me what that call from your father was about."

"Can't a father call a son to say hello?"

"Give me a break, O'Neil. He called to give you some information."

"What if he did? He was a cop, remember? Cops have all kinds of contacts."

"How come you didn't tell me you'd gotten in touch with your father about what's been happening to me?"

"It didn't seem important to tell you, not until I found out if he could pick up some information on Moratelli."

"And he did, but you won't tell me what it is."

"Dammit!" Time was flying, and Conor's gut told him that from now on every second counted. "Beckman," he growled, "get out of my way."

"Why would you think your father would know anything about Moratelli?"

"I just told you why. Because my old man was a cop. He used to work the streets where—"

"Where what?"

Conor took a breath. ''Where you can dig up information on low-lifes like Vince.''

Miranda's eyes fixed on his. ''I know there's more to it.''

''Miranda . . .''

''And now you want me to stay here like a good little girl, and sit on my hands all by myself while you play detective.''

''You won't be by yourself. I've told you that. I've arranged for security until I get back. It's already in place. You heard the call I made, and the confirming one that came in, a little while ago.''

''Do you ever listen to yourself? The way you spoke to whoever it was you telephoned—''

''An associate,'' Conor said. Hell, it wasn't a lie. Thurston was an associate, in a way.

''And the words that trip off your tongue. Contacts. Associates. Security.'' She made a face, as if she'd smelled something unpleasant. ''There are times you sound like an actor in a bad spy movie!''

''Will you calm down?''

''I am calm. I'm very calm. I'm just tired of being lied to.''

''I haven't—''

''Oh, please, spare us both that wide-eyed routine! You haven't been honest with me and I know it.''

He knew he was supposed to deny it, assure her he was second cousin to an Eagle Scout, but he wouldn't. No more lying, not after Eva gave him some answers.

''Miranda,'' he said softly. He took hold of her shoulders, feeling the rigidity in her body. ''Sweetheart, you're right. There are things I haven't told you.''

''Then, tell me now.''

''I can't.'' She tried to pull away from him but he wouldn't let her. ''But I promise, I'll tell you tonight.''

''Everything?''

''Everything.''

She sighed, and he felt some of the tension ease out of her.

''No more lies, Conor.'' The anger in her words was gone, replaced by a weariness that almost broke his heart. ''Please.''

He took her face between his hands and raised it to his.

''Trust me one last time,'' he said, ''that's all I ask.''

She looked up. His eyes were steady on hers, and filled with promises enough to last a lifetime. She smiled tremulously and he kissed her. Then he undid the locks on the door and picked up the manila envelope with the photograph inside.

''Afghanistan Banana Stand.''

''Afghanistan Banana Stand?'' she said and, just as he'd hoped, her smile warmed. ''What's that supposed to mean?''

''It means that you lock the door after me, put the chain on, and don't open it for anybody or anything, unless you hear those words. I'll be back, before you know it.''

He kissed her again, and then he was gone.

It was chilly out, and felt more like early fall than late spring.

Conor zipped up his jacket and turned up his collar. He knew he should get moving. Everything was set. He'd had Thurston make sure that Eva was at home, though he'd warned him against alerting her to his visit.

''You want to tell me what's going down?'' Harry had asked, and Conor had said he wasn't sure, which was damn well the truth.

But something would go down, tonight. Eva was sitting on a secret and he was going to get it out of her, any way he had to. Conor's mouth thinned. And if Hoyt got in his way . . .

He had a million reasons for putting his fist through Hoyt Winthrop's teeth, every one of them named Miranda.

Conor looked up and down the street. He'd made a specific request for Hank Levy to watch over Miranda and Hank had phoned, to assure him he was in place along with Dave Scotti, another good man, to cover the service entrance.

Well, then, why was he wasting time? He knew, just *knew*, that the tangled skein of the Winthrop's secrets was about to unravel.

Yet, he had an uneasy feeling about leaving Miranda alone.

But she wasn't alone. Her door was locked, and Scotti and Levy were watching over her.

Conor turned up his collar, tucked his hands into his pockets, and headed for the Winthrop mansion.

Far above the street, in Miranda's apartment, the shrill ring of the telephone pierced the silence.

Miranda jumped. Hand to her heart, she reached for the receiver.

"Hello?"

"Good evening, Miranda."

Her heart slammed against her ribs. She knew that unctuous voice, would know it anywhere.

"What do you want?" she whispered.

Vince Moratelli laughed. The evil sound felt like a trail of slime across her skin.

"Your mother knows what I want, darling. Why not ask her?"

The connection was broken and the dial tone hummed in her ear, Miranda started to tremble.

"Conor," she whispered, as she hung up the phone, "Conor, where are you?"

She thought of the message written in Spanish, that had something to do with her mother and secrets, thought of Moratelli's whispered words as they had oozed through the telephone.

Your mother knows what I want.

She had received the threat, but Eva was the target. She had been, all along.

Miranda looked at her watch. Less than ten minutes had crawled by since Conor's departure. He'd tell her everything, he'd said, when he returned, but why should she wait? Eva had answers, and she wanted them now.

Someone was downstairs, Conor had said, watching over her. Miranda smiled tightly as she headed for the door.

Whoever was down there, she hoped he was in the mood for a little visit to Fifth Avenue.

Conor knew he'd caught Eva off guard, from the way her lips formed into a thin, unyielding line. She wasn't any happier to find him waiting in the entryway than Jeeves had been to find him on the doorstep.

"Mr. O'Neil." Her gaze flashed to the envelope he held in his hand, then to his face. "You should have telephoned first. I'm afraid my husband and I are expecting dinner guests."

Conor smiled pleasantly. "This won't take long."

He didn't wait for an invitation but pushed past her, into the foyer. The painting of Miranda was gone. A watercolor in a heavy gilt frame hung in its place.

Eva brushed past him. "Indeed, it will not," she said briskly. "This way, please."

The library was the same as it had been, weeks before. Once they were inside, she shut the door, folded her arms, and looked at him.

"Well? What is it that brings you here uninvited, Mr. O'Neil?"

"You're direct, Mrs. Winthrop. I admire that."

"And I admire brevity. What is the purpose of your visit?"

Conor smiled. "I was wondering . . . what was it like, at The Black Cat?"

The color drained from Eva's face. She seemed to age a dozen years as she staggered backwards to brace herself against the paneled wall.

"The what?"

"You're a good liar, Eva, but not good enough. Why did you lie about your birthplace?"

She stiffened, but only for a heartbeat. Then she reached past him and flung open the door.

"I think you'd better leave."

"It was stupid, pretending you were Argentinean, when the truth was so easy to discover." Conor opened the envelope and drew out a photo. ''I have something for you. A little souvenir, you might say.''

''Get out!''

''Come on, Eva, aren't you curious? It's a picture, from your country.''

''My country,'' she said coldly, ''is the United States of America. And I would remind you, Mr. O'Neil, that my husband is—''

She fell silent as Conor held out the photograph. Her gaze shot to it, then to his face.

''What—what is that?'' she whispered.

''You tell me.''

He lifted his arm and slowly waggled the photo back and forth. After a moment, Eva took it from him and looked at it. The sound of her breathing seemed to fill the room.

''Where did you get this?'' she asked hoarsely.

''Someone had it delivered to your daughter this afternoon.''

She nodded. ''Well, I don't—I don't know why you've brought it to me.'' Her hand shook as she held out the photograph. ''A picture of a street in the middle of nowhere . . .''

''It's over,'' he said, almost gently, and he slid the other photos from the envelope and held them in front of her.

She looked at him, and he could see the fear in her hazel eyes. He almost felt sorry for her.

''What's over? I don't know what you're talking about.''

''If you tell me the truth, I may be able to help you.''

''Why would I need your help? So I lied about my birthplace. Well, so what?'' She slammed the door shut and leaned back against it, her posture one of regal defiance. ''That was a long time ago. Is there a law that says Colombians can't enter the United States, especially when they're married to U.S. citizens?'' Her chin lifted in a gesture that reminded him of Miranda. ''We have friends in high places, Mr. O'Neil. Have you thought of what the president will say, when my husband informs him that you've been harassing me?''

''Actually,'' Conor said softly, ''I've been thinking about

what he'll say when he finds out the wife of his ambassador-designate used to earn her living as a whore."

There was an instant of electric silence and then Eva flew at him, her fingers curved so that her blood-red fingernails flashed like talons. Conor grabbed her by the wrists and forced her further into the library.

"*¡Condenado,*" she screeched, "*hijo de puta!*" She pulled free and wrapped her arms around her middle. Terror and rage flashed in her eyes. "You son of a bitch! I knew you were going to ruin everything from the second I laid eyes on you."

"Who's blackmailing you, Eva? Tell me what's going on, and maybe I can get you out of this mess."

"I will tell you nothing. Not a word, do you hear me?"

"Have you told Hoyt?" His question made her breath hitch. "I thought not." Conor's expression hardened. "Give me what I want, and the information will never leave this room."

Her eyes were fixed on his, her body as taut as a stretched wire. The air almost vibrated with tension. She was hanging on to his every word.

This was the moment he'd been waiting for.

"I want to know why de Lasserre's after Miranda."

"How would I—"

She stumbled back as Conor moved towards her.

"You fuck with me," he said, "so help me God, I'll toss you to the wolves."

Eva stared at his face. His eyes were cold and flat. She had seen eyes like those in what she'd begun to think of as a life that had belonged to somebody else. But it wasn't somebody else's life, it was hers, and it had caught up to her, as she'd always feared it would.

"All right," she whispered. She folded her arms around herself again, as if to let go would mean she'd break into a dozen pieces. "But first, you have to promise me that no one else will ever learn what I tell you—and that Edouard de Lasserre will never bother me again."

Considering what he had in mind for the son of a bitch, it was an easy promise to make.

"Done." Conor sat down on the arm of one of the silk chairs that flanked the fireplace. "Now, let's hear it."

Eva took a deep breath. "Very well." Her accent, always before barely noticeable, had grown stronger during the past minutes, and more pronounced, as if she were giving up not just the truth but herself. She looked straight at Conor and though her face was flushed, her gaze was steady. "I was born to a mother who was a factory girl." She smiled bitterly. "I had many *tíos,* uncles, who would stay with my mother for a week, a month . . ." She shrugged and drew a deep breath. "One day, when I was perhaps twelve, one of the 'uncles' had business in a town called Santa Teresa. He took us with him."

"Drug business?"

Eva laughed. "That *is* the business in Santa Teresa, Mr. O'Neil." Her smile faded. She shivered and rubbed her arms briskly with her hands. "I don't know what happened between them, only that they quarreled and he left us there. My mother had no money and so she sold herself at El Gato Negro, so that we could eat."

"And she stayed on," Conor said, when Eva fell silent.

She nodded. "She died in a drunken fight when I was almost thirteen." Her eyes flashed. "I make no apologies for what I did then, Mr. O'Neil. What other work is there, for the daughter of a *puta?* Yes, I worked at El Gato Negro until I'd saved enough money to go to Bogota—and then I met my soldier."

"Beckman."

"Yes. He was very young and very innocent, and when I told him he had taken my virginity and that I was pregnant with his child . . ." Eva's hand slashed through the air. "He married me and brought me to this country."

"Why did you lie about your birthplace?"

She shrugged. "I wanted to bury my past. Buying a phony passport was easy enough, and Beckman was stupid. He believed whatever I told him."

"Even that Miranda was his," Conor said softly.

"It would have been better if she had been born dead," Eva said bitterly.

"Jesus Christ, do you hear what you're saying? She's your daughter!"

"She is no good."

"And what are you?" Conor's mouth twisted. "You lied your way into marriage, cheated your way into this country, found that pig, Winthrop, molesting your very own flesh and blood, and you did nothing except punish the girl by sending her away."

"Ah, I see. You have chosen to believe Miranda's version of the story."

"She told me what happened."

"She is a liar and a tramp!" Spittle formed in the corners of Eva's mouth. "She is the one who lured Hoyt to her bed."

Conor's laugh was brutal. "You can't really believe that."

"Why would I not believe my husband? The blood in his veins is as blue as the sky."

"And the blood in Miranda's veins is yours." A muscle knotted in Conor's jaw. "That's why you didn't believe her, isn't it? You believe in the sins of the fathers . . . only in this case, it's the sins of the mothers."

"What I think is none of your concern, Mr. O'Neil."

She was right. His only concern was Miranda's safety.

"Tell me why Edouard de Lasserre's been threatening Miranda," he said.

"Because I would not do as he demanded."

"Which was?"

"Do you know anything about the manufacture of cosmetics, Mr. O'Neil?"

"No."

"Papillon makes perfumes, colognes, lotions and sprays which contain fragrances. To make them, we import huge quantities of fresh flowers." She smiled a little. "Colombia's economy has expanded, in recent years. It exports drugs—and magnificent flowers. The flowers must be hurried through customs, or else they wilt and die. Because of our reputation and my husband's connections, Papillon has been granted something called a 'line release.' It means shipments we receive from Colombia come into the United States without being searched by U.S. Customs."

"And?" Conor said, wanting to hear it from her lips, even though the picture was coming together with breathtaking swiftness.

"And, de Lasserre wanted me to permit him to use our shipments to smuggle in cocaine. He said it would be profitable for us both."

"But you didn't want to risk it."

"Certainly not. I have everything I could possibly want. A successful business, a magnificent home, a husband with a fine old name . . ."

"And a daughter you don't give a crap about," Conor said through his teeth.

"If you think to shame me," Eva said coldly, "I assure you, you cannot. Miranda is the one mistake of my life."

"What you mean is that she's the reminder of who you really are, Mrs. Winthrop." Conor smiled tightly. "Go on. De Lasserre asked you to smuggle drugs and you said no. What happened next?"

"You know what happened next. He sent me a threatening note, and then he began sending notes to Miranda. He thought he could make me change my mind, you see." She shrugged her shoulders. "The man's a fool."

Conor's hands fisted. He jammed them deep into his pockets. "Let me be sure I understand this. He's threatening Miranda, to get at you."

"Yes. He assumed that since I had bought him off when he married the girl, I could be coerced into giving him what he wanted again."

"Five hundred dollars," Conor said, very softly. "You really put a high price on her, didn't you?"

"It was not five hundred, it was twenty-five thousand. I am not without feeling," Eva said stiffly. "Besides, I knew the marriage was an error."

"For Miranda, or for you? It wouldn't have done much for

your reputation, would it, if word got out that she'd run off with a piece of sleaze like de Lasserre?''

At the other end of the room, the door eased slowly open.

''I tell you again, this is not your concern, Mr. O'Neil. Your only business is to see to it that my husband gets his appointment. That was the reason you were sent to Paris, the reason you forced my daughter to return to the States. It is why you reentered her life, because it was your obligation to do whatever was necessary on behalf of my husband and me. Now, all that remains is to stop de Lasserre from ruining everything for us. We cannot afford any scandalous headlines, do you understand?''

Conor could feel his rage building with every beat of his heart. He wanted to grab Eva Winthrop, shake her until her bones rattled, tell her that she was a poisonous harpy who ought to be on her knees, thanking whatever gods existed for having let her give life to the miracle that was Miranda.

But things were moving too quickly now. Eva had said no to Edouard de Lasserre, and he wasn't a man you said no to without paying the consequences. Eva was safe, but Miranda was all too vulnerable.

So he took a deep breath, fixed a smile to his lips, and looked at Eva Winthrop in a way that made it clear they were in this together.

''Making sure you and your husband get what's coming to you is all I'm interested in,'' he said.

''I'm pleased to hear it.'' Eva was almost her old self now, standing straight and tall, a look of elegant *hauteur* on her face. ''I'll wager this has been a far better assignment than most that have come your way.''

At the far end of the room, the door flew open and hit the wall. Conor spun around, in a crouch . . . and saw Miranda, standing in the doorway.

His heart dropped when he saw the look on her face. ''Baby,'' he said quickly, ''it's not what you think!''

''Yes, it is,'' she said, giving him a smile that hit him like a kick to the groin. It was the same smile that Hoyt had captured in the painting that had hung in the foyer, a smile that spoke of pain and betrayal. "It's exactly what I think."

"Miranda." He moved towards her, his face grim. "Goddammit, I told you to stay put."

She laughed, a long trilling sound that was as phony as her smile.

"I don't ever do what I'm told. Just ask my dear mother. Besides, then I'd have missed your wonderful chat with Eva."

"Miranda," he said, reaching out to her, "sweetheart . . ."

She slapped his hand away before he could touch her, and now he could see the glitter of tears on her lashes.

"Was it?" she said, in a gravelly whisper. "Was it what she said, Conor? A better assignment than you're used to getting?"

"No!"

"It wasn't? You mean, it was just run of the mill, what we had? What I thought we had?" Her voice broke and tears rolled down her cheeks. "Goddamn you," she said, "goddamn you to hell, O'Neil."

Her hand flashed through the air and slammed against his cheek. It was a hard blow that stung his flesh and rocked him back on his heels, but it felt as if it had penetrated straight into his heart.

She'd misinterpreted what she'd heard but hell, whose fault was that? He'd lied to her, time after time; he deserved the blow and more, and when she pulled back her hand to hit him again, he didn't try to stop her. But she didn't hit him. A cry ripped from her throat and she turned and ran from the room.

"Miranda!" He started after her, but Eva flung herself in front of him.

"Just a minute, Mr. O'Neil. I want to know what you intend to do next. You promised me you would take care of Edouard de Lasserre."

"Get out of my way, damn you!"

"Not until you've answered my questions."

Conor cursed, grabbed Eva Winthrop by the shoulders and shoved her aside.

"Miranda," he yelled, as he ran into the hall.

Where was she? The hall was empty, and the foyer was, too. He raced to the front door, yanked it open—and almost collided with Hank Levy.

"Where is she?" Conor snarled.

Hank's jowly face was grey. "I'm sorry, O'Neil. Hell, it all happened so fast—"

Conor grabbed him by the shoulders. "Where the hell is she?"

"She went running out of her apartment. So I followed her. I left Scotti back at the building, to keep an eye on things, just in case."

"Dammit, man, just tell me!"

"I was across the street here, watching the front door. Somebody came out of the side entrance. Jesus, I didn't realize it was the girl."

"You lost her?"

"A car came up, black Mercedes, tinted glass so I couldn't see inside. The door opened. I yelled . . ." Hank gave a wheezing sigh. "Hell, Conor, somebody snatched her."

Chapter Twenty

Flying. Miranda was flying, soaring though the skies.

And she was blind.

No, not blind. Blindfolded, that was it. There was a cloth tied around her eyes. She couldn't see, but she knew she was in an airplane. She could hear the low rumble of its engines, feel their vibration resonating in her body.

She didn't remember getting onto a plane. A car. She remembered that. She'd heard Conor and Eva, talking about her as if she were a problem they'd been coping with, and she'd run blindly from the house while Conor pounded after her.

The car had come out of nowhere, running up onto the sidewalk, the door opening.

"Hello, pussycat," somebody had whispered, and a hand clamped around her wrist.

After that there were only her screams and a rag jammed over her mouth and nose and the smell of something sweet and awful.

Then there was darkness.

How long had she been unconscious? An hour? A day? Terror swept through her and with it, a wave of nausea. She moaned, tried to gasp for air, but there was a gag in her mouth. Her hands were bound, too, and angled painfully behind her.

The terror rose again and ripped from her throat in a silent scream.

Behind her, she heard the whisper of laughter.

"Easy, pussycat. We don't want you should hurt yourself."

Hot breath feathered against the back of her neck. Miranda froze, her heart was the only part of her that was moving as it banged erratically against her ribs.

"That's it," the voice whispered.

Leather creaked. Whispers floated on the air. Someone eased into the seat beside her.

"We was wonderin' how long it would take you to wake up and join the party."

Don't move, she told herself frantically, oh, don't move. Just sit still and don't let him see how frightened you are.

A hand stroked lightly over her face. She couldn't help it; all her promises fled at the feel of those unseen fingers moving on her skin like the soft brush of tiny spiders. She bucked back against her seat, twisting in a desperate attempt to escape, but it was useless.

The man next to her laughed, and she felt him lean closer.

"Now, pussycat, this ain't no way to make friends." A hand touched her thigh, eased up over her belly. "It'll go better for you if you act nice, you know that."

Miranda sobbed against the gag in her mouth as the man cupped first one breast and then the other.

"Nice. Real nice. I'm a tit man, myself. 'Course, my pal, here, he ain't so specialized, you know what I mean? He likes tits, ass, everythin'. Ain't that right, Vince?"

Vince? Vince? Bile flooded her mouth. No, she thought, no, please, no . . .

"Hello, darling."

God. Oh God. It was him. It was Vince Moratelli.

"Come on, Joey."

He sounded civil. Polite. As if they were back at the party, where they'd met.

"Don't monopolize the lady's time. It isn't nice. Tell you what. You go sit in the back, read *Penthouse* or something. I'll sit here with our guest and entertain her."

"Aw, Vince. I was just havin' some fun."

"Who's in charge here, Joey? You? Or me?"

"You, but—"

"Get moving!"

Joey let out a sigh that stank of decay.

"I'll see you later, pussycat."

"Joey," Vince said in a warning tone.

"Yeah, I'm goin'." Joey chuckled and leaned closer. "You got a knight in shinin' armor to protect you, pussycat. Ain't that nice?"

Vince Moratelli, protecting her? Miranda stiffened as leather creaked again and Vince settled into the seat beside her. Moratelli had sent her that hideous picture, said those hideous things, and now he'd helped kidnap her.

But he'd stopped the other man from touching her.

Maybe it was going to be all right. They'd kidnapped her, but that didn't mean they intended to hurt her. Money. That's what they wanted. That's what kidnappers always wanted, wasn't it? They'd ask Eva for ransom and she would pay it because she and Hoyt couldn't afford scandalous headlines, wasn't that what she'd said to Conor?

Conor. Conor, who had deceived her. Who had never meant anything he'd said, whose kisses had been lies . . .

"I do want to thank you, darling, for having made things so nice and easy for us. Though I suppose it was serendipity, that first your boyfriend leaves your place and then you come flying out the service entrance of your mother's house, just when we were trying to figure out how to go in and get you." Moratelli sighed. "Just listen to me, prattling on. I haven't even asked you how you feel."

"Mmph," she said, into the gag.

"Ah. The gag's in your way. I understand." He patted her shoulder gently, like a father or an older brother. "We'll take it out soon, I promise. After we land and get settled. But first, you're going to take another nice little nap."

No, she screamed, or tried to scream, but she couldn't. There was the sudden sharp sting of a needle in her arm, and then, once again, there was only darkness.

When she awakened the next time, she was sitting in a soft, deep chair and the drone of the engines had gone.

Where was she? A house? A room. It was cool; she could hear the whisper of an air conditioner, and way off in the distance, a deeper sound. Waves, maybe, beating against a shoreline.

"You awake, darling?" It was Vince; she could hear the rustle of cloth, feel the whisper of breath against her face and she knew he must be squatting down beside her. "Not feeling too good, huh? Well, you'll feel better soon. Take off her blindfold, Joey."

She trembled as the cloth was ripped away. She didn't want to look, didn't want to see anything. Dialogue from a hundred bad movies chased through her brain. You weren't supposed to look at your kidnappers, not if you wanted them to let you live.

But she already knew their identities. One was named Joey. And the other was a man she'd prayed to never see again.

"Open your eyes, Miranda."

Moratelli's voice was soft, and surprisingly gentle.

"Come on, darling. You might as well take a look. We both know you can identify me. Besides, I think you're going to be surprised. This isn't half as bad as you've probably imagined."

There wasn't really any choice. Slowly, she opened her eyes. She saw Joey first and he was as she'd pictured him, small and dark, with a furtive look that was frightening. She thought he must have been the kind of boy who'd gotten his kicks torturing defenseless animals and pulling wings off butterflies.

"You like what you see, huh, pussycat?" Joey said. He

grinned, showing a mouthful of yellow teeth, and she looked quickly past him.

Vince smiled as their eyes met.

"Miranda," he said, nodding his head.

For one insane second, she almost smiled back at him. He looked just as she remembered, tall and good-looking, with a civilized smile and dark, pleasant eyes.

"Look around you," he said. "You'll see that there's nothing to fear."

It was true, there didn't seem to be. She was in a living room that was big and bright. The ceiling was high, with exposed wooden beams and a huge skylight that seemed filled with stars. A fireplace stretched the length of one wall. The furnishings were handsome and looked expensive.

"Nice, isn't it?"

Her gaze flew back to Vince and he frowned.

"For heaven's sake, aren't I foolish? You can't answer, not with that gag in your mouth, can you, darling? Joey, undo Miranda's gag, if you please."

She took a deep, ragged breath as the gag fell from her lips. Her throat felt raw and parched and she swallowed painfully.

"Joey," Vince chided, "I think you must have had that on too tight." He bent down and knelt in front of her, his expression one of deep concern. "Are you all right, darling?"

It took effort to work enough moisture into her mouth to speak.

"Mr. Moratelli . . . "

"Please, there's no need for such formality. Call me Vince, won't you? It's much more appropriate, considering how well we're going to know each other."

Joey let out a high-pitched giggle. "Oh, that's good, Vince, that's really good!"

Vince sighed and shook his head. "You'll have to forgive Joey, Miranda. His manners are sadly lacking."

"Mr. Moratelli. Vince." She swallowed dryly. "Vince, please, you're making a mistake."

Joey giggled again. Vince shot him an angry look.

''Go put up some coffee,'' he said. ''Miranda and I want to talk. Now, darling, what do you mean, I'm making a mistake?''

''I know you want money.''

''Well, we all do, don't we? Even you, with your privileged upbringing, must understand that.''

''What I'm trying to say is, if you let me go, I'll see to it that Eva pays you whatever it is you've asked.''

Vince smiled. ''That's very kind.''

''Plus a bonus, for—for being so cooperative.''

''Do tell.''

''Yes. And I swear, I'll never tell her or anyone else that you were involved in this.''

Vince rose to his feet, folded his arms and rocked back on his heels.

''I don't understand, darling. You say your mother will pay extra for your safe release.''

''Absolutely. As I said, she'll pay whatever you've asked, plus—''

''But I haven't asked anything, Miranda.''

''No, not yet. I'm talking about when you get around to contacting her.''

''Ah, I see.'' Vince smiled. ''Sit forward, will you, so I can undo that rope around your wrists.''

Miranda scooted towards the edge of the chair. She could see Joey measuring coffee in the kitchen. He was horrible, a human weasel, and he made her skin crawl. Vince did, too; she tried not to shudder as his fingers brushed her flesh as he untied her hands, but at least he was reasonable.

She had to concentrate on him, direct her plea to him.

''How's that? Better?''

She nodded, flexed her hands and put them in her lap. The blood was pouring back into them and the pain was sharp, almost breathtaking, but she sensed it would be better not to admit it.

''Much better. Thank you.''

Vince gave her another of his radiant smiles.

''Good. Now, what were you saying, Miranda?''

"I was saying that if you'd just let me go—"

"I'm afraid that's impossible."

"Why? Why is it impossible?" Miranda heard the hysteria mounting in her voice. She stopped, took a breath, and started over. "You're in charge, you said, isn't that right?"

"Absolutely."

"Well, then . . . "

He moved, so suddenly and swiftly that she had no warning at all. He grabbed a fistful of material at the round neck of her cotton shirt yanked down hard and ripped the fabric to the hem. Miranda screamed. She reached for the torn edges of the shirt but Vince grabbed her hands in one of his and squeezed. She could feel the bones of her fingers scraping against each other.

"Joey was right," he said conversationally. "You do seem to have lovely breasts."

"Don't," she said, in a high whisper of a voice that couldn't possibly have been her own, "oh don't, please don't . . . "

His hand closed on her bra and it tore in half.

"Ah," he breathed.

"Mr. Moratelli. Vince, please. I beg you . . . "

"Joey? Come here a minute, would you?"

The little man came scuttling over. His lips curled up, revealing a yellow grin, as he peered at Miranda.

"What'd I tell you? Great tits, right?"

"Excellent tits. Stand up please, Miranda."

She shrank back deeper into the chair. Vince sighed, grimaced and hauled her to her feet.

"Please, don't make this more difficult than it need be."

She dug in her heels but he was strong, far too strong for her to stop him. She struggled futilely as he dragged her along after him, through the living room and down a bright hallway. At a doorway, he paused, shifted position, and shoved her ahead of him into a huge bedroom.

One wall, entirely made of glass, looked out over a perfect blue sea. The other walls were mirrored, as was the ceiling. The sole piece of furniture in the room was a huge four-poster bed, set on a platform.

"I love this room," Vince said, "don't you?"

Miranda began to scream. Vince sighed and shook his head. "It's a waste of effort, darling. No one can hear you. We're on a private island, surrounded by miles and miles of ocean. You'll only scream yourself hoarse and anger me in the process."

"Me, too," Joey said. "Jeez, Vince, she's hurtin' my ears."

"Do you hear that, Miranda? Do you want to hurt Joey's ears? Stop that noise at once, or I'll be forced to let him stuff another rag down your throat."

He meant it, she knew. The thought of being gagged again was more than she could bear. Miranda clamped her teeth into her bottom lip. Her screams died away and became a soft, keening whimper.

"Good girl. Now, Joey, there's a closet in that wall, do you see the outline of the door just in back of that mirror? You'll find some silk scarves inside. Pick some pretty ones. What colors do you like, Miranda? Pink? Blue? Well, you choose them, Joey, one for each wrist and each ankle, and bring them here. Get on the bed, darling."

"Vince," she said, her voice quavering, "Vince, please . . ."

"Didn't you hear me, Miranda? Step up on the platform."

He started towards her. Quickly, she scrambled backwards, up the two steps on the platform.

"Now, lie down."

"No! No, don't . . . "

Vince shoved her, hard. She fell onto the bed and he moved quickly, sat down beside her and grasped her wrists while Joey trotted over with four silk scarves.

"Excellent," Vince said. "Take her hands. That's it. Tie them to the posts at the corners of the bed. Very good, Joey. Now her ankles . . . "

The men worked quickly and efficiently. When they were done, Miranda lay weeping and sobbing with fear, spread-eagled before them, her breasts exposed and her life in their hands.

“There,” Vince said, standing back and looking down, “that’s fine.”

“Perfect,” Joey said. He grinned, reached down and ran his knuckles over her breasts.

“Now, Joey,” Vince said sternly, “what did I tell you?”

“Come on, Vince. We got her all to ourselves for, what, another couple of hours?”

“A day, at least. And we have to take good care of her.”

Joey chuckled. “I’ll take good care of her, you can bet on that.”

“Vince,” Miranda whispered, “Vince, please, don’t let him . . .”

“I won’t, darling, I promise. But he’s right about one thing. We do have time hanging heavy on our hands.” He smiled, and her breath caught at the sudden cruelty in that smile. “I wouldn’t want you to become bored.”

“Don’t,” she said, as he moved towards her. “God, please, don’t!”

She cried out as he bent down and opened her jeans. His hand slid under the denim, his fingers stroking her flesh.

“Lovely,” he whispered.

“Vince, please, I beg you . . .”

“She’s beggin’ you, Vince. How can you turn her down?”

Vince’s smile tilted. He put his other hand over his bulging fly.

“Lovely,” he said again, and began to rub himself.

A long, terrible wail rose from Miranda’s throat.

“Gag her, Joey,” Vince snarled. “And then turn your back.”

“Aw, Vince . . .”

“Do as I say, damn you!”

The little man did as ordered, then turned away, his shoulders hunched. Vince opened his zipper. Whimpers burst from Miranda’s throat and he laughed.

“Not yet, darling.” Smiling, he reached inside his pants and drew himself out. “See what I have for you?” he whispered, as his hands began to move along his own flesh. “Not now, we have to wait.'' He groaned as his touch on himself quickened. ''But I promise, later, after—after . . .''

He groaned again, and Miranda shut her eyes as he ejaculated. There was a silence, and then a sigh, and she heard the zipper snicking shut.

''Miranda? Open your eyes and look at me.''

She shook her head wildly from side to side, the gag biting into her mouth, the bile bitter in her throat.

Vince's fingers closed on her chin, hard. She gasped with pain and her eyes flew open.

''Remember the picture I sent you, bitch? The one with the knife, shoved into your cunt?'' His teeth drew back from his lips. ''This time tomorrow, I'm going to make it real. Oh yeah, I'm gonna put a blade right up where you live, little girl.'' He laughed and leaned closer, until she could smell his sweat. ''But first, we're gonna make you a movie star. That's what all you models dream of, isn't it, becoming movie stars? Well, tomorrow we'll do it. We'll make you a gen-u-ine movie queen.''

''Vince?'' Joey said plaintively. ''Can I look now?''

Vince sighed, let go of Miranda's chin, and straightened up. ''Yeah, you can look.''

The little man turned around. His face was flushed.

''It's not fair,'' he whined. ''Why do I have to wait? I could just do some stuff, get off like you did.''

''De Lasserre doesn't want her spoiled, you know that.''

De Lasserre. De Lasserre. Miranda moaned against the gag. The name tolled with the resonance of a funeral bell.

Vince winked. ''An old friend of yours, right? He told me to take good care of you, loosen you up, get you ready.'' He chuckled. ''And I will, I promise.''

''He gets to fuck her first, right?''

''He's the boss, Joey. The boss always gets his first. We'll handle the video cameras and when he's done, we'll get our chance.''

"Just so's I get to do her," Joey said petulantly.

"Right after me."

The little man shivered with pleasure. "And then the big finish," he whispered.

"That's right." Vince looked down at Miranda and smiled. "And what a finish it's going to be." He leaned closer. "You know what a snuff film is, darling?"

Miranda felt her flesh turn cold. Vince laughed.

"She knows, Joey. That's too bad. I was kind of looking forward to explaining that, in a way, a snuff film's an actress's greatest performance, because when it's over, so is she." Vince smiled. "Then, we take your body out on the boat and feed you to the sharks."

"Jeez," Joey said, licking his lips, "you keep talkin' about it, I'm gonna come in my drawers."

Vince chuckled. He grabbed a blanket from the foot of the bed and drew it up over Miranda.

"There you go," he said softly. "We wouldn't want you to catch your death of cold, would we, Joey?"

Joey snickered. Vince clapped him on the shoulder and the men began to laugh. They were still laughing as they sauntered from the room.

Crisis-time in New York wasn't like crisis-time in Libya, or in the middle east.

On an opponent's soil, a man working on his own was a man without access to necessary resources.

Conor stuffed his hands into his jeans pockets and squeezed them until he could feel his nails digging into his palms.

But by God, a man on his own was also a man who could get something done without it ending up a three-ring circus, which was what this thing was rapidly becoming.

Miranda had been snatched more than a day ago and the Winthrop library was jammed with bodies. Cops, FBI agents, city officials, Hank Levy and Dave Scotti . . . and for all he knew, there were more to come.

The door opened and a pair of detectives from the local squad strolled in, self-important in dark suits that didn't quite fit over their bellies. They went straight to Hoyt Winthrop, who was standing alongside Eva, his arm around her shoulders with a look that said "I am a worried Daddy" on his aristocratic face.

It was all Conor could do to keep from heading across the room and punching out his lights.

But it wouldn't do any good. Oh, he'd settle that score, but now wasn't the time. The son of a bitch wouldn't get away with what he'd done to Miranda. Now, though, the only thing that mattered was finding her—finding her before de Lasserre did what the photo he'd had sent to her in Paris had suggested.

Jesus. He couldn't think about that. He couldn't think about the dead cats, either. Conor patted down his pockets, cursed himself for not having a cigarette and for being such an ass.

Why had he left her? Why?

Hank Levy was a good man, so was Scotti, but he should never have left her alone.

If only he knew where to start looking. They had the Mercedes' license plate: Hank had managed to get a partial and the computer at the Department of Motor Vehicles had done the rest, but so what? The Mercedes had been stolen; the owner knew nothing. And despite a nationwide alert, nobody had reported spotting the car.

Conor felt his pockets again, cursed under his breath and began pacing the room. The damned circus was getting bigger. Another pair of uniforms had just marched in, followed by the precinct captain, and here came the mayor himself, surrounded by his retinue of ass-kissers.

"Hoyt," the mayor said in the deep tones that had won him the election, "all the city's resources are at your disposal."

Hoyt offered his hand along with a grave smile.

"Thank you, Your Honor. Eva and I are very grateful, aren't we, dearest?"

Eva, pale and regal and plastered to her husband's side, nodded brokenly as she drew a lace handkerchief from her pocket.

"Yes," she whispered, "oh, we must find my poor baby!"

Enough, Conor thought grimly. He pulled his phone from his pocket, moved into the hall, and punched in a number. A second later, Harry Thurston snapped a crisp hello in his ear.

"Harry, I've had enough of this crap."

"Calm down, Conor."

"Don't tell me to calm down! You should see what's going on here, goddammit. It's a fucking joke."

"You know that what you're seeing is nothing but surface glitter. Beneath all of it, we're hard at work."

"There's nothing new?"

"Nothing. De Lasserre disappeared after he left for Charles de Gaulle airport yesterday."

"There's no record of him anywhere?"

"We're checking. He's not a fool, Conor. He probably used a couple of bogus passports. We'll find him, but it takes time."

One of the uniforms scurried from the library, spotted Conor and headed for him. The cop was just a kid, probably fresh out of the academy. He had a round face and freckles and his eyes glowed with the excitement that came from rubbing shoulders with the rich and infamous.

"You know where the kitchen is? The mayor wants some coffee."

Conor glared at him, got to his feet and walked into the foyer.

"By the time you find him," he said into the phone, "it may be too late. The guy's a sicko. He's not going to hold Miranda as a negotiating tool, I'm telling you, he's going to hurt her. Big time."

"If you have any ideas, I'm listening."

Conor ran his hand over his face. The only idea he had involved killing Edouard de Lasserre the slowest, most agonizing way possible, but to do that, he had to first find him. And he had to find Miranda. God, if anything happened to her . . .

"You see?" Harry said gently. "You can't come up with anything we haven't already thought of. Think positively, my boy. We're narrowing the search, minute by minute."

"Sure." Conor smiled bitterly. "We've almost done Europe. All that's left is the U.S., Asia, Africa and the fucking Caribbean." *The Caribbean!* Conor's breath caught. "Harry," he whispered, "dammit, Harry . . ."

"What is it?"

"Get back to Amalie de Lasserre."

"I told you, our people spoke to her. She doesn't know a thing."

"She does," Conor said. He was trembling; he could feel the adrenaline pumping through his veins. "When I talked with her, she said Edouard had been in the States on business."

"So?"

"She also said he'd been checking some property he owned, in the islands."

"And you think . . . ?"

"The islands, Harry. People say that, they mean the Caribbean."

Harry whistled. "I'll get back to you, ASAP."

Conor slammed down the phone, reached into his back pocket and took out his wallet. The picture he'd taken from the file at Miss Cooper's School for Young Ladies was still there, only a little the worse for wear.

He stared at Miranda's face, at the sweet, girlish smile.

"I'll find you, sweetheart," he whispered, "and when I do, I'll never let go of you again."

A few hours later, he was in a helicopter, urging the pilot on as the craft lifted off for an island nobody had ever heard of except for an irritated Amalie de Lasserre, who'd finally dredged its name from her memory.

* * *

Miranda's arms and legs ached. Her wrists and ankles felt chafed from her constant twisting against the silken bonds that tied her to the bed.

Everything felt raw, including her throat. The gag seemed to be soaking up all her saliva. Her lips felt swollen, too, as if the skin might split at any minute.

How much time had passed since Vince and Joey had tied her up and left her? There was no way to tell. For all she knew, night had turned into day again. She'd tried finding a way to keep track of the passage of time, but it was impossible. Vince had returned just once, to turn on a lamp in the corner and draw heavy drapes across the windows. The drapes blocked out everything, even sound, though sometimes she thought she could hear the distant beat of the surf.

Or was it the beat of her heart?

It could be. She was wild with fear, caught up in it in a way that would have been unimaginable before she'd raced out of Eva's house and been dragged into the car. The notes, the picture—they'd been terrifying but not like this. Never like this. A picture wasn't real, it wasn't the same as lying here, spread-eagled and half-naked, remembering Vince's hands on her, and on himself, and the things he'd said about what would happen to her after Edouard arrived.

No. She couldn't think about that. She had to think about something else, about being found and rescued.

About Conor.

Tears blurred her eyes and slipped down her face, into her tangled hair. Conor. Oh, how she'd loved him. Trusted him. But he hadn't loved her. He'd used her, deceived her.

She made a soft, choking sound as she began to weep. Had he? She'd overheard his conversation with Eva, but she might have misunderstood.

If only she'd listened, when he'd tried to explain. If only she hadn't run away . . .

"Ah, *ma petite,* how good it is to see you again."

Miranda's eyes flew open, her body jerking in startled response to that soft, well-remembered voice. She twisted her head on the pillow and the blood in her veins turned to ice. Edouard was coming towards her, his handsome face set in the smile that had once seemed so charming, his trim body draped in the Armani he'd always favored—and a cold cruelty in his eyes that sent her heart thumping against her ribs.

''For shame, Vincent,'' he purred. ''You have put a gag in Miranda's lovely mouth.''

''Yeah,'' Vince said, leering over Edouard's shoulder, ''she was making too much noise.''

''Surely, she understands that we are surrounded by sea and sand, and that no one can hear her.''

''Sure, but she screamed anyway. It hurt Joey's ears.''

Edouard sighed. ''Does the gag bother you, my dearest Miranda?''

Miranda nodded.

''Do you wish it removed?''

She nodded again.

''You must not scream, if I remove it. Poor Joey is quite delicate.''

Miranda bucked against the bindings. Edouard smiled.

''I take that as a yes,'' he said, and he leaned down and took off the gag.

She gasped and drew air deep into her lungs.

''Poor darling. The scarf has left marks beside your beautiful mouth.'' Edouard sat down beside her. ''Better now?''

''Water,'' she whispered hoarsely.

''Of course.'' Edouard snapped his fingers. ''Vincent, a glass of water for my beloved.''

Vince brought the water in a tall tumbler. Edouard took it, put one hand beneath Miranda's head and raised her from the pillow.

''Here,'' he said gently, ''that's it. Drink. Not too quickly . . . ah, you have spilled some on the blanket.''

''I'm—I'm sorry,'' she whispered. ''But I was so thirsty . . .''

Edouard swept the blanket away.

''It is no matter, darling Miranda. Why would we need this

blanket, anyway?'' He smiled into her eyes and, as he did, he laid his hand against her throat. ''We are all friends here, yes?''

''Edouard. Edouard, please, please, let me go. I don't know what it is you want, but—''

She gasped as he turned his hand so his knuckles pressed into the hollow of her throat. For an instant, the pressure was terrifying; she knew that he had only to deepen it and her breath would be cut off. But then he smiled and the pressure lessened; his hand drifted slowly down her skin, to her breasts, and he cupped first one and then the other.

''What I wanted, beloved, was respect.''

''I never showed you any disrespect, Edouard.''

He laughed. His hand was moving again, down her abdomen to her belly. She told herself not to think about it, or about Vince, looking down from beside the bed and breathing hard, or Joey, who'd come sliding into the room and was standing by the door, watching, his beady eyes gleaming.

''Miranda, *ma petite,* let us show some honesty, now that we have reached such an important juncture in our relationship. I gave you my name, took you into my home, and how did you repay me? By cringing when I touched you, just as you cringe now. By crying for your mother and running off with her, as soon as she appeared.''

''Edouard, please, I was only a child.''

''Your mother was no better. Calling me names. How dared she?'' Edouard leaned towards her, his eyes bright with hatred, the phony smile vanished from his lips. ''I am the Count de Lasserre and she—she is nothing. I knew it, in my heart, and I set out to prove it.''

''Edouard, God, will you listen?''

''Eva Winthrop,'' Edouard de Lasserre said, spitting out the words. ''Wife of Hoyt, founder of an empire—and all the time, she was nothing but a whore. A Colombian *putain,* with pretensions of grandeur.'' He stood up and jerked his chin at Vince. ''Turn on the lights.''

Vince grinned. ''Here we go, Joey.''

Lights blazed on overhead. Miranda blinked and tried to turn her face away from the glare.

"Get the video cameras and the tripods. You know where to place them."

"Edouard," Miranda sobbed, "Edouard, please . . ."

De Lasserre bent down and back-handed her across the face. She felt blood well at the corner of her mouth.

"Shut up, *putain.*"

"Edouard, don't do this. Please, please, just tell me what you want!"

"It is too late for begging, Miranda." Edouard shrugged off his suit jacket, folded it carefully and lay it over the back of a chair. "I offered your mother one last chance, but she chose to ignore it."

"What last chance? I don't know what you're talking about."

He undid his tie and put it on top of his jacket.

"No, no, Vincent," he said impatiently, "don't put that tripod there. Further back, near the wall."

"Edouard," Miranda said desperately, "what chance did you offer Eva?"

"It doesn't matter, beloved." He smiled as he stood over her and stripped off his shirt. His torso had thickened; she remembered that he'd been lean and muscular but now there was a power to his shoulders and chest that seemed almost brutish. "Eva denied me a business opportunity, but I will deny her the pleasure of her daughter. As for the film we make today—it will be a memento, if you will, a little reminder of our marriage that I shall always cherish."

Still smiling, he kicked off his shoes and opened his belt.

"No!" Miranda sobbed as she struggled against the scarves, her body arching up from the bed. "No, you can't really mean to do this, Edouard!"

He sat down beside her. "First I will have you," he whispered, "and then, though it pains me to do so, I will give you to Vincent and to Joseph who deserve something for their role in this, *n'est-ce pas?*" He reached out and moved his hand over her, his touch lazy and loose. "And then I will take you again, Miranda, but this time, when I climax, you will die." He bent towards her, his breath hot and wine-scented on her face. "I promise, darling, I will make this extraordinary. You will feel such joy, such pleasure, that your death will be a small price to pay for—"

Miranda's head shot up from the pillow and she spat into his face.

Edouard reared back. Slowly, he raised his arm and wiped the spittle from his cheek.

"So much for pleasuring you," he said coldly. "And so much for dying quickly. I shall prolong my climax, Miranda, and Vincent, who is really quite clever, shall prolong your death." He stood, unzipped his fly, and nodded at Vincent. "Untie her ankles and strip her."

Miranda screamed, even though she knew no one could hear her. Vince worked at the scarves that bound her feet while Joey held her legs down. They were strong, the both of them, but terror made her strong, too. She kicked out, hard, and she heard Vince warn Joey to hold her tighter, and she kicked again and again and suddenly she felt her foot smash into something.

Vince grabbed his eye and stumbled backwards.

"Bitch," he snarled. "Joey, for crissakes, hang onto her!"

She kicked again, lower this time, and Joey doubled over in agony, but by then Vince had staggered back to the foot of the bed and grabbed both her feet.

"I've got her now, Mr. de Lasserre," he yelled, and someone ripped off her jeans and her panties and Edouard's face loomed over her, and his hands clasped her thighs and forced them apart—

The door crashed open. Miranda looked up and saw a miracle.

Conor!

She breathed his name, afraid to say it aloud, afraid it was a dream and not reality. But then he looked at her and said, "I'm here, baby," and she began to cry because he was real, and because she'd almost lost him.

She lost track of things after that. There was a lot of shouting and a blur of bodies, and she shut her eyes against it. When she opened them again, Edouard and Vince were both lying very still on the floor. Joey was on his knees in a corner, babbling incoherently.

And she was in Conor's arms.

"I love you," he whispered.

"I know," she whispered back, and she smiled through her tears and knew that she'd never have to be afraid again.

Epilogue

The house was big, and old, and it still needed lots of repairs, even after almost five years.

You couldn't take a shower on a cold winter morning without running the risk of turning into an icicle, and the basement leaked, if the rain was too heavy.

They'd put a lot of money into the place already and, as Conor sometimes said, they'd have to put a lot more in, before it was all fixed up they way they wanted it. And Miranda would sigh and say, yes, he was right, and they'd look at each other and say, well, maybe they should sell this house and buy something newer, now that his law practice was beginning to do so well.

But each of them knew that they never would.

The house was big, and old, and it needed work. But it rang with laughter and shone with happiness, and it was the first real home either of them had ever known.

They loved it.

And they adored Susannah, who'd been born three years to the day after their wedding. Conor said it was a good thing their daughter looked like her mother because he'd feel sorry for any kid that looked like him but now that Miranda was pregnant again, she lay in his arms in the dark of night, her hands lightly cupping her belly, dreaming of the little boy she carried, one she just knew would be the perfect image of his daddy.

Sometimes, on a summer's evening such as this, while she sat curled beside her husband on the creaky glider on the back porch, crickets chirping in the meadow and the baby tucked safely away in the nursery upstairs, she thought about what a miracle it was, that life had given her this chance at such happiness . . .

That it had given her Conor.

He was her passion and her strength, and his love had changed her life forever. Her past had faded away, even the kidnapping. Conor had made it happen, not just by loving her or rescuing her but by vanquishing all her ghosts. Edouard was dead, and so was Vince Moratelli. Joey would be in prison until he was an old man.

As for Hoyt . . . she'd never seen him again. But Conor had, and a couple of days later, the papers had reported that Hoyt Winthrop had decided to decline the appointment offered him by the President and to sell his interest in his securities firm. Winthrop, it was said, had decided to devote his money to good works and to lead a life of seclusion.

By some amazing coincidence, after Conor spoke with Eva, she, too, had opted to perform charitable deeds. The week after Hoyt turned down the ambassadorship, Papillon announced it was going to use the entire profit from its new cosmetics line, Chrysalis, to endow a fund for abused and neglected children.

''As a mother,'' Eva said, her eyes damp with emotion (but her mascara intact) during a *Twenty-Twenty* segment, ''I know how much it means, to give a child a good start in life.''

Miranda, who'd watched the televised interview from the safety of Conor's arms, had laughed.

''What an actress,'' she'd said. ''She knows she couldn't buy this kind of publicity for Papillon at any price.''

But tears had risen in her eyes and it had taken Conor to kiss them away.

Oh yes, Miranda thought as the old glider creaked and swayed, Conor O'Neil had surely changed her life.

She smiled, thinking how she had changed his.

Conor wasn't running around the world anymore, playing those dangerous games for Harry Thurston and the mysterious members of the Committee. Days after he'd rescued her, Conor had stumbled through an explanation of what it was he really did for a living and she'd let him, trying to look stern while she'd watched him blush, but it hadn't been much of a revelation. By then, she'd begun to figure things out and, to tell the truth, learning the man she loved was a man who worked just outside the law had delighted her—once he assured her he was giving it up.

There was something about being married to your very own James Bond that was almost sinfully exciting.

Once, a year or so ago, she'd asked him if he missed his old life. Did he have any regrets?

Conor had smiled, taken her in his arms and told her with words and with his body that this life, the one they'd made together, was the only one he wanted.

It was how she felt, too.

For the first time ever, she was part of a family. There was her husband, and her baby; there was Jean-Phillipe, living in California and happily out of the closet, directing films instead of acting in them and being, as Susannah insisted, the very bestest uncle in the whole wide world. There was Conor's father, who was doing his best to learn how to give love unconditionally. There was the unborn child in her womb, who would make the magic circle complete.

But always, always, the center of her soul, the very heart of her, would be her husband.

Miranda moved more closely into the curve of his arm, and laid her head on his strong shoulder.

"Conor?" she said softly.

Conor looked at his wife. Her head was tilted back and she was smiling and his heart kicked the way it always did, the way it always would, at the knowledge that she was his.

He smiled back, shifted into the corner of the glider, and drew her onto his lap.

"What, baby?" he murmured.

Miranda lifted her hand to his cheek. There was so much she wanted to tell him, but she didn't have to. He knew what was in her heart.

"Nothing," She took his hand and brought it to her lips. "I just like to say your name."

Conor's arms tightened around her. "Do you have any idea how much I love you?"

The answer to his question was in her kiss.

Low on the horizon, a creamy white moon slipped from behind a screen of lacy clouds and caught in the branches of an old apple tree. Conor rose to his feet with his wife still in his arms.

"Let's go to bed," he said, and as he carried her into the old house and up the steps, the cricket chorus swelled and swelled until the night was alive with song.

ROMANCE FROM FERN MICHAELS

DEAR EMILY (0-8217-4952-8, $5.99)

WISH LIST (0-8217-5228-6, $6.99)

AND IN HARDCOVER:

VEGAS RICH (1-57566-057-1, $25.00)

Available wherever paperbacks are sold, or order direct from the Publisher. Send cover price plus 50¢ per copy for mailing and handling Penguin USA, P.O. Box 999, c/o Dept. 17109, Bergenfield, NJ 07621. Residents of New York and Tennessee must include sales tax. DO NOT SEND CASH.

CJ 8

YOU WON'T WANT TO READ JUST ONE—KATHERINE STONE

ROOMMATES (0-8217-5206-5, $6.99/$7.99)
No one could have prepared Carrie for the monumental changes she would face when she met her new circle of friends at Stanford University. Once their lives intertwined and became woven into the tapestry of the times, they would never be the same.

TWINS (0-8217-5207-3, $6.99/$7.99)
Brook and Melanie Chandler were so different, it was hard to believe they were sisters. One was a dark, serious, ambitious New York attorney; the other, a golden, glamourous, sophisticated supermodel. But they were more than sisters—they were twins and more alike than even they knew . . .

THE CARLTON CLUB (0-8217-5204-9, $6.99/$7.99)
It was the place to see and be seen, the only place to be. And for those who frequented the playground of the very rich, it was a way of life. Mark, Kathleen, Leslie and Janet—they worked together, played together, and loved together, all behind exclusive gates of the *Carlton Club.*

Available wherever paperbacks are sold, or order direct from the Publisher. Send cover price plus 50¢ per copy for mailing and handling to Penguin USA, P.O. Box 999, c/o Dept. 17109, Bergenfield, NJ 07621. Residents of New York and Tennessee must include sales tax. DO NOT SEND CASH.